LUKE IRONTREE & THE LAST VAMPIRE WAR

Book 0 - The Centurion Immortal
Book 1 - Dark Fangs Rising - March 22, 2022
Book 2 - Dark Fangs Raging - April 19, 2022
Book 3 - Dark Fangs Descending - May 17, 2022
Book 4 - Blood Empire Reborn - August 23, 2022
Book 5 - Blood Empire Avenged - September 20, 2022
Book 6 - Blood Empire Infiltrated - October 18, 2022
Book 7 - Blood Empire Burning - November 15, 2022
Book 8 - Ancient Sword Falling - March 21, 2023
Book 9 - Ancient Sword Unyielding - August 22, 2023
Book 10 - Ancient Sword Shattering - January 4, 2024

The Luke Irontree Historical Adventures
Rise of the Centurio Immortalis - April 5, 2022
Fall of the Centurio Immortalis - May 31, 2022
The Moonlight Centurion*
The Highway Centurion*

*Forthcoming
Titles and release dates may be subject to change.

ANCIENT SWORD SHATTERING

LUKE IRONTREE & THE LAST VAMPIRE WAR
BOOK 10

C. THOMAS LAFOLLETTE

EDITED BY
SUZANNE LAHNA

ANCIENT SWORD SHATTERING
C. Thomas Lafollette

A Broken World Publication
13820 NE Airport Way
Suite #K395495
Portland, OR 97251-1158
Ancient Sword Shattering
Copyright © 2024 by C. Thomas Lafollette
ISBN 978-1-960766-06-9 (ebook);
ISBN 978-1-960766-07-6 (paperback)

Cover Design: Ravven
Developmental Editing by: Suzanne Lahna
Copy/Line Editing & Proofreading: Amy Cissell

CONTENTS

To Me
You and I have come a long way together, Luke.
*I put down over a million words in this adventure on the way to finishing my
first series. It's not to say there won't be other Luke Irontree adventures
someday, but this one is done.*

PRONUNCIATION GUIDE & AUTHOR'S NOTES

Pronunciation: Latin names and words are mentioned throughout the book and are intended to be read with the classical Latin pronunciation. For instance, "c" is always pronounced hard, like a "k." "U" is always a short "oo" sound. "V" typically sounds like a "w." There are plenty of resources on the internet if you wish to learn more about Classical Latin pronunciation.

- Lucius – Loo-kih-oos
- Silvanius – Sihl-wahn-ih-oos
- Ferrata – Fehr-rah-tah
- Jung-sook — Yoong-sook
- Jan – Yeahn
- Roxiustanta - Roks-see-oo-stahn-nah
- Surena - Ser-rehn-nah
- Selene - Sehl-lee-nee
- Eusebius - Yoo-see-bee-oos

Latin Words: Latin words are used for effect and to add to the "flavor" of the story, not to reflect Latin grammar/declensions/conjugations.

Luke sat on his mount of silver, staring out over the smoldering ashes of his captured fortress. Resting his elbow on his knee and his chin on his fist, he watched his friends and packmates disassembling the vampire's base, salvaging everything worth taking. Even through his fugue, he appreciated the pack's waste not, want not ethics.

They'd defeated the vampires yet again, but at what cost? Pablo, his best friend, was in a coma. Pieter had severe burns. Misha had died saving Pieter and the rest of his tank crew. Delilah had taken a slash to the side that was an inch from killing her.

He couldn't get the images out of his head.

Pablo trapped under a massive pile of rubble. The burnt stench of Pieter's flesh. Delilah's screams as her trembling hands tried to stem the bleeding and Simone's sobs as she pressed rags to the wound. They still hadn't recovered Misha's body from the tank.

A shift in the wind swirled a haze of smoke and ash around him. The only concession he made was squinting and narrowing his nostrils. Out of the corner of his eye, the blackened, smoldering husk of the Sherman tank mocked him and his grief. The armor meant to protect his friends had nearly been their death, trapping them inside the burning steel oven. The shifting breeze brought wafts of burning oil tainted air.

He'd hoped to avoid anything like the hellish battles of World War I and II, but this battle had been a weird combination of modern mechanized war and an old-fashioned fort siege. They'd pulled it off, but there were too many injured and too many dead. He was still waiting for the final tally from Maggie and her medical team.

Her primary goal had been to stabilize the worst of the injured so their enhanced werewolf healing could take over. Once they were in a relatively stable condition, they could be moved back to Portland for more advanced medical treatment.

He hated everything about what had happened and how the battle had ended. His fury burned brightly in his chest like a glob of molten lead. Wishing he could pluck it from his chest and quench it on a vampire, he instead held it tight to his bosom, protecting it and nurturing it.

Using it on some random fanger would be a waste of a hatred so pure and intense. The dark entity. The god of the vampires. Saubarag. Luke would quench his towering wrath in the god's body. From now on, vamps were an incidental target. From now on, he'd tear through anything, vampire or werewolf, standing in his way to destroy his true target. He couldn't keep snipping off pieces of the snake's tail. It was time to lop off its head.

Saubarag must die.

A small piece of Luke at the back of his mind wondered at the hubris of killing a deity, but humanity had killed plenty of gods. History books and museums were littered with their ideological remains. He just planned to take a more direct and personal role in the killing of this god.

Luke wanted to watch the light fade out of Saubarag's eyes then spit on his corpse when he finished. He'd come through nearly two thousand years of pain and vampire-killing drudgery to this point. He'd earned the right to meet the one who'd unleashed this blood-sucking hell on earth and end him with his own hand.

A pair of werewolves emerged from a nearby tunnel, a body on a stretcher held between them. As they spied Luke and his dark visage, they swung wide around him on the way to their destination. Judging by the sheet over its face, they'd recovered another body and were taking it to their temporary morgue.

Grinding his teeth, he stared at the covered corpse until the stretcher bearers disappeared from view. Shaking his head, he looked west, checking to see where Sol Invictus was on his journey across the sky. It wouldn't be long now before the god and his sun chariot would disappear for the day. Then, he could begin his search for the dark god of the vampires.

He wasn't sure how long he stared at the horizon, ignoring everything around himself as he fixated on his losses, but the scent of coffee roused him from his stupor. Someone had brought him coffee and a plate of food, setting it on a nearby crate of silver. He hadn't even noticed their presence, let alone heard them if they'd attempted to talk to him.

"Luke, dōšagīh, it's time." Roxi reached out, taking his hand in hers.

He nodded, picking up his tray. "I'll be ready shortly."

She smiled sadly, then sat next to him, resting her head against his left shoulder. He mechanically scooped the food into his mouth until the spoon scraped against an empty plate. Taking a swig of coffee, he grimaced. It was still a touch too hot to be drinkable, but at least light scalding was a feeling other than the dark maelstrom of emotions spinning in his gut.

"Just set the tray aside, someone will be along to collect it," Roxi said, standing up. She gingerly stepped down the pyramid of crates to the ground, waiting for Luke to follow.

Grabbing his sword and rudis, he followed her, stopping to clip them onto his belt. He pulled the rudis, its silver inlay and cutting edge catching the first rays of the moon's light. He stared at the shimmer, then looked up, trying to locate the moon, his mistress, the moon goddess Selene.

"She's ready for us, Luke."

As if she were eavesdropping, and she probably was, Luke felt the goddess's presence infuse his inner being. For a moment, a bit of the worry and tension loosened, though he clutched his rage close. Without welcoming her fully in, there was only so much she could do to lighten his mood. And he wasn't ready to let her see the ball of hatred he'd been nursing close to his breast. The bit of ease he'd gained from her was enough to let him straighten his spine and nod at Roxi.

Heaving a sigh, he turned and stalked around his mountain of silver, heading toward the tunnel entrance where a line of chained vampires was being forced from their underground hiding place. Some of the vampires, fearing Luke's retribution or the sun's, had hidden in an out-of-the-way bunker. Luke's people had found them while they were dormant for the day and chained them with shackles, like the ones they used to render a werewolf's powers inert.

They shuffled forward, dispirited and staring at the ground. Sam had a crew of their packmates functioning as prison guards, shoving them forward if necessary with a butt of a shotgun. There was enough anti-vamp ordnance assembled to turn every vampire into a smudge in the dirt if he ordered it.

Luke stopped and waited, his feet spread wide and his rudis held behind his back with both hands. He glared at the vampires, the muscles in his face tight with anger as he clenched his jaw.

"Halt!" Sam called, stepping forward. "They're ready for you, Luke."

He nodded, and she moved up next to him, flanking him on his left while Roxi flanked him to the right. Taking a step forward, he brought his rudis around and pointed at a vampire near the front. "You, step forward."

Rhonda shoved the vampire forward with her shotgun since the vamp was too busy searching the dirt and pebbles for an escape route to realize it'd been picked by Luke.

"Look at me, fanger," Luke said, his voice deadly calm. The vampire, despite its trepidation, slowly raised its head and eyes. "Do you know who I am?"

The vampire nodded shakily, its breath hissing in and out in short bursts. Though the vampire didn't need to breathe to exist, the autonomic terror-response had taken over.

"Say it," Luke ordered.

"The slayer…" the vamp whispered.

"Say it loud enough for your little friends to hear."

"The slayer. The demon… The wood-fanged demon. The Centurion Immortal…"

Luke nodded curtly. "Good. I'm glad we don't have to play games. You know who I am. You know I have no mercy for your kind. You have seen my works." He raised both of his arms and gestured around at the ruined and still smoldering fort. "Look upon them and despair."

The vampire lowered his eyes.

"Look!" Luke barked.

Its body trembling, the vamp lifted its head slowly, almost against its will as it responded to the authority in Luke's voice and looked around. A swirl of ashes spun over the ground and into the vampire's face as it drifted by.

Luke chuckled humorlessly. "That's likely one of your leader's remains you're coated in. Unless you want to join them, I'm going to give you one chance to talk, one chance to live."

"Li…live?" The vamp's voice trembled, though a small thread of hope wound its way through the word, sparking a light in its eyes. "How…how do I know you're not lying?"

Luke took a step forward and lowered his head, staring into the vampire's eyes. "You don't, but right now you're not in a position to worry about it, are you?"

Luke's proximity made the fanger's body quiver, but it managed to shake its head.

"Shut up," a nearby vampire hissed. "Say nothing."

Luke's eyes flicked to Rhonda then the offending vampire. She noisily chambered a round and shoved the barrel of her Winchester M12 into the back of the blabbermouth. The vampire didn't seem cowed but did shut its mouth, glaring daggers at Luke and the fanger he'd selected.

A feral grin spread across Luke's face. "If you value your immortal existence, you'll ignore your friend. They don't have your best interest at heart. Now I'm going to ask you a simple question.

Answer truthfully, and I'll let you go so you can find the deepest darkest hole to hide in where I maybe won't find you someday. Do we understand each other?"

The vampire nodded almost eagerly.

"Shut. Up," the other vampire hissed.

Rhonda poked hard with the shotgun. But instead of pushing back against it or shutting up, the vampire lurched forward, leaping into the air toward the potential traitor. The vamp had enough chain to let it get its hands on the traitor's chin and the back of its skull. With a lighting fast twist and a sickening crunch, it ripped the traitor's head off. Before gravity reclaimed it, Rhonda fired.

The vamp hit the ground screaming and writhing. Rhonda had missed the heart, but still filled the vamp with wood and silver. A slight sting wound its way from Luke's arm to his brain. Glancing down, he saw a bit of splinter sticking from a small dab of blood. Picking it out, he flicked it away and looked at Rhonda. She shrugged sheepishly, mouthing "sorry" at him. He gave her a faint nod.

Pointing his rudis at the now beheaded corpse of his potential informant, he formed the incantation in his head and squinted at the body. Light wound its way down the wood and silver blade and connected the tip to the body with a dancing thread of pure golden light. A moment later, the thread grew fat and a globule of light slithered up the thread until it hit the tip of the rudis. The wood sword flared brighter until the golden glow disappeared into his arm. The headless vamp dissolved into a pool of reddish-black goo.

The small wound on his arm disappeared, leaving a drop of blood. He swiped it carefully onto the tip of his finger and held it up. He could practically feel the hungry stares from the fangers as they looked at the smear of red on his forefinger. After a moment, he popped the finger in his mouth, licking the drop from his finger. Someone in the fanger crowd groaned lightly. Snorting quietly, Luke stifled a chuckle.

He was sure many a vamp dreamed of draining him of his blood. None of them knew his blood was toxic to their kind. No vampire that had ever fed on him had lived long enough to spread the word.

Once the blood was gone, the vampires returned their attention to their comrade rolling and groaning on the ground. Roxi could have it later. Leaving it alive and in agony would let the others know what awaited them if they didn't cooperate or tried to stop their friends from cooperating. Luke looked around the crowd. All but one lowered their eyes, their gazes flicking back and forth from the vampire on the ground and the dirt in front of them. He marked the one who stared back, venom in its eyes. No baby vamp would have the guts to fix that gaze on him in this situation and maintain the vitriol.

"Who is going to be brave enough to answer my question and earn their freedom?" He looked around the crowd, but no one seemed to be interested in volunteering. So, he raised his rudis, nearly everyone flinched away from the gesture, and pointed toward another vamp near the front. "You."

Ahmed shoved the selected vampire forward.

"You know the deal. Are you willing to earn your—whatever you call this stolen existence—back?"

"Fuck you, butcher," the vampire spat out.

Luke shoved the rudis through the air and yanked back, this time without even thinking about the incantation. The vampire exploded into a shower of goo, splattering him, Roxi, Sam, and the nearby vampires. A surge of energy ran through him, lightening his physical exhaustion. Next to him, Sam groaned, wiping vampire corpse from her face and arms and cursing under her breath. On the other side, Roxi stood still and glared at the vampires, her rudis in her hand, dangling by her leg.

"As you can see, I have no qualms about ending you on the spot. If you've ever had any doubts about my willingness to drain you of your essence and leave your remains where they fall, get rid of them now."

"We're your prisoners. Don't we have rights?" the staring vampire spat out.

"Rights?" Luke barked a harsh laugh. "What rights do you give your victims? What rights have you afforded me? You held me captive and forced me to fight for your amusement. You're not signatories to the Geneva Convention. This isn't a formally declared war. I'll shove this blade into any one of you"—Luke raised the rudis in his hand and yanked the life from another nearby vampire, sending its dusty remains drifting on a gust of wind—"any fucking time I want. Don't speak to me of rights, just answer my fucking question and maybe you'll earn your right to scurry away."

The vampire's eyes opened wide, and it gulped, visibly paling in the dim moonlight.

"Do we understand each other?" Luke asked.

The vampire nodded vigorously.

"What about the rest of you? Are we clear on your rights and what I think of them?" Luke stared back over a crowd of eager bobble heads. "I don't care who gives me the information I want. I just want it. And the quicker someone gives it to me, the better the chances are I won't end you. Got it?"

They all nodded back, most of them looking up, though not meeting Luke's eye, for the first time since being dragged from their hole.

"I want the dark entity. Your god. Saubarag."

Several of the vampires flinched, others returned their gaze to the dirt. Luke gave them a few moments, but no one spoke up.

He reached out with his rudis and angrily yanked the stolen life essence from the body of another vampire into his. It slapped to the ground, adding to the pool created by the other young vampire. "We're not starting off very well."

"You don't know him…" one of the vamps muttered. "He'll destroy us."

Picking the vampire next to the one who'd just spoken up, Luke drained it, splattering the speaker in a shower of explosive goo. He didn't know why some of them exploded but was glad for the timely assistance. Coated in the remains of his former comrade, it trembled uncontrollably, and its eyes bulged.

"Saubarag"—the fangers twitched again at the mention of the name—"may destroy you at some date in the future. But I *will* destroy you right here and right now. You are currently alive only at my forbearance. I don't care if I have to kill every one of you. I'll just go find some more fangers. Eventually, someone will tell me what I need. But it won't do you any good. You'll be dust in the wind." He pointed to the growing pool of muddy, bloody vamp remains. "Or a shitty slick of mud." He spat into it.

The vampires looked at each other furtively, wondering who would be the first to betray their god. Hoping to encourage them and remind them of their stakes, he slapped the flat of his rudis into the palm of his other hand over and over. Each time the wood hit skin, the vampires flinched.

"You have one minute to make a decision before I start killing," Luke said, nodding toward Sam. Out of the corner of his eye, she set the timer on her phone.

He continued slapping his rudis into his palm while staring coldly at the vamps assembled in front of him. Deciding not to wait, he targeted the fanger next to the one who'd spoken up and yanked its essence. It puffed out and blew all over the vamp who was already coated in the sludge of its neighbor. The combination made for a nasty, dust-coated mess.

"You said we had a minute!" it protested.

"Pray I don't alter the deal any further," Luke replied, his voice deadly quiet.

"I don't know where the Dark Lord is. I swear. But I know who does..." The vampire broke, its spine curling in a slump.

"You better talk fast." Next to him, Sam's phone alarm went off.

"The Emperor knows. Find him and he can tell you where to find..." It rolled its hand, afraid to mention Saubarag.

"The emperor?" Luke hitched an eyebrow up.

"Constantius. He has a house outside of Bend on the Deschutes River." The words tumbled from the vampire's mouth almost faster than it could form them.

Luke narrowed his eyes, a sneer spreading across his face. "Tacky decor? White carpet and towels?"

The fanger nodded its head so hard Luke thought it might fall off and roll away.

"We burned that place to the ground weeks ago. You better give me something I don't already know in a hurry, or you've reached the end of your immortality." Luke pointed the rudis at the vamp, twitching the tip of it side-to-side crisply. "Tick tock. Tick tock. Tick. Tock. Your time is running out…"

"That's all I know! Please, I swear!"

"I believe you," Luke replied.

"You d—"

Luke angrily yanked his sword back, and a glob of golden light connected the vamp to the wood sword, and then the vampire poofed out and blew away in the evening breeze. Some of the vamps jumped away, one falling after tripping on the chains shackling it. Others squeaked and moaned in fear. Only one vampire, in the back row, stood stock still.

It slowly raised its head, staring back at Luke. "Eusebius. That's who you want."

Eusebius. Constantine the Great's Christian zealot. The likely orchestrator of Luke's exile from the Roman Empire. Eusebius. Constantius's lapdog.

"Eusebius?" Luke said quietly, but he was sure the vampire could hear him.

It gave a firm nod.

"Constantius's lapdog?"

The fanger snorted. "Eusebius plays the part, but he's Constantius's sire. 'The Emperor'"—the vampire sneered—"gets to play the important man, but the power resides with Eusebius, and Eusebius reports to the Dark Lord."

"How do I find Eusebius?"

"That, I don't know. But if you've stayed true to your past practices, you probably have the answer in your possession. Did you take the computers from Constantius's house before you burned it down?"

Luke nodded.

"You'll likely find his address somewhere in one of them."

"They'll kill you for this betrayal," another fanger hissed.

Luke snatched its life force away. That seemed to catch the vamp willing to speak off guard, as it flinched away from the fanger who'd just threatened it.

"Continue," Luke commanded.

"There are lists of properties and assets. Constantius kept them, as do a few higher ups. They include properties and hiding spaces. It's not a full directory of all vampiredom, but you should be able to find what you need there."

"Do you have a password?"

"No. I'm not important enough for that. I've given you all I know of use. And no one here knows anything more than I do. They're all fairly low-level newer vampires."

Luke swept his gaze over the remaining vampires. None of them had the steel to speak up. Most of them slouched to look as small as possible, several shaking in fear. He couldn't sense any vampire of real power. The fanger was probably right.

"Is this true? If anyone has any tips on Eusebius, speak up now." Luke hoped someone would have something, but all he saw was shaking heads. He turned his head toward Sam. "Document them and add them to our registry."

"Right." She pulled out her phone and moved close enough where she could get a good photograph of each individual vampire.

When she finished, Luke placed his hands behind his back, the rudis dangling casually between a couple fingers. "You're the first vampires I've ever set free. This is your one shot at mercy. Spread the word. I want Eusebius." Sam nudged him on the shoulder, shoving a phone at him. It was on with its phone number displayed on the screen. "If you have any tips, you can call this number." Luke read off the burner phone's number. "But if I ever see you again, you will be the first to die."

"What should we do with them?" Sam asked.

"March them out the gate and a few hundred yards from the camp, then cut them loose. I want them to spread the word about what happened here. The vampires' night is over. I'm coming, and I'm taking them all down." He turned back to the vampires. "You better run, and I mean run fast! Run and hide in whatever hole you can find. Run until you're as far away from me as you can run, then run some more. Do you understand me?"

The vampires nodded eagerly.

"If anyone of these blood sucking bastards so much as looks over their shoulder, you're free to open fire."

"Got it," Sam replied. "Get them marching toward the gate."

Rhonda nodded, shoving the nearest vampire to get it moving. Luke didn't need to watch the chain gang shuffle away, though the jingling of their chains serenaded him as he stalked across the fort's yard toward the gap in the wall they'd destroyed during their siege. Roxi jogged to catch up, matching his purposeful stride.

She waited until they were outside the fort before breaking the silence. "Luke…" She paused. "What's going on? How are you doing that? I've never seen anything like it before."

He shrugged. "I don't know." He walked for another dozen paces before stopping and turning to face Roxi. "I just began chanting the incantation in my head during the melee after we had to abandon our tank. Then I stabbed a vamp in heart as it tried to attack me. The power slammed through the blade into me. It happened again a few times until I pointed at one running away and then I saw the line of light connecting it to me just before it exploded."

"And it transfers the power to you?"

Luke nodded. "Completely."

"You have to be practically vibrating with the energy right now." She gently ran her hand down his shoulder.

He gave a half-hearted one-shouldered shrug. "I guess."

Roxi pulled him into a tight embrace, cradling the back of his head with a hand. "I know you're hurting, dōšagīh. I am, too." She kissed him softly on the cheek. "We're all here for you."

Laying his head on her shoulder, he nodded and drew in a deep shuddering breath. "I'm so angry, Roxi. I feel like I want to destroy everything around me."

"I can understand that. When was the last time you felt this angry? I mean good and burning rage filled anger?" She stroked his neck soothingly.

"I don't know. Decades. Maybe centuries," he mumbled into her neck.

"You've been numb for so long. I know. I've felt it, too, until we met. But I think there's been an undercurrent of anger slowly building up over that time, and now that you've come out of your numbness, you can feel it, and it's found a target."

"Saubarag."

"Right." She pushed back a little and cupped his cheeks, kissing him gently. "Anger can be a powerful tool. Keep it focused and remind yourself to let it go once it's been spent upon its target. Alright?"

He nodded weakly. "I'm just afraid it'll fill me up and consume everything good I've found lately."

"I know. But I don't think it will. You're too good of a person, too good of a soul for it to best you. You're too strong. Remember who you are. Remember the soft and gentle man who I love and who Maggie loves. Focus on your friends and the connections you've made. Keep the inferno of your anger ready and targeted. If you keep your goal in mind, it will serve its purpose then you can let it go."

"I guess."

"Do you trust me?" Roxi asked softly, running a thumb over his cheek.

"With everything I am and ever will be." The words were softly spoken but laced with steel and surety. He trusted her with his everything. They'd struggled across two millennia to be together. He'd threatened a god to save her. He knew without a doubt she'd do the same if it came to it.

"Good." She pulled him into another kiss, this one a bit more serious than the earlier one. "Now where are we heading?"

"I want to see Pablo."

Roxi nodded, grabbing his hand. Together, they strolled under the moonlight, saying nothing, toward the medical facilities set up in the shadow of the fort's northern wall. The shade it provided against the brutal daytime summer sun of Oregon's high desert helped protect the wounded. It could still be hot in the tent, but at least it helped some, especially if there was a breeze blowing through the large tent.

Maggie walked out from the tent and met them out of earshot of anyone with supernatural hearing. "It's good to see you."

"You too, Maggie. Do you mind if I head into the tent and say hi to a few people?" Roxi asked.

"Not at all. Visitors are always good for the injured. They could use their spirits raised."

Roxi nodded, squeezed Maggie's shoulder on the way by, and left them to have some privacy.

"How is he?" Luke asked.

"The same. Still unconscious."

He slumped.

Maggie took his hand, squeezing it. "That's good though. His vitals are strong. The breaks are set and healing. Now all we can do is wait and hope."

He nodded. He knew she wasn't just spinning a lie to soothe him. She'd never do that. His friend was alive, at least.

"Ready to go in?" Maggie asked, a look of supreme kindness on her face.

He could only nod, not trusting his mouth to make any noises other than utterances of pain. She led him in by the hand. As he approached, Roxi's laugh drifted out of the tent along with the laughs of several other people. The sound chiseled away a bit of the dark mood encasing him.

They stopped by a section cordoned off by clear plastic sheeting. The burn ward. Only Katya remained inside. She'd tried to stay in the tank to free Misha, even escaping the grasp of her rescuers once to climb back in the burning hulk of the Sherman tank.

"How is she?" Luke murmured.

"Holding steady. We're keeping her unconscious for now so her body can work. I think she'll pull through."

"Good." He sighed, shaking his head. She'd wake to a world where her partner was gone, dead to help a pack they barely knew.

After that, Luke dug deep to find his "commander's" face so he could walk the tent, talking with the wounded. He was glad most of his people were werewolves. Otherwise, the tent would have been far fuller.

Most of the light injuries had already healed. Those with more serious ones were among the ambulatory wounded. They didn't need to be in the hospital tent and could heal elsewhere while they awaited any final corrective work that would likely have to be postponed until everyone returned to Portland.

Pulling up a chair, Luke sat next to Roxi by Pieter's bed. "How are you doing?"

Pieter held up his gauze wrapped hands. "Can't say I'm a fan of my new mittens, but Doc assures me I'll be able to take them off soon. I got off light." He sighed and slumped a little, his eyes flicking towards the section of the tent where Pablo was cordoned off. He straightened back up, plastering a smile on his face that did little to push away the pain in his eyes. "I'll be able to help out before too long."

Maggie, who stood next to Luke, squeezed his shoulder. "Just being cautious. Infections are unlikely, but I'd like to give the skin more time to heal before you go out and try to do work."

It was probably a good idea to force Pieter to stay confined because he would insist on doing whatever he could to help out. Though a task would help him keep his mind off Pablo. Even if his hands weren't ready, he'd find a suitable job for Pieter to distract him from his troubles.

He reached out and squeezed Pieter's knee. "I'll find you something to do—with Maggie's clearance, of course."

Luke felt for Tony. Both of his partners had been injured. Though he longed to be here with Pablo and Pieter, he was one of the few wolves left in charge of Portland while most of the pack and their allies were making war in the high desert of eastern Oregon.

Pieter shrugged. "Whatever you say. I'm good at following doctor's orders."

Luke managed a half a smile for his dear friend before standing up to work his way down the line of cots, exchanging pleasantries and heaping praise on those who'd been hurt in their cause.

Stopping next to Tutyr's bed, Luke nodded at him.

The god smiled up at Luke through his bushy, unkempt beard. "Hello."

"How are you feeling?" Luke asked, sinking into a chair next to Tutyr.

"Good. Be up in no time."

Maggie chuckled politely. "As soon as you can stay awake for more than an hour, we'll discuss it."

Tutyr sighed, slumping in his bed, and stared toward his feet. "Very tired. Would like to curl up with Alfie."

Luke thought he understood. The god had spent most of his time with Luke and the Portland pack as a giant dog who Gwen had named Brutus. His preferred bed was an extra-large dog pillow they'd bought for him, which he shared with Luke's orange tabby cat Alfie.

"We'll let you get back to resting," Luke said, standing.

Tutyr nodded and wiggled so he was laying down. A few moments later, his breathing leveled out, and he drifted into another round of exhausted sleep.

Luke only had one more patient in the main room to visit. Sitting next to Simone, he laid his arm around her shoulders and gave her a hug, kissing her temple. Delilah, a light sheen of sweat covering her face, rested with her eyes closed, a furrow running down the middle of her brow. No doubt, she was probably judging something Luke had done. The thought brought a moment of lightness before the darkness crashed back in. He'd even take her stern scoldings if it meant she didn't have to suffer the pain of her wound.

"How is she?" he asked.

"In pain, so Maggie keeps her under. Though, she's healing much faster than a human would, thankfully." Simone reached out and ran her knuckles gently down Delilah's cheek.

"Ọ̀ṣọ́ọ̀sì?" Luke asked.

"Yes. He is taking care of his hunter. I don't know how. You have your wooden sword, but she's never explained how her connection to the god works." She exhaled, a note of exasperation coloring it.

Nodding, he stood up and bent over Delilah's bed, kissing her forehead before whispering, "Get well soon. I need you to keep me on the right path."

After he visited the last patient, Luke stood in the doorway of the tent, staring out into the blank brownness of the dry landscape.

"Are you ready to see Pablo?" Roxi asked softly, holding his hand.

"No," Luke whispered, shifting his eyes to the ground in front of him. "But I guess we should."

She kissed his cheek and led him to Pablo's bed. He looked like he slept peacefully. The bruising could easily be mistaken for the shadows of the dim tent. Next to Pablo's head, Maggie set down a folding chair, gave Luke a sympathetic smile, then departed to make the rounds.

He stared at the chair for a minute, then slumped into it, staring at the floor between him and Pablo's bed. Sighing, he reached over and grasped his friend's hand, careful not to disturb the IV providing fluids. Not sure what he could say, he just sat holding Pablo's hand gently.

"I'm sorry," he whispered, shaking his head. "I should have never wandered into your pub all those years ago. I should have..." He choked up, his eyes burning with unshed tears.

His head falling forward, he carefully pressed the back of Pablo's hand to his forehead, the tears now flowing. In the background of his mind, he heard a curtain being drawn. The light dimmed a bit as someone gave him the illusion of privacy. Behind him, Roxi rubbed her hand over his back soothingly.

Once he cried himself out, Roxi stuffed some tissue into his free hand. Setting down Pablo's hand gently, Luke blew his nose and dried his eyes and cheeks, stashing the tissue in his pocket.

"I'm sorry. You're one of the best friends I've ever had. I know it's inadequate, but I'll make the bastard who did this to you pay. I'll make sure he can't do this to anyone else. I'll make sure you wake up to a world that's less dangerous." He stopped, holding his breath for a moment, until the burn in his eyes lessened. "Please come back. Tony and Pieter need you. The pack needs you. I…I need you."

He reached out and squeezed Pablo's shoulder, then leaned over and laid a kiss on his forehead before standing up. He turned, but before he could decide where to go, Roxi pulled him into a fierce hug, rubbing the back of his neck softly.

"It's not your fault, dōšagīh. But you are right about one thing. We'll remove the entity responsible from the world so it can't harm any more innocents and people brave enough to stand up and fight it. That's a promise we can make."

They stood there for a while, just holding each other until someone cleared their throat from outside the little secluded area by Pablo.

"Luke, Sam said she needs you back inside the fort," Patrice said quietly.

Roxi turned her head. "Let her know we'll be along shortly."

"Will do." Patrice moved away to deliver their message.

"Are you ready to deal with people?" Roxi asked.

"I will be in a moment." He gave Roxi a final squeeze, then stepped out from behind the curtain blocking them from view.

Maggie waved him over. He nodded and joined her, his head down as he stared at the floor. Taking his hand, she led him out of the main tent to a smaller tent.

"You can go clean up if you need to," Maggie whispered, kissing his cheek.

He stepped into the small tent with its sinks and sanitized water and turned on a faucet. The cold water felt good on his flushed skin. After he'd patted his face down with a nearby towel, he stepped out and found Roxi waiting for him.

"Maggie had something to do in the tent." She raised an eyebrow questioningly as she appraised him.

"I think I'm ready now. I just needed a moment to wash my face and pull myself together." He wasn't truly ready, but he knew he had to do what was expected of him. And he still had a job to do, no matter how much pain he was in. Smiling softly, he turned toward the nearest entrance into their captured fort. Roxi fell in next to him.

He didn't feel the need to talk to her, but her presence soothed him, nonetheless.

Once they stepped out of the shadows and into the moon and artificially lit central courtyard, they had to dodge the hive of activity. The armored vehicles had arrived to take the captured silver to Portland. The mountain of silver-stuffed crates he'd sat on earlier was much diminished as the pack loaded them with haste.

He grabbed a passing packmate. "Where's Sam?"

"Um…" She looked around, then stopped, pointing. "She's over by the main entrance."

"Thanks." He picked up his pace, weaving through people as they carried their captured prizes to staging areas.

"Hey, Luke!" Sam called, waving once she spotted him.

He waited until he stood next to her. "Looks like the silver trucks arrived."

"Yup. Also, the big rig is ready to load up with all our goodies." Seeing his eyes dart around, she added, "It's parked outside. Figured we'd get the silver out of the way before moving it in. Just not that much space after we blew up a lot of the ground."

"What about the medical evac?" Roxi asked.

"They're here, too. Though, they're parked out by the med tent."

Luke rubbed a hand through his dirty hair. "Anything else we're waiting on?"

"No. I think we've got everything cleaned out of their storage. All the vehicles we have in motion are here."

Luke's eyes drifted to the piles they'd assembled. "Do we have enough capacity?"

"I think so. Holly says she's got a backup plan if we don't, but we'll have to wait until we're loaded to see if we need another truck and trailer."

"We'll want to be careful not to overload them. We don't want to have any issues when we pass through any of the weigh stations. I don't know how we'd explain the heavy armaments and hundreds of guns."

Roxi snorted. "We'd look like gun runners, that's for sure."

Sam chuckled. "Technically, we *are* gun runners."

"When do you think we can finish the evacuation?" Luke asked.

"I think a couple hours should do it. How do you want to handle the vehicles?"

Luke scratched his beard. He couldn't wait until they returned home so he could take a shower. "I'm not sure if one giant caravan is a good idea."

"We don't have a lot of options. There isn't a wide variety of roads out here. That leaves only a few options," Sam said.

"I guess you're right." He stopped and looked around the compound, counting up the vehicles. "Let's split it into two groups. We'll send one north to I-84 and the other will take back roads toward Bend. We'll want to ensure we have enough protection for both groups."

Sam arched her back backwards, stretching through a yawn. "We should be good on that. We have all four of the road runners ready to go. That'll give us two per caravan, plus we'll ensure every vehicle has at least one armed person for protection."

"I don't want to sound overly confident, but we should be able to make it back to Portland safely. I don't know how much of a response they can mount at this point." Roxi gestured around the yard. "We took out a huge number of their people and captured a lot of vehicles. As long as we don't dillydally, we'll be home and tucked in bed before they can get around to a counterattack."

"You're probably right, but it's better to be cautious," Luke replied, looking at Sam. "Anything else we need to decide at the moment?"

"Nope. Let's get everyone their assignments," Sam said.

They split up and organized the various parts of their evacuation caravans, ensuring there were enough people to drive their new vehicles and to crew all the defensive needs. Once they'd finished a couple hours later, they gathered near the exit. Luke was about to speak when he saw Owen jogging toward him.

"You get everything finished up?" Sam called.

Owen stopped, wiping a hand across his sweaty brow. "We're wired up. Give the word, and this place will become a crater."

"Good," Luke said vehemently. The sooner he could exact his

vengeance on this fort and all it had taken from him, the better. Maybe it would provide a bit of salve for his gaping psychic wounds.

Owen held up the remote. "Do you want to do the honors?"

Luke shook his head. "No, you can have it. I just want it done."

Raising an eyebrow, Owen shrugged, tucking the remote in his pocket. "I'll go in the last car out of here then and blow it sky high once we're far enough away."

Luke nodded as Rhonda jogged up.

Panting, she took a moment to catch her breath. "We're loaded up. Maggie has all the patients out, and her medical tent is down and loaded."

"Right," Sam said. "I'll go check with the last couple of task captains. Y'all wait here so I don't have to go looking for you." Without waiting for an answer, she jogged off.

Not in the mood to talk, he stared distractedly into the distance while Owen, Rhonda, and Roxi chatted.

A few minutes later, Sam returned. "Alright, everyone is reporting finished. We can load up and get out of here."

"Good. You and Rhonda will lead the first caravan. Roxi, Owen and I will take the second caravan. Owen, you'll ride in the tail road runner. Roxi and I will take the lead road runner."

"Right," Owen said, nodding. "Who's going to drive?"

"Patrice is with the medical caravan," Rhonda said.

Mary waved as she approached. "I can drive if you need me. I'm pretty good behind a wheel if we need to do any evasive driving."

"Thanks, Mary. That would be great." Sam looked back and forth between Mary and Owen, smirking. "As long as you two can keep your minds on the job."

Owen rolled his eyes. "I think we can manage, but thanks for your concern. I'll ensure it's duly registered."

Mary slid up next to him, stealing a quick kiss. "I just need a route and a navigator."

"You'll have someone," Sam replied. "I think that covers it. I'll get everyone to their vehicles, if you give the final go ahead, Luke."

He nodded. "Let's get out of here. I'm tired of looking at this shithole."

Nudging a rock out of his way, he turned and headed toward their temporary motor pool. The sooner he saw this place disappear in his rearview mirror, the better. He needed to get home so he could attempt to mend the wounds this place had caused, and the first step was distance.

Luke rode in the back of their road runner, his mind drifting as Roxi and Connor talked in the front seat. Connor had volunteered to drive since Roxi wasn't ready for serious driving on American roads, and Luke couldn't muster the concentration, though he'd be ready to fight if called upon. He would always rally to protect his people.

At first, the monotonous nighttime landscape of sagebrush and dirt lulled his mind as they moved north. He found his eyes drifting towards the moon, slightly less full than it had been on the night of their attack. The goddess, though busy with her own tasks and the increasing worship of the werewolves, no doubt kept an eye on him. She'd taken a special interest in him over nineteen-hundred-years ago and had always done right by him, even when there was little she could actually do.

Her support had helped him in the impossible task of protecting humans from the bloodthirsty bumps in the night, allowing him the modicum of success he'd achieved. When he'd set out from his home in the forests of Belgian Gaul as a seventeen-year-old, he never thought he'd get mixed up with the gods. Yet here he was, one goddess watching over him while another god lived with him.

Brutus, back in his dog form, rested his head on Luke's lap as he dozed. Too tired to focus on it and simply not wanting to at the moment, he'd deal with the revelation of the dog's identity later. The fact that an ancient god had functioned as his oversized pet for a couple years was too much on an exhausted mind and a bruised spirit.

Even the occasional tiny town did little to draw him out of his head until they hit Burns, Oregon, where they'd be heading north toward John Day and Pendleton before turning west on I-84 for their final run to Portland.

Something tugged at his awareness—something dark and hungry. At first, he thought it was his mood coupled with his own hunger. It had been quite a while since he'd eaten his rations that evening. By the time he found something to stuff in his mouth, the feeling had disappeared in the rearview mirror. Shrugging, he returned to his lackadaisical stare, looking out the window but seeing little but a blur of passing high desert.

He barely noticed when the town of John Day came and went. But when they hit Pendleton, the same feeling came over him, though a bit stronger. He didn't think he was hungry, and the darkness didn't fit his foul mood. It felt like it was coming from outside of him, from something…distant. Though, a tiny piece inside him reached out as if like sought like.

His mind snapped to alertness. The hunger felt fresh and raw… and searching, as if it was hunting. Twisting around, he looked to see if he could spot the vampires. As strongly as the sensation hit him, they must be near. But as they moved through Pendleton, the feeling diminished, then reappeared but coming from the other side. No matter where he looked, he couldn't find the source.

"You alright back there, dōšagīh?" Roxi asked.

He grunted, shrugging in response. When Roxi searched his face, he gave her an expression that encapsulated his confusion. Seeming to understand, she smiled softly and nodded, returning her attention to the road ahead of them.

Once they passed Pendleton, he returned to his thousand-yard stare until the next town of size. Once again, the sense of hunger washed over him. He looked around but came up with nothing as they passed a few cars with humans in them. After the sensation went away, he settled back in, though he thought he caught Roxi's concerned stare in the rearview mirror. Yawning, Brutus settled his head back onto Luke's lap. Luke absentmindedly scratched behind the dog's ears.

He'd hoped to get some sleep on the way back to Portland, assuming there was no call to fight, but every time they drove through the increasingly large towns as they neared Portland, the overwhelming hunger washed over him. The later into the night they drove, the hunger would sometimes feel dulled and mostly satisfied, yet it never receded entirely.

By the time they approached Troutdale on the outskirts of Portland, Luke's irritation overwhelmed him as he shifted in his seat and fidgeted. Brutus, annoyed with his restless pillow, found another position to sleep in, though he cast a miffed eye at Luke periodically, accompanying it with a huff.

Once they hit Portland, the feeling became too intense to ignore as he worried at the skin of his thumb with the nail on his forefinger. Finally, the sticky, slick sensation warned him he'd drawn blood. As his eyes flicked about, his breathing grew shallow. The lights along I-84 seemed to blink in and out harshly as his eyelids twitched, trying to manage the light levels.

Although the omnipresent feeling of hunger pulsed up and down in strength, it never entirely went away. He couldn't escape it. After a while, he feared he would never escape it, but he sighed in relief after they pulled off I-5 at the Rosa Parks exit and pulled into the North Portland Pack's territory. By the time they pulled off on Luke's street, the sensation was almost gone. Though, he couldn't be sure if some small part still sought him out or if it was the shadow of too much stimulation lingering.

"Luke, we're home," Roxi said, turning in the passenger seat.

He shook his head, finally recognizing the house they were parked in front of. "Don't we need to take care of the car?"

"Connor will stash it in the garage."

"But—"

"Luke. Grab Brutus and take him inside. I'll be along shortly." Roxi's voice was firm and crisp.

He responded to the natural authority in it and exited the car with the dog, who indicated he wanted a brief walk. Tired and loopy, Luke snorted then chuckled. "The jig is up. I'm not entirely invested in picking up your poop anymore. You can use the toilet like the rest of us."

Brutus huffed then squatted on the lawn. Luke shook his head, grumbling about perfidious gods.

Luke folded his arms across his chest. "Be careful I don't make an appointment with the vet to get you snipped."

Brutus growled, scratching grass over his mess. Luke perked up once Connor pulled away, the high-powered engine rumbling down the street.

Roxi stopped next to Luke. "He couldn't wait to use the toilet?"

Luke shrugged. "I guess not. I threatened to take him to the vet to get him snipped, but he didn't think much of that idea."

Now that they were home and the constant sensation of a dark hunger no longer plagued him, his shoulders slumped in exhaustion. Sliding the key into the lock, he pushed the door open to the sound of a cat's meow. Alfred trotted toward them, winding his way through Brutus's legs before stopping just out of reach from Luke. The cat raised his nose and sniffed at Luke, his ears back a little.

Luke moved into the living room and scooped up the cat who tensed for a moment before relaxing. "What's up with you, buddy?"

Roxi waved Brutus through the door to go find his kibble bowl. At the sound of kibble rolling around in a metal bowl, Alfie wiggled and Luke set him down so he could go join his friend for breakfast.

Before Roxi could open her mouth, he peeled off his hoodie and headed toward the bathroom. "I need a shower."

He needed a few minutes to clear his mind before Roxi asked him what was going on now that he was home. After he stripped down, he turned the water on as hot as he could stand it. He had too much grime, blood, smoke, and grit permeating his being. Letting the hot water cascade over his head, he tried to find his center but couldn't home in on it after an utterly discombobulating night. Something had changed. Something was wrong. Yet, he couldn't figure out what. Once his inability to pinpoint it grew into frustration, he soaped up and scrubbed his body until his skin tingled.

When he emerged from the bathroom, Roxi lay across the bed in nothing but a robe, her hair wet from the shower she'd taken in the other bathroom. She patted the bed, a concerned smile doing little to counter the dark rings under her eyes. They both needed a lot of sleep.

"What's going on, dōšagīh? I don't know if I've ever seen you this…disconcerted."

Luke laid down next to her, resting his head on her shoulder. She enfolded him in her warm embrace and stroked his damp hair, humming one of the soft melodies she knew would sooth him.

He inhaled slowly until his ribs stretched the muscles of his chest, then exhaled explosively. "I don't know. I'm so exhausted, Roxi. I just have nothing left to give at the moment."

She squeezed him, kissing the top of his head. "Alright. Let's get some sleep and talk about it when we're more coherent."

Groaning, he rolled off the bed, tossed his robe aside and crawled under the blanket. Roxi joined him a moment later, spooning him, pressing her nude body against his. The skin-to-skin contact lulled him to sleep.

LUKE WOKE UP, groggy and sore. The vague recollections of nightmares haunted his awareness around the periphery. Rolling over, his arm searching for Roxi, he found nothing but disturbed sheets and a cool patch of mattress.

Shaking his head, he swung his feet off the bed, sitting up. A faint scratching on the door was followed by a familiar meow. Groaning, Luke stood up and pulled out a T-shirt and a pair of pajama bottoms. Once he emerged from the bedroom, he scooped up Alfie and scratched the cat's ears as he purred aggressively. The scent of coffee drew him toward the kitchen.

Roxi, wearing short shorts and a ratty T-shirt, reached into the cupboard for a coffee cup. "Good morning, dōšagīh."

Luke gently set his old furry man down so he could take the cup of coffee. Sitting at the table, he inhaled the dark, roasty aroma, a smile curving his lips.

"I have some food being delivered," Roxi said, sitting across from him.

They sat there in companionable silence as they drank their coffee and waited for their food. This, more than anything, provided Luke with a sense of rightness that helped fill a bit of his spiritual well. Nearby, Brutus noisily crunched his bowl of kibbles while Alfie wound his way through Luke's legs, accepting the occasional scritch whenever Luke dangled his hand within range.

Roxi waited until after they'd finished breakfast before read-dressing last night's car ride home. "How did you sleep?"

A dark cloud passed over Luke's eyes. "Like shit." He sighed. "I had nightmares all night. Dark, weird ones." He tried to focus in on the details but they slipped away like sand through fingers. "They're just a lingering sense of…wrongness."

"I'm sorry." She reached across and squeezed his hand, then rubbed her thumb over the back of his hand. "Do you think it had anything to do with your…fidgetiness on the way home?"

"I don't know." He slumped, his brow furrowing as he tried to put his thoughts in order.

"What was going on? You were so… I don't know how to describe it. 'Out of sorts' doesn't seem strong enough."

He looked at the table in front of Roxi. "It was like…" Shaking his head, he sighed. "Like I could sense vampires but more. I could feel their hunger. At first, I thought it was my own hunger after not eating much. But there was a darkness to it that felt unwholesome. Then, as it got later into the night, there was a satisfied, almost sati-ated tone to the hunger, but it never went away. The hunger… It was all-consuming. When we hit Portland, it was overwhelming. I thought I was going to crawl out of my skin. It wasn't until we were deep into North Portland that it finally went away."

Roxi's brow furrowed, and her eyes looked troubled. "Do you

think it has anything to do with your…" She rolled her wrist, needing a physical gesture to help her find her thoughts. "Well, let's say your sudden increase in abilities?"

He thought about it for a few minutes. "Maybe. I don't know. It could be. So much has happened in the last few days, and I definitely haven't had time to sort it out."

"That's understandable. I mean… You drained vampires without actually sticking them." She shook her head. "I've been doing this for as long as you, and when I saw you do it for the first time…" She shivered, her black, curly hair vibrating around her beautiful face. "It made every hair on my body stand on end."

"When it first happened during the fight, I was too busy trying to survive to think about it. I just kept using it because it worked, and it was keeping me alive. Then when we questioned the vampires… I was too tired and angry to think about it. I just used it to get what I needed at the time."

Roxi nodded thoughtfully. "Maybe that was part of it… The drive home, that is. That was a lot of vampires you drained and incorporated. Maybe it was too much. Like drinking too many coffees."

Luke tilted his head to the side, contemplating it for a moment. "Maybe. Maybe it tuned me into the vampires too much. I looked for them whenever I felt them, but it was just civilians going about their lives. They had to be running around in the cities hunting and feeding. Maybe I overdosed on vampires."

Roxi chuckled. "I didn't think that was possible, though neither of us seem to drain a lot of them at once. Usually just enough to heal our wounds and keep going."

"It's not always easy to get a downed vamp when everyone is staking them. We haven't tried taking captives before." He snorted, shaking his head. "The team is very good about putting them down quickly."

"Maybe it's time for a change in strategy. If what you felt was authentic, then this city is still full of vampires."

"We've kept too many people busy with too many tasks outside the city, and the vampires have reestablished a foothold in Portland." He sighed.

Roxi reached across the table and took his hand in hers. "We're not going to win this war clearing out a neighborhood at a time. I'm sure that base had plenty of time to disgorge a new army of blood-thirsty monsters before we shut it down."

"No," Luke said, clenching his jaw. "We're not going to win this war that way. I'm tired of fighting a losing rearguard action."

"What do you have in mind?"

"I want to turn this city upside down and shake it until we get what we want."

"And what do we want?"

"Saubarag."

"Hey, Luke, I'm home!" Gwen called, shutting the front door. She scooped up a meowing Alfred and hugged him, scratching his ears and chin.

"We're in the kitchen," Roxi replied.

Luke stared at the half-full coffee cup sitting on the table in front of him. Gwen had stayed at Olivia's house a couple extra nights to give Luke and Roxi time to recover after their disastrous victory in southeastern Oregon.

Roxi looked the sixteen-year-old up and down. "You dyed your hair."

"Yeah. So?" Gwen said snottily.

Luke noticed a slight momentary twitch in Roxi's cheek. He didn't like the increased level of bad attitude his ward seemed to display to Roxi, but he couldn't deal with it now. He could barely deal with himself as his grief and anger threatened to overwhelm him.

"Just noticing it, that's all. It looks good. Pink is a good color for you." Roxi smiled warmly at the teen.

Gwen's eyes narrowed slightly, possibly looking for some slight in Roxi's comments she could be angry about. When she found none, she relaxed, some of the tension draining out of her shoulders. Finally, she looked at Luke. "What's wrong? Are you hurt, Luke?"

"He's uninjured, physically," Roxi said. "Um. There were some casualties."

Luke, tears burning at the corners of his eyes, stood up and pulled Gwen into a hug, resting his chin on the top of her heard.

"W-who?" Gwen asked.

"Delilah…" Luke mumbled.

"What…" Gwen's voice quavered, as her body tensed. Delilah had been the first person outside of Luke she'd bonded with. "Is…is she…"

"No," Roxi jumped in. "She's alive, but she took a bad slash. She'll heal though."

Gwen's body relaxed slightly, though she shook, a sniffle punctuating the start of her own tears.

"Pieter…" Luke said.

"He's almost healed from his burns," Roxi added.

"Pah…" Luke choked, blinking furiously as a tear streaked down his cheek. "Pablo."

"Pablo? Oh, no…" Gwen whispered, squeezing Luke hard. "What happened? Is he…"

Roxi licked her lips, watching Luke with worry in her eyes. "A tunnel collapsed on him, and he was struck by a beam. He was badly injured. He's alive, but he's still unconscious."

"But won't he heal? He's a werewolf."

"His body has healed the injuries, and the doctors are working to correct any of the bones that have healed poorly, but Maggie says that sometimes the brain can take longer to heal or…"

"Or not at all," Luke said, his voice shaky and thin, tears running down his cheeks.

"Oh, no…" Gwen's body shook as she cried.

Roxi stood up, stepping toward them, but Gwen tensed up. So Roxi walked around behind Luke, placing her hands on his shoulders, and pressed into his back. Luke wasn't sure how long they stood like that, but eventually Gwen pulled away and shuffled off to her room, Alfie trailing behind her.

Without Gwen there, he sagged into the chair, and Roxi sat on the ground next to him, resting her head on his leg. He just stared at the table. Eventually, he remembered he had coffee and picked it up. Grimacing at the initial cold sip, he drank the rest anyway because it was something to occupy his mind.

Roxi finally broke the silence. "We should go see him."

Luke nodded, clenching his jaw.

"Would you like to go now?"

He thought about it for a bit. "I guess so."

Roxi stood, offering a hand to him. Grasping it, he stood up and fell into Roxi's open arms as she stroked his hair and hummed a sad melody.

After a while, he sighed and pushed pack. "I guess we should get this over with."

He didn't want to see Pablo. Not like that. He'd visited too many friends in the hospital in his nearly two-thousand years. But he'd never been so reluctant to make the visit before. When they'd first met, he'd warned Pablo about the dangers but had let him join the hunt, anyway. Now Pablo was in a coma and the best news Maggie could give Luke was that his best friend was still alive. Still hanging in there. Maybe he'd heal his way out of a brain injury, maybe… Luke felt shitty for thinking of it, but if Pablo didn't heal, he hoped his friend would pass quickly instead of lingering.

Roxi gave him a squeeze and pushed him away to arm's length. "Go splash some cold water on your face, and I'll see if Gwen wants to come."

Five minutes later, they piled into the pack loaner car, Roxi behind the wheel, and headed to the pack's medical clinic. After they parked, Luke was the last out of the car, staring at the dashboard while Roxi and Gwen waited in the shade of a tree near the entrance. Taking in a deep breath, he expelled it noisily, squeezed his eyes shut tight, and climbed out of the car, rallying himself to visit his wounded friend.

As he approached the door, Roxi held out a hand to him, and he took it. Gwen held the door for them. Maggie, sitting behind the desk near the front door, stood up and hugged Luke fiercely.

"How is he?" Roxi asked quietly.

Maggie gave a half shrug. "About the same. Stable, no changes."

Roxi squeezed Maggie's shoulder. "Can we go visit him?"

"Of course," Maggie replied, turning and leading them down the hallway to Pablo's room.

When they entered, they found Tony sitting in a chair near the head of the hospital bed on the opposite side of the room.

"Gwen, it's good to see you," Tony said. "Roxi. Luke."

"Is it alright if we visit?" Roxi asked.

Tony nodded tersely, then stood up. "I'll give you some privacy. I need to take a walk." Just before he exited the room, he stopped and fixed his hard eyes on Luke. "If he makes it out of this, no more. No more hunting. No more vampire wars."

Luke couldn't raise his eyes to make eye contact, but he nodded sadly to acknowledge Tony's words. Without another word, Tony pulled the door closed behind him, the crisp sound of his heels on the hard floor fading as he walked away.

Gwen walked over and squeezed Pablo's hand then left the room, shutting the door behind herself. He didn't know what his ward was thinking or feeling, but Pablo had been one of the first pack members to reach out and bond with the kid when she was skittish and afraid of werewolves. When they had a moment, he'd have to take her out for lunch and check in with her. He had nearly two-thousands years dealing with grief, and he still had trouble managing it; he had no idea how Gwen was doing.

"Don't worry," Maggie said, "Tony will come around. You'll see."

He didn't hear any conviction in her words, though he appreciated her effort. Tony meant what he said. Though, Luke would gladly give up hunting with his best friend if it meant he was alive and well. He'd miss Pablo by his side, but he'd rather miss him by his side and have an alive friend than the alternative. He'd even give up seeing his friend if Tony demanded it. There wouldn't be a deal he wouldn't take if it meant Pablo woke up and was OK.

"I need to make the rounds," Maggie said, hugging Luke and kissing him on the cheek.

Roxi stopped Maggie before she could leave and hugged her. "Thanks, Maggie."

Luke stood still, staring at the floor. With a squeeze of his hand, she sat in the chair next to Pablo's bed, scooping up his hand. As she stroked his hand, she talked to him, saying nothing of importance, just speaking as if they were making conversation. After a while, Luke tuned it out as he warred with himself and the guilt he felt for bringing his friend to this impasse.

He knew the logic of the situation, that if Pablo hadn't gotten involved, Luke would be dead. He knew it was Pablo's own decision to join as an adult with three-hundred-plus years of experience. But Luke couldn't deny the what ifs and the reality laying in the bed a few feet away. If he hadn't come into Pablo's life, he'd likely be alive and well, unbothered by vampires.

When Roxi touched his shoulder, he startled.

She lifted his chin with her finger, her eyes full of compassion. "I'll step out so you can be alone with him."

He nodded, moving out of the way. Once the door clicked shut, he had no idea how long he stood there in silence, the only sound the beeping of machines. Finally, he collapsed into the chair Roxi had sat in earlier.

Taking Pablo's hand, he pressed the back of it to his forehead. "I'm sorry, Pablo." He could feel the unshed tears burning in his eyes. "I'm so sorry." The tears fell, and he sniffled. "If I could do anything to make this right… If I could switch places…"

He couldn't complete his thoughts. The words felt empty. He couldn't change the reality of the situation. All the experience and resources—the skills, the strength, the power, the money, the property—meant nothing, not that they meant much to him at the best of times. They were merely tools to use in his pursuit of his goal of ending vampirism. But none of it could help Pablo. He would have gladly given it all to have his friend awake and healthy.

This was the danger of friendship. Pablo's friendship had saved him, not just from death at the hands of the vampires, but his *life*. Pablo had led him back into the world of the living, had become his friend and his family. Luke had met Maggie and been brought into the pack because of Pablo. He hadn't just been a means to an end, another tool to use in his war against the vampires. He'd become a reason to fight for. A reason to live for. And now it was all for naught. His best friend lay motionless in a hospital bed. A slow rise of his chest and a steady beep of a heartbeat on a machine his only signs of life.

Luke hated feeling helpless. But nothing made him feel more helpless than situations like this. A tight spot, he could fight his way out of. Civilians being taken advantage of by vampires, he could free them. Hell, he could even dress a lot of wounds. But a brain injury? He might as well try to stop the tides or stop the sun from rising.

He wanted to talk to his friend, but he couldn't make the words come out. Unlike Roxi, he couldn't find the head space to make conversation like his friend was there to reply. He sucked at small talk at the best of times. At a time like this? With his best friend in a coma? He couldn't find the place where he could make the words happen. He just hoped his presence would be enough for Pablo as he sat there, holding Pablo's hand to his head.

The door cracked open, and Roxi poked her head in. "Luke? We've been here an hour. And Tony is back."

Luke sighed. Tony wouldn't come back into the room with Luke there. He couldn't blame him. His anger was justified. Standing, Luke laid Pablo's hand across his stomach then bent over and kissed his friend's forehead.

"I miss you, buddy. Please come back." With one last look to his friend, he turned and left the room, Roxi trailing behind him.

CHAPTER
FIVE

Simone nervously tapped on the steering wheel of Pablo's black Toyota Tundra crew cab. Delilah had a spare set of keys for it, and Pablo had said they could always use it. Delilah, still not ready to return to action, had given Simone the keys.

"Where do you want to start?" she asked.

Luke shrugged. "I don't care. Pick a neighborhood and drive. I'll tell you when to stop."

"Just like that?" Simone asked, her French accent growing thicker along with her nerves.

Roxi, sitting behind Simone in the backseat, reached forward and squeezed her shoulder. "Trust him."

"You know I trust him," Simone replied. "This is just…"

"It'll be OK, Simone." Sam buckled herself into the front passenger seat. "Let's go to Southeast Portland if you need a place to drive toward. We've always found plenty of fangers hanging around Belmont and Hawthorne. And we have a couple teams out working in southeast if we need to call in back up."

"Right." Simone pulled out into traffic and turned on to Lombard Street heading east toward I-5. Fifteen minutes later, they pulled off I-5 and merged onto Belmont Avenue. "Now where?"

The strong buzz of vampires had swarmed over him as soon as

they'd driven a mile south on I-5. It was virtually constant, but there was a slightly stronger pull toward the southeast. "Keep going east, then we'll take a right in a bit. I'll give you a heads up."

"OK," Simone replied, sounding a bit unsure.

Once they neared 30th, Luke called for the right turn then a left a couple blocks later. They'd cleaned out many a house in this exact area in the past.

"Be sure to write the address down, Sam. I'm curious if it's a house we've raided before." He paused, tilting his head to the side. "Turn right at the next block, then park. We'll walk back."

"And you're sure?" Sam asked. She'd only been slightly less skeptical than Simone when he'd said he wanted to go out and hunt by feel alone. Though Simone's nerves could be chalked up to hunting directly with Luke along with the fact that Delilah still wasn't fully recovered from her wound.

"Very," Luke replied, a small surge of nerves settling over him.

It had been a long time since he'd done a street-by-street house hunt in this neighborhood. They'd left that task to the street teams and the newer people, now that he had a small army of hunters to lead. He also didn't want to fail in front of his friends now that he was testing the boundaries of something new.

And after nearly two thousand years of stasis, a change in his abilities was cause to be nervous.

When they parked and jumped out of Pablo's truck, Luke checked his gladius and rudis, both strapped to his back. That was something else he hadn't done in a while. Since they'd been fighting in remote areas where he was surrounded by friend and enemies with no civilians around, he'd kept the weapons in the open.

"Am I covered?" he asked, trying to look over his shoulder.

"Here." Roxi took his hood and draped it to cover the pommels of both weapons.

Roxi got away with wearing a lightweight three-quarter length trench coat that stopped at her knees. It was still summer, though they were getting close to the arrival of autumn, but few people questioned odd wardrobe choices in Portland, even a slightly out-of-season jacket.

"You both ready?" Sam asked.

"Let's do it," Luke said, almost as a pep talk to himself.

As soon as he took the first step, the nerves washed away now that action was imminent. It had always been that way for him. Roxi caught up while Sam and Simone tucked in behind them.

Luke focused on his vampy senses, homing in on the house he wanted. He didn't know how many fangers were inside, not exactly. But as he concentrated, narrowing his senses, he thought the numbers were within their ability to handle.

They stopped in the shadow of a large tree a few houses down from their target.

"What's the play?" Sam asked.

Luke chuckled. "Normally, I'd say we just kick the back door down and turn them all to sludge..." He stared down the street for a moment. "Roxi, Sam. You two are on the front door. Give me and Simone time to slip around back. Then you two walk up to the front door and knock. Or pick the lock and let yourself in."

"Just like that?" Sam asked.

"Just like that," Luke said.

"OK."

Luke waved Simone after him. Together, they slipped into the side yard and let themselves into the backyard through the gate. Simone, her eyes wide, looked everywhere, her movements twitchy and anxious. He couldn't blame her. This was the first time she'd been paired with him on something like a house raid since she'd joined them. Any of the raiding she'd done after she'd moved to Portland had been while he'd been imprisoned and removed from the map in the vampires' arena. Since he'd emerged, it had been large-scale operations.

They stopped at the corner of the house before swinging around to the back.

Luke reached out and laid his hand on Simone's forearm. "Don't worry. There's not that many inside. We're just going in for a little chat."

She nodded briskly.

"Let's go," he whispered, reaching over his shoulder to draw his gladius.

Simone pulled out a stake, leaving the machete on her hip in its scabbard. Luke led the way, ducking under a couple windows before stopping at the edge of a sliding glass door. Reaching out, he pushed the handle, and the door slid a little. They'd left it unlocked.

Shaking his head, he smirked. The vampires in this city needed a healthier sense of fear. Fear... He knew once the vampires inside the house realized who had come looking for them, they'd react in terror. He swallowed the saliva pooling in his mouth at the prospect of the terror of vampires and shook his head.

Turning his head, he made eye contact with Simone. She nodded at him. He slowly slid the door open and stepped inside, waving Simone in after him. Carefully, he slid the door closed behind them and locked it.

"What the fuck... Oh shit!" The vampire, its eyes wide, turned around and sprinted out of the kitchen. "Run! Hunters!"

Simone yanked the machete out, taking a couple steps away from Luke so she had room to work if she needed to. Luke raised a hand, waving her back. She nodded and lowered her weapons, though she still looked like she was coiled like a mousetrap, ready to spring into action.

Moving toward the door leading out of the kitchen, Luke raised his hand next to his mouth. "I'm not here to kill. I'm here to talk."

He waited. Somewhere deeper in the house, he could hear a panicked conversation, though he couldn't make out anything.

"I swear," he called out. "You talk. You give me the information I want, or as close to it as you can, and you can leave. Unharmed and still undead."

"Bullshit!" a male voice yelled back.

Sam chuckled. "I think your reputation is working against you."

Grumbling, Luke clenched his jaw. "I guess so." He tipped his head toward the stairs leading up. "If you don't want to talk, we can do this the other way. I can kill you all and find some vampires who are smarter than you."

A window shattered, and Simone jogged to the sliding glass door. "Luke, this way."

Luke joined Simone at the door as someone landed gracelessly on the lawn. They came up clutching a bloody forearm, a long gash the source of the blood. With a growl, Luke yanked the door open and pointed his rudis at the vampire and drained it, a trickle of golden light linking the body and the tip of the rudis for a brief moment before the vampire puffed into powder and floated about on the light summer evening breeze.

Stalking out into the yard, he looked up into the terrified faces of two vampires. He raised the rudis, two lines of light connecting to it, and drained them before they could even move.

"Shit," he mumbled. "Simone, can you have Sam and Roxi sweep through the upstairs? You watch the front door. I'll watch this side of the house. If they can spare any vamps and capture them, great. If not, we'll try another house."

"Right." Simone disappeared into the house.

A couple minutes later, Roxi poked her head out the window. "Looks like these three were the only ones here. Why'd you kill both of these?"

He shook his head, pursing his lips. "I tried to only drain one, but it connected to both. Damn it."

Roxi snorted, shaking her head and trying to contain her laughter. "Let's sweep the house and move on."

Luke nodded and plopped down on a nearby patio chair. A few minutes later, his three companions emerged through the sliding glass door, a few laptops tucked under their arms. They also probably had some pilfered cell phones stashed in pockets for the tech team to go through.

"What now?" Sam asked.

"I guess we try again." Luke stood up and headed toward the side gate.

He didn't bother looking over his shoulder to see if anyone was following. He could hear their breathing and the sound of equipment jingling. Fifteen minutes later, they parked out of the way of another house. They could have stopped at several along the way, but Roxi and Sam thought it would be better if they moved further away from their first house in case they'd attracted any unwanted attention.

This time, they swept in quieter and rounded up four vampires who'd been too distracted with their bottled blood. Picking up a discarded bottle, Roxi peered at the label, then turned and showed it to Sam, who stood next to her. Simone kept the cluster of vampires contained with her shotgun pointed at them.

"No wonder they were easy to round up," Sam said, handing the bottle over to Luke.

He spun it around and checked out the white label. Human female blood. Heroin. That would explain the docility of the four vampires. They had either just been on the nod or were about to be, though the adrenaline of four vampire hunters busting into their nest seemed to be keeping them somewhat alert, at least for three of them. One of them periodically drifted off, their head snapping back up only to start the process over again.

Luke set the bottle aside. "I don't know if we'll be able to get anything out of them in this condition."

Sam shrugged. "Don't know unless you ask."

"Simone," Roxi said, nodding toward the one dozing off yet again.

Together, they dragged the vampire away from the others. That seemed to wake it up. It tried to thrash about and get away, but the strength of a vampire hunter and a werewolf kept the stoned vampire in check. They stopped along the wall opposite the other three. Backing away from each other, they held the vampire's arms out wide.

Sam stepped in, leveling her shotgun at the remaining three fangers. "I think our new friends could use an object lesson."

With a curt nod, Luke pulled his rudis out and focused on the undead heart of the vampire they held. Soon, he felt the connection but also, to a lesser extent, three more connections. The three vampires behind him whined. Scowling, he tightened his concentration on the one in front of him. The other three more tenuous threads snapped. He thought he heard the vampires behind him sigh in relief. In a matter of moments, the thread disappeared into Luke's rudis and, through it, into him. The remains of the vampire sluiced to the floor, splattering on the laminate wood flooring. Roxi and Simone danced away, trying to avoid any unwanted vamp goo being splashed on their shoes and pants.

Luke turned around. The three vampires huddled together, holding each other, their already pale faces even paler.

"Do you know who I am?" Luke asked.

One of the vampires nodded; the other two just stared down at the floor.

"Who am I?"

"Y-you're the…" The vampire swallowed. "You're the w-w-w…"

"Say it," Luke barked out.

"The Wood-Fanged Demon."

"And do you know what I do to vampires?"

"M-m-murder us."

Luke tsked, shaking his head. "Semantics. Can I murder murderers? I bring justice to the souls stolen and the humans robbed of life. But today's your lucky day. I want something more than your undead lives. And if you give it to me, I'll let you run away and find a deep dark hole to hide in. You saw what I can do. There's no escape without cooperation."

"What do you want?" the vampire stammered.

"Information. I want the location of the dark entity."

"The what?"

"I want the one you all fear. The one you grovel to. Saubarag."

The vampire didn't so much as flinch, a note of confusion joining the fear contorting its face. Luke wasn't sure what to expect when he used the name of the god who'd transformed himself from a tiny god in a smaller pantheon into one of the supreme dark powers on earth. Luke had only just discovered it a few days ago. But he had no idea what the rank-and-file vampires knew about the one who controlled them. Neither of the other two vampires did anything besides tremble.

If a vampire could pee—Luke didn't actually know if they could urinate—they'd be pissing themselves in fear. These were probably, at best, low-level foot soldiers. Newly turned thralls or victims. They wouldn't know anything important. If Luke actually found someone in the first few houses who did know something, it would be a major miracle. Today didn't look like it was going to be their day for divine interventions.

Careful not to stab himself, he folded his arms. "If you can't give me that little sneak thief of a god who calls him Saubarag, give me Constantius or Eusebius."

Those names seemed to strike a note where Saubarag hadn't.

"I see you recognize them. Where can I find them?"

"I-I-I don't know," the vampire said.

Luke pointed to one of the other vampires. "You. Do you know?"

The vampire shook its head vigorously.

Aiming his rudis at the other one, he asked, "You?"

It shook its head weakly. A growl rose in Luke's throat as he turned around and stalked across the room. Spinning around, he jabbed his sword to the cluster of vampires. "Run."

They didn't move.

"I'm going to let one of you go. And it's going to be whoever is the fastest. Spread the word. The Wood-Fanged Demon is coming. If you want to live, I want information. Now Run!" Luke's anger, always bubbling under the surface lately, spiked. Jabbing out with his rudis, he quickly drained one of the vampires, the surge of power only serving to stoke his fury.

As the other two vampires were drenched in the sloppy remains of their companion, they shot to their feet, slipping on the sludge that was their friend and clawing at each other to gain some advantage over their competition.

One vampire tumbled backwards, allowing the other to stumble toward the window, often using all four limbs to make forward progress. Not even stopping to kick out the window, the fanger hurled itself headfirst through the window, sending jagged shards flying everywhere.

Stepping toward the window, Luke looked down into the backyard. The vamp twitched on the ground, trying to claw its way toward escape. The headlong fall from the window must have cut important things in its neck as a dark shiny patch spread from its oddly bent neck. The sound of thumping feet flying down the stairs turned into a noisy thud and roll as the other fanger tripped and fell down the rest of the stairs. A moment later, the sliding door thumped in its frame.

Luke pointed his rudis out the window and held the incantation firmly in his mind but didn't unleash it. As soon as he saw the other fanger approach its mostly dead friend, Luke unleashed the incantation.

The vamp on the ground exploded, drenching the other vamp as it jumped over what was its last companion's body. It fell to the ground, clawed back up, and sprinted out of sight. Most young vampires just turned to goo and sluiced down to the ground. But every once in a while, a young one would explode. Despite losing a lot of the sludge that ran through its veins, this one made a ridiculously large mess.

Snorting, Luke bent over and grabbed the shirt the vamp he'd drained had worn and wiped down the rudis before putting it away. "We should sweep for any computers then get out of here."

"OK..." Sam said, nodding shakily, and disappeared with Simone.

Roxi waited until she no longer heard their friends. "How are you doing, dōšagīh?"

He thought about it for a moment. "I don't know. Angry." Looking down at his hand, he squeezed them into fists to hide the slight tremble in his fingers. "I'm feeling a bit...over charged."

She nodded, pursing her lips. "You've drained a lot of vamps the last few days. Have you ever done that before?"

He thought about it but had trouble focusing. "I don't think so. I never take more than I need to heal. Usually, we just stake most everything and go. I never get a chance to glut. Is Sam OK?"

"I think she's a bit nervous about the shift in your powers. You suddenly have a new tool and have been using it a lot. They're probably used to one way of doing things with you. Now..."

He furrowed his brow and stared at the floor, the dark pool of vampire goo slowly spreading. "That's probably true."

"Luke. We're ready here," Sam called from downstairs.

"We better go, in case anyone called the authorities after the little window dive." Roxi rubbed his back reassuringly, then guided him toward the stairs.

He descended absentmindedly, thinking about Roxi's words. His new ability to trigger the rudis's power without direct contact was a powerful tool, but it was too early to know what the side effects might be. Following quietly, he let his friends guide him out the back, around the side of the house, and back to Pablo's truck.

Focusing on how he felt physically, he ignored the quietness of his friends and the lack of their usual banter. Though that could be explained by the missing loved ones not healed enough to be there. His body buzzed like he'd drank too much coffee. Focusing, except through the lens of his anger, was difficult. But he could feel the vampires more directly than he ever had before when it was just a general sense of nearness and directionality.

"Luke? Luke? Luke!" Sam called.

He shook his head and looked up.

Sam narrowed her eyes as she assessed him. "What do you want to do now? Hit another house? Call it for the evening?"

"Let's keep working. I doubt we'll get an answer so easily, but we need to make sure the vampires know about the changing situation and that word gets back to someone willing to betray their master for survival."

Sam's eyes flicked to Roxi briefly. She nodded lightly.

"OK. Simone. Start driving. We'll find another neighborhood to hit next."

Normally, he might have been annoyed Sam had checked in with Roxi to get confirmation before executing Luke's plans, but he didn't have the focus available for it at the moment. When the effects of too many vampires wore off, he'd have to check in with Roxi so they could have a long talk about what was going on with him.

Twenty minutes later, they stopped in another neighborhood. He had no idea which one. He hadn't paid attention until he called out that he felt some vampires, though he'd felt them the entire trip. But by then, he figured they'd traveled far enough.

He couldn't tell if it was his new senses picking up the constant sensation of vampires or if there were just that many in Portland. With the size and proximity of the fortress they'd blown up a few days ago, probably both. Once they returned for the evening, he'd talk with Roxi and see what her perceptions were so he could figure out a baseline for himself.

As soon as his feet hit the ground, he focused on the task of hunting. Hunting and killing seemed to be the only thing his body and mind could coordinate on, especially as juiced up as he was. But now that it was time to hunt, he felt like a leashed dog waiting to be unclipped so he could run and sink his fangs into his quarry.

Like the previous house, they found no one who could tell them anything of value, so they let one run free and killed the rest. Eager to get another raid in, he urged the team to move on so they could find another house. It yielded the same results.

He tried to talk the team into finding another house in the dying darkness as the sun threatened to emerge any moment. But Sam, backed by Roxi, overrode him. After giving in, he quietly sat in the backseat of the truck and brooded.

As they wound their way through the surface streets of Portland, he wondered how far he could use his new ability and pulled out his rudis.

"Luke, what are you doing?" Sam asked. "It's not safe to play with swords while we're driving."

"I'm curious about something." Rolling down his window, he pointed the tip of the rudis out toward a house and concentrated. The pull felt harder and more difficult to maintain, but then it snapped back, almost shoving him across the backseat. But the seatbelt kept him in place. A large golden globule flew out of the house he'd targeted and connected with the tip of his sword.

Energy surged through him and he practically vibrated, bouncing in his seat like a hyperactive child. Someone sighed, but he didn't pay attention to who. No one spoke or even turned on the radio.

Without something to focus his mind on, it skittered about from subject to subject like a hummingbird looking for nectar. When they dropped Roxi and Luke off at his house, he immediately walked in and took a shower, hoping the calming steam would bring him down enough he could get to sleep, though he felt the edge of exhaustion creeping up on him.

As the water began to cool, he didn't feel noticeably more relaxed. Shutting the water off, he toweled off and crawled into bed next to Roxi. At first, he tried to settle in but couldn't seem to find a comfortable spot. Normally, if he had trouble falling asleep, it was due to his mind fixating on something, but now, it flitted about without direction. Mumbling, Roxi rolled over and laid a hand on Luke's shoulder. The heat of her hand soothed him enough he could slip into sleep.

CHAPTER
SIX

Luke woke up with a gasp, tangled in the sheets. Bolting upright, he tried to breathe through his pounding heart rate and bring it down.

"What? Are you alright, dōšagīh?" Roxi asked groggily.

"I don't know. I'll…I'll let you sleep." He swung his legs out of bed and grabbed his robe.

Shutting the door quietly, he used the bathroom, then headed through the living room toward the office.

Gwen was on the couch playing video games with Alfie laying against her leg. "You're up early."

Luke ran a hand through his sweaty hair. "Yeah. Having trouble sleeping. I'm going to head down to the gym."

"OK."

He grabbed the book that triggered the secret entrance to his underground gym and lair, shutting it after himself. Quickly changing into some workout clothes, he headed to the treadmill, hoping to burn off some of the excess energy of draining so many vampires.

At first, he started off at a reasonable warm-up pace. But it felt too sedate, so he punched the up button. He could only manage a couple minutes at the upped pace before he became antsy and reached for the speed button again.

Once again, he hit the button, but this time, nothing happened. Looking down, he stared at the speed. Sixteen miles per hour. He'd reached the unit's maximum speed, and he wanted more. He'd searched for a while to find a treadmill that could even go that high, though he'd never really used the maximum speed except for the occasional sprint workout. Now, he'd been at maximum for several minutes and felt like he could go faster and still sustain his pace.

Huffing in annoyance, he forced his eyes away from the speed indicator and stared ahead, letting his mind drift to the thought of chasing down vampires. Though, he had to keep himself from getting carried away as his feet hit the end of the treadmill and his stomach bumped into the control panel.

Sweat poured from his skin, soaking his clothes and dripping on the treadmill. His breath raged in and out of his mouth as his body pulled in as much oxygen as possible to keep up with this sustained punishment. He wondered if he went outside if he could run the entire street at the posted speed limit of twenty-five miles per hour.

The thought forced a gasping chuckle from his lips.

He stumbled a couple times, and when he nearly lost his balance on a third stumble, he backed off the speed until he finally walked on wobbly legs. He nearly fell into the rail but caught himself before he slipped off the end of the treadmill.

He grabbed a towel and wiped at the sweat, but it quickly replaced itself faster than the towel could handle. He tossed the towel aside and grabbed another as he staggered toward the mini fridge.

His hand trembling, he pulled a water from the fridge but struggled to open it. Finally, the cap fell to the floor, plinking off the top of the appliance. He shoved the bottle into his mouth and chugged as much as he could, reaching halfway before he came up gasping for air.

Blinking hard, he tried to clear his vision from the sweat blurring it. But it didn't clear and now the edges were graying. He looked down at his shaking hands, water sloshing inside the bottle as his knees gave way. Grasping for the wall with his empty hand, he slid to the ground, and the bottle fell from his hands, tipping over and spilling water over the floor. The cold spilled liquid soaked into his shorts and provided a modicum of relief before he passed out.

A TERRIBLE STENCH dragged him from a weird, gray netherworld.

"Luke… Luke…"

His name sounded like he was hearing it through water. The pop of fingers against his skin further brought him back to awareness.

"Wha…" he mumbled.

Blinking hard, he saw blonde hair waving in front of his face as his hand made contact with something below his nose.

"Let's give him a second to finish coming to," a woman with an accent said.

A low murmur of voices, like bees swarming a flowering bush, kept him from sinking back under. Once his vision cleared, he saw three faces staring at him, all of them looking worried.

"Luke? Can you understand me?" Maggie asked as she dropped something into her pocket.

"What is that stench?" he asked.

"Smelling salts. You passed out."

"How long?"

Maggie looked at Roxi.

"I don't know. It's about noon. I woke up at eleven and you weren't in bed, so I went looking for you."

"I couldn't sleep, so I came here to burn off the excess energy, then…" He closed his eyes and concentrated, his hand moving to the damp material of his shorts. "I was running on the treadmill, then stopped to get a water." The light flickering off the empty glass bottle, now standing, drew his attention.

"And now…" He gestured around him with a shaky hand.

"How do you feel?" Maggie asked, turning to the side to grab something.

"I…I don' t know." He tried to get up, but Roxi lurched forward and pushed him back onto his butt.

"You stay put until Maggie can examine you. You had us scared witless." There was still a deep furrow in Roxi's brow. Gwen nodded along.

Sighing, he relaxed his muscles and sagged against the wall next to his fridge. Maggie pulled out a stethoscope from her bag and put it on.

"Just breathe normally, please," Maggie said clinically, moving the stethoscope from his heart to various other parts of his chest. "Now breathe deeply."

When she finished with the listening device, she put it away and pulled out a flashlight she shined into his eyes as she held his eyelids open. Next, she popped a digital thermometer into his ear until it beeped. She sat back, her eyes narrowed as she assessed him.

"What's going on with him?" Roxi asked.

"His pulse is elevated, his temperature is up, and his pupils are dilated. If I didn't know any better, I'd say he'd overdosed on a powerful stimulant like cocaine."

Luke chuckled halfheartedly. "Sorry, but no rootie tootie booger sugar for me."

Gwen giggled nervously, and he winked at her.

Roxi stared at him, her face serious with no trace of amusement. "You did overdose. On vampires. You must have drained dozens in the last handful of days with at least twelve or so last night."

Luke started laughing weakly, but it didn't stop as it built. Roxi's face shifted from serious to stern as her brow furrowed and she crossed her arms. Maggie looked vaguely puzzled behind her professional façade, while Gwen just looked confused. When it had tapered off to just a few uncontrolled chuckles and snorts, he took a deep breath to calm himself.

Shaking his head, he exhaled loudly. "Sorry for laughing. It's just so absurd. How fucking stupid is it that I overdosed on vampires? As if all the other things the rudis does to us aren't bad enough…"

No matter what new side effect of his immortality and the tool he was forced to use to maintain his existence, the prison Mithras trapped him in never ceased to amaze him at its depths and peculiarities. Even after nearly two thousand years. He'd burn the hateful stick if he could, if it wouldn't destroy him.

"Is he going to be alright?" Roxi shifted so she was looking at Maggie.

"I'd like to say yes, with some time to detox, but with this… I just don't know. I've never treated someone for a vampire overdose. I'd say I didn't even know it was possible, but I don't even know that much about what your wooden swords do or how they work and affect you." She looked annoyed at not having the answers she wanted.

Roxi gave a half shrug. "I'm sorry I can' t help you much. I've never taken in that many vampires before, or anywhere close to it. Nor have I discussed the tool with any medical professionals, certainly not in the modern age."

"I don't know," Luke said, then paused for a yawn. "It kind of makes a perverse sort of sense. On the one side, if we don't take in a vampire, after a while, we go through withdrawals. So now we know the flip side is true. Too many fangers—overdose."

"Is there anything we can do?" Roxi asked.

"Keep him hydrated, let him rest, and lay off the vampires for a while." Maggie shrugged, her brow furrowing deeply in frustration. "That's the best I can do for a suggestion. It's not like you two conform to standard medical needs, even for supernaturals."

"Can we move him upstairs?"

"I think so."

Luke cleared his throat. "I'm right here, you know."

Roxi reached over and patted his knee. Rolling his eyes, he caught a knowing, sympathetic glance from Gwen as the adults in the room talked around him. Whatever. It wasn't like he'd intentionally overdosed. It was a new and untested power. He'd just have to be more careful with it until he learned more about it.

"Luke?" Maggie asked. "Do you feel well enough to move upstairs?"

"Yeah. I think so." He set his hands down to push himself off the ground but couldn't quite coordinate it. "Here. Give me some help up."

He held both his hands up. Roxi and Maggie stood up, each one taking one of his hands, and helped him to his feet. Roxi, quick as lightning, slipped under his shoulder, keeping her grip on his hand.

"I'll help you up the stairs. Gwen, can you go make sure the doors are open and Alfie doesn't get underfoot, please?"

Gwen nodded and ran toward the door, opening it before storming up the steel spiral staircase that led to the entrance in his office on the main floor of the house.

Luke did his best to control his own body but quickly realized his coordination was off, and he needed to rely on Roxi's strength and guidance. By the time they made it into the living room, sweat beaded on his forehead and dripped down his back.

"Here will do for now," he gasped out between ragged breaths. Smacking his dry lips, he tried to draw moisture into his mouth. "Can I have some coconut water?"

Roxi helped him down onto the couch as he sagged into the cushions of the couch. Before he could orient himself, an open can of coconut water was thrust into his face. Carefully, he gripped it in his hand, but spilled some over the rim thanks to the ongoing tremble.

"Dammit." Luke handed the can over to Roxi.

"Sorry," Gwen mumbled.

"No. It's not your fault I can't control my muscles right now."

"Gwennie, dear, go get a plastic cup and a straw. We can fill it halfway. That should be easier for him to manage." Maggie turned to Roxi. "Do you have any electrolyte tablets or drinks? Coconut water is good, but he'll likely need more to help replenish his body as it comes down."

"Yeah. We have some in all our kits. We have it in case we find any vampire victims."

Maggie nodded, smiling at Roxi. "That makes sense. Keep his food pretty simple for a bit. Nothing too heavy or greasy."

"Can do," Roxi said. "Is there anything else we should do or anything we should keep our eye on?"

"No. Just check his pulse and temperature every so often to

make sure they're steady or going back to normal ranges. If you get a spike in either, call me immediately."

Roxi stood up and pulled Maggie into a tight hug. "Thank you, Maggie. Thank you for coming so quickly."

"Of course." Maggie kissed Roxi on the cheek. "You've got my number if you need it." She stepped back. "I guess I should get into the clinic and check in with everyone."

Luke looked up at Maggie, pain in his eyes. "Give us a call if there's any news about... One way or the other."

Maggie hugged Gwen as she walked by. "Of course. Take care."

Gwen grabbed the can of coconut water and poured some into the cup, dropping a straw in it. "Here you go."

He was able to handle the partially filled light cup and sucked it empty, handing it over for a refill.

"Be careful not to drink too fast. I don't want to have to chase down Maggie if you aspirate your drink." Roxi fixed a tired smirk on her face.

Nodding weakly, he took a bit more time before handing over an empty glass.

"I've got one of the electrolyte tabs dissolving in some cold water right now," Gwen said.

"Thank you." Roxi smiled fondly.

"Ice, please," Luke mumbled, yawning widely.

Despite his elevated pulse and the constant sheen of sweat, he felt a bit better. The tiredness falling over him felt more natural, unlike the moments before he passed out on the floor.

"Are you hungry, dōšagīh?" Roxi sagged into a nearby armchair with a heavy sigh of relief.

"I don't know. I think I'm just thirsty right now."

As if to answer his need, Gwen reappeared with a jug filled with ice and water hazy from the dissolved tablet. She refilled his coconut water glass and handed it to him, setting the jug on a coaster.

The ice-cold water felt amazing sliding down his throat, relieving the constant heat causing his perspiration. Letting Gwen refill his cup, he worked his way through the jug, forcing his eyes to stay open. Once the straw sucked air, he set it down on the coffee table and allowed his body to sag to the side. Grabbing a throw pillow, he stuffed it under his head and moaned lightly in happiness that he was no longer forcing himself to stay upright.

"Are you alright, dōšagīh?" Roxi asked, sitting up from her relaxed slouch.

"Yes. I'm just tired. No fainting this time," he mumbled as he let the lead weights in his eyelids respond to gravity. "Wake me up when it's time to go hunt vampires…"

WHEN HE WOKE, he groaned as the shifting light of the television pierced his eyes, and his head throbbed. He thought he could hear his blood pumping through his ears.

"How are you feeling?" Roxi asked from her place in the armchair.

"Blech," he replied, closing his eyes. "My head is going to explode."

"Hangover or something we need to seek medical attention for?" Concern filtered through her voice.

"Hangover… I think." He wanted to lie there and maybe go back to sleep until his headache disappeared, but a different ache made itself persistently present. He needed to make a trip to the bathroom.

Forcing himself into a sitting position, he waited until his head quit spinning before attempting to get all the way to standing.

"Here." Roxi held out a hand to help him rise. Without him noticing, she'd climbed out of her chair and moved to his side.

Taking her hand, he groaned as he rose. He set his other hand on her shoulder as he waited for the dizzy spell to pass. Not worrying about his dignity, certainly not where Roxi was involved, he let her guide him to the restroom. When he reemerged, he felt lighter and a bit steadier on his feet as he shuffled back to the couch.

He looked around for his phone so he could check the time. "Is it too late to get out on the streets?"

Roxi raised an eyebrow, quite possibly higher than he'd ever seen her raise one before. "Luke. Dōšagīh. It's six a.m. You slept through the afternoon and night. You've missed the window to hunt vamps for the day. But. I'm not letting you out tonight either. You can barely walk."

"I'll be fine —"

"Dōšagīh. Take the day off. Rest. Recuperate. I've spoken with Sam, and she's got the teams working on the new catch and release protocol."

"But I can sense —"

"The werewolves can handle it well enough with their noses. If I need to, I'll call Maggie over and have her sedate you. You're not going out tonight. You have well-trained friends. Let them carry the burden while you recover."

He sighed and sagged into the cushions of the couch. "Fine."

A moment later, Roxi joined him, picking up his hand and flipping it over. Laying two fingers across the underside of his wrist, she concentrated. "Still a bit high, but much better." She scooped the thermometer off the coffee table and poked it into his ear. "And almost back to normal."

"That's good, I guess."

"Maggie said you could return to duty as soon as your temperature and pulse were back to normal ranges. Unless something else crops up, you should be fine by tomorrow night. Is that soon enough?"

"It is." Tomorrow night, he'd see what he could do while protecting himself from his new power. Convenience was no reason to endanger his life and his mission. He grabbed her hand and raised it to his lips, kissing the palm of her hand. "Thank you for taking care of me."

She smiled warmly at him, love filling her eyes. "How could I do any less when you took such good care of me after you found me and brought me back to your manor?"

"There's no balance sheet between us, Roxiustana Surena."

"I know, dōšagīh. But the fact is, I owe you my life. You challenged a god to save me."

"It seemed a small thing to have you by my side. I'd go much farther to save you if I had to." And he would. He'd challenged

Mithras to save her from the deadly compulsion he'd placed on them, returning them to a status quo. But he'd kill a god if it meant saving her. And that's what he planned to do. A god stood in the way of their happiness and the happiness of any human who wanted to live a life free of the exploitation of fanged predators.

The other humans he'd fought for were an abstract concept. Leaning in to Roxi and laying his head on her shoulder, he sighed in contentment and reached up to stroke her cheek. He'd do terrible things to protect their future together and let the rest of humanity reap the benefits of the results.

It may not be the most noble of goals, but a humanity that would never know why it was safer wouldn't care one way or the other. They would survive, and he would love.

CHAPTER
SEVEN

After the initial overdose, they stuck to mostly regular methods of making examples of vampires—stakes and their anti-vampire ordnance. With Luke recovered and staying in Portland for a while, the pack was able to increase their reach with all the extra bodies he normally took with him on his away missions. The only thing keeping them from being at full strength was the people still out with wounds and injuries from their assault on the vampires' fort.

And grief.

There was still too much of that going around for their lost pack-mates, friends, and family. Though visiting Pablo was a Herculean struggle, he forced himself to go every day, despite the continued cold shoulder Tony gave him.

Luke could barely stand seeing his friend so pale and frail as he lay motionless, his chest steadily rising and falling as a nearby machine beeped. But Pablo had saved Luke's life with the friendship they'd built, and he would never abandon his friend no matter how uncomfortable, angry, and grief-stricken it made him. He had to dedicate some of his strength to talking to his unconscious friend. Then, when he returned home, he could be weak in Roxi's arms. He didn't know where he'd be without her and their love for each other.

The best he could do for his friend, since he couldn't magically heal him, was to make sure the entity that had caused Pablo's condition was never allowed to do it to anyone ever again.

In contrast, the visits with Delilah were more enjoyable and less emotionally arduous. As she healed, her mood improved. As she neared the point where she'd be medically cleared, she grew more excited to rejoin her friends on the street.

But night after night, Luke and his raiders grew no closer to finding a vampire who knew anything of substance. So they kept hunting, killing, and sending out survivors to spread the tale. However, it seemed like the pickings weren't growing slimmer. The city practically pulsed with the undead.

Since they'd returned to hunting and clearing the city, Luke turned over the operation to Delilah who was now well enough for the light duty of desk work and managing their hunting. He was glad to have her back, though he wouldn't be fully happy until she could return to the hunt with him. Though one added benefit of her recovery, beyond his own feelings, was Simone's brightened mood. With Delilah out of the clinic, Simone was practically giddy.

"Look at him run!" Simone said, a wicked grin on her face as they watched their chosen "lucky" vampire sprint away from the house they'd just raided.

"They're very good at running," Roxi said, sounding disgruntled. "That seems like all they're able to do." She twisted her sword in the chest of a dead vampire that lay at her feet, stepping back as she yanked her sword free.

"Another gooey mess." Luke stepped back as the vampire oozed into the carpet. He looked up and glanced around the room. "When was the last time we dusted a vampire?"

He waited, but no one seemed to have an answer as they looked back and forth at each other. Taking a moment for himself, he tried to pinpoint the last older fanger they'd dusted.

"Not since the first night back from the fort," he concluded. "What are they playing at?"

"I don't know." Roxi shrugged. "But we've killed a lot of their senior vampires over the last couple years. Maybe those they have left are out of position trying to hold down their own territories with all the new vampire hunters your videos have unleashed."

That seemed plausible, but for some reason it didn't seem to sit right with Luke. The conclusion they'd come to was that the vampire hierarchy was bent on his destruction and had dedicated vast amounts of resources to it. That fort couldn't have been cheap or easy to build out in the middle of nowhere. He had to wonder if they'd pulled back their older vampires to prepare for some other plot to take him out.

Luke opened his mouth to voice his concerns when Sam's phone rang, and she raised a hand to forestall him.

"This is Sam." Her eyes narrowed. "What? Slow down. Where?"

Luke, Roxi, and Simone stood quietly, watching Sam as her eyes widened and her jaw dropped.

"Right. We'll get moving right away. Call me back in ten with an update." Sam ended the call and shoved the phone back into her pocket. "We have to get moving ASAP. I'll explain when we're on the road."

They all stared back at her.

"Move!" Sam led by example, dashing toward the front door.

Luke, adrenaline dumping into his system, went on high alert, bringing up the rear to make sure nothing jumped any of his people as they fled the house they'd just cleared.

Once they were buckled in, Sam gave Simone directions then waited until they were rolling.

Luke, tired of being patient, leaned forward, stretching the seat-belt until it clicked to hold him in place. "What's going on, Sam?"

She twisted around in the front passenger's seat to look back at him. "One of the teams is in trouble. They called in an emergency to Delilah."

"Did she give you any details?" Roxi asked, setting a hand on Luke's thigh.

"Not much beyond that. Just that they'd encountered heavily armed resistance. Delilah is trying to get more teams headed that way. Once she's got that taken care of, she'll try to gather more details."

"Right." He fidgeted with his fingers. "Where are we going?"

"It was the team on Mt. Tabor," Sam replied, turning to give Simone the next round of directions.

"That's an odd neighborhood up there. Not a lot of roads in or out, and the layout isn't great either," he said, sinking back into his seat. "I don't like it. It's probably a trap."

Sam gave him a few tight nods. "Yeah, I don't like it either. But what choice do we have? Let's just hope the location doesn't suck."

Luke's eyes flicked about as they drove deeper into Southeast Portland. Clenching his jaw, he forced himself to keep his lips tightly closed instead of telling Simone to speed up. They didn't need to get pulled over on the way to a rescue mission. Once Sam's phone rang again, he tensed up more, waiting to hear what the updated situation was.

"Right. Right. Text the address… It's already waiting?" Sam nodded along to whatever Delilah was saying. "OK. Thanks, Dee."

Holding up a hand to stop anyone from interrupting her, she punched in the address on the truck's GPS then turned around. "Delilah has the teams converging at a spot on the south side of the hill, along with a backup team assembling on the north side of the hill."

Luke had caught a brief glimpse of the location before the GPS had returned to showing their next turn. The house the team had disappeared at was in one of the worst possible locations—backed up against the rough hillside in a curved street that ran along the extinct volcano's edge. He didn't remember the on-the-ground layout of the street; it had been ages since he'd been there in person. He just remembered thick hedges and weird elevations on both sides of the street.

"Any updates on the situation?" Roxi asked.

"No. Nothing new. I have the address the team checked in at before they penetrated the house's perimeter."

Luke could barely hear the words coming out of their mouths.

Since tapping into a new level of his powers, Portland had felt alive —or undead—with too many vampires. He was starting to get used to it, at least a little. It still made his skin crawl, but now at least it felt like a background sensation.

But as they neared Mt. Tabor, the sensation smacked him in the brain. Panting, he gripped his left wrist tightly but gasped when he'd pinched too tight.

"Luke, what's wrong?" Roxi asked, gently rubbing his shoulder.

"Vampires. Too many." He forced himself to take in a deep breath and hold it for a few seconds to collect himself. "The closer we get, the thicker the feel is."

"What do you mean?" Sam's brow furrowed. "Are your senses getting even more acute?"

"I don't know." He thought about it for a second. "I don't think so. Let me see if I can put it into words… Since we came back from the fort, my range has increased drastically. When we're moving through a neighborhood, I can feel the tug and pull when we approach vampires. I can feel them fade and recede into the background when we pass by them. There's never a break or a moment when I'm not feeling vampires."

He paused, narrowing his eyes while he looked for an analogy. "It's like cell phone towers. You get more bars the closer you get, then the bars go away until you're handed off to another tower. I'm still feeling that right now. But ahead. On Mt. Tabor, I'm sensing a massive dark cloud waiting for us. The closer we get, the nastier it feels."

Rolling down the window, he poked his face toward the onrushing air and tried to breathe in the cool wind to keep his gorge from rising.

"Roxi, do you feel it?" Sam asked, her eyes flicking back and forth between the two hunters in the back seat.

"Luke's description works. I can feel it too, but much weaker. I still get breaks in the sensation when we get far enough away from a vampire house. Right now"—she rolled her eyes up in contemplation —"I can feel a pressure at the back of my head. It's almost like when the hairs on the back of your neck stand on end but you don't know why? Something wicked that way sits."

"It's bad?" A ridge of worry formed in the middle of Sam's forehead, running from her nose to her hairline.

"It's bad," Luke said. "Really bad."

"What's our count tonight on active teams? Do we have more backups we can call in?" Roxi asked.

Sam fished her phone out of her pocket. "I'll call and tell her to activate everyone and call in our allies."

Once Sam finished with Delilah, she called Holly so she could alert the pack's other regional allies. Luke, now that he had his stomach under control, sat, leaning to the side so he could watch the GPS unit. They were nearly there.

"Looks like we're the first ones here. What's the plan?" Sam asked.

Luke shook his head. "I don't know. Not until we get a better idea of the situation."

Soon enough, they'd get their first look. Simone parked along the street at the spot the GPS indicated.

Luke stared out of the front window, blinking rapidly, trying to clear his watering eyes. "It's almost like a palpable stench."

"Hey, Sam," Roxi said. "Doesn't it look a little too dark?"

Sam leaned forward, staring out the window. "Yeah. It's hard to tell through the trees, but there are hardly any houselights on."

He exhaled quickly. "I hate to ask this, but I need one of you to put your wolf skin on and see if you can sneak up there and get an idea of what awaits us."

"I'll go. My fur is darker," Simone said, unbuckling before peeling her clothes off.

As soon as she was naked, she shifted into her full wolf form. Sam opened her door and slipped out, making room for Simone to jump to the ground. Next to Luke, Roxi opened the small sliding window in the back of the pickup and the canopy, then crawled in, her scale mail rustling.

Grumbling and cursing, she stopped about halfway in. "Luke. I need you to push me the rest of the way in."

Luke's mood lightened a little. "Are you stuck?"

"Ugh. Yes. I am. My hips are too wide. Now push me in."

"They're such lovely hips, though," he replied with a smile.

"I know. I've caught you looking at them enough, but that's beside the point. Push me in."

"OK." He surveyed the situation. "I think you're going to need to twist your hips some so they're angled a bit better. Let me see if I can help you raise the side closest to me."

"Alright."

Luke slid over, ducking his shoulder to wedge it under Roxi's right hip, then pressed up, trying to keep his force directed to just the one side. As he turned his head to make room for Roxi's hip, he caught Sam, a fist stuffed in her mouth as she choked on her own laughter, recording the scene on her cell phone. A grin raised one corner of Luke's lip, and he winked at his friend.

With a grunt, Roxi slid into the bed of the pickup with a thump that shook the large pickup. "Sam. Delete the video."

"What video?" Sam gasped out between chortles.

"The one I know you're recording."

"Fine. I'll delete it." Sam made eye contact with Luke and shook her head as she tried to clamp her lips shut over her broad grin. "Deleted."

"Send it to me," Luke mouthed.

Sam winked and nodded.

"Just remember, Samantha. I'm the one in the back with the shotguns." To emphasize the point, Roxi poked the butt of one of their Winchester M12s into the cabin of the truck.

Luke grabbed it and set it out of the way so it wouldn't be visible to any random passersby. Shifting in his seat so he could reach easier, he took the next shotgun and the one after that.

"Only three?" Luke asked.

"Figured we can sort out Simone's when she gets back. Didn't want to have to stash one or leave it in the front if she was going to stay a wolf." Roxi poked her head back into the cabin, sticking her tongue out at Sam before disappearing again. A moment later, she shoved a wad of cloth through the window. Next came their ammo bandoliers and three satchels with additional reload.

Luke pushed the pile of trench coats and ammo out of the way and extended a hand toward the window. "Ready?"

"Yeah, Roxi. Why don't you climb back through the window," Sam encouraged, her phone in her hand, ready to lift and record at a moment's notice.

"Fuck you, Sam. Come let me out the back."

"I mean… We wouldn't want anyone to see what we have in the back. Now would we?" Sam tried her best to make her tone as reasonable as possible but just couldn't hide the jocularity just below the surface.

Roxi's eyes narrowed, her glare serious. "Sam. You're a friend, so I'll do it gently, but I'll fully knife you."

Luke, trying to hide his smirk, opened the door and walked around back to let Roxi out. Scowling, she stormed by Luke and climbed into the back of the truck. When he rejoined them, Roxi sat with her arms crossed and stared out the window, grumbling under her breath.

Sam, choosing the wiser path of withdrawing from the engagement, turned around to stare out the front window and watch for Simone's return. Moving their gear out of the way, Luke slid next to Roxi and rubbed her leg. After a minute, Roxi huffed and turned toward Luke, leaning into him.

"I suggest you keep that video Sam sent you for personal use only, Roman." She looked up at him, batting her eyelids flirtatiously, though the eyes were hard as agates.

"You know I'd never do anything to humiliate you."

She reached up and patted his cheek. "Good man. Sam, I will trust you to only use that in moments of dire need."

"You can trust my discretion, Roxi." Sam winked jauntily before turning back around to watch for their wolfish friend.

A minute later, a dark blur darted across the street into the shadows of the bushes and trees running along the sidewalk. Sam stepped out of the truck, leaving the door open. A moment later, a medium-sized wolf with dark black fur jumped into the front seat.

Shaking her fur, she sat then shifted into her human form. Once she was dressed, she panted for a few moments then slouched.

"What did you see?" Luke asked.

Simone turned to look into the back seat. "It's eerie as fuck," she said, her French accent thicker than normal. "The porch lights are out, and there aren't any lights on in any of the houses. The streetlights are out too. Some looked broken. And with all the trees and bushes? It's dark up there."

"Did you see or hear any vampires?" Roxi asked.

"Yeah. And smelled a lot too. And…" She gulped, shivering a little. "And more. Death and decay. Dead bodies."

Sam, still standing on the sidewalk, leaned further into the truck. "What were the vampires doing?"

"I only saw a few. They were staring out the front windows of a few houses. I caught the gleam of the light on the occasional set of fangs as they watched me walk through."

Luke jerked around, his eyes narrowing. "They saw you?"

Simone shrugged. "Yeah. If there were as many as you said, someone was bound to see me and sneaking looks sneaky. So, I just walked through the neighborhood. I figured they have plenty of werewolf stooges, but they probably can't tell werewolves apart."

Roxi nodded appreciatively. "When subterfuge fails, be bold and act like you belong. It's spy craft one-oh-one. Good job, Simone."

"Merci."

Luke caught Simone's eye and conveyed his respect with a nod and a small smile. "Did you see any werewolves or living humans?"

"No. Unless they had them hidden deep inside those houses, the only sensory contacts I made were vamps."

"OK." Luke checked the time. Still plenty of darkness left. Pulling up his map app, he expanded the neighborhood and looked at the street situation. "How deep did you go?" He handed the phone forward.

She looked at it briefly, then held it up. "I looped up here around Thorburn, then back through Ash, then up around Pine, then back on Stark. As far as I can tell, it's all vampires."

Luke, stroking his beard, whistled. "That's a lot of houses."

"Yes. It is."

"What are you thinking?" Sam asked.

"I think we're going to have to push through and get to that house and see if they've got our people there." He looked around the cab of the truck. "What other choice do we have?"

CHAPTER
EIGHT

L uke stared at the crowd of people all wearing their lightweight summer trench coats. He snorted, trying to contain laughter at a sudden thought. They looked like a Columbo and Castiel cosplay convention.

"Our teammates are waiting for us. There are a fuck ton of vampires between us and them. Do you intend to let them get away with keeping our friends?" He waited until everyone shook their heads. Normally, if this were a movie, this would be the place he rallied them into loud, raucous cheers, but the team all knew that stealth was the order of the day without even being told. He was proud of them. "But we've dealt with stiff odds before. You all know your assignments. Let's go get our friends."

The team risked a few murmurs and pats on the back before breaking up into the platoons. Satisfied, Luke turned around and moved through the crowd until he was on the edge of the group. Roxi and Sam joined him, forming up on his left and right. He nodded at them, then proceeded across Southeast Stark Street and jogged east until it turned into Thorburn Street.

That was the signal which was quickly relayed to the other teams.

The rest of their people split up, half crossing the street to join

Luke, Roxi, and Sam and the other half splitting into two groups. One would sweep up to the next street which was perched on another wooded rise that overlooked Thorburn. The rest shifted into wolves and disappeared into the wooded slope that rose on the right side of Thorburn. As the street curved northeast, Luke moved into the center of the street. Roxi and Sam dropped back and spread out a bit.

Luke pulled his shotgun out from under his trench coat and rested the barrel on his right shoulder. "Hey! Why don't you come out and play?" he called, strolling forward nonchalantly.

Behind him, doors were bashed in on the left side of the road and shotgun blasts shattered the quiet of the eerily dark neighborhood. The light of muzzle flashes punctuated the unusual darkness. Luke whistled a tune as he strolled down the street, waiting for anyone to see what the new commotion was. Out of the corner of his eye, he saw some movement as someone darted out of view of the window.

"What? Are you scared of the Centurio Immortalis?" He stopped and pumped a shell into the firing chamber and fired it into the air in front of him. "Hey-ay-ay! Come out and play!"

"Offspring? Really, Luke?" Sam said.

He could practically hear the shake of her head.

"Luke…" Roxi said, her tone carrying a warning.

Shadows formed in front of him as they emerged from around the curve of the street. Off in the distance, a wolf howled, raising the hairs on the back of his neck and a smile across his face. Lowering his shotgun from his shoulder, he took aim down the street, angling the gun up somewhat as if he were lobbing artillery shells, and fired. The angle gave him some extra distance, but nothing happened. Normally, he wouldn't be so wasteful, but the ammo team had increased their production rate with the influx of pure silver ingots. Walking forward at his same sedate pace, he waited until he judged he was within a better angle and fired again.

This time, he was rewarded with screams of shock and pain as the shadows broke rank and shoved against each other. He quickly grabbed two shells from his bandolier and shoved them into the magazine on his shotgun. Another howl sounded behind him.

"Ready?" he asked just loud enough for Sam and Roxi's super-natural hearing to pick up, strolling along as he had been.

"Yup," Sam replied from just behind him and to the left.

"Yes," Roxi said from his right.

Once he judged their distance close enough, he burst into a sprint without warning. Sam's and Roxi's feet slapped the pavement as they joined him. Adding a rising growl and yell, he charged toward the line of vampires, raising his shotgun, and opened fire, quickly spraying shots left, right, and center. Two more shotguns barked to life behind him, though they didn't try for as wide of a fire pattern as Luke since they were behind him. After the sixth shot, he quickly slung the empty gun over his shoulder and pulled out the other. He pumped through all the shots in it as the vampires in front of them scattered.

A few tried to raise guns to respond, but the chaos of the sudden charge had caught the inexperienced vampires—likely young ones based on recent trends—completely off guard. Once the last shot rang out from Luke's shotgun, he pulled his swords, both wooden and steel, and slammed into what remained of the front line of vampires.

Roxi joined him a second later with a high-pitched war cry. Sam, who'd slowed just enough to quickly assemble her naginata on the run, was only a couple seconds behind Roxi.

On the sides, their friends and allies boiled out of the shadows and houses they'd broken into, picking up those vampires who'd broken rank and tried to make a run for it. Off to the right, he heard the rustling of bushes as a few vampires tried to break up the hill and were intercepted by his wolves working that flank. In front of Luke, a vampire raised a handgun. Staring down the barrel, Luke's eyes opened wide as his jaw dropped. But before the vampire could pull the trigger, a long shaft with a sword blade on it swept forward, lopping the vamp's hand off along with the gun.

If the vampire had been faster or hadn't hesitated, he might have been able to put a bullet between Luke's teeth. Shaking off the brush with catastrophe, Luke redoubled his efforts, annoyed with himself for letting his mind slip at a crucial moment. Finally, as he stood in the middle of the street huffing and puffing, he lowered his swords as the last opponent in front of him fell into a pile of goo.

A crackle sounded in his earpiece. "Target secured."

Luke pushed the talk button on his radio. "All teams. Phase two." He yelled out the orders again for those who weren't using their radios in their wolf forms.

Before moving out of the street, he took a moment to drain a single vampire to top up his energy. He darted out of the way as the last vampires were staked and the werewolves attached to the other end cleared the street, melding into the shadows.

"That was a bit noisy," Roxi said, her brow furrowed and her lips pursed. "Are you worried the police will show up?"

He snorted. "The police gave this city to the vampires years ago. They aren't going to call in any in case the word gets out to the media or other outlets."

"Still," she replied.

Sam chuckled nearby. "Welcome to city operations with Mr. Subtle."

Luke narrowed his eyes at Sam. "Hush, you."

Roxi shook her head.

Raising a hand to stifle the banter, he looked around for Simone. "Simone?" She slid out of the shadows, her tongue lolling out in a pant from the earlier skirmish. "I need you to run ahead and see what's happening."

She nodded and slipped out onto the sidewalk, then loped along the curve of Thorburn until she disappeared from view in the darkness. Behind him, the team quieted down as they waited in silence, the metallic clicks and slide of loading ammo the only sounds. Pulling his shotguns around, he used the time to refill the guns and his ammo belt from his satchel. He hadn't had time to reload during the fight and still had plenty of ammo. The near silence, eerie in the middle of a city—even up on an ancient, dead volcano—spiked his anxiety. Simone should be back soon.

Wolves perked up their ears, tipping their heads toward the direction Simone had disappeared. Soon, Luke picked up on what they'd noticed. An occasional yip broke the silence, growing louder each time as it neared. Nails and pads hitting pavement soon joined the quiet barks. Peeking around the fence he hid behind, he saw a black wolf running toward them.

Simone angled toward Luke and picked up her speed, her muscles bunching and releasing until she leapt over the fence and slid to a halt on the lawn behind him. Her tongue hanging out as she panted hard, she jogged over to Luke, then sat down, shifting to her human form.

"They…are…" She stopped for a second, trying to calm her heavy breathing. "They're gathering not far from the house we think our people are being held in."

"Did you see how many?" Luke asked.

"A lot. I didn't stay to count, but more showed up while I watched, running up from the other way."

"Armed?"

"Yes. Most with guns, all with something." She dragged the back of her hand over her sweaty brow.

"Good. Thanks. Catch your breath while you can." He grabbed the talk button for his radio and pressed it. "Enemy reforming, well-armed. Proceed to your next spots. Wait for the signal unless engaged."

Simone slipped back into her wolf form, stretching her paws in front of her with a wide yawn. Around Luke, groups moved in various directions, some walking around the fence into the next yard, some disappearing further back into the side yard. Within a minute, he was alone with Roxi, Sam, and Simone as they waited. Not wanting to wait until the vamps drew closer, he pumped a round into the chamber and rolled to his knees so he could watch over the fence.

Off in the distance, figures darted in and out of the shadows, moving from bush to bush and yard to yard as they approached his position. Ignoring them for the moment, he looked deeper down the street, then pulled out his night vision scope. He hoped the night had cooled enough so he could distinguish the low body temperature of the vampires from the ambient heat of a warm summer night.

Fortunately, there was enough of a difference for him to notice a few more fangers working their way down the street.

He clicked the radio. "Snipers, remove their eyes, starting from the back."

He'd barely released the button when the first shot cracked out, a scream in the distance replying. Another shot rang out. He'd grown quite fond of the sound of the Steyr SSG-69 sniper rifles they'd stolen from the vampires. Jung-sook, in particular, had mastered the weapon after a few years of steady use. All the different terrains and conditions she'd been forced to shoot in had turned her into one of his deadliest weapons.

With his scope in hand, Luke tried to locate the scouts the vampires had sent out but couldn't find any. Either Jung-sook and Connor had eliminated them, or the survivors had found enough cover to stymie their adversaries. Keeping under cover, he refocused his attention down the center of the street, waiting for the main horde to descend. Every once in a while, one of the Steyrs would ring out as they found more viable targets.

Though he didn't see the main force, he did catch some flashes of movement as more enemy scouts tried to assess the situation. He never saw any scouts returning to their own lines, though. Robbed of their eyes, the fangers had to make a move.

A grin spread across his face as bigger clusters worked their way along both sides of the road. The sniper rifles continued to find targets, keeping the enemy honest. Still, the main force delayed. Turning around, he looked back toward Stark Street, then west toward the downtown, holding his breath. He squinted but saw no blue and red lights in the distance. He couldn't entirely dismiss his worry that the vamps could be delaying as they waited for more heavily armed and trained assets to be moved into position, but so far, the cops seemed to be blissfully, and likely intentionally, ignorant of the situation. But they hadn't heard from any of their own scouts watching the rear, and they knew their business well enough not to be caught or taken by surprise.

Soon, they'd have to spring the trap, or they'd let the groups advancing move past their positions. His vampire sensitivity was higher than it had ever been, but it still wasn't tight enough to pick up the detailed movements of those nearby. Either that, or the sheer weight of vampires gathered around this hill and spread out over the city rendered everything else null and void.

"Let's fall back," he whispered to his friends.

"Won't they see us?" Sam asked.

"If they do, they'll likely just assume we're the scouts they'd already sent in. Simone, keep out of sight."

She nodded, then sprinted toward the fence separating this yard from the house next to it. Aiming between a couple of trees, she sprung into the air and disappeared behind the fence. Luke took off toward a bush, Roxi and Sam falling in behind him. Once they rounded the fence of the next house, Luke waved Simone to the next one and then one more before settling in.

Finding a place where he could hide but still monitor the situation, he pulled out his night vision scope and resumed his surveillance. The repositioning and the steady fire of the snipers bought them more time to carry out their attack. They needed the main group of the vampires to take the bait. If they launched the attack too early, not only would they lose the element of surprise, but all those who hadn't come forward could fall on their exposed rear.

He'd almost given up hope when he swept his scope across the road for the umpteenth time. Something drew his attention back toward the center of the road. At first, a few large groups tried to move in a concealed manner, darting from bushes and trees to shadows and patches of darkness. Then a few more large groups joined them until a vast horde moved forward, taking up most of the narrow road.

"Cease fire for the moment," he whispered into the radio's microphone. He'd have to rely on his team's knowledge of the plan and their wolfish hearing to pick up the command.

Once the sniper fire ceased, the groups who'd been moving under the threat of bullets out of the darkness, poked their heads out, looking down the street to where Luke and his people were concealed and back toward the larger group moving up on their rear.

Luke pushed the talk button again. "Wait for it…"

The vampires were growing a bit more courageous now that the sniper rifles had stopped firing. A few were so bold as to step out into the street to get a better view. When no shots punished them, several more grew overconfident. One dashed back toward their own lines, though he couldn't see who they were speaking to, not in the low detail of the night scope.

When it looked like enough had swallowed the bait, he sent out the order, "Go."

Stepping into the street, he didn't bother with any banter or theatrics, instead charging forward with a raised shotgun, a yell on his lips and a breeze moving through his hair. Charging an armed mob of vampires wasn't the best idea. He wished he'd brought his helmet.

His packmates sprung out from their hiding places in side yards, on roofs, and the brush, hitting the vampires on both flanks. The trap achieved the necessary result of creating chaos and packing their enemy tightly into a cluster. It helped to nullify the vampires' numeric advantage and made it harder for them to bring their guns into the fight for fear of shooting their comrades.

Once he emptied both of his shotguns, he drew swords and waded in with Roxi at his side and a bipedal Sam on the other side with her naginata. Simone had changed from her full wolf to her bipedal form and was shredding any vamp that came into reach. Together, they kept the fangers bottled up.

Though they had taken a lot of the vamps' guns out of the fight, the occasional shot rang out followed by a pained yip or howl. He just hoped that they weren't using too much silver ammunition. But the sharp screams and piteous moans of his werewolves spoke to the possibility. It did, however, spur the werewolves on to new levels of ferocity.

Unprepared for the ambush and the intensity of Luke's allies, the vampires near the end began to turn tail and run. Luke had insisted they leave the route open so the vampires would be more likely to run than fight like caged animals if escape was cut off completely. Once the first few fangers made a dash for freedom, the desire to keep fighting crumbled as the trickle became a flood, allowing Luke and his people to clean up those who hadn't fled.

Stepping back from the fighting for a moment, Luke fed more

shells into his shotgun for the next round. Others followed his example as the fighting dwindled to a few last pockets that were quickly put down. Sam, still in her bipedal form, used her pack link to direct their medic teams toward the wounded. Any dire cases were treated, but most of the rest were gathered up and helped along as the team reformed to block the street.

Leaving Sam to organize the movement of the wounded, he moved to the front line and called advance. They effectively blocked the entire street with teams on the flanks moving to check out houses and yards to ensure they were cleared of any fanged squatters. Occasional growls and the rustling in the bushes along the hill to the right attested to pockets of activity on that flank which advanced along with their general move forward.

When they reached the address their raid team had last reported in at, they found an open door and signs of a hasty retreat. Luke signaled for Roxi and a couple of werewolves to join him and sent two other teams around the left and right sides of the house to root out any hiding vampires. He waited until the teams disappeared around the sides before climbing the steps into the house.

He was not prepared for what he saw.

CHAPTER
NINE

The kitchen table had been dragged out, so it blocked the entry hall. On it sat four bloody heads.

Turning around, he stepped outside to get some fresh air before he threw up. It wasn't the first time he'd seen severed heads presented in such a way, but it had been a long time since it had been friends. The two werewolves that had come in with him shoved past him and puked in the bushes.

Once the smell of vomit became worse than the smell of blood and dead flesh, he returned to the house. Roxi had pushed the table back and was walking around it, examining the heads.

"Anything of note?" Luke asked.

Roxi, still bent over and looking closely at the heads, replied, "A few buckshot wounds—some with silver burns. But the worst part is here." She pointed to skin where the heads had been separated from the bodies. "There are burn marks all around the edges. Looks like silver burns."

He sighed, shaking his head. "So, they're using silver-infused blades now. Fuck." He moved forward and peeked around the table. "Let's move this table back out of the way."

Together, they picked up the table and moved it into the corner of the kitchen, careful not to disturb the heads or send them rolling.

Luke, needing to feel skin contact, grabbed Roxi's hand. "I'll go find Sam and keep the rest of the pack out of the house for now."

Roxi laid her forehead on his hoodie and armor covered shoulder. "I'll see if I can find a tablecloth or sheet or something to cover them."

Squeezing her hand and letting go, he exited the house, pushing the door mostly closed. He found Ahmed. "Where's Sam?"

"Over there." He pointed back toward where they'd just come from.

She wasn't hard to miss with her long spear propped against her shoulder as she pointed her giant wolfy paw down the road. He stopped and waited for her to acknowledge his presence after she finished silently delivering her orders through the packlink. Though he was a member in full standing and part of the pack's leadership group, he'd never be able to experience the packlink and the closeness it could create. But it was only a minor regret. He'd never known it nor thought of having it, not until very recently when the pack took him in and made him a part of their large found family.

Sam raised a brow questioningly.

"We found our team, but it's not good. All four are dead." He stopped and looked around, moving closer to Sam. He tried to keep his voice low enough so only Sam could hear. He didn't want the others losing their cool and doing anything stupid because of the desecration of their packmates. "The fangers cut their heads off. Roxi is holding down the house so no one else can go in. She was going to cover the heads out of respect."

A low growl rumbled deep in Sam's throat as her paw gripped her naginata tightly. He squeezed her shoulder reassuringly.

"You ready?" Luke asked, gesturing back toward the house with his head.

She nodded and followed him. She must have given an order because the werewolves milling about setup to cover both approaches to the house. When they entered the house, Roxi waited with a blanket, holding it up for Sam. Taking the offer, Sam shifted back to her human form and let Roxi wrap her in the borrowed blanket. She propped her naginata against the wall and followed them into the kitchen.

Roxi had found a dark sheet. It was better than a white one, but he could still see the shiny sheen of absorbed blood.

Sam sighed, rubbing her forehead. When she lifted her head, weariness caused her face to droop. "I was afraid of this when we came upon this neighborhood, but I hoped…"

"Me, too." Luke slid up next to her and wrapped an arm over her shoulders, pulling her in for a one-armed hug. "Roxi, did you find the bodies?"

Roxi nodded jerkily. "Uh, they're in the basement along with those of the people who lived here. At least that's my guess."

Luke's jaw dropped. "They didn't even keep them alive as blood bags?"

She gave a one-shouldered shrug. "They're as dry as husks. They fed until they drained them, then tossed them aside. I'm sure the story is the same throughout the rest of the neighborhood."

Sam nodded. "Yeah. That's what's been reported through the packlink of those who've been in the houses. A whole neighborhood…"

Walking away for a moment, he stared at the dated floral pattern of the wallpaper, wanting to kick the wall. He restrained himself since it would ultimately be a futile and painful gesture. "It's not just the neighborhood." He turned around and made eye contact with Roxi and Sam. "It's the whole city. It's being murdered around us. Every neighborhood we've driven through has a large vampire presence. I've no doubt they bought some of the houses, but most are paid for with blood and murder."

"Do you feel more vampires? Nearby, I mean." Sam looked nervously toward the door.

He nodded, clenching his jaw lightly. "It's a non-stop surging sea of sensation. In the immediate vicinity, it's been thinned out a bit, but not far away, maybe the next street or two over, there are more. And beyond that range… Too many."

A knock on the door drew their attention as Ahmed poked his

head in. "Luke, Sam, we're getting some reports of more vampires sniffing around at the end of the block."

"Which end?" Luke asked.

"Both."

"Damn it." He spun to face Sam. "What's the word on the wounded?"

"We were moving them back to where we parked so we could move them to the clinic for triage and treatment."

Ahmed cleared his throat, tapping the earpiece in his ear. "I'm getting calls from them. They're reporting a large group of vampires moving toward them."

"I'm hearing the same on the packlink."

Luke bit off a string of curses. "Get them back here immediately. Where's our backup team?"

"They haven't reported in. I'll send a few wolves to check it out."

Ahmed, still standing in the door, perked up, looking outside to the southeast. "I hear gunfire in that direction."

"Fuck it all. If we can't hold either side, we're trapped up here. Sam, you organize the extraction of the wounded back here and the scouts to see what's going on. Roxi, you and Ahmed get everyone here ready to fight again. I'm going to call in to Delilah and see how she's doing on the general mobilization."

With Luke's crisp orders, they leaped into action, leaving him alone in the house with the dead bodies and severed heads. He didn't like it, but he needed quiet, and judging by the yells from outside, the house was the best he'd manage for now.

He dialed Delilah. "Hey, Dee. We're about to be in some serious trouble. How goes getting us some more help?"

"Well, hello to you, too. I've got some pieces moving into Portland. Can you hold out?" Delilah replied.

"I'm in a neighborhood, not a fort. But I'll figure something out… Look. It's going to get hairy up here. Don't split your forces. Get everyone in one spot and open us a corridor so we can get off Thorburn Street. Southeast Stark Street is the best option to get us off of Mt. Tabor. That's where most of our vehicles are parked."

"Got it. I'll come bail you out. Keep Simone alive for me."

"I'll do my best. Call me with any updates. If you don't hear from me, assume I'm busy keeping everyone alive." He hung up and headed outside.

Sam ran up to him. "Luke. The backup team is fighting for its life. They're trying to retreat to us but are having trouble disengaging."

Growling, he shook his head and crossed his arms. "Split the teams. Half to help out the backup team, the other half to extract our wounded and get them back here. You lead one team. Roxi will handle the other. But leave me four or five wolves. I need to figure out a defense and need some eyes and ears."

"Got it. Any help coming?"

He nodded, pursing his lips. "Delilah is efforting, so we're going to be on our own for a bit."

"Great." She tossed aside the blanket, standing naked in the summer night, and sighed wearily. "I guess I better get to it." She shifted to her bipedal form.

Luke ducked back inside the house and grabbed her naginata, bringing it to her. Roxi had already departed at a jog with her people, sweeping down to protect the wounded and bring them to safety.

Sam waded through the throng of werewolves waiting, her naginata serving as a flag. As she passed, a steady growl started low, raising the hairs on his arm. Thrusting the naginata into the air, the growls crescendoed and turned into blood curdling howls. Moving down the center of the street, her people fanned out to each side, shotguns pumped to the ready for those who were still in their human costumes, though a fair few had shed their clothes in favor of their bipedal form, if they had one. The time for subtlety had passed. It was time for shock troops.

Ahmed and four of their packmates joined Luke as they watched Sam break into a jog and then a run.

"I pity anyone on the receiving end of that," Ahmed said. "Now what did you need us for?"

"Everything is going to shit, and we need to see what kind of defense we can organize. Delilah has reinforcements gathering, but we might be on our own for a while until they get here."

Ahmed snorted, crossing his arms. "So, situation normal?"

Luke finished the phrase. "All fucked up."

CHAPTER
TEN

Luke sat low against the floor of the house, feeding shotgun shells into his M12. His ammo belt was empty, and he was having a harder time finding more in his satchel which now felt suspiciously light.

"Roxi, how are you on ammo?" he called across the front room.

She was taking a breather while someone else fired out the window. "Not good." She reached into her satchel, rummaging around int it for a moment. "I'm out." She shoved the last shell into her shotgun's magazine.

"In the house!" someone yelled from outside.

Luke held up a hand. "Ceasefire."

"In the house! Let's talk."

He waved everyone down and out of their windows. Rolling onto his knees, he peeked out of the window. A shadow emerged from behind a tree on the other side of the street.

"What do you want?" Luke yelled.

"You." The light gleamed off the vamp's fangs as it grinned. Looking to the other windows, it called out, "Send out the centurion and his whore and everyone else can go home. Plus…"

"Why do they always insist on calling me a whore?" Roxi rolled her eyes.

He smirked at Roxi. "It never goes well for them. They must have a death kink or something."

"…we'll let our hostages go."

That got Luke's attention as his head snapped back to the fanger who now stood entirely clear of the trees' protection. Two burly looking vampires dragged out someone who appeared to be well tied up. Tossing them onto the ground, one of the fangers reached down and grabbed the hair, pulling back and revealing Ahmed.

Luke froze for a moment, then turned and looked frantically around the room, somehow hoping to see Ahmed safely—as safe as they could be trapped in the house—tucked in one of the corners waiting for his turn to shoot at the vampires. He hadn't realized that Ahmed wasn't there. He'd hoped it was some trick of the fangers. Turning his head back to look out the window, he saw the fear and desperation in Ahmed's eyes. Luke's stomach dropped.

"Luke, what are we going to do?" Sam hissed.

"I don't know."

"We have plenty," the vampire called, gesturing behind him.

Soon, there were three more trussed up hostages laid out on the ground.

"And since we have spares…"

Someone else stepped out of the shadows and pulled out a katana. The two burly vampires grabbed Ahmed off the ground.

"No!" Luke yelled.

The silver blade caught some light, gleaming, as it arced down into Ahmed's neck. The head, as if in slow motion, dipped forward, then fell to the ground, bouncing a couple times before rolling away. The vampire stopped it with its boot.

Looking down at the head, the vampire caught Luke's gaze, then pointed to another of the hostages.

"NO! Stop!" Luke screamed.

The blade sliced down, and Gracie's head fell to the ground. Crying and growls filtered through the roar of blood pumping through his ears.

"Now you know I'm serious. Send out the centurion and his woman." He gestured again, and they lifted another hostage, but he held up his hand and stopped the blade from falling. "I can go all night… Well, until we run out of hostages. It's up to you."

"No…" Luke said lowly.

Reaching over his shoulder, he pulled his rudis free. Hands without faces reached out to stop him, but he shoved them aside and stalked toward the door.

Sam blocked the door. "Luke, you can't go out there."

He reached toward the doorknob, but she pushed his hand away. "Move."

"Luke. No." Sam folded her arms across her chest.

Roxi moved to Luke's side, placing a hand on his shoulder. "Sam, let him go."

Too focused on what had happened outside moments ago, he nearly missed the battle of wills as Roxi and Sam stared at each other. Finally, Sam nodded and sighed, then stepped out of the way.

Opening the door, Roxi stepped back and pulled out her sword. "I'm by your side, but don't do anything too extreme."

He gave her a tight nod and stepped through the door, stomping down the steps and sidewalk out to the street.

"Drop your weapons," the vampire who'd ordered the deaths of his packmates said.

"No." Luke raised the rudis, forced the incantation into his mind and directed it and his wrath toward the fanger.

It exploded, spraying its neighbors in a fine cloud of powder. Before the other vampires could recover, Luke widened his focus and directed the tip of his rudis toward the vampire who'd wielded the sword that had decapitated his packmates. The vamp covered the hostages and slopped to the ground in a squelchy mess. The fangers holding his friends were next. Once they were turned to goo, the hostages used the opportunity to roll away from vamps to put Luke between them and their captors. Calls rang out from the house and feet slapped on the porch as people sprinted out to get the hostages to safety.

"Someone fucking attack him!" yelled someone.

To his right, a handful of vampires surged from their line.

"I've got them," Roxi said, unsheathing her rudis so she had two blades to work with.

Another group, this time from his left, dashed toward him. Snarling, he swung his rudis around and charged, yanking out their stolen life essences as he barreled into the crowd. Before he made contact with the line of vampires, he yanked his gladius from its scabbard, then started cutting. As he drained vampires on the fly, pulling in their energy, he sped up, moving faster than even the vampires could keep up with.

He no longer saw individual opponents, just a mass he needed to eliminate. At one point, he thought he heard a gunshot as he stumbled, but instead of causing pain, it merely stoked his anger. With a broad focus, he yanked the power from an unknown swath of vampires and the brief moment of discomfort disappeared, replaced by more energy and power.

"Just fucking swarm him!"

Normally, that would have concerned Luke, but he only felt the exhilaration of combat and the joy of meting out death. As he spun, he realized he'd been cut off from Roxi. And while she was fast and deadly, she wasn't working at the new hyper levels he was. Soon, she would be overwhelmed.

Though the vampires had him surrounded, those in the front row were reluctant to enter his kill zone. None had escaped. And they could see the gooey results on the ground and splattered on those who hadn't yet met their own fate. Since he was in the eye of the hurricane, he took a second to find Roxi.

The circle around her tightened.

"No!"

Opening his focus, he yanked back the rudis, cutting a massive corridor open. Not waiting for the vampires to fill it, he dashed forward, parrying weapons thrust in his way and resorting to the simple expedience of draining everything in front of him until he thought he could feel the atoms that made up his being vibrate at a higher frequency.

The thought of Roxi wounded or dead spurred him on as he swung wildly with the rudis, indiscriminately draining every vampire in the arc of his swing and ten feet back. He couldn't see or focus. All he knew was he moved toward Roxi, sliding in the pools and rivers of dead vampire goo he was creating en mass.

"Roxi!" The words sounded slurred even in his own ears.

"Luke!"

He thought he heard fear in her voice.

"No!"

He stopped, thrusting both his sword and rudis out to the sides. Slowly spinning in a circle, he opened his field of concentration and pulled in the power of every fanger he could get a hold of until he could no longer stand and fell to his knees. More. He had to drain more. To protect Roxi and his friends… He tried to raise his arms to keep the rudis linked to vampires.

Sagging backward, his head spun and legs gave up holding him upright. He couldn't focus his eyes, but he thought he saw stars and tree limbs, blurry as they were, above him.

"No…"

He struggled to get up but couldn't make his muscles coordinate. Soon, the vampires would fall on him, and he'd be dead. Panting, he tried to roll over so he could push off the ground but only managed to twitch his body. Warm tears streaked down his face as he wondered if he were melting. Every tremble of his body squelched and felt gooey.

"What's wrong with him?" Ahmed asked.

No, Luke thought. That can't be him talking. He'd just watched his execution.

The stars and the trees were eclipsed by a cloud of wild, curly black hair and a face lined with weariness and worry. Roxi.

"He's taken in too much vampire energy." She placed the back of her hand across his forehead. "Bloody hell. He's burning up. Sam, we need to get him out of here."

"Simone?" Sam said. "Go bring up the pickup. Fast."

"Hold on, Luke. We'll get you to help," Roxi said, pushing the sweat drenched hair from his forehead.

"Get the bodies off the street and get them ready for evac," Sam called.

Pain surged through his body, and it quaked violently as he choked.

"Someone help me roll him over, fast." Roxi slid to his side and, with the help of another set of hands, rolled him over.

And just in time. He heaved up what was left of his dinner onto the blood drenched street. Before he could gasp for air, he vomited again with wracking, heavy, body-clenching force. Soon, it was just dry heaves that got weaker as his strength faded.

"Is he going to be OK?" someone asked.

"I don't know. Can someone get me some water? He's going to need it," Roxi replied.

His body relaxed now that he wasn't heaving out his guts, allowing him to gasp in air with huge gulps.

"He...he just exploded all the vampires," someone nearby murmured.

"It was the freakiest shit I've ever seen, and I've seen a lot," someone else replied.

He couldn't tell who was speaking. Every voice except for Roxi's sounded distorted and distant.

"Dōšagīh, I want to move you. Are you done?"

He wobbled his head in what he thought was a nod. A weak groan fell from his lips as he was lifted into the air by his wrist and ankles.

"Careful, don't slip in all this shite," Roxi instructed. "Don't drop him. Easy. Set him down carefully on the quilt."

Nearby, tires screeched to a stop.

"We're going to move the makeshift stretcher into the back of Pablo's pickup," Sam called.

Luke jostled as he was hoisted off the ground, the poles of their improvised stretcher smashing into his sides. He wanted to groan in pain but couldn't spare the air or the energy.

The end of the stretcher thunked as it was dropped onto the tailgate of the pickup. They slid him in until all he could see was the blurry top of the inside of the canopy. The pickup jostled as someone climbed into the back with him before the tailgate was shut and the canopy door was lowered.

Roxi took his hand in hers. He'd know the feel of her hand in his anytime, and apparently in any condition. With the other hand, she brushed away sweaty hair once again and crooned a sad song to him as the truck rumbled down the road. He couldn't tell how long or how fast they were traveling.

He couldn't concentrate on anything except the song on Roxi's lips. Focusing on staying conscious, he existed in a gray nothing where he could see nothing but the vague outline of Roxi next to him. Sound, sight, and sensation—she was all that was keeping him anchored to the here and now.

"GET HIM ON THE GURNEY," Roxi said. "Careful."

"Oh, God, what happened to him?" Maggie asked.

"It's not his blood," Roxi said.

"That's a relief. I've got a room prepped for him. Let's roll him inside." Maggie held the door as he was pushed into the pack's clinic. "Now, move him over to the bed."

"Stay here. I'm going to need some help getting him out of his armor." Roxi unzipped the hoodie then tugged on the leather thong keeping the front half of his armor closed.

"I've got some shears," Maggie said, handing something to Roxi.

"No…" he mumbled.

"Luke, dōšagīh, the hoodie is ruined and you have plenty of leather thongs." Not waiting for him to approve, she cut off his hoodie and clipped the leather cord. "Let's roll him to his side."

After Roxi cut the leather holding the back closed, she had the two who'd functioned as orderlies help her remove his armor. Then she clipped off his armor padding and t-shirt. He shivered hard.

"He's burning up," Maggie said. "What happened?"

"We got in a bad spot, and he pretty much single-handedly wiped out the vampires by draining them."

"Like the last time?" Maggie asked.

"Yes."

He struggled to breathe, his inhalations rasping in his throat. A cold instrument pressed into his chest in a few spots.

"His pulse is way too high and erratic. Lift his head for me."

Maggie slipped an oxygen mask over his nose and mouth. Though it didn't relieve the tightness in his chest, the oxygen eased his gasping slightly.

"What can we do?" Roxi asked.

"I don't know. If this were a normal human malady, I'd be able to deal with it. But this is entirely new to my experience. And probably to anyone's. They don't teach you about vampire overdoses in med school." Maggie sounded frustrated and scared.

Rasping for air, he started trembling. Then he shook until finally he couldn't control his body as he violently spasmed. The beeping sound of the heart monitor speed up then shrieked. And then he knew no more.

CHAPTER
ELEVEN

The first thing that filtered into his awareness was the smell. It didn't smell like Portland. Like the clinic. Or his home. It was a familiar one. It brought him a sense of peace and contentment. He basked in that aroma and sense of comfort, not wanting to open his eyes and find out he was either at the clinic, or—he wasn't sure if it was a bad or good option—dead.

Next to him, someone flipped the page of a book, then set down a ceramic cup on a saucer. Cloth rubbed on cloth as they shifted position. In the background, a faint beeping disturbed the harmony of the other sounds he'd cataloged.

Forcing his eyes open, he slammed them shut immediately as light poured into them, sending sparks through his brain. This time, he opened them only a crack, letting them adjust. He was in his room at the farm.

"Welcome back to the world, dōšagīh." Roxi appeared at his side and bent over, kissing his forehead. "You gave us a scare."

"What?" His voice sounded dry and raspy.

"Here." Roxi grabbed a glass of water and laid the straw across his lips. "Slowly."

He followed her instructions, only sucking in a bit of liquid. The cold water felt refreshing as it slipped down his throat. He took another sip, taking more.

"How do you feel?" Roxi asked.

"I don't know," he rasped. "Alive?"

Roxi chuckled. "You are alive. If just barely."

"How long?"

"Tonight would make it five days." She bent over and kissed his cheek.

"Five?"

A wave of fear flashed across Roxi's face before it settled back into gentle placidity, which almost worried him more than the fear. They'd faced plenty of near-death experiences together and journeyed closer to the line than most, even stepping over it a few times. But the calm façade was the face one saw when they were about to hear the news they were terminal.

"What's my prognosis?" he asked.

"I don't know. You're in uncharted territory. I'll go fetch Maggie so she can examine you." She patted him on the arm, then turned and left without saying anything else.

While he waited, he flexed his muscles to ensure his body was still in working order, or at least that he wasn't disabled in some way. All his limbs responded, though he had to be careful not to flex too long or too hard for fear of the cramps threatening his contractions. Overall, he felt alive, even if his body felt like it had been worked over with a baseball bat—or twenty.

He was halfway to standing when the door opened and Roxi and Maggie walked in. Pausing his motion, he felt as if he'd been caught with his hand in the cookie jar. His body trembled, unable to hold him in the in-between position, and he fell back onto the mattress.

"What do you think you're doing?" Roxi asked, a scolding eyebrow raised.

He breathed heavily. "I needed to go to the bathroom."

"You're catheterized at the moment, so you don't need to get out of bed," Maggie said. "We didn't know how long you'd be out."

He'd been too out of it to feel the tug and pull of the catheter as he moved. Sighing, he unclenched his muscles, letting his body sag fully into the comfort of the bed and pillows. He was too tired and depleted to even feel embarrassed at his gaffe.

The last few years had been a series of events where he learned to deal with the humiliation of his circumstances, though this one felt rawer since it was in front of both of his girlfriends. Then he reminded himself that he needn't worry about such things, not with them.

"I'll wait outside, Maggie."

"Thank you," she replied.

Once the door closed, Maggie sagged onto the chair next to Luke's bed. "You foolish man."

"Wha—"

"What were you thinking?" Maggie interrupted.

"There wasn't much of a choice."

"I know. Roxi explained it, not that it helps." She shook her said. "It seems like you've found a new way to abuse yourself with this power." She held up a hand to forestall him. "I know. It was for the good of the pack. But what about those who love you? What about Gwen? Roxi?" She paused. "What about me?"

"I'm… I'm sorry, Magdalena."

Maggie sighed and ran a hand over her face. "I'm sorry for scolding you."

He looked up at her, pleading with his eyes. "I just didn't know what else to do. I couldn't watch them butcher their prisoners—our packmates."

"I know. But does it always have to be you?"

"If not me, then who?"

She rubbed her eyes. They had dark rings under them and looked red. "I'm sorry. I was scared for you. I love you. I'd be devastated if I lost you."

He reached out, untangling the blanket from the IV in his arm, and grabbed her hand. "I am sorry for making you worry and for causing you pain. You've been so good to me. But I couldn't look you in the eye or myself if I let anyone else suffer on my account. It's not who I am."

"I know. Your sense of justice is one of the first things that attracted me to you." She caressed his cheek and jaw. "I just some-time wish you were a little less zealous about it, but you're right. It's not who you are. And I can't ask you to stop being who you are on my account. You're more than just mine. You're Roxi's. Gwen's. The pack's."

He blushed, his breathing shallow as he tried to fight off the tears that wanted to form in his eyes. Pablo and Delilah had been the first to draw him out into the world of the living with their friendship, but it had been Maggie's love that had reminded him just how sweet life could be.

The old Luke would have tried to talk himself into fleeing from her for her own good and so he wouldn't have to feel the pain…or feel at all. But that Luke was dead and he wouldn't let himself resurrect him.

He didn't fight for an ancient god or some nearly intangible mission. He fought for love. For the love of his extended family of the pack. For the love of his dearest friends. For the love of his adopted daughter. For the love of the women he loved. For the love of life.

It was a terrible responsibility. But he was right about one thing. Who else could do what he could do? He stood as a bulwark against the encroaching darkness. Not gods. Not governments. Not nations. He'd raised up a powerful army that could continue the fight long after he was gone. But he didn't want them to fight an indefinite war.

He was the only one who could bring down the dark god of the vampires. The god who only saw his creation as a road to power—to corruption. The destination Saubarag had in mind was chaos and pain.

Luke didn't know if Saubarag wanted to rule the world. He didn't care. The only route to peace and to end the predation of humanity was through Saubarag's body, such as it was. Something had shifted. He didn't know if it was his mindset or his new power, if he could use it without destroying himself before he achieved his goal… All the parts had to be brought together. They all must serve him.

Saubarag brought undeath.

Luke would bring true death.

He just didn't know if he'd live to enjoy a world free from the dark god.

CHAPTER
TWELVE

Maggie had been unhappy about his vital signs, though they'd been better than when he'd been brought in. His heart rate was still erratic and his oxygen levels were below optimum. She wanted to run more thorough tests after they moved him back to Portland, but he was well enough to get out of bed and move about the farm as long as he didn't exert himself too much.

Gwen insisted on playing cards with him whenever he sat in the sitting room, which he didn't mind. He knew it was her way of reassuring herself that he was still alive. Though he appreciated it, he did get tired of seeing the worried looks on everyone's faces and fearful glances every time he so much as sneezed or stumbled. He couldn't tell if he was annoyed with everyone else or at his own frailty.

After the kid had beat him at another round of cribbage, he called it quits, removed the IV bag from the downstairs stand, and headed upstairs for a nap. The stairs only added to his exhaustion, though he wouldn't let anyone else know. He couldn't handle any more pity.

Opening the door, he paused when he saw Roxi sitting in the chair by the head of the bed.

"Luke, we need to talk before you take your afternoon nap."

"OK. Give me a moment first."

Roxi nodded.

He sauntered into the bathroom to take care of business then returned to the bedroom, hanging his IV bag, then slipping under the covers. Sighing contentedly, he wiggled to get comfortable. "What about?"

"I spoke with Selene last night. I think you need to talk with her and let her examine you."

"But—"

Roxi held up a hand, cutting him off. "Your malady isn't medical, though it's showing various medical-type symptoms. The cause is supernatural. Maggie can try to treat the symptoms, but there's no human sickness causing your problems. And right now, our best source is Selene."

He mulled over what she'd said for a moment. "You're probably right. If I'm going to actually get on the mend so I can get back into the fight, it won't be human medicine that'll 'cure' me."

Roxi relaxed, her shoulders dropping and her brow smoothing. "Good. I was worried you'd argue about it. You can occasionally be stubborn when it comes to your own health."

He chuckled. "I've heard that before, but I'm trying to do better. I have plans, and I need to be healthy if I'm going to end this war."

She raised an eyebrow. "End it?"

"What else are we fighting for?" He took in a shaky breath. "I can't keep this up indefinitely. I can't see people I lead be..." He paused, clenching his eyes shut. "I can't witness what happened the other night again."

Looking down, he saw his hands trembling, so he clenched them into fists and slid them under the blankets. Roxi stood and walked around the bed to the other side, slipping under the covers to snuggle up next to him.

"I know, dōšagīh. That was rough, even after all we've seen. You just scared us. I've been doing this as long as you have, and I've never seen anything like what you're doing. It's..." She exhaled, the air hissing between her teeth. "It's exhilarating and profoundly terrifying. You could destroy the vampires, but the power is destroying you."

He rolled over, resting his head on her shoulder. "I'm scared, too."

"I hate to say this, but"—she kissed the top of his head—"I'd rather fight vampires forever than lose you. I've finally found you, and I'll fight anyone to protect you. Including you."

"I know," he whispered. "I love you more than I can say."

Roxi nodded, squeezing him tightly, and stroked his hair. "Just rest in my arms. Tonight, we'll speak with Selene."

LUKE WOKE up from his nap in an empty bed, the other side cool with time. At some point, Maggie must have been in to remove the IV. Rolling out of bed, he stumbled into the bathroom to relieve himself, then returned to his bedroom and pulled on whatever was on top of the drawers he opened—shorts and a T-shirt. Because he was chilly, he pulled on a robe and slipped into a pair of slippers. If he had a pair of jelly sandals, he'd be all set for a Big Lebowski convention.

Since he was still weak and shaky, he was forced to grip the handrail tightly as he descended the stairs.

Roxi poked her head out of the kitchen, a smile spreading across her face. "Ah, good. You're awake. I was about to get you. I made a run down to The Birk for burgers."

His stomach grumbled at the thought of burgers. "Funnily enough, I'm a bit hungry. I feel like I haven't eaten anything solid in weeks."

"Then come sit down and dig in." She beckoned him over and disappeared back into the kitchen.

When he rounded the corner, there were a few people already gathered around the table. Roxi was handing out burgers to Maggie and Tutyr, whose shorts, slippers, and robe matched Luke's attire.

"Luke." Tutyr nodded, and his beard shifted in such a way to indicate he might be smiling under it.

"Tutyr." He pulled out a chair next to where Roxi set her burger down. "How are you doing? Up and about, I see."

"Still weak, but better each day," he said, his accent thick but understandable.

Luke was the reason for the god's weakness. When they'd fought Saubarag, Tutyr had shifted into the shape of an Aralez—a winged hound-wolf whose lick could heal injuries and even revive the dead, if legends held true.

Tutyr had been a weak god even in Luke's days in Rome's legions. And the only reason he'd heard of him—beyond the tale Selene had told him about the creation of the werewolves which involved Saubarag tricking Tutyr—was the time he'd spent in the Caucus Mountains and later the steppes. He'd never even claimed the potential power base of being a god involved in the creation of the werewolf.

Somehow, through time, he'd become trapped in Saubarag's prison-arena in the mountains of Wyoming. That's where Luke had found them when he'd been freed from the prison. Though, the god had disguised himself as a dog and kept the shape until revealing himself a few weeks ago.

Once Luke sat down and dished up some fries, everyone commenced eating. The simple joy of sharing food with loved ones eased a bit of the soul weariness that seemed to be trying to drag him under. The casual conversation and friendly banter felt simple and homey. It felt good.

It might have been the best burger Luke had ever eaten, though he struggled to finish it and left most of his fries uneaten on the plate. Tutyr had no trouble finishing his food, licking his fingers with gusto. When Luke caught him eyeing the uneaten fries, he slid the plate toward the god.

Tutyr reached for the plate but stopped his hand halfway. "Are you sure?"

"I'm willing, but my stomach says stop. You can have them so they don't go to waste."

"Many thanks." He dumped the fries onto his plate and squirted more ketchup on them before digging in. When he cleaned his plate, he pushed back in his chair and patted his stomach. "American burger and fries are very tasty."

Roxi raised an eyebrow. "Certainly better than dog kibble."

Luke snorted, covering it with a cough.

"No, no. Kibble good, too. Burger is just better."

No one seemed to know how to respond to the admission that he liked kibble. He'd certainly eaten enough of it during his time as an overly large dog.

Standing, the god took his plate and rinsed it before placing it in the dishwasher. "I go for a stroll now. Settle belly." He patted his stomach again.

He didn't wait for anyone to say otherwise and walked out of the kitchen, the front door clicking shut as he departed.

"I have to say. It's really weird having your former dog eating at the table with us," Maggie said.

"I don't know if I can really call him my former dog. He was a god who hid out as a dog and crashed at my house." Luke followed Tutyr's example and did his dishes before sitting down again, his breathing labored.

Roxi groaned. "Ugh. The number of walks I've taken him on and cleaned up after him."

"Oh, God…" Maggie said. "Me too."

Luke shook his head. "I'm too tired to think about it." He grabbed Roxi's hand and squeezed it. "I hope whatever you're planning doesn't require much exertion because I don't have it in me."

"We'll help you out. We just need to go a bit beyond the cabins," Roxi replied.

Nodding, he stood up. "I'm going to go hang out in the sitting room until it's time. I don't think I have the energy to make it up the stairs."

He left the room and sank into a comfortable wingback chair near the fireplace, though there was no fire burning. It was cooler in the Coast Range but not that cold. Soon, he drifted off to the pleasant murmurs of Roxi and Maggie conversing in the other room.

LUKE STARTLED awake as someone gently shook him.

"It's time."

He opened his eyes to the smiling face of Roxi framed by a dark window with only a bit of moonlight filtering through. Accepting her help up, he used the downstairs restroom then put on a pair of sneakers before meeting Maggie and Roxi on the farmhouse's porch. They formed up on each side of him and provided helping hands and balance as they descended the few steps to the ground.

They took it slowly as they walked toward the edge of the forest that surrounded the property. Halfway there, Luke needed to take a break, leaning up against one of the small cabins used to house pack-members during events, or in some cases, house the wounded when there wasn't enough room in Portland. Only a few cabins had lights on at the moment.

"This sucks." Luke swiped a hand across his sweaty brow.

"Take as much time as you need. Selene is patient," Roxi said.

Nodding, he pushed off the side of the cabin, wobbling to a standing position. "Might as well get moving. Maybe she'll be able to help, and I'll have my energy and strength back."

After that, he saved his breath for huffing and puffing as he toddled, with Roxi and Maggie's help, to a small clearing in the woods. It had been a favored meeting spot for Luke to speak with Selene.

He expected to be the first to arrive at the clearing, but Tutyr in his aralez form already waited. The large, winged wolf-dog hybrid lay on the ground in a very dog-like pose, his tongue lolling out.

Roxi pulled out a camping chair she'd had stashed aside and set it up for Luke. Sinking into it, he exhaled in relief.

"Do you want me to call to Selene?" he asked.

Roxi squeezed his shoulder. "No. I'll do it."

She stepped into the middle of the clearing, standing between Luke and Tutyr, and lifted her face to the sky. A calm, beatific expression spread across her closed-eyed face. A moment later, a silver blur shimmered next to Roxi, resolving into the moon goddess. She immediately strode across the clearing to stand in front of Luke. Her normal placid face showed lines of worry.

Kneeling before him, she took both of his hands in hers and stared at him blankly. Maggie and Roxi waited while Tutyr lumbered over to lay next to Luke, his head resting on his paws. Though he didn't feel better, the goddess's presence still brought a calm over him and his breathing eased.

Selene, her eyes focusing, nodded to herself, then stood up. "He's burning up inside. His body can't handle that much vampire energy. A life force is a powerful thing, even one that's been tainted by vampires and Saubarag's corruption. He's dying."

Maggie gasped, putting her hand over her mouth. Roxi seemed to lose a bit of the steel in her spine as her shoulders slumped and her head dipped.

Hearing the words, Luke slumped in his chair, his momentary calm melting into wretchedness. He'd just started living and wanted time to really do it, but now it appeared his time was up, and he'd leave his mission unfulfilled. He snorted, shaking his head. His mission. It was Mithras's mission. Luke just wanted it done so he could live a life free of its brutal taint—a life of his own.

A handful of years ago and he wouldn't have cared if his time had finally come to an end. He probably would have looked forward to a final note. Now the end of his seeming immortality sank into him like hot lead. Nearly two-thousand years stalking the earth and suddenly he didn't have enough time to *live.*

"Is there anything you can do, My Mistress?" Roxi asked, desperation in her voice and eyes. "Is there anything Mithras can do?" Her eyes flicked to the aralez on the ground next to Luke. "Is there anything Tutyr can do? He's healed Luke twice now."

"But it's cost him each time," Selene replied. "Maybe at one time, but he doesn't have his old power and is greatly diminished." The goddess pursed her lips, an odd expression for the normally serene deity, and looked on at Tutyr. "There is something I would like to try that could help both Lucius and Tutyr regain their vigor. But I'll need both their permissions."

"Could?" Maggie asked. "What does that mean? What are the odds? The dangers? The consequences?"

Selene turned to Maggie and caressed her cheek. "This is

uncharted territory, Magdalena. A first and an experiment. Dangers? No more than Lucius has faced too many times, though that is hardly a balm. It could do nothing or heal him. It could harm them both, hastening the inevitable. I just don't know, but I can think of no other solutions and if this works, I can return both of them to health."

Maggie stared into Selene's eyes, hope, fear, and hopelessness shifting across her face in equal measures. Finally, she reached up and squeezed the goddess's hand and nodded.

Luke, a sad, soft smile on his face, thanked Maggie with a nod.

Tutyr raised his head and nodded hard once before setting his head back on his paws.

Luke snorted and let out a sardonic chuckle. "What's the worst that could happen? I die? I give my consent, My Mistress."

Folding her hands in front of her, she nodded. "Very well. I'll need your rudis."

"I don't know if I have it here."

"It's in the closet of your room," Roxi supplied. "I'll go fetch it. Is there anything else we'll need while I'm there?"

"No, my child. The rudis is all we'll need."

Roxi nodded and jogged out of the clearing.

Running her hand along Maggie's cheek, the goddess gave her a reassuring smile. "Fear not, Magdalena. I believe this will work, and your love will have his health restored."

Maggie, tears brimming in her eyes, nodded and smiled sadly. "Thank you."

They heard Roxi before they saw her as she broke branches and rustled leaves running through the woods. Slowing at the edge of the clearing, she strolled to the goddess, then dropped to one knee, holding the rudis up to the goddess with the blade laying flat across both palms.

Selene grasped the blade by the handle. "Thank you, my child. Now please take Magdalena into the woods."

"We can't be here for Luke?" Roxi asked.

"Normally, it would be fine, but I'm unsure of what might

happen and want to ensure your safety in case something goes awry."

"Of course." Roxi held out her hand to Maggie and together they walked into the woods.

Bending over, the goddess scratched the aralez behind the ears and around the neck. "I'll need you to resume your human form, my friend."

Tutyr blurred into the shaggy-haired man in a bathrobe Luke had joined for dinner earlier. Like Luke, he wobbled a bit on his feet but steadied himself.

"We three must all stand near one another." Selene offered her hand to help Luke rise from the chair. Holding the wooden sword by the handle and point down, she moved it so it was in between the three of them. "Lucius, grab the blade at the hilt guard. I suggest your off-hand. Tutyr, grasp the blade at a lower point. Leave some separation between your hands. Both of you be careful not to cut your hands, not yet anyway."

They obeyed. Luke hoped it wouldn't take long. His arm trembled. He didn't even have the strength to hold it out away from his body for long.

"Concentrate your wills on the rudis." She placed her other palm on the pommel of the sword, wrapping her long, elegant fingers around it, and closed her eyes.

The goddess, who always had a bit of a glow, burst out with a silver aura that forced Luke to squint. The glow joined with the rudis and slid over it until it touched Luke's hand. He could no longer move it as if it no longer belonged to him. His fist was locked around the blade.

At first, he felt a gently tugging in his core, then a much more insistent one until something broke loose inside him. Whatever it was wound its way down his arm in shuddering halting waves until it hit his hand and joined with the silver energy of Selene with a golden glow of its own.

Silver and gold wound down the blade like a twisted cable until it met Tutyr's hand.

"Grip tightly and move your hand toward Tutyr's," Selene said, speaking directly into Luke's mind.

The blade bit into the flesh of his hand with a sharp slice of pain as he ran his fist down the rudis. The red of his blood joined with the silver and gold threads and wound together into a cord twisting the three together. The heel of his palm met the top of Tutyr's hand at the midpoint of the blade, joining a fourth line to the rope of energy, this one green.

As their blood mingled, the cord wound itself around their hands, binding the three of them together and burst into white light.

Perspiration broke out on Luke's forehead and ran down his back as his weak muscles trembled. He squinted against the brightness of the white light as it expanded and encompassed them. Clenching his teeth, he hoped to keep his insides where they belonged as their combined power surged in and out of him like storm-driven waves. The vibrations of it hummed in his ears and blurred and shook his vision. If his hand wasn't clamped to the blade and his body forced into rigidity by the combined essence of the cord, he'd have fallen into a boneless heap on the forest floor.

He thought he saw Selene's lips move, but he couldn't hear anything or make out the words falling from her lips. Across from them, Tutyr stood with his eyes clamped shut and his mouth open as he panted heavily.

The surges running through him grew harder and more aggressive, pushing forcefully outward. He felt like if they hit him much more violently, he would explode. When he thought he could take no more, the electricity running wild through him found a stasis and settled. The white light lessened until it faded altogether. The four colored threads pulled back and disappeared, leaving four hands on a bloody wooden blade.

Luke's legs wobbled and his head grew faint. The world spinning around him, he slumped to the ground and faded into unconsciousness.

It had been three days since Luke had gone through the ritual with Selene and Tutyr, and he felt better than he had in a while. Some of Selene's serenity must have lingered after everything was done. Maggie insisted he stay at the farm for another few days so she could monitor his stabilizing vitals and to ensure he actually recovered. According to her checks, his stats had returned to near baseline numbers.

Though he thought it had just as much to do with preventing him from running out and doing something stupid while under the influence of whatever had happened to him. And as much as he wanted to get back into the fight, he still tired too easily. If he was being honest with himself, his body still didn't feel right. His vitals might be returning to near normal levels, but his body would take more than a day or two to be trustworthy again.

She'd said fainting was never a good thing. Waking up a touch on the giddy side was also apparently bad. Roxi, betraying him for his own good, had joined forces with Maggie to keep him out of the action and resting until he received a medical clearance.

They'd explained he could hold out for a few more days since the team had suspended operations because of the deaths and the dangerous shift in the situation. Planning didn't require a lot of energy. Though they didn't accept that reply, insisting they were immovable on the subject. Giving in, he'd settled into three days of relaxing in one of his favorite places with his favorite people and Tutyr.

Luke did feel quite a bit better and used the opportunity to take walks in the woods with either Roxi or Maggie. He even got to know Tutyr a bit, teaching him how to play cribbage.

The god seemed much revived, as far as Luke could tell. He'd only known him as the dog Brutus. His brief relationship with Tutyr had been forged in fire and pain when the god had helped rescue him from the netherworld trap Saubarag had sucked him into.

Again, Luke owed his life to Selene, though he knew she didn't keep a tally. The goddess was gracious in all things when it came to him and her children, the werewolves, as they came back to her.

He'd come close to death too many times in the last few years, only to get a last-minute reprieve. His luck and allies could only hold out for so long, and if he didn't end this soon, it might run out. That wasn't something he really wanted to face at the moment, though brushes with dead were practically an old friend after two-thousand years. At least he felt secure in the knowledge that if he did succumb to death, the fight would go on, and the people he cared about would be taken care of, inheriting all he had.

After a quiet day, Luke broke out whiskey as he, Roxy, Maggie, and Tutyr played cards in the quiet sitting room. Tomorrow, they'd pack up and head back to Portland.

"Luke?" Roxi grabbed the bottle and added another splash of the brown liquor to her glass. "What exactly happened after we left?"

Maggie nodded. "All we saw was a bright white light, then we found you and Tutyr laying on the ground."

Maggie still had trouble with acknowledging Tutyr since she'd learned he was a god, even if he wasn't the most powerful or well known. Selene's occasional presence and kind nature no longer seemed to bother the doctor anymore as she'd gotten to know the goddess and grown to understand her connection to Luke. She wasn't there yet with Tutyr. It also didn't help that she'd first known him as a mangy but magical dog Luke had adopted and nursed back to health.

"I'm not entirely sure myself. She somehow took the excess power from draining all those vampires and redistributed it, giving it to Tutyr so he could heal."

Tutyr, who was quiet and uncomfortable in people's presences, nodded. "That is what she did, pretty much. I do not understand her powers, though she has grown more powerful than when I emerged from that shit hole the vampires kept me in and first met her."

"Do you not know her from… You know…" Maggie asked, making a hand gesture to try to encompass what she was struggling to say.

"No. I've wandered the earth for centuries, keeping to myself. Once my people dwindled and disappeared, swallowed up by others who replaced me with their one god, I saw no point to staying there or associating with beings of power." He shrugged then laughed bitterly. "I guess I wasn't forgotten entirely."

"Saubarag?" Roxi asked.

"Yes, him. He was petty little godling, always cradling slights to his chest. I guess he never forgave me ruining his attempt to use werewolves as dark army. Now he's trying to make us all pay for emotional wounds he took millennia ago." He sighed heavily. "I should have never taken him seriously when he said he wanted to make bridge between wolves and humans. He killed my dearest aralez to advance his sick scheme. At least in that, I denied him. And for that, he has never forgiven me."

Luke took Maggie's hand in his. "I, for one, am grateful that the aralez you sent were your best. Otherwise, history could have been a lot different."

"Who knows?" He sighed again. "This is melancholy discussion. I'm going to take a walk." He set his cards neatly on the table and walked out the front door.

"He's an odd one," Roxi said after a while.

Luke set his whiskey glass down. "I don't know. He's spent centuries by himself, possibly as a dog. Even for a god, that kind of loneliness has to be taxing. Then he was captured by his arch enemy and tortured, possibly without knowing who was doing it only to find out who it was as it tried to destroy us. I think he's doing alright, all things considered."

"Yeah. I guess." Roxi shrugged. "It's hard to know what gods are thinking or why they do what they do, especially in this day when so many of the ancient ones are weak and likely untethered from old power sources and the rules and restrictions attached to them."

"Do you think he's a danger? Especially now, if he's been… restored?" Maggie asked, worry furrowing her brow.

"I don't think he's a danger to us," Luke replied. "He's fought hard to protect the pack and counter the vampires. He's saved many of us from Saubarag, including me twice directly. He may not be entirely stable, but I feel like he's firmly on our side."

Nodding along, Roxi reached out and squeezed Luke's hand. "I agree. He's done too much for us to doubt his integrity. At worst, he's the enemy of our enemy, but I think he's an ally and a friend. He's proven himself too many times for us to start doubting him now. Though, we can still keep an eye on him, just to be safe."

"That sounds fair," Maggie said. "Where will he live now that he's… Well, now that he's not a dog?"

"He can move into my guest room for now, if he wants," Luke replied. He was glad he had the extra room. Prior to Gwen moving in and taking over the previous guest room, he'd used the spare room to store a few unused items he'd ended up getting rid of or moving into the basement lair.

Roxi gathered the cards and shuffled them. "It's probably for the best. He's comfortable in the house. Alfie likes him, and it'll keep him around people he feels safe with. Plus, we can keep him out of mischief until he settles on what his future is going to be."

"I'm looking forward to getting back to Portland and seeing the kid and the cat." Luke picked up his glass for a drink.

"You'll have to wait one more day—" Maggie started.

Luke interrupted, "I'm not cleared yet?"

"As much as I'd like to keep you for observation, you'll have to blame Holly this time. She wants to meet with you and the rest of the leadership team and figured this is as safe a place as we have."

Luke couldn't disagree with Maggie, though he did want to get back to his home. He just hoped Holly wasn't getting cold feet after all these years working on the front lines of Luke's vampire war, though he couldn't blame her if she was. They'd taken some brutal casualties lately. Having a handful of packmates beheaded would make anyone balk at continuing the fight.

He sighed. Ahmed…

"If Luke's done being lost in his head, are you all ready for another around?" Roxi asked.

"I am," Maggie replied.

Luke shook himself out of his dark path and nodded. "I'm ready."

Tomorrow wasn't too long to wait, and there was little he could do by fixating on it. Either way, Holly wouldn't beat around the bush. It wasn't her style. For now, he'd enjoy the company and the cards and see about another glass of whiskey. Tomorrow, he'd see which way the wind was blowing.

LUKE SAT QUIETLY, watching everyone who'd been called to the farmhouse get settled. The air felt thick with grief, anger, and tension as people tried to make small talk to pass the time and avoid delving into sad topics before they were forced to by the meeting. Though he kept an eye on it, no one flashed him an angry stare or a glance that was anything other than kind or curious.

The kitchen was crowded, standing room only. Luke's leadership team was there, comprising Roxi, Sam, Delilah, Pieter, Owen, and Simone. Jamaal had set up his computer and a projector if anyone needed it.

Luke missed Ahmed's presence and likely would for a while to come.

Lauren, Owen's sister and the Coast Pack packleader, had driven out from the coast. Maggie, who led the medical team, was already there. Mary, who hadn't returned east, showed up with Owen. Tutyr, standing separately from everyone else, leaned up against the counter, out of the way. Pablo's absence was conspicuous.

Without his best friend there, Luke felt like he was missing an arm. That was another reason he longed to return to Portland. As much as he dreaded seeing his friend lying motionless in a hospital bed, he owed his buddy whatever friendship and company he could provide and would reach him through the coma.

Sam stood up and called out, "If everyone has drinks and snacks, let's get situated so we can start."

"Thanks for meeting out here," Holly said. "I wanted to ensure we had absolute privacy and security. I'll turn this over to Pieter, since he has the most important news."

Pieter cleared his throat and sat up straight, his elbows resting on the table and his hands clasped in front of him. "Since I'm not sure how to warm up to the subject, I'll just break it to you quickly." He made eye contact with Luke. "Jan has been spotted—"

"Where?" Luke interrupted.

"Here. Portland." Pieter's knuckles throbbed red from his intense grip.

Luke clenched his fist under the table. "Fuck. Here? Just what we needed. Did you see him?"

"Not personally, but it was one of my most trusted people from Belgium. They knew Jan well and would recognize him instantly."

"And you trust them?"

"Explicitly," Pieter replied.

"Shit. I guess we'll have to keep an eye out for him."

"There's more," Sam said.

"He was spotted with a group of scary looking individuals," Pieter said.

"Scary how?" Luke asked. "Vampires? Gangsters? What?"

"She wasn't sure if they were vampires. She was too far to tell that, but she said they looked like military types. Muscular. Wary. The kind of people who moved like trained killers."

Luke stared at Pieter. "How many?"

"She counted a dozen, but there were more vehicles that matched the ones they got into. It could be as many as twice that if they were all there."

"And they might have a base somewhere nearby with more." Luke shook his head. "Fuck. Fuck, and more fucks."

"We've decided to postpone the memorial services," Holly said, nodding to Sam.

"We thought it might be too trackable to hold a bunch of funerals for those who were murdered in the line of duty," Sam said. "Though we'll do a private memorial after the meeting for those here."

"I know Portland is huge, but we felt an overabundance of caution was warranted," Holly added.

Frowning, Luke nodded. "It's probably the smartest move."

Holly leaned forward, her brow furrowed, and held Luke's gaze. "Is Portland dying?"

He wasn't expecting that question. "What do you mean?"

"The vampires are worse than ever. Based on the reports you've sent me, the city is literally being swarmed under. Now this Jan shows up with some sort of dangerous cadre? I'm worried the pack is quickly becoming out matched, even with you and Roxi to lead us. I'm afraid, Luke." Holly paused as Sam reached over to hold her hand. "Terrified might be a better word. The pack has spent years building our holdings and homes in North Portland. We've lost so many people to this fight. I'm scared we'll lose our homes next."

He couldn't help but feel for Holly. She was an excellent leader and kept her people front and center in every decision she made. He admired her.

She continued, "I just don't know what to do. If we abandon our businesses to flee until this thing is over, we might lose our livelihoods. If we leave our human employees and friends to keep them open, we leave them vulnerable without the pack's full defenses. North Portland is safe right now, but for how long?"

Luke nodded, a furrow of sympathy on his brow. "It's a hard place to be in. It seems like only bad options are available to you. I'll do whatever I can to help you make the decision and execute it."

Holly gave him a weak smile and the barest of nods.

"Holly, dear," Lauren said. "You have the full support of the Coast Pack if you need to evacuate. We can even provide more volunteers to help fight. We've been training our people for a while in case we need to defend our territory."

Owen set his hand on his sister's shoulder. "I've spoken to our friends on the Wind River reservation. They'll help out, too."

"Some of my pack is willing to make the trek over as thanks for helping Maine get rid of that camp," Mary said.

"I've been working the phones while we've had the teams off the streets," Sam said. "Our allies have more interesting tales to tell."

Luke's stomach flopped as worry wriggled in his guts. "What kind of tales?"

"It seems that a lot of them have stopped finding vampires in their cities. Contacts have dropped to almost zero in several territories. All the vampires showing up in Portland had to come from somewhere." Sam looked around the table, letting her message sink in. "They're thankful for the relief in their territories and willing to send trained people to bolster us."

"Don't forget," Jamaal spoke up, "all the people out there who've been watching our videos. We've even been receiving videos of their vampire kills. I've contemplated setting up a 'Vampire Kill of the Week' contest. Anyway, if we put the word out, I'm sure we can attract some freelancers."

Luke chuckled. "That's probably more accurate to the origin of the word than it's used now." He momentary levity dropped from his face as he returned his gaze to Holly. "I'm scared too. I've never seen anything like this. Ever."

"Me neither," Roxi said. "The vampires are only a tool. They're here for one purpose and were sent by one entity." She paused as everyone hung on her words. "To kill Luke before he kills Saubarag."

"Can you actually do that?" Holly asked. "Kill a god? He's an actual god, right?"

Holly had only met Selene. Despite her initial skepticism, she'd agreed, and like many of the werewolves Luke had interacted with since joining the pack, had come away changed from the experience.

Tutyr stepped forward for the first time and spoke the first words he'd said since everyone showed up. "Saubarag was small god. Weak and reviled. Sneak thief and liar. Now… Now he's something different. I don't know what's left of original Saubarag, but what's replaced him is…terrifying in its power and its willingness to break anything to achieve its goals. Including your city."

"You're a god, right?" Holly said, a desperate hope filling her eyes. "Can you stop him?"

Tutyr shook his head slowly. "Once upon time when we were both in our original times and contexts." He reached into the pocket of the sport coat he'd picked from the Pack's spare clothes' storage, pulled out a few dog kibbles, and popped them into his mouth, crunching them loudly. "He is more powerful than I ever was. Far more powerful than any divine power I've ever met.

"When I fought him alongside Luke and Roxi, I touched his awareness briefly. I don't think there's much left to his sanity. Much like my friend here"—he gestured toward Luke—"Saubarag isn't an infinite vessel. He can only hold so many stolen souls. But unlike vessel, such as pitcher, excess doesn't just spill over the side returning vessel and liquid to level of stasis. He's trying to hold on to every soul his minions have stolen. I'm afraid it's cracking."

"What do you mean?" Holly asked. "Can we just let him break? Will he disappear then? Can he die?"

"I don't think he'll break like dropped jug. I don't know how he's maintaining himself now, other than letting his monsters drain more souls which he collects. Maybe he's using them to patch himself. But he'll break at some point, and what results could be cataclysmically bad. Dark eldritch horror bad."

"He sounds like one already," Holly said.

"No." Tutyr huffed. "I don't have direct proof, but I suspect at some point he ate Ahriman like he did nhang when they first warped it into the first vampires. If he managed to do it at height of Ahriman's power, he could have vast darkness churning under surface, working its own will and evil. I am afraid he wants to turn your city into hell on earth. If he breaks Portland's defenders—you—he'll move to next city and consume it without enough resistance to even give him indigestion."

"Dear goddess…" Holly murmured, her hands shaking.

Silence hung heavy in the room, fear tainting it as people looked around the room at their friends and loved ones.

Finally, Holly collected herself and looked at Luke. "What can we do? If we evacuate, we risk alerting our enemies. If we stay, we risk them finding us. How do I get my people out of this without losing everything?"

He wasn't used to seeing Holly this wholly discombobulated, and it shook one of the foundations he'd found comfortable about Portland. She'd been a rock, and he'd trusted her to provide sound civilian leadership while he handled the more militaristic aspects of pack life. That had been the balance since he'd joined and Holly had agreed to stand with him.

"We call in our allies. As many as can come. We'll put out the word to the internet and unleash everyone who has learned from our videos. Whatever it takes, we'll protect our people and territory long enough for me to end this once and for all."

"How? How can you end this?" Holly asked, a thread of hope returning to her voice.

"I'm going to end the vampires by killing their god. There's only one mission that matters from here on out, and that's to end Saubarag."

Jamaal raised a hand. "I think I can help with that. All the work we've been doing has paid off, and I think I have a reliable tip on the location of someone high up in the vampire organization."

Luke raised an eyebrow in curiosity. "Who?"

"One Flavius Constantius."

A wicked grin spread across Luke's face. If the road to Saubarag allowed him to kill Constantius on the way, he'd gladly travel it.

[WORK IN A BIT from Jamaal about the vampire informant sending a location for Flavius Constantius]

CHAPTER
FOURTEEN

"Go! Go! Go!" Luke yelled into radio to activate the rest of his people while waving his team on.

A vampire sprinted out of a bush, running with all its supernatural speed toward a large house that could almost be classified as a mansion. Acting on the tip Jamaal had received from their mysterious insider in the vampire camp, they hoped to capture a fanger who actually knew where to find Saubarag.

Luke had taken a week to help with his recovery while allowing time to carefully scout the location their mysterious source had directed them to. The delay had also allowed them the space to bring in a few of the offered allies to bolster their patrol teams and this raid. Despite all the logical and smart moves, he still chafed at the delay.

Doing his best to keep up with his werewolf allies, he sprinted over a well-manicured lawn. They'd made it through the surrounding woods undetected, but the security at the perimeter had been far better than Luke had been expecting. Despite being annoyed at tripping an alarm, he had hope they'd actually acquire a high value target. They just had to close the net before anyone could escape.

Pulling around a shotgun on the sprint wasn't the easiest of tasks, but Luke managed it without losing too much speed. He pumped a shell into the firing chamber and readied the weapon for action.

The vampire was opening up distance on them. It was no doubt familiar with the terrain, but even that didn't explain its speed. It must have been a sprinter or athlete in its human life and freshly juiced up on some exceptional blood, possibly laced with some sort of stimulant.

Leaping over a short bush like a hurdler, it didn't even lose a stride as it hit the ground. Smarter than the average vamp, it didn't waste time or energy looking back. It knew who was there and what they did to vampires, which no doubt fueled its run.

Most of Luke's werewolf allies had opted for their bipedal forms, which were tougher and better for fighting, but they weren't the fleetest of foot. Those few who'd gone with their full wolf forms were catching up to the fanger, though not fast enough to stop it from reaching the house.

"Demon!" the vamp screamed as it neared the house. "Wood… fanged…demon."

Luke smirked, the dark place in his heart feeling satisfaction in the evocative nickname the vampires had given him. None of them knew his current documented name—some bland combo of common names Luke used for taxes and his driver's license that he sometimes had to think about—or the name he used as his current identity in his own mind and with his friends, Luke Irontree. Only a few vampires knew or remembered his old name, Lucius Silvanius Ferrata.

He hoped to capture one of them tonight.

A window on the second floor of the house slid open, and the screen fell to ground. Something thin, dark, and shiny poked out.

"Gun!" Luke shouted.

He raised his shotgun to his shoulder and fired toward the window. The gun barked, the muzzle flame flashing in the night. Nearby, one of his wolf friends grunted. He couldn't tell who, but a quick look over his shoulders showed that no one had dropped back or fallen. They must be using standard non-silver ammo in whatever gun it was.

Grabbing one of the smoke grenades Owen had procured, he yanked the pin and slowed down. Drawing back his arm, he hurled the grenade toward the window. It had been a long time since he'd regularly thrown things like a pilum, but he still had the knack. The canister flew through the open window.

The shooter, only seeing a grenade shaped device flying at it, jumped out of the window. A second later, smoke billowed out.

The front door opened quickly as the running vampire approached the steps. Leaping over them, the fanger landed inside the doorway and kept running. One of Luke's werewolf friends, hot on the vamp's tail, leapt after it but slammed into the hastily shutting door with a yelp.

Recovering quickly, the wolf slammed its body against the door, digging in to keep the vamps from shutting it. A second wolf slammed into the door, leaning against it and stopping it from advancing toward the frame. A split second later, the fast bipedal wolf—it looked like Simone at this distance in the dark—smashed into the door, shoving it backwards. She hit it so hard, it flew open, scattering the vampires as she tumbled to the ground.

The two wolves leapt into the room and over Simone, snarling and snapping to protect Simone and drive back the vampire. Another pair of wolves pounced on the vampire that had jumped out the window, tearing it to shreds. A moment later, one of the bipedals slammed a stake into its chest to end it permanently.

Since the entrance was breached, Luke slowed enough to feed a shell into his shotgun and top it off as he aimed for the door. The three wolves—Simone had quickly recovered and sprang up—wreaked havoc with any vampire that tried to challenge their right to the entryway. They didn't advance, holding the space as their allies approached.

Luke's werewolves boiled into the house, advancing past Simone and the other two werewolves. Staying in place, they protected the entrance while catching their breaths.

Luke hoped the teams on the back and side entrances were having similarly good luck. If everyone did their assigned jobs, the teams roving in the woods would have a boring night. But if any fangers slipped through, they'd be there to make sure no one would escape. They'd assigned the volunteers drifting into town to the woods teams to work with his more experienced and reliable wolves. It promised to be the best option to test their enthusiastic allies.

Dodging the wolves in the doorway, he tucked out of the way and let the other wolves move into the house while he took a breather. That lawn was a longer dash than he'd wanted. Yet another reason to dislike lawns, though it had made for decently easy running.

The werewolves worked their way through the first floor, tearing apart any vampire or werewolf henchperson that dared resist them. One team took up their station at the stairs leading up to the next floor. Luke had wanted to ensure the first floor was cleared before splitting their forces. In a house this size, there would likely be a basement too, so his people had been advised to find the stairs down as quickly as possible. The basement would be the strongest place for the vampires to hide and defend.

Delilah, stopping and wiping a hand across her sweaty brow, bent over for a second to stretch. "Damn. Being on the injured reserve was not good for my conditioning." She stood up, stretching, but hissed as she grabbed her side. "Still a bit tight around the scar," she said by way of explanation.

"We find our target?" Luke had briefed everyone on their target, though he'd had to rely on ancient depictions since there wasn't any modern photographic evidence to his appearance.

"Not yet. We've only found a few older ones to dust. Most of the hired help is freshly whelped and messy. Anyway, I think we've found the stairs down. I've got a team checking the last couple rooms on this floor."

Luke wiped a drop of sweat from his eyebrow. "Good. Did the teams at the other doors get in?"

Delilah twisted gently, stretching her torso. "Not that I saw. I'll go let them in. Do we hit the second floor first or split and go up and down?"

Footsteps thundered on the stairs from the next floor up, and

Pieter poked his head over the railing. "Luke, we got a problem here!"

"I guess that solves that problem. Finish securing the first floor and send me some backup. Looks like I'm headed upstairs." He took off, jogging to where Pieter stood by the wall next to the stairs.

A shot barked out, and Luke dove to the side out of habit. Rolling back to his feet, he ran out of view of the stairwell, making for Pieter. "How many?"

"I saw at least three as they moved by the top landing, but it was hard to tell. They were moving fast and looked armed."

Nodding, Luke handed Pieter his shotgun and pulled around the AK-47 he liked to carry for situations like this. Though they had massive supplies of silver thanks to their bloody battle at the vampire fort in southeastern Oregon, he didn't want to waste it firing blindly. Plus, he could only carry so many shells and they had no idea what waited them below.

Racking a round, he reached up to make sure his helmet was secure. "Gather the teams. I'm leading the way."

Before anyone could protest, he stepped into the open. A shot splashed into the wall next to him, spraying splinters and drywall dust. "I'm coming up. Drop your weapons and live. You've got one chance. Anyone armed and fighting dies."

He punctuated his statement by firing a short burst upstairs. A blur dove out of the way. Mounting the first step, he fired another burst. With each step he took, he fired another few rounds. Someone braver than his friends leaned into the stairwell and fired. Ducking his head, Luke grunted as buckshot hit his chest, knocking him back a step.

A low growl rumbled in his throat. Aiming up, he held the trigger and sprayed left to right and back until the AK clicked empty. With a quick, practiced motion, he grabbed the magazine, flipping it, and rocked the magazine taped to the other side into the magwell.

Instead of the slow advance, he fired off a few rounds, then sprinted to the top, yelling as he went. As soon as he hit the top step, he leapt forward, tucked the gun into his stomach as he landed and rolled, and came out behind the vampires who'd been firing at him from the top of the stairs. From his knees, he took aim and put three bursts into three of the vamps before they could get out of their crouched positions. The fourth leveled an AR-15 at Luke as he swung his barrel around to take out the last vamp.

The vamp sneered at Luke, a gleam of hatred in its eyes. Luke dove to his left as the first shot rang out. A second never sounded. A werewolf tackled the shooter and yanked the gun from its grasp, smashing it in the face with the butt of the gun.

As the vamp lay stunned, the werewolf grabbed a stake from its bandolier of stakes and ended the vampire. Storming noisily up the stairs, a platoon of werewolves joined Luke and the first wolf. Half of them dashed past Luke to set up a defensive position while the other half staked the other three fangers. Picking himself off the ground, Luke took a second to survey the situation. They had a long hallway and what looked like another set of stairs leading up at the other end of the hall.

Luke walked to the top of the stairs and called down, "Send up the next platoon."

Behind him, doors crashed open as pissed-off werewolves didn't even bother trying the doorknobs, instead kicking them open. If any doors remained on their hinges after they were done, he'd be surprised. He didn't blame them.

The pack was still upset about the number of injuries and deaths sustained in their recent assault and the beheadings. His werewolf family was very interested in extracting payback, even it was just a door owned by a vampire.

Luke, spotting Pieter overseeing his platoon cleaning out the hallway, walked up to him, grabbing his shoulders. "Call if you need backup. I'm going to go see what's up with the basement."

Pieter nodded crisply. "Right. Good luck."

A few shots rang out down the hall. No one seemed bothered by the shots, so he guessed they'd used the pack link for the "all-clear" to indicate it wasn't one of their people who'd been shot.

Once he descended to the ground floor, he found Delilah and Simone with their teams, watching the closed door that supposedly lead downstairs. "Any news?"

"No. All quiet," Delilah said. Simone growled low in her throat, and Delilah nodded. "Too quiet."

Luke raised an eyebrow as he looked at his friend. "Do you understand her wolf communication?"

"Well enough," Delilah replied, smiling at her girlfriend.

He was happy they'd found each other and had such a solid relationship. They both deserved each other.

"I can understand that. Have you opened the door?" he asked.

"No. Didn't want to alert them that we might be curious about what was hidden behind it." She shrugged. "Also didn't want to catch a bullet between the teeth."

He snorted and lowered his voice, "Stand back and clear out some space behind me. I'm going to take a look."

He wished he had Roxi by his side. She was an absolute terror in situations like this, and between the two of them, he felt like he could take on the whole world with her. But they'd decided leading the teams hunting the forest for any vamps trying to escape or infiltrate their lines would be the best use of her stealth skills, especially with a bow and arrows if she needed to take down someone silently. She'd also asked Tutyr to join her. In his dog form, he'd be particularly useful in the dark.

"On my mark, give me five seconds then follow me down, but watch out for me," he said.

"Got it." Delilah looked around at the werewolves hanging around. "You heard the man."

Simone chuffed.

Chuckling, Delilah smirked. "Right, follow Luke into danger as he does something bonkers."

He suspected their level of communication wasn't that sophisticated, but Delilah was using it to get a second whack at making fun of him in her friendly manner. Though she wasn't always the most jocular of people, he appreciated her stepping up to pick up a little of the slack with Pablo still in the hospital.

Tapping the door frame lightly, he decided to use the AK-47 again and pulled the partial magazine, replacing it with another taped together double magazine. Pulling back the charging lever, he pointed it toward the door as he reached toward the doorknob.

With a quick inhalation, he pulled it open briskly and let go. Someone must have caught it since it didn't bounce into the wall. Forcing his mind back onto his task, he opened fire, firing blindly down the stairs toward the bottom.

"Mark," he said loudly to be overheard over his firing. "Here goes…"

CHAPTER
FIFTEEN

Thundering down the stairs, he kept up his steady fire, spraying short bursts at different angles to make sure no one had a safe spot to fire back from. A high-pitched shot answered, and he grunted as it ricocheted off his shoulder, cutting a gash in his hoodie.

When his gun clicked empty, he quickly flipped the magazine and kept firing. A few more shots missed him. Once he hit the bottom, he found a spot to tuck into, maintaining his periodic bursts of fire. Soon, his team would be coming down and he needed to keep the way clear. Once the other magazine came up empty, he just dropped the AK. Someone coming behind would pick it up and return it to him. Stowing it was time he didn't have.

He yanked around the Winchester M12 and opened fire. The tight confines of the hallway were perfect for the short trench gun and would allow him to show the vamps why the Germans of World War One feared the weapons so much. Silver would almost assuredly find a new home in such conditions.

A flash of movement twenty feet in front of him drew his eye, so he fired. Someone screamed in agony a split second later. A vamp rolled on the ground, more preoccupied by the silver burning inside its body than staying hidden in its nook.

Hurtling from its hiding spot, a vampire probably hoping Luke was sidetracked by its downed comrade broke from cover, dashing down the hallway.

Luke fired. The fanger exploded into dust. As he jogged down the hall toward the first vampire he'd shot, he kicked out, catching the fanger in the teeth as he passed. Someone else could finish it off. Keeping his finger on the trigger guard and the barrel pointed down the hall, he grabbed two shells from his ammo bandolier and reached across the gun to feed them into the magazine.

A whimper ahead drew his attention as he advanced. Swinging the barrel of his gun toward the sound, a fanger curled up in the nook of a doorway. Its hands shot into the air, surrendering.

"Please don't kill me. I have information," the vampire begged.

Luke nodded, keeping his barrel leveled at the vampire as he glanced ahead to watch for any danger.

"We got him," Delilah said quietly. "Let's go, fanger. Move real slow, and you won't have any problems."

Now that the vamp was taken care of, Luke pushed it to the back of his mind and resumed his march down the hallway. Once he found a turn in the hallway, he stopped and fed some more shells into his Winchester.

A faint scrape of leather on concrete drew his attention. Delilah's shoes had rubber soles, and the werewolves had wolfy paws. He raised his fist into the air, halting all activity behind him. A quick glance over his shoulder told him the vampire was no longer in the hallway. Luke didn't want the vamp to remember its loyalty to its fanged siblings at the wrong time.

"I heard gunfire near the stairs," someone whispered ahead. A moment later, something thudded to the ground.

Letting his mind tune into his vampy sense—he actually could this far outside of Portland in the rural lands near the Coast Range. Since the battle at the fort, he'd been able to pick up the proximity of vampires in a more refined way that nearly allowed him to gauge their distance with relative accuracy.

He stayed hidden, back against the wall before the turn, and waited. With one hand still on his gun, he held up the other and signaled six vampires coming. Behind him, a quiet growl broke the silence. He whipped his head around and glared down the hall. The growling stopped immediately. Sure that Simone was already on it, he'd have to check in with her to make sure the team was reminded not to break discipline.

The approaching vampires stopped. They must have heard the growl. One of the vampires reversed course rapidly.

"*Shit,*" he thought.

The vamps weren't as close as he wanted them—he wanted them in meat grinder range—but they were within range. Pivoting into the other section of hallway, he didn't wait to acquire a target. He just fired, then pumped another shell into the firing chamber and squeezed the trigger again.

By the time the second shot echoed down the hall, he spotted his mistake. Just because they were close didn't mean they were straight ahead. The tunnel took another zag, returning to its original direction.

He beckoned his team after him and sprinted forward, hoping they were keeping up. Sliding around the corner, he took a quick aim and fired down the hall as he slammed into the wall to stop himself. He fired once more but hit nothing.

A vampire broke from cover and sprinted away from Luke, but not fast enough. Its remains splatted onto the ground, creating a slick. Another vampire thudded into the hall as if thrown, landing against the wall, and fell to the ground in a heap. It sprang to its feet, but Luke drew a bead and fired.

But while he'd focused on the free vampire, three fangers dashed down the hallway. Luke opened fire, taking out the one in the back as it puffed into dust. As he dashed past, he cast a quick glance in the nook they'd been hiding in. A vampire with its throat cut lay on the ground. That must have been the thump from earlier. Thus was its punishment for speaking and breaking their cover. The injury wouldn't kill it, but it would incapacitate it, leaving it to be killed or captured by the vampire hunters.

Before he could fire again, they turned down another hallway.

"Get the master out of here!" one of the remaining vampires shouted.

That's exactly what Luke wanted to hear. He sprinted down the hall as fast as he could, only slowing to take the corner. There were only occasional offset doorways he'd passed so far. He'd left them for his team to break into and clear out. He doubted there was much of immediate interest in them, though they'd sweep them for any valuables and technology. He wanted to find something that actually looked like a safe-room or strong room. So far, it just looked like a shitty basement apartment building.

Around the next corner, he caught a glimpse of black hair flying out behind the fleeing vampire and fired. The vamp took another turn, the silver buckshot peppering the wall where it had been standing a moment before.

"Dammit," Luke bit out.

He didn't slow down. Though he had supernatural foot speed compared to a human, an old vampire could outrun him. An empty shell flew out of the ejection port as he pumped the shotgun, but it was his last shell. He couldn't stop and reload or even slow to do it on the fly if he wanted to keep close enough to the vamps to find out who the "master" was. He hoped it was indeed their intended target but only keeping up would let him find out.

Taking another corner, he skidded to a halt. A vampire stood facing him down at the other end of the corridor. The vamp held a semi-automatic pistol in one hand and a short, curved sword in the other.

Luke blinked hard, his jaw opening slightly. The face. The beard. The long black hair. It had been a thousand years since he'd seen that face, directing a band of vampires that had cut down the party of vampire hunters he'd joined in Samarkand.

"Come to meet your death, hunter?" the vampire said through a thick accent that spoke of its origins in Central Asia.

A sneer-like grin spread across Luke's face. "No. Just to extract one I missed a long time ago." Reaching up, Luke tugged down the zipper on his hoodie, revealing the lorica segmentata. "Do you recognize this armor? The last time you saw me wearing it was in the mountains south of Tuva and Mongolia."

The vampire barked a humorless laugh. "Small world. So, you're he? The one called the wood-fanged demon?"

Luke nodded once. "You can put down the gun—it won't penetrate the armor—and you and I can handle this like civilized beings. Sword to sword."

"Maybe it won't, but you've got a face I'd love to put a bullet in." The vampire raised his aim.

Luke charged forward, lowering his head to present the top of his helmet and the wide, plunging neck guard. The vampire fired, and Luke grunted as the bullet hit him in the chest. Staggering, Luke regained his balance and kept running.

The second shot slammed into the neck guard, forcing Luke's head up and exposing his face. Desperate for a quick distraction, Luke hurled his empty shotgun at the vampire's gun hand. The third shot went wide, plowing into the wall.

As the vampire juggled to knock the shotgun out of the way, Luke yanked his gladius out. His shotgun clattered to the ground. The fanger swung the handgun around, but instead of pulling the trigger, he dropped it and brought his Kilij—a curved, single-edged sword originating in Central Asia—up to counter Luke's sword strike aimed at its head.

If the vampire had hesitated for a second longer, relying on the gun, it would have been dead. As it was, the vamp was unprepared for the strength and speed Luke could bring to bear, especially with the additional power he'd been siphoning from the fangers he'd consumed.

The vampire, at least a thousand years old, drew on its longer sword as well as all its speed and experience to escape Luke's initial attack and regain a bit of the momentum. It had been a while since Luke had crossed swords with an enemy who actually knew what to do with one. Not since Le Mousquetaire.

He almost found himself enjoying the give and take. The vampire had expanded his study beyond just the techniques of his human youth sometime in the earlier medieval period and presented some different attacks. But Luke had studied longer and had kept up his sword play. He doubted the vamp had fought anyone talented with a sword who wasn't one of his bloodsucking compatriots.

A smile spread across the vamp's face, his fangs pointed and sharp. Luke found the corners of his lips edging upwards.

"Why are you smiling?" Luke asked, feinting towards the vamp's guts.

The vampire blocked the upward slash and riposted. "While you're wasting your time displaying your sword knowledge, the master is making his retreat. Either way, I win."

Growling, Luke parried the counter and slashed wildly toward the vampire's head. It dodged, ducking. But it had bought Luke a split second. He used it to slam into fanger with his shoulder. Already slightly off balance from the quick duck, the vampire tumbled to his ass. Instead of following the attack, Luke stepped back and pulled his rudis.

"Either way, you're wrong." Luke didn't wait for a reply, forcing the incantation into his head and through the rudis.

The vampire's eyes went wide and his jaw dropped, but as its chin reached the bottom of its movement, it flaked away. Unlike some older ones, this one still held its form as pieces dried up and fell off, puffing into little clouds as they hit the ground.

A vicious grin spreading across Luke's face, he kicked out, hastening the vampire's final dissolution. It puffed into a cloud of dust, settling on the concrete floor of the underground corridor.

But before the vampire hit the ground, Luke was already gone, sprinting down the hallway.

"Luke!" someone shouted. "Hold up. Wait for backup!"

Not bothering to even turn to pitch his voice, he just yelled back, "Can't. We'll lose him."

He hoped their werewolf hearing would catch his words. Keeping his senses alert, he barreled past doors that didn't cause any shift on his perception of the location of the vampires until he slowed at a corridor.

Staring left then right, he wasn't sure which one was the right choice. He'd told Pablo in Seattle, when all else failed, follow the

Gandalf principle by letting your nose choose. In this case, he picked the corridor that stank more, at least in the sense that the vampire tug was slightly more pressing to the right.

Once again, he slowed, but this time because he could feel a group of vampires approaching, or rather he approached one that felt relatively static. Wary of an ambush, he stopped and ducked into one of the periodic nooks that split off from the hall and led to other rooms.

Peeking out, he didn't see anything, so he slipped from his hiding place and stalked down the corridor. Ahead, he heard people talking angrily, but he wasn't close enough to distinguish their words.

Stopping at a corner that turned to the left, he backed up to the wall, his rudis and gladius held down by the sides of his legs.

"Master, hurry! He's got to be getting close."

A haughty voice replied, "Surely Subutai stopped him."

"Has anyone been able to stop him?" The replying voice verged on panic. "He's not just a vampire hunter; he's a disaster. A plague unleashed upon our kind. He's not just a demon, he's a devil. If we don't move, we'll be his next victims."

"But, the safe room," the haughty voice whined.

"Nowhere is safe from the wood-fanged demon," a third person snapped. "Either you move, Master, or we'll carry you."

Taking in a slow deep breath to slow his heart, Luke prepared to move around the corner. The one he wanted was there. But before he could lift his foot off the ground, the sound of padded feet and nails on concrete drifted down the hallway after him. Snapping his head around, he relaxed as a group of werewolves sprinted down the corridor.

He raised a hand and gestured for them to slow down, then brought a finger to his lips to indicate silence. A few seconds later, they stopped behind him. He held up a hand to indicate three or more people were around the corner. Not waiting for a response, he turned and entered a short corridor that almost immediately turned to the right.

Not bothering to slow down, he stepped around it. Not more

than forty feet in front of him were six well-armed vampires surrounding a seventh. That must be the one.

"Constantius! Where are you going in such a hurry? I just want to talk," Luke called.

One of the werewolves behind him chuffed. It was true. Luke did want to talk. But in Constantius's case, there would be no catch and release after Luke got him to talk. The vendetta was truly personal beyond the role of vampire hunter and vampire.

Too many times had the man tried to deny Luke his life and freedom, interfering in his pursuit of life and love beyond his current circumstances—first with Marpesia and then with Roxi. He had no idea if the petty schemer had caused more strife in his life, but it didn't matter. Constantius would finally pay for what he'd done to Luke…after he beat the location of the petty imperator's master out of him. Saubarag must die, and Constantius would help Luke do it whether he wanted to or not.

"Go, move!" The rear vampire tried to chivvy his master along.

"Don't you want to chat just for old time's sake? Like when you captured and tortured me. Twice. I promise. I only want to ask you a few questions. Answer them and you'll have a future." Luke didn't add that it would be a very short and painful one, but now was no time for semantics.

Luke walked hard down the corridor, his swords swinging. The motion caught and reflected light from his blades, capturing the eyes of the bodyguards and their master who kept looking back, fear in his eyes. The only shift in his demeanor occurred when one of his bodyguards placed a hand on him to hurry him along. Then, the anger at being touched by what he no doubt considered a being beneath him replaced the fear.

The son of Constantine the Great hadn't changed much since Luke had met him when he was a teenager and Luke was already over two-hundred-years old. Constantius was still a weak man standing in the shadow of his betters. Then it had been his father and Luke. Now, it was a dark and twisted god.

Deciding to change the dynamic, Luke broke into a jog, then a run. The vampire bringing up the rear barked out some commands, then turned around. Two of his comrades stopped and joined him, forming up on his left and right. The other three continued their fruitless attempts to get Constantius to run. The best he'd manage was a brisk walk. Running must be beneath one such as him.

Luke itched to slide his rudis between the boy's ribs and drain him. He practically salivated at the thought, wanting to make it slow and painful.

"Flavius Constantius, I'm beginning to think you don't want to join me for a brief conversation," he called after the fleeing emperor. "Have I said something to offend you?"

Shaking his head, Luke raised his swords at the three vampires, who held their swords at the ready. He looked over his shoulder to his werewolf friends and said, "I'll try to open some space for you. If you can slip by, make a dash for them. The one in the middle is who I want."

"Not so fast, hunter," the lead bodyguard sneered. "You'll have to get through us first."

He wasn't sure why the trio didn't charge at him, other than they were buying more time for their master. Maybe that and the handful of werewolves Luke had with him caused them a moment of pause. The rumble of their growls would stop anyone from being too aggressive.

"Stay back," Luke commanded. "Your priority is getting to Constantius. I'll handle these flunkies."

These three weren't the average vampire chumps they typically fought. Without proper sword training, the werewolves would just get in his way and get somebody unnecessarily hurt. The body language and movements of these vampires conveyed their abilities. Their weapons appeared to be a part of them, and their auras gave off a fine patina of age. It was moments like this that made him wish Roxi was by his side. The two of them would be able to handle them. As is, it would be a difficult fight by himself.

Falling back on the old tried and true, he charged into battle, not allowing the space for his opponents to choose the start of the engagement. At the last moment, he swerved to the right and sprang off the wall, bringing his gladius down in a brutal thrust at the right-most vampire.

The fanger hastily parried the thrust and backed up. The middle vampire lunged over slashing at Luke's midsection. But he was prepared for that and swept aside the blow with this rudis. Tipping to his left, Luke slammed his shoulder into the middle vamp who staggered into the vamp on the left.

Once Luke's feet touched the ground, he swung a backhanded slash to his right at the first vampire he'd attacked. The vamp had recovered and had lunged in, but quickly had to adjust to block Luke's slash. The other two vampires backed up, maintaining their blockade of the hallway. He'd only managed to push them back a handful of feet.

Tightening his grip on the rudis, he longed to just drain them, but he'd already taken one without truly needing it. After passing out once and nearly dying another time from using the rudis on too many vampires, he felt justifiably concerned about what would happen if he overdosed a third time. He didn't know if four quick vampires would be enough to create problems. It's not like he'd studied the issue and knew the limits on his body. He'd only gained this ability a few weeks ago.

A flick of his eyes at Constantius fleeing increased the urge to succumb to the simplest of solutions. A quick drain of the three old vampires, and he'd be able to obtain what he wanted. But a week ago, he'd been on his deathbed—the closest he'd been in a long time. A tremor of longing ran down his arms…

Drawing in a sharp breath, he gripped his swords tightly and hissed out his breath between his teeth, stuck between victory and life.

Narrowing his eyes, he flicked his gaze to the left, leaning slightly that direction. The fanger there tensed and lunged forward with a thrust. Pushing to the right, Luke brought the rudis around in a quick arc and knocked aside the blow enough to allow him to step into the thrust. The tip of the vamp's blade slid into his hoodie and screeched across his armor as Luke stepped past the vampire and pivoted.

Too close to get a proper thrust with his gladius, he brought it down and across the vampire's back, the blade biting deep. The fanger screamed and arched his back, staggering forward. Using the opportunity, the werewolves yanked the vampire forward into their waiting claws and teeth. One down.

The two remaining vampires backed up and fanned out, swords raised and at the ready. Their eyes flicked back and forth to each other to ensure they were still there to cover their side.

Luke flicked his gladius briskly, sending splatters of blood flying through the air. A few spatters landed on the face of one of the vampires. The moment it cringed, Luke twirled the gladius once and charged down the middle of the hall.

Keeping his rudis up and to his left, he slapped aside the hastily raised sword of the vamp he'd splattered with blood. A drop must have flown into one of its eyes. It swiped at it with its empty hand while trying to keep up with Luke's gladius. The vamp blocked, parried, and dodged a series of thrusts and slashes while Luke did his best to keep the other vampire at bay.

Sensing the movements of his opponent to the right, Luke dropped low and rotated to his left. The vamps weren't expecting it. The one on the right overshot his thrust and moved by Luke. The one on the left slashed over Luke's head as he dragged the gladius through the vamp's quad. Blood welled up and spilled down its leg as it staggered backwards.

Using his momentum, Luke tucked and rolled forward, just in time to avoid the other vamp's swing at his head. He came up to his knees, then sprang to his feet near the vamp with the wounded leg. As he stalked forward, the vamp backed up, while his comrade did his best to keep an eye on both Luke and the werewolves who were now at his back.

Lunging forward off his right foot, Luke thrust his rudis at the wounded fanger, who backed off hastily. Planting on his left foot, Luke swung his gladius in a deadly arc behind him as he pivoted. The feint caught the vamp off guard. It barely parried Luke's slash, backing off to open more distance.

And that's what Luke wanted. The vampire momentarily forgot

his surroundings, and the werewolves pounced. In short order, they turned the vamp to mincemeat.

Luke smirked at the remaining vampire. "Last chance…"

The vampire's eyes flicked between Luke and the werewolves, then he turned and sprinted as fast as he could with an injured thigh, hobbling and hopping to compensate. Luke raised the rudis to drain the vamp, but the werewolves, sensing wounded prey, bounded after it and cut it down in seconds. Shrugging, he jogged after them until he cleared the mess they'd left, then dashed down the corridor.

He hoped the recalcitrant former Roman emperor had kept the bodyguards' progress slow and inefficient. The weasel was the kind of vampire who would squeal and give up the information about Saubarag's location to save his own skin. Luke had never had the chance to be truly in charge of Constantius's fate. The one time he'd been able to turn the tables on him—thanks to Pisakar and Marpesia—he'd had to let the boy go or risk an all-out battle he wasn't prepared to fight.

Wondering how far he'd have to run before he found anything, Luke picked up speed. The panting and low growls of his werewolves vibrated down the hallway behind him. After another turn, Luke slid to a stop. Through the last door was a large open concrete-floored room. Once he stepped through the door, he could see various luxury cars parked along the walls. Ahead, a pair of red taillights grew distant in the dark.

Luke stopped, planting his fists on his hips, his swords pointing forward. "Fuck!"

He stared as the lights faded to nothing. There'd be no way to drain them at this range. He couldn't even tell what direction they'd gone. Shaking his head at himself, he should have risked draining the three bodyguards. If he had, they might have caught Constantius before he disappeared. He fumed at his timid decision, air hissing in and out of his mouth as he stomped in a short back and forth. The werewolves gave him a wide berth as they moved into the room to investigate any unseen dangers and whatever prizes they could take.

He had no idea how long he stared out the large open garage door, but his heart rate had slowed to normal by the time he turned to find out what his companions were up to. The werewolves had left him alone, more curious about the fancy cars lining the walls of the neat and clean garage.

Sighing, Luke looked around for a rag to wipe down his blades. "See if you can find the keys. We're taking the cars."

Heading toward a bank of tools, he found a rag and stowed his sword. They'd gone far afield in his chase, far beyond what the initial mission parameters had been, and he needed to check in. He tried the radio but got nothing but static, so he pulled his cell phone out and gave it a try. No signal.

While the crew looked around for the keys, he jogged out the garage door until he thought he was clear enough. The garage opened out onto a road that wound down the side of the hill. The garage itself had been built into the lush, forested hill. Holding his cell phone up, hoping the extra couple of feet would help, he still had no reception.

They weren't that far away from Highway 26 and cell reception. This wasn't the old days when you'd lose cell reception as soon as you left town. They'd been able to use their phones up until the last couple of miles approaching their target when total silence had been the order.

Running back inside, he found the werewolves clustered in a little office that was situated in an out of the way corner. They'd found some coveralls to put on and had shifted into their human forms. Perhaps they could check in through their pack link. He didn't know if the density of the hill or the distance from the main house mattered. One of these days, he'd have to break propriety and ask for those kinds of secrets. It would come in handy for planning and safety reasons.

"Did you find the keys?" Luke asked.

"Sure did," Ramon said, holding up a set.

"Communication question. Can you communicate with the rest of the pack from here?"

Ramon shrugged. "Don't know. Haven't tried."

"I can't get any cell reception. The radios don't work either.

We're inside a hill, but I should have been able to get something from outside.

"The fangers might have some sort of jammers set up," a werewolf Luke didn't recognize said.

Luke wouldn't be surprised if they had. If they were trying to hide Constantius, keeping this place way under the radar would help. "You might be right. Let's see if we can find something of that sort. In the meantime, can you reach out to the rest of the pack? We're a bit out of bounds for this mission, and we need to let them know what's up."

"Sure thing, Luke." Ramon looked off into the distance. "Sorry, must be a bit too far."

"OK." Luke pointed to the wolf he didn't recognize. "You and Ramon run back and make contact. Alexa and I will see if we can find what's jamming us."

"Righto!" Ramon gestured with his head and stripped out of his coveralls. The other werewolf followed suit, and they changed to their full wolf forms, which were faster and would provide better offense than a human if they needed it.

After the pair had left, Alexa held up a set of keys, jingling them. "What are we going to do with all the new rides?"

"Have Jorge and his crew strip them of any identification or tracking devices and sell them off on the black market." Luke shrugged. "Fuck it. We might keep them for the pack. The spoils of war."

The more he thought about it, the more he liked the idea. He'd sacrificed his precious old Volvo to fake his death and advance their plot against the fangers. Maybe it was time for him to take a little payback. A smirk on his face, he left Alexa in the office and strolled out into the garage. Starting with the nearest line of toys, he stopped in front of a Maserati.

What the fuck did Constantius need with all these cars in Portland? The minds of vampires were almost unfathomable to him, save for their need to feed and dominate. But weak boy emperors were a subject he'd become well versed on after what historians called the Crisis of the

Third Century. There'd been a fair few then. Opulence and crude displays of wealth were viewed as necessary so others wouldn't overlook them. If you can't manage great deeds, loud wealth would suffice.

Perhaps Constantius needed his toys. Perhaps he wanted to rule Portland after taking it from the vampires' greatest enemy. And in the hierarchy of the bloodsuckers, a set up like this would earn him much jealousy from those he dominated.

Snorting, he continued his shopping trip, his hands behind his back as he strolled leisurely down the line of automobiles. Most of the vehicles were thoroughly modern luxury vehicles—a Bentley, a couple of Benzes, a few Italian sports cars.

He chuckled, shaking his head at how ridiculous he'd look rolling up to hunt vampires in a fucking Bentley. It would be big enough with plenty of trunk space…

No. He laughed. It would be too ridiculous and far too conspicuous. He kept walking. He almost missed it, tucked back in a dark corner, but a stray beam of light flashed off a metallic light blue finish.

The corner of his mouth quirking up, he stared at a cherry 1968 metallic blue Mercury Cougar. Checking the door—it was unlocked —he popped the hood. A clean, completely rebuilt 289 cubic inch engine stared back at him. Peeking back into the side window, a gear shifter with an eight-ball stood proudly from the hump running down the center. He guessed it was a three speed.

He didn't need a sedan. The team could follow in bigger vehicles.

"Hey, Alexa, see if you can find a set of keys for an old Mercury Cougar. This one's mine," he called.

It wasn't the rarest of cars, or even of its model run. It wasn't the biggest engine they'd put in the Cougar, but it was a quick little car that could practically fly.

"Luke! Catch." Alexa tossed a set of keys.

Snatching them out of the air, he opened the door and sank down into the low seat. The keys slid in like magic, and a moment later, the Cougar purred. A shiver ran down Luke's spine as the car's powerful motor vibrated the vehicle. Pulling carefully out of the corner and around a couple cars nearly blocking him in, he revved the engine as soon as he cleared the luxury obstacles.

Mashing his foot on the brake, he revved the engine then slid it into first gear and spun the tires on the smooth concrete before pulling his foot off the brake. He shot forward, a laugh escaping his lips. He spun the steering wheel, applying just enough brake so he could whip around in an aggressive one-hundred-eight-degree spin.

Then he raced to the back end of the garage. Before he slammed into the wall, he yanked the wheel over and spun some donuts in the garage. When he finally let the car rest, he rolled down to the end of the garage and turned it off, stepping out.

Alexa strolled up, her hands in her pocket. "That's some pretty good driving."

"Thanks. I don't get much call for that kind of skill, but it's always a good one to have in your pocket."

"I can see that." Her ears perked up. "Someone's coming." She paused for a moment then relaxed. "It's OK. It's pack."

A moment later, a small group of six werewolves burst through the door from the long, winding corridor into the garage. They were running like someone had set their tails on fire.

Still on the run, Sam transformed mid-stride into her human shape. "Luke..." she panted. "North Portland... Our houses. The vampires."

"What?" Luke's jaw slowly dropped and his eyes grew wide as realization dawned. "Gwen?"

Bending down and resting her hands on her knees to catch her breath, she continued, "Don't know. Just got an emergency call from Holly. She's organizing rescue teams and what defenders we have. I've got everyone else evacuating the mansion to head back into town."

Luke had already started toward the Mercury. "Take whatever cars you can find keys for."

He only had one thought going through his mind—get home to protect Gwen and Maggie.

SEVENTEEN

He slid into the open door of the Mercury, pulling the door shut behind him, and fired it up. Slamming the gear into first, he whipped the car around, the tires squealing, and aimed for the garage door, the only thought in his head to get to his family.

As he pulled into the dark rural night, he frantically fumbled for the brights but couldn't find them until he bumped a protrusion on the left side of the footwell. He tapped it, and the brights added more light to the winding road ahead of him. The extra light added a touch of focus to his terrified brain as he struggled to force the machine to his immediate needs.

The lightweight pony car flew down the road, reaching ridiculous speeds on the narrow lanes. As soon as he approached a corner, he slowed down just enough and aimed for the inside of the corner, sweeping across both lines to ensure he hit the best line through every set of curves. At this time of night, the roads were deserted this far from Portland.

Every straightaway, he pushed the Cougar to its fullest. He thanked the vampires for taking such good care of the car. It handled like a dream. As he shot east on the narrow roads, he debated how to get home. If he took Highway 26, it would be faster since he could truly open up and let the car fly. But the chances of running into a cop were much higher.

If he aimed toward Cornelius Pass or Germantown Road, he'd be less likely to run into a cop, but the roads were windy and dangerous and would add time to his trip. On a straightaway, he checked his phone to see if he had a signal yet. He did.

Using his voice command, he tried to dial Maggie and then Gwen, but got neither. Next, he tried Roxi to see if she'd broken free of the dead zone around the mansion.

"Luke? Where are you?" she asked by way of greeting.

"I'm heading back home. I'm sorry I couldn't wait for you."

"I understand. Have you heard anything from Gwen?" There was a rare note of panic in her voice.

"No. I was hoping you might have. I've tried both her and Maggie." The gaping maw of worry in his gut opened a bit wider.

"Have you tried Zel?"

"No. I will now. Bye." He hung up before she could respond and dialed Zel. "Zel. Luke here. Do you know what's going on?"

"Luke? No. There are sirens everywhere. I can see fires nearby. Holly issued a stay in place until called upon order."

"Have you talked to Gwen or Maggie?"

"No." They choked up, sniffling and crying. "They're not answering."

"Shit. I'm on my way. Keep trying them. Call me if you get an update."

Through their sobs, they managed to agree.

That settled it. He took the next turn that would take him to Highway 26. When he finally pulled onto 26, he put the pedal down and ran the car as fast as he could without blowing the engine. Tapping the steering wheel anxiously, he kept the car in the left lane unless he was forced to swerve into the other lane to avoid someone not paying attention. If he didn't have to keep both hands on the wheel, he'd have deployed rude gestures as he flew by them.

As he rounded the curve that led down the hill toward Portland proper, a set of red and blue lights flared to life behind him.

"Fuck!"

With both sets of index fingers tapping the steering wheel, he ignored the cop and thought through his options. Drifting into the middle lane, he used gravity to get a bit more speed from his car, then shifted over to the right lane. The cop followed him.

He couldn't quite tell what kind of cop car it was. Most likely, it was one of the newer small SUV models. The Cougar was more nimble and could outmaneuver it, but he wasn't sure if he could outrun it, not with the beefier engines they put in police vehicles just for situations like this. He kind of wished he had one of the ugly blockade-busting roadrunners Jorge had assembled. A set of caltrops wouldn't go amiss at the moment.

Slowing slightly to make the last curve into the Vista Ridge Tunnel, Luke put his foot back down as soon as he straightened out. If he stayed in this lane, it would dump him off on I-405 South.

Checking his rearview mirror, the cop was close, but not too close. He probably had called in the pursuit and was waiting for instructions or backup. Hopefully, the ruse would work.

His gut tightened as he neared the point of no return. Slamming on the brakes, he swerved hard to the left, nearly losing control of the car but regaining it—the back end fishtailing a bit—as he slid into the left lane to exit onto I-405 north.

The car next to him slammed on its brakes and swerved away from him into the right lane. A moment later, the cop smashed into the back of the car that'd just changed lanes. The cop car swerved to the side until its tires caught and it flipped, rolling a few revolutions until the concrete barrier stopped it abruptly and violently.

Luck had been on Luke's side. He slowed enough to take the tight curve of the on-ramp to I-405 North. Quickly merging onto the freeway and over to the left side, he took the exit into industrial Northwest Portland. It would add a couple minutes, but it might be more cop free, especially if the one following him had called in his location as moving toward 405 South.

He opened up the gas, letting the Mercury Cougar fly down Highway 30 past warehouses. Not even slowing, he blasted through an empty red light and kept going. When he approached the ramp leading up to the St. Johns Bridge, he cut off an oncoming car as he sped through another red light and crossed traffic up the ramp onto the bridge. Thankfully, his world remained free of blue and red lights.

Forced to slow to make the turn, he revved the speed as soon as he straightened. Groaning in annoyance, he saw two pairs of brake lights ahead. They belonged to a couple of semi-trucks heading across the bridge. Why they weren't in a single lane like they should have been boggled his mind.

He slipped into the left lane, then danced across the center lines separating him from oncoming traffic and back. He didn't see any headlights, so he yanked the wheel and kicked it into third gear as he accelerated into the lane belonging to the other side of the bridge.

Speeding past the trucks, he earned a couple honks from their air horns as he whipped back into the proper lanes. Driving through the downtown St. Johns neighborhood slowed him down until he turned onto Lombard Street. He couldn't mash the pedal all the way to the floor, but the lack of traffic let him move quickly.

In the distance, he could see the telltale glow of fires toward the Portsmouth and Kenton neighborhoods. It was too many to be a coincidence or an accident. As his foot lifted from the pedal, he scanned the horizon. Everywhere he looked, he found more fires, more destruction, more deaths. He hoped there would be none, but he wasn't that naïve…

Desperation squeezing his heart and returning the pedal to the floor, he gripped the wheel tightly and forged ahead.

Tires screeched in protest as he straightened out the wheel and he pulled onto his street. Ahead, flames danced into the night, a haze of smoke joining them while the oppressive feel of nearby vampires laughed at him.

The brakes screamed as he stopped near his worst nightmare — his house engulfed in flames with his loved ones potentially trapped inside. Before he could get inside, he had to clear the vampires preventing him from finding his family.

He had his gladius out of his scabbard before he'd even cleared the door. Jamming the blade into the back of the first fanger he encountered, he twisted and yanked it out, moving on before the first one had even fallen to the ground.

The second vampire held a machine gun pointed toward Luke's house as it watched the flames. Taking it in the back of the neck, the head flopped forward and bounded off the gun on the way to the ground. With his left hand, he snatched the barrel from the hands of the vamp and tucked it into his shoulder. Propping it up with his right forearm, he moved his left hand to the grip and pulled the trigger.

The first shots ripped into the side of the skull of the nearest vampire. Sweeping wide, Luke fired the gun in short bursts, hitting his targets most of the time since there were so many packed in too tightly. Those he didn't hit dropped to the ground, trying to figure out what was going on.

He had no idea how many were gathered around his house. He couldn't think logically enough to count them off. He just had to get through.

When the gun clicked empty, he dropped it and dashed to the next vampire, slicing its head off. A shot rang out, bouncing off his armor-covered chest and knocking him backwards. Air whooshed from his lungs as he slammed into a tree in the strip between the sidewalk and the street.

Shoving his back against the tree, he bounced forward and reached over his shoulder to pull his rudis. The light of the fire glinted off the metal of the gun, so Luke resorted to the fast option and drained the vampire holding the weapon. It exploded into a pool of goo, showering a few vampires near it.

The dull throbbing in Luke's chest subsided as he pulled in a lung full of smoky air. He coughed, lashing out with his steel-toed boot and catching a fanger in the face. Hopping up, he landed hard on the vamp's head and crushed it.

After his initial brutal onslaught, the vampires still alive scrambled to their feet. A couple, despite the guns they held, charged at him with feral screams. Grunting, he sidestepped the first and hooked it around the neck with his arm and swung it around. He opened enough space, then jammed the rudis into the vamp's back and heart.

With a violent throw, his gladius hurtled through the air, spinning end over end at a vampire as it raised a gun toward Luke. The blade's edge caught it on the face, and blood cascaded down from the cut, obscuring its vision. Snatching the gun out of the air from the first vamp, he cracked off a quick shot at the second vamp charging at him and hit it in the face, knocking it off balance as it careened into a nearby hedge.

Luke opened fire and advanced. He swept a burst or two at chest level, then fired off a couple shots at a vampire that tried to get off the ground. Despite the non-silver ammo, it did good work knocking back opponents and damaging flesh. Best of all, it leveled the playing field just enough.

Once he'd emptied that gun of ammo, he flipped around and caught the barrel, ignoring his burning hand and teed off on a vampire that tried to leap up at him. The fanger slammed face first onto the concrete sidewalk.

Luke dropped to his knee quickly and brought the rudis down into the vamp's back, ending its immortal life. "Maggie! Gwen!"

Not for the first time, he wished he could use the packlink to communicate, but at the moment, he'd settle for shouting loud enough that one of the werewolves would hear him and know he was there to help.

In short order, he'd collapsed on the vampires like a ton of bricks and tore through them, killing and maiming several. The few left in front of his house were either too wounded to get up or were faking it. One or two managed to skedaddle out of his path. A few shadows sprinted away from him, running in the street and keeping close to the cars to provide less of an area to shoot at.

With the house burning and the front door inaccessible, he had no time for panic. Focusing on the task, he shunted off every emotion that would get in his way and forced himself to ignore his growing terror.

"Gwen! Maggie!" He scooped his gladius up from the ground on the run and made for the side yard and the gate. It swung open in the night wind generated by the flames, a few embers smoldering on the wood.

He burst into the backyard and cut down two vampires quickly. There were only a few more in the backyard. Jabbing his rudis toward them, he forced the incantation into his mind and drained them. As the light globules floated toward him, something slammed into his back, knocking him forward.

Swinging around trying to keep his balance, the line of vamp energy sizzled through the air and hit the attacker, frying its face and neck—leaving nasty burns—on its path to Luke's rudis. In the light of the fire and the energy coursing off his rudis, heads and eyes whipped around to stare at Luke.

He'd seen a lot of scared vampires in his day, but he'd never seen that many terrified to their core, though he couldn't tell if it was the dark waves of fury pouring off his face or the glowing, hissing blade. In their eyes, he probably looked like Anakin Skywalker showing up to kill the younglings.

Uncorking the towering inferno he'd contained within him as all the injustices the vampires had perpetrated against humanity and him and his loved ones, he let it all radiate out through his eyes and the magic, wooden sword. The air around him sizzled as spurts of lightning and sheets of dark waves flashed off of him, fighting for dominance. The very air pulsed with deadly energy seeking a place to connect to and ground. In a trickle, then a flood, the vampires loitering around his backyard broke and ran.

Instinct told him to chase them down. But love kept his feet firmly planted and reminded him of his mission. Cutting off the power to his blade, the last of the energy fizzled away, returning the sword to a mere object. Sheathing both swords, he ran to the back corner of the lot and opened a sealed compartment built inside a stone temple and pushed a button.

"Come on..." he muttered.

It had been a few years since he'd used the elevator that descended to a small room at the back of his underground training facility. A groan rose from beneath him, as did a series of artfully arranged rocks that hid the top of the elevator. A gush of cooler air flowed up and out. He heaved a sigh of relief, then climbed in and reversed the direction before it even finished its ascent.

"Go, go, go…"

While it had been used mostly as a freight elevator to bring in larger objects to his underground lair, its primary purpose had been as an escape option. In an emergency, it even had its own power supply—a bank of heavy batteries that were regularly charged from his home electricity.

As the elevator bumped down, he slipped his gladius from its sheath. Licking his dry lips, he reached out and gently slid back the grating that blocked the entrance to the elevator. He cracked the door leading into the training facility. Heat, though not as intense as that raging above, swept through the crack—along with screams of fear and anger.

"Someone kill the bitch wolf and grab the kid!" a familiar voice shouted.

The anger he'd banked earlier after chasing off the vamps returned in a flash. Shoving the door in, he burst into the back of the sparring floor, assessing the situation on the fly.

Gwen had her naginata and was using it well to keep a wide area open as she moved through a variety of the Japanese and Chinese forms Sam had taught her. The wounded vamps were a good indication of her effectiveness. Nearby, a pale wolf in bipedal form swiped at a vamp that'd gotten too close.

A stutter slipped into his step. He'd never seen Maggie's bipedal form—he didn't even know she had one. When they'd first started dating, he'd figured it would be impolite to ask. Then, after a while, he never really thought of it. It didn't matter.

She was a non-combatant—a healer. After all she'd gone through, it was bad enough she had to deal with the wounds generated in the fight against the vampires, but he'd never wanted to see her join the actual fight.

He slammed into the nearest vampire, beheading it as it tumbled away from him and into one of its comrades. The distraction of its headless friend allowed Gwen to slip in and slice the naginata's sword-like blade across its throat, turning it into a gory Pez dispenser.

In quick succession, Luke put down two more and turned to the door that led to the spiral staircase up to his office.

A familiar face to match the familiar voice stared back at him, his mouth hanging open and his eyes widening.

"You…" Jan van den Bergh pointed with a shaky finger.

Compared to the flames above, the fire of hate burned brighter in Luke's heart. He let out an incoherent war cry and charged toward the man who'd killed his own father and murdered his own pack-mates in his rise to power. The vampires standing between Luke and his target dissolved in a flurry of blades.

From inside the back of his jeans, Jan pulled out a pistol and raised it at Luke. Ducking his head to present the top of his helmet and the neck guard, he kept up his charge. He knew every inch of this space intimately.

A shot barked out, plowing into the mat in front of Luke. Another shot fired. Air whooshed out of his lungs, but he kept on. When no third shot came, he looked up and saw the back of the patricidal piece of shit as he fled up the metal spiral staircase.

The smell of roasting meat wafted from the stairs. Luke bounded up behind them, avoiding touching the rails as the whole thing shook and swayed a bit. It wouldn't be long before they collapsed in the fire.

The heat radiating from the doorway knocked Luke back. He thought he saw a shadow leaping through a wall that had fallen, but he couldn't be sure. Backing up, he turned and sprinted down the steps, leaping out of the way as they tipped over, wedging on a beam that still hadn't collapsed.

His enraged rampage had cleared out most of the attackers, allowing Gwen and Maggie to take out the last couple as he ran up.

"We've got to get out of here. The whole place is going to collapse." He stopped, panting.

Taking a moment to assess them, he saw red in Maggie's fur and hoped it was vampire blood and not her own. A cut along Gwen's cheek leaked a bit of blood, but it would heal quickly on the young werewolf. A hollow pit of despair threatened to open when he didn't notice his fuzzy old man Alfie.

He winced as something behind him crashed. The roar of the fire intensified as the ceiling burned, though it hadn't yet spread this far in the underground lair.

"Where's Alfred?" he asked desperately.

Shaking, Gwen let her Naginata fall from her hands and thump to the floor of the sparring mat. She ran back to a closet in the back corner and opened it. A scared orange tabby darted out, but she scooped it up, using her enhanced werewolf speed. The cat struggled for a moment, then settled in. Luke ran to another closet and pulled out his spare cat carrier. Gwen dumped the cat into it, shutting the door to lock him in.

With the cat safely located and contained, he breathed a small sigh of relief. He turned to assess the fire. The flames were creeping along the rafters deeper into this portion of his underground facility, passing into the sections where there was no house above. They didn't have long.

"Maggie, can you shift back? I have a car waiting outside," Luke said, resting his hand gently on her furry shoulder.

She didn't move or respond. She just stared at the dark, glistening slick as it spread wide, staining the straw-colored mat.

"Maggie..." He gave her a gentle shake. Still nothing. "Gwen, grab your weapon and get ready to move. Back left corner."

"OK." She scooped up her naginata and jogged to the corner where Luke had emerged a few minutes prior.

Moving to stand in front of Maggie, he cupped her furry cheeks and stared into her eyes. "Maggie. It's OK. You protected Gwen. The vampires are gone, but we need to go."

A loud crack emphasized his point.

"Luke..." Gwen said.

Peeking over his shoulder, what he saw made his stomach dropped. Flames licked at a snapped beam.

"Maggie. It's time to go."

She blinked and shook her head, seeming to recognize him. In an instant, she shifted to her human form. "Luke... I...I killed them... So many."

His heart ached for her. Rubbing a thumb over her now hairless cheek, he poured all the love and empathy he could muster into his eyes. "I know, but you helped save Gwen. We need to go, though. The roof is about to come down on our heads."

She looked around him, her eyes widening as if seeing the fire for the first time. He ran over to a cabinet against the wall and pulled out a robe for her, draping it over her shoulders. She tied it clumsily and let herself be guided over to the door by Gwen.

Soon, they gathered in the tight confines of the elevator. Giving Gwen his sword, he borrowed her naginata. If anything awaited them above, its extra reach would allow him to force them back and create enough space for them to get out.

"Run to the sidewalk, then go left. There's a blue classic sports car parked by the curb half a block down." He reached into his pockets and gave the keys to Maggie. "If anyone is hanging around, don't wait for me. You start the car and get out of here. Go pick up Zel and get yourselves to the farm. Do you understand me?"

"Yes," Maggie mumbled.

As the elevator opened up to the night, Luke braced his muscles, the naginata ready in his hands. A quick survey through the slowly increasing opening showed nothing but a burning house. He sighed. All his stuff...

It didn't matter, not really. It was all replaceable. He had what really mattered right behind him — his kid, his girlfriend, and his cat.

CHAPTER
EIGHTEEN

After the four of them piled into the stolen car, Luke dashed over to Zel's house, slowing as he approached to see if any fangers awaited his arrival. Thankfully, he saw none, nor did he feel any in the nearby surroundings.

Zel ran out of the house as soon as Luke stepped out of the car and walked around to help Maggie out. They threw their arms around him, tears washing over their cheeks.

"Thank you! Thank you for saving them," Zel said around sobs.

He didn't know how to respond without further frightening them or sounding too casual or blasé. Instead, he wrapped an arm around Zel and squeezed them firmly. When they stepped back, wiping their eyes, their brow furrowed.

Luke reached down to offer his hand to Maggie, who took it mechanically.

"Is she alright?" Zel asked.

"Physically, she's fine. Just a few scratches that've probably already healed." He turned to Gwen. "Can you go set your weapon and the cat on the porch, please? Then come back and help me with Maggie."

Gwen nodded and jogged up to the porch, then returned to take

Maggie's hand and guide her toward the house. Luke waited until they stepped inside, and the door shut behind them.

"She had to fight to defend herself and Gwen. When I found her, she had shifted into her bipedal form…"

"Oh no…"

"I know. I never wanted this to happen to her. I…"

Zel reached out and set a hand on his forearm. "You can't accept blame for all the actions of the vampires. We all fight to protect our family."

"I just didn't want it to be on the front lines and physically for her." He clenched his jaw, his cheek muscles flexing. "I need you to pack up whatever you need and get Maggie and Gwen to the farm. Make sure you're not followed. They probably won't, not with the level of effort they put into this massive assault, but just be cautious. I have a feeling we're going to need the refuge."

Zel nodded firmly. "Right. She's going to want to help with the wounded."

"I know, but she needs some rest and a little time first. I have a feeling she'll be seeing plenty of wounded up that way before long." He looked off in the distance, finding too many areas with all the signs of fires. "I need to get going and link up with Holly to see what we can do to help our people and evacuate."

"I understand."

Luke followed Zel into the house so he could give Gwen a fierce goodbye hug. Then he kissed Maggie on the forehead. He told them both he loved them and asked them to check in when they arrived safely.

Before the door had even closed behind him, he had Holly's number ringing. "This is Luke. I'm back in town. I'm having Zel take Maggie and Gwen up to the farm."

Holly exhaled in relief. "I feared the worst when Maggie didn't check in. Is she OK?"

"Physically. She's in a bit of shock right now. Zel is taking care of her."

"Good," Holly replied, packing the single word with a palpable sense of relief.

He opened his mouth to speak but paused when a thought smashed into his head. "Is the farm safe?"

"It is. We're evacuating all of our wounded up there."

"How?" Luke asked.

"I'll explain later. Right now, we have to do what we can to save our people."

"Where's the rally point? The rest of my strike force should be back in town soon, if they're not already here." Luke slid into the driver's seat of his stolen car.

"Yeah. I've been in constant contact with Sam. They're headed to the warehouse down on Swan Island. I'll meet you there as soon as I can break free."

"Right. See you soon." Luke fired up the car and tore through North Portland, anger making his foot heavier and his turns more aggressive.

He arrived a couple minutes after his assault team. They'd stolen an impressive collection of cars, though they would have to leave them in the empty warehouse until they could be stripped of any tracking devices the vamps may have put on them.

Once they assembled, Luke, Sam, and Holly organized the group into large teams to sweep through the neighborhoods inhabited by the pack members to check on ones that hadn't reported in yet.

As Luke led his people, most of them spent a lot of time watching the eastern horizon, waiting for the first rays of sun to drive off the vampires. But even without vampires causing mayhem, the fires they'd set wouldn't go away with the rising of the sun. Those would linger, causing damage and wreaking ruin.

But fire wasn't the vampires' only ally that night. They'd encountered their fair share of werewolf henchpeople. Most of the people who hadn't reported in had been asleep and had no idea what was going on. Those people were reported in as safe and given orders to evacuate to the farm.

When they approached a burning house with firefighters working, they asked about any rescued people. What he did hear was too many reports of evacuated bodies and wounded people which turned a dark night darker.

One group of people that were conspicuous by their absence was the cops. All the flashing lights had belonged to the few ambulances and fire trucks being overworked far beyond their capacity. There were few if any cops providing any kind of support, but Luke didn't find that unusual. The vampires had created and taken advantage of a lot of bad apples, and consequently, the whole bunch had spoiled.

Either way, he was left with more questions than he had answers for and no time to investigate them, not when the lives of his people were on the line.

They worked tirelessly through the remainder of the night. Where the fire department was working, they moved on. There were too many houses burning with no one there to fight the fire. The vampires' attacks had overwhelmed the fire department, and they were probably waiting for backup to arrive from other jurisdictions, if they were coming at all. In a normal situation, they'd have likely already been there.

CHAPTER
NINETEEN

L uke paced around the kitchen at the farmhouse, his hands clasped behind his back. The leadership team had taken a break from coordinating the massive evacuation of their community from North Portland to assess where they were and what they needed to do.

"I just don't get what happened," he fumed, making a turn to pace the other way.

Sam rubbed her tired eyes and yawned. "The best I can figure is the vampires hit several industrial sites with explosives. Places that would attract a lot of attention from their local fire departments and necessitate calling in reinforcements from neighboring departments. Once those fires were burning hot and deadly and had pulled in a bunch of firefighters, they hit us in North Portland."

Holly, staring down at her coffee cup, lifted her head to watch Luke pace. "When they're using firebombs and other accelerants, it doesn't take long for a house to go up when there are no fire trucks available to put out the fire."

"I don't know what kind of resources they pulled in to accomplish this," Roxi said, "but this is the biggest single coordinated attack I've seen of its kind. Frankly we're lucky the pack didn't lose more lives."

Holly groaned. "It was too many lives, even if it could have been more. Too many…" Her head settled into her hands. "We're refugees and hunted in our own city."

"How, though? How?" Luke asked, finally stopping his pacing. "How did they hit us so precisely? We keep North Portland clean of vampires. They probably knew that was our home base, but without the ability to sweep through the neighborhoods sniffing out werewolves, how?" He gripped his hand into a fist, wanting to strike the counter, but forced it to open.

"Werewolves?" Roxi asked. "But wouldn't you notice if a strange werewolf was sniffing around your house?"

Sam nodded sadly. "Yeah."

"And there's no way human thralls would be able to figure out who was a werewolf and where they lived," Roxi added.

Pieter rubbed his temples as he stared at the empty wood of the table in front of him. "Jan."

"What?" Holly asked.

"Jan," Pieter repeated. "According to Luke, Jan was personally leading the assault on Luke's house."

Luke looked for his glass of whiskey, finding it on the counter on the other side of the kitchen. "I've thought about the encounter"—he peeked into the sitting area to make sure Gwen hadn't snuck downstairs to eavesdrop—"and it wasn't just to burn my house down. And it wasn't to kill me, since they very deliberately drew me out of town to set this whole thing off. They wanted to take Gwen hostage."

Roxi whistled. "This was more sophisticated than just an attack on our homes. It was also a direct strike at Luke and an attempt to gain significant leverage over him."

Luke nodded.

Pieter pushed off the table and looked around at everyone. "And that has all the markings of Jan. It was at once brazen and subtle. He's exacting revenge and trying to prove himself to his masters. But he couldn't do it on his own. He had to have inside help. The surgical precision of their strikes into our territory only makes sense if he had a database of pack members."

"Do you think any of our people or the Belgians who've joined us would betray us in that way?"

"There's no way anyone in the pack would," Holly said firmly, then looked at Sam, her eyes begging for reassurance. "Would they?"

"No," Sam said sadly.

"I would like to say all my people were safe, but after what happened"—Pieter scraped his hands over his face—"I'll never be able to trust that fully again."

"Does it have to be an intentional betrayal?" Roxi asked. "Does it have to a betrayal at all?"

Everyone turned to look at her, hope blossoming in a few eyes while a few others anticipated something new and possibly worse.

"We've been running roughshod on the vampires' tech resources. Is it possible they've finally turned the tables on us?" Roxi, her face drawn with dark rings under eyes, looked from person to person.

Sitting slumped in a chair, Jamaal sniffed, wiping at his eye. "It's possible. No system is one-hundred percent airtight. I've tried to make ours as secure as possible, but they could have found something I didn't think of or some other chink in our armor. I'll get my people to tear every line of code apart. We'll scour everything to see if they broke into our system."

Luke, grabbing his whiskey, settled into his seat next to Roxi. "That brings me back to the question I had for you, Holly. How is the farm safe? I know you've got guards posted and other security measures, but should we be expecting unwanted visitors at any moment?"

"The farm is off the books. It's never been on them. My ancestors were some of the first settlers who colonized this area." Holly's voice came out nearly monotone.

This whole thing had been a huge blow to all the work she'd spent decades on. Her safe haven for LGBTQ+ werewolves had been violated in a horrendous way.

"But people have been here. Both your original pack and the Belgian additions," Roxi pointed out. "If our guards and lookouts haven't seen anything out of the ordinary, it kind of lends back to what I said earlier. It may not be a betrayal of loyalty, but an attack slipping through our security."

"I know," Jamaal snapped. "I'll get to the bottom of it. Dammit."

Holly perked up, fierceness driving away the haunted look in her eyes. "Jamaal. Did you and your people do everything possible to secure our digital safety?"

He paused for a moment, then nodded.

"Did do everything to make sure any holes were closed?"

He nodded again.

"Is there anything else you could have done?"

"There's always something…"

"Something that would have actually worked or made a difference?" Holly's gaze practically sizzled through the air.

"I mean…no."

"No one here blames you, at least any more than we all are blaming ourselves." Holly looked around the room slowly, holding each person's gaze for a moment before moving on to the next. "We're all blaming ourselves, wondering what we missed or what we could have done better. But I know every one of you has poured your hearts and souls into protecting this pack. We've lost battles before. Just not one this badly. As much as we want to wallow in our pain and self-recriminations, we're still under assault. We still have a mission. We still have people to protect and relocate."

For the first time since they gathered, the people gathered around the table felt their purpose return. Holly was right. They'd all blame themselves, but they had too much to do and even fewer resources to accomplish it. Luke knew he'd forever hold the pain of failing the pack, the people who'd taken him in and given him a life and a family when he was adrift in the world. But he couldn't let it break him or distract him from giving his all and moving forward.

"Holly is right." Luke stood up, leaning over the table, and looked at his friends. "We're all in pain. And it's the kind of pain that can beat you down and never let you up again. I've seen it before. Seen it destroy good people who couldn't find their way out of the pain. I've been that person, though I managed to fight my way out again." He paused, a small, sad smile gracing his face. "You all helped me find the light again. We'll always carry this, but we can either let it destroy us or we can use it to make ourselves stronger."

Luke reached down and gripped Roxi's hand as he stood tall. "We're all family here. None of you are alone in this. I know it's asking a lot of you, but we all have to dig down and keep going. If we curl up into balls and hide, our family will suffer. There will be time to rest and heal down the road, but right now, we have to slap a bandage on our hearts and march on."

Purpose filled the eyes looking back at him. Hands reached out to touch and hold those sitting next to them. They were a team with a job left undone. They just needed someone to hold them up and together.

Resolve in his eyes, he looked at Holly. In her eyes, he saw a plea and trust. She nodded faintly. He'd always looked to her to oversee him and to integrate him and his purpose into the pack, but that time had passed.

All his years and experience had led him to this moment.

Taking a deep breath, Luke let his eyes drift to the ceiling for a moment before he exhaled and addressed the room. "Holly. You'll continue the evacuation and coordinating with our allies on getting our people settled. Your second priority is to gain a true assessment of their military standing. I know it's not the softest word, but this is war. I need fighters, support staff, and supplies. We need to mobilize everything. If they balk, remind them that we're paying for their quiet cities with our homes and our blood. They can fight the vampires here or they can wait until we're vanquished and taste defeat in their own cities."

Holly, her jaw set, nodded.

"Roxi, I need you to organize scouts and spies. We need to see what's left. Your priorities are our armories and the silver ammunition production."

"Right," Roxi said. "Also, we can perform any extractions if we find out that any of our people are in unsafe territory."

"Good. I want you to take Jung-sook with you. She has some new ammo with a bit of silver in it."

Pieter raised his hand. "I'd like to go with Roxi as well. I'm the best person to smoke out my brother and identify him. Then we can put Jung-sook's new bullets to good use."

Luke raised an eyebrow, assessing his friend. "I'd have figured you'd want a direct chance to reward him for his transgressions."

Pieter shook his head, sighing sadly. "No. I've seen what hatred and the desire for vengeance does to a person. Jan deserves swift justice for his crimes. A bullet through the heart will more than satisfy that need. Then I can think upon him no more."

Luke held Pieter's gaze for a moment then nodded. "Very well."

He knew his friend would always think about his brother and the patricide he'd committed. Apparently, Pieter didn't want to add fratricide to the mix, though at this point, Luke was sure Jan would have no compunction about murdering his own brother.

"Sam, I'll need you to coordinate our forces and integrate any recruits we get in."

Delilah, who'd been sitting quietly next to Simone, looked up. "What about us? And you?"

"I'd hoped you'd join me in a little mayhem project."

Delilah raised an eyebrow. "Mayhem?"

"I want to build a handful of fast strike teams and rain pain and chaos on the vampires. We'll return to the old ways. Sweep in, maximum damage, and disappear into the night to hit somewhere else. I want you to lead a team. We need to create as much chaos as possible so Roxi can sneak about."

A feral grin split her face. "Yes."

Luke turned to Simone. "Do you feel comfortable leading a team? You have the nose to track down a nest or any wandering vamps, and I'd trust you to lead any mission."

Simone exchanged a brief look with Delilah then nodded seriously. "I'm ready."

"Great. Jamaal's teams are working over some of the cars we just liberated. We'll use them. One change we'll be making is instead of hitting lots of neighborhoods, we'll stick to one neighborhood then everyone will move onto the next. If we get in trouble again, I don't want a repeat of Mt. Tabor. We need to be close to each other in case we have to collapse in and rescue one of the teams."

Luke stood up straight and looked each of his people in the eyes. "When we're done here, we'll assemble our teams based on the skill assessment. The sneakiest people go with Roxi. The toughest and hardest fighters go with me, Delilah, and Simone. Sam, you assemble our best logistics people to help you coordinate everything. And no untested, unvetted outsiders on these teams."

He reached down and grabbed the glass of whiskey he'd poured and tossed it back, exhaling loudly as the alcohol burned down his throat. "I don't have to tell you to be careful. We all know what's at stake. They burned down our homes and killed our friends and family. They are trying to destroy the last resistance to their hegemony. If they break us here, they will have a virtual free rein in any and every city they want to make their home. If we break, there will be no place left to run to.

"We have to give it our all, because that's the only thing that's going to keep us alive, keep each other alive. Although we all have individual tasks, we are teams. We work together, we succeed together." An angry grimace spread across his face. "We destroy the vampires together."

R amon dashed out of the house, skidded to a halt, and lit the Molotov cocktail he'd made in the kitchen after they'd rousted out yet another nest of vampires. The wick caught, and he hurled it into the open door.

While he did that, Luke ran out to his new stolen 1968 Mercury Cougar and pulled off the top layer of the magnetic fake license plates they'd affixed to all their new cars. The simple magnetic mat was one of his favorite tools they'd used to help keep them off the radar.

Before Ramon could even buckle his seatbelt, Luke had the car in gear, tires squealing and smoke rising from the pavement. Behind him, one of the luxury sports cars made a similar exit.

So far, they'd hit three houses in rapid succession without a hitch. The vampires seemed to have grown complacent in the days after their brutal victory in North Portland.

"Get me check-ins on the other teams in the neighborhood." Luke hit the corner hard, the tail of the Cougar drifting a bit as he screeched around it.

Before Ramon could get a message off, both their phones started ringing. Snagging it out of the console, Luke tossed it to Ramon.

"Luke's phone, Ramon speaking." Ramon paused.

Luke might have been able to listen in, his hearing was good enough, but not when he was whipping around corners with little regard to the rules of the road.

"OK. OK. Got it. Hold on a second. I'll tell him." Ramon held the phone away from his head. "Delilah's reporting a bunch of cop cars coming this way, lights on."

"From what direction?"

"She says mostly from the north."

"OK. Tell everyone to blend in and make their way east then north. We'll rendezvous at the meetup spot on NE Columbia Boulevard." Luke slowed down so they could blend in now that they were far enough away from the last scene of the crime.

"Got it." Ramon relayed the information and hung up. First, he sent a group text which went out to the designated non-drivers. After he received the confirmations, he made two calls to the teams that didn't check in. One person picked up, and Ramon gave them the information. When he finished, another call came in—the last team.

Once they confirmed that all the teams were still operating, Luke heaved a sigh of relief. The action of battering their way into homes, killing as many vampires as possible in only a few minutes, then torching the place had kept his brain busy. But as soon as they left their targets, the anxiety and worry kicked in again. He couldn't deal with another failure like on Mt. Tabor.

"Ramon, now that everyone's clear, send a text to Pieter to find out their location." He didn't want to bring down heat wherever Roxi and Pieter and their team were working. Of the teams, theirs was the only one working without true destinations since their targets were more flexible.

A few minutes later, a vibration alerted Ramon to a message. "He says they're currently working their way to the warehouse down on Swan Island. I wonder what's taking them so long."

"It's nothing but roads, warehouses, fences, and train yards down there. It's not like they can sneak through the forest and check out our warehouse."

"I guess that's true. What neighborhood do we want to hit next?"

Luke thought about it as he wound his way through neighborhood streets where he could avoid the main thoroughfares the cops would be using. "Let's plan on shallow Northeast and North Portland. I want to see if the fangers have already moved into houses in their captured territory. Send out the order. We'll rendezvous, then head out. Let's stay west of NE Fifteenth and north of Killingsworth, but I don't want to go west of Denver. That should keep us busy but far enough away from Roxi not to foul up anything they're doing on Swan Island."

"Sounds good to me," Ramon replied.

"I'm glad you approve."

"Sorry, I didn't mean to presume…"

Luke shook his head. "No, I should apologize. It was snarky, and you don't deserve that. After everything that's happened over the last couple of months… I've let my anxiety get the better of me."

"That's understandable, man. No worries. Want me to relay that message?"

"Please. And send a second one to Pieter so he can let the other team know we're nearby if they need some muscle."

"Roger that." Ramon grabbed his phone, his fingers flying over the keyboard. "Shit. Luke, I've got a message coming in from Sam. Top priority she says."

"Fuck." He debated whether he should pull over or keep going but decided they needed to use the night while they had it and forged on. "Dial her up."

Ramon called Sam, then held up the phone between them with the speakerphone on.

"This is Luke, go ahead, Sam."

"Sorry to break in, but we have a potential rescue operation," Sam said.

"And Roxi is busy on Swan Island," Luke replied.

"Exactly."

"Give me the details."

"We got a text message from an unknown number claiming to be from a family being held in a house in Overlook. Said they managed to lift a phone from one of the vampires."

Luke narrowed his eyes. It sounded too convenient. "What

confirmation do we have?"

"They sent a selfie. I know the family, and the house is theirs. It's one of the families we haven't heard anything from."

"Shit. So…are you saying authentic?"

"I am."

Luke looked around for a place to pull over. Once he was parked, he reached into a pocket and pulled out a small notebook and a pen. "You said the house was familiar?"

"Yes. I've been over before."

"OK. Give me a rough layout and dimensions."

Sam relayed the information to him, though she was uncertain on a few points. "That's the best I can do."

"It's better than walking in completely ignorant. Do they have any idea how many vamps are in the house?"

"They can sense at least six, but there are also strange were-wolves. They guess around another six."

"Hmm, twelve or more. That could get hairy. Anything else?"

"Yeah. There are two children in the house. They've got them separated, that's why they haven't tried anything, beyond the fact that they're not fighters."

"Do they know where they're being held?" Luke hoped they were still on site.

"Not far away is all they know."

"And based on the picture you sent me, the parents are in the basement?"

"Yes. It's unfinished, so there are no egress windows," Sam added.

"I guess we're going to need the siege van."

"The what?" Sam asked.

"The siege van…you know." Luke rolled his wrist to indicate what he was talking about even though Sam wasn't there to see.

"I don't. Are you sure that's what it's called?"

Luke sighed, dropping his face into his hand. "Sam, don't make me say it."

"I don't know what you're talking about. We give things specific names so we can easily identify them. If you don't use the right name, how do I know what one you're talking about?" Sam's voice sounded matter of fact, but he could hear the humor squeezing out between the cracks.

"Fine." He shook his head. "We need the…the Penetrator."

"The what? I didn't hear you." She sounded extra smug.

"Dammit, I'm going to revoke your naming rights."

"No, you won't," Sam said confidently.

"I'll do it. I'll appoint someone else the official namer of code names, mission names, and other namings."

"No, you won't."

"Just send me the Penetrator van, OK?" Next to him, Ramon sniggered, doing his best to keep it contained with his hand over his mouth.

"Say it with some verve. Weren't you a theater kid?"

"You know I wasn't. And neither were you."

"I could have been," Sam said matter-of-factly.

Luke sighed. "Yeah, you could have been. Fine." He drew in a deep breath and sat up straight in the driver's seat, holding out a hand in a mock imitation of a serious thespian. "I call upon thee! To summon the PENETRATOR!"

Sam busted out laughing in high-pitched squeals. Ramon, no longer to restrain himself, joined her, guffawing in the passenger seat. It took Sam nearly a minute to get herself under control.

She sighed and let out a last chuckle. "It's already on the way, big guy, but I really needed a laugh. And I'm sure the recording will come in handy with morale a bit low."

Luke shook his head. Of course she'd recorded it. "Great. Thanks."

"Anything else you need?"

"Not at the moment. I'll let you know if anything changes." He hung up the phone and pulled back onto the road. "Don't say a thing about this."

Clamping his lips together to contain another laugh, Ramon nodded and looked out the window until he could get himself under control.

"We're gonna go in tonight?" Ramon asked.

"I think we have to. Right now, we know the children are near, but if we leave it until tomorrow, they could be moved by then. Damn, it's getting late and dawn isn't that far away. I was hoping to hit some fast raids, then get out of town. An operation like this could put us into daylight and take long enough to give the cops time to respond." Luke gripped the steering wheel tightly as he tried to think of all the ways to run the mission and how it could go wrong.

"I hate to suggest it, but do you think we should split up the team?" Ramon sat quietly, his eyes moving over to Luke, then back straight ahead.

"What do you mean?"

"Well, if we're worried about cops, send part of the team deeper into Northeast than you initially planned. Have them hit as many houses as they can to raise a ruckus. Hopefully, that'll draw off the cops and give us more time to hit the house and get our people out."

Luke didn't want to split up the team and move them into two different areas where it would be difficult to link up if something went badly. It's probably why it hadn't even entered his mind or been subconsciously dismissed before it could even be mulled over. But now that Ramon said it, Luke knew it was the right plan.

"I hate to split the team, but it's the right move. Thanks for suggesting it. We'll send them out near I-205. That way, they can jump across the bridge into Washington and make their way back to the farm."

"Thanks for listening," Ramon said.

"I always try to listen, even if I'm feeling a bit surly." Luke reached over and patted Ramon's knee. "Thanks for putting up with me tonight."

"I'm just excited to get to work with you directly."

Luke nodded, acknowledging him. "OK, Ramon, send out an emergency change of plan. We'll keep the same rendezvous point, but the mission is changing. Relay the basic sketch, including your change to tonight's procedures. Once everyone confirms, I want you to look at the house and the surrounding territory on the maps street level."

"Got it."

CHAPTER
TWENTY-ONE

Luke stared through his night scope binoculars in the direction of the house. It was less than ideally situated right on the bluff that overlooked Swan Island and smack dab in the middle of the block. The houses along this stretch of Willamette Boulevard were mostly big, old houses that cost a lot of money. This wasn't going to be an easy raid.

Going with a smash and grab might be their best option. Scream up Willamette Boulevard, park out front and crash through the door, though they couldn't leave drivers in the cars to keep them hot and running. Maybe if they hadn't split the teams, but it was a necessary evil.

He hoped. Fortunately, his people had a lot of experience hopping fences. He couldn't rely solely on the front door without sending at least a few people to scope out the back and prevent any unwanted escapes.

Ramon tapped his shoulder. "Luke, the Penetrator is here."

Luke rolled his eyes, dropping his binoculars. "Where?"

Ramon pointed over his shoulder. A black van finished parking and turned off its lights and engine. Sam, dressed in tight black clothing, popped out of the passenger side and walked up to him, hands in her pocket.

"Fancy meeting you here."

Luke smiled warmly at his friend. "What are you doing here?"

"My team has the logistics under control for the evening, and I figured you could use an extra hand."

"We could." He pulled Sam into a hug. "Let's deploy our siege kits."

"You mean our *penetration* kits."

Rolling his eyes, he chuckled. "OK. Let's go over the plan."

He relayed the plan to her, leaving space for her to interject ideas and thoughts, which she did frequently. They'd done similar missions tons of times together, but Sam's knowledge of the house was coming in handy as they sorted out the raid. Within a few minutes, they had a workable plan and relayed it to their people, deploying them to their positions.

"Is everyone in place?" Luke asked Ramon, who was functioning as his radio by using the packlink. They didn't want to risk having too many verbal conversations. With hostages and at least a dozen guards—vampire and werewolf—Luke figured they might be paying more attention than the residential raids they carried out. They'd alerted the parents inside to huddle in the corner to avoid any stray bullets.

He'd sent Delilah to lead the team providing the distraction raids so he wouldn't have to worry about coordinating with another human. Besides, she was the right leader for the mission. He trusted few people as much as he trusted her to get the job done.

Ramon stood next to Luke in his sweatpants and sweatshirt, ready to shuck them and go full wolf if need be. "Yeah. All teams checking in."

From there on out, Ramon would hang by his side, taking Luke's hand signals and relaying them to the team.

Looking through the cage protecting the cabin of the black van, he gave a thumbs up, then checked his helmet to make sure it was snug. Along with Ramon, he had six other werewolves packed into the back of the Penetrator with him. The engine started, the driver reaching to a switch on the console, and the van rose a few more inches.

Carefully, they pulled out onto the narrow side road and aimed for Willamette Boulevard. They waited for a car to pass, giving it plenty of time, before pulling into the outside lane that ran right next to the bluff overlooking Swan Island.

This time of night, traffic was light. The few bars that even stayed open to two had closed an hour ago. Inside their target, the vampires had to be getting a bit sleepy as the sun grew close to predawn.

The driver turned to address those in the back. "Hold on."

Luke grabbed a bar above his head they'd installed for this purpose. A moment later, the van turned hard and slammed over the curb, shaking the whole vehicle. Slamming on the brakes, they slid to a halt, leaving deep tire ruts in the once perfect lawn. Once the driver put the van in park, a low intensity red light turned on in the back.

The two wolves in the end of the Penetrator kicked the doors open and stepped out, holding them open. The next pair ran out carrying a black, steel battering ram and dashed to the front door of the house. Another pair ran out, taking post on either side of the door, shotguns at the ready.

As Luke dropped out of the van, the first pair ran to join the rest of the wolves at the door. Luke jogged up as the battering ram was drawn back. A second later, it was slammed violently into the door, shattering the glass panes at the top and sides as well as a good chunk of the door frame. Thankfully, the fangers hadn't reinforced the door.

The werewolves weren't sparing anything in their efforts to save one of their own families. The pair with the battering ram ran away from the door, the next pair immediately filling their spot, sending shotgun blasts into the doorway. A moment later, the battering ram thunked onto the floor of the siege van.

Luke, pumping a shell into his shotgun, flicked off the safety and stepped into the doorway as the way was cleared for him. A vampire poked a gun out from behind a wall. Luke fired, and they jerked back.

A shot ricocheted off his shoulder armor, and he cringed involuntarily. In a split second, he had another round in the firing chamber and discharged it in the direction the shot had come from. Screaming rewarded his ears. A kill would have been better, but pain inflicted on his enemies was a close second.

Jogging forward, he braced up against a wall to make room for the rest of the front door team. Ramon followed him, posting up at his back with his shotgun pointed the opposite direction.

Luke smirked as he saw the shadow of someone writhing on the ground from around the corner where the shot came from. With the rest of the team in the house, Luke feinted a step around the corner, then dropped to his knee and fired. The first vampire that had fired at him had bought the feint and stepped around the corner, handgun at the ready. But Luke's shot was faster, catching it in the chest. It splattered to the ground, splashing on the restored oak floors.

Holding his position, he waved the next team to advance. A pair of werewolves swept past him, pointing their guns around. Two shots rang out, followed by an all clear. Luke, reaching down to his left hip, grabbed his gladius and took care of the vampire he'd shot earlier, drenching a hall rug with reddish-black sludge.

If they were able to dislodge the vampires from Portland, he didn't envy the owners their cleanup bill, though he doubted they'd hold it against him since he was rescuing them.

Stepping carefully around the mess he'd just made, he backed up next to a door and switched his safety on. A quick flick of his eyes told him Ramon—his shadow—was ready. He smashed back the butt of his Winchester M12 into the door just above the doorknob, sending it flopping open.

Not even bothering to see if anyone was in the room, Ramon stuck his shotgun in the door and fired. Luke cringed at the maneuver. The children probably weren't on the first floor, but he had to trust to the pack's link. So hopefully Ramon had checked it before firing.

Luke whipped his head around and looked up as a loud crash sounded from upstairs and shook the house. It was followed by a second. The roof teams had breached the roof and would soon be smashing through the ceiling.

Wolfish snarls were followed by a yelp of pain. He hoped it wasn't one of his werewolves, but he couldn't rush off to check. He had to clear the first floor first. He waited at the second door but heard no more shot from Ramon. They repeated the procedure.

Ramon yelped and staggered back as a gunshot answered. Luke took a deep breath and pivoted on his foot and opened fire. An answering shot slammed into his chest, his air wheezing out of his chest. Shaking his head, he pumped another round into his gun and fired. An answering scream warmed his heart as he grabbed a shell, shoved it into the magazine, and pumped it directly into the firing chamber.

A vampire seized on the floor, silver smoking from a hole in its torso. Luke had no idea how silver hadn't found its heart, but he remedied it himself and emptied the shell he'd just loaded. The vampire poofed out. After he checked the closets, he ran out and found Ramon sitting on the ground, holding his shoulder.

Moving his hand briefly, Ramon showed Luke the bloody hole in his upper chest near the shoulder join on his left side. It wasn't a deadly wound, but it made it damn hard to pump a shotgun.

Luke scooped up the shotgun, loaded shells to top it off, then loaded his as well. "Go wolf."

Ramon nodded and shifted, leaving his sweats on. They ripped at the seams and hems but stayed on. It was probably easier than trying to take them off with a fucked-up shoulder. Hopefully he'd heal quicker in his bipedal wolf form, but even with one working arm, he'd be far more deadly than with a gun and arm that couldn't work it properly.

Pushing himself off the ground with his good arm, he grunted and checked out the wound. Though still open, the bleeding had largely stopped. Normally, Luke would send a wounded wolf off to take care of a lighter task, but Ramon was his communication relay. Others could potentially handle it, but at this point, it was better that they stick with the original plan.

Luke led the way back to the entryway. The rest of the entry team assembled. The first floor was theirs. Pointing to Ramon, Luke held up two fingers. Phase two. A pair of wolves departed to hold the front door, and another pair ran to secure the back door.

An angry rumble swept down from upstairs as a giant wolf leapt over the banister, slamming into Luke's side. Air whooshed out of his lungs. Out of instinct, he raised his arm just in time to block the wolf from ripping out his throat. A weak scream ripped from his throat as the wolf latched onto his forearm, shaking its head viciously from side to side.

Balling up his fist, he slammed it into the wolf's neck. It felt like a column of rock shifting under the skin as it clamped down harder. Luke struggled to draw in a breath, the weight of the wolf keeping his chest pinned to the ground. Each of his punches grew weaker. If he didn't keep his arm up, they would dive in and rip out his throat.

A shadow fell over Luke, and a shotgun blast rang out. The wolf flopped over, its teeth still clamped around his arm. With the weight gone, he drew in a breath of air and let it out as a whimper of pain.

"This is going to hurt, Luke," Rebecca said, setting aside her shotgun. Bending down, she grabbed the wolf's jaws and pried them off Luke's arm.

As the teeth ground out of his bones, he nearly passed out.

"Someone get the medic," Rebecca called. She darted away, returning a few seconds later with a towel she gently wrapped around his arm.

"Vampire..." Luke wheezed.

"What? Oh shit..." Rebecca concentrated for a moment. "I sent out a call to save a body if we can. Don't know if any are left, but hopefully we find one."

Ramon, peeking into Luke's sight, held up a wolfy paw and gave a thumbs up and a nod to confirm Rebecca's message. Luke nodded weakly, blinking his eyes hard to keep from blacking out. A moment later, Isabelle slid to a stop next to him and quickly dressed his wound.

Shotguns blasted above them on the upper level.

"Damn them." Rebecca scowled—Ramon growled in acknowledgement—as she looked up at the ceiling. "I'll send the message again."

"They better hurry," Isabelle said. "Fuck, he's already bleeding through the bandages."

Luke screamed once as they removed the bandages, then grayed out for a second. When he became aware again, a hand pushed into his chest, keeping him down.

"Don't move, Luke. We've got your arm immobilized. I've got a couple clamps in your arm. There was an artery I missed. Sorry."

"We've got the word out for a vampire," Ramon said, having shifted back to his human form. "There's none here. We were too efficient. We've secured the house for now."

"Move out of the way, Ramon." Sam's voice was thick with authority. "Alright, let's load him on the stretcher. Someone find where he dropped his sword."

Ramon held it up. "It's right here. I moved it out of the way."

Sam leaned over him. "We're going to load you into the Penetrator and roll you down the road. The kids aren't here; a couple vampires dragged them off. The parents are going wolf and will track them. We'll follow. Then you can drain them. Two birds, one stone." She stood up. "Alright, lift him carefully. Ramon, bring the sword. You're still by his side."

TWENTY-TWO

As they loaded him into the van, Sam's words filtered through his pain-addled brain. He could drain the vampires. But he didn't need to wait to find them. If there was a nearby house, he could do it as they rolled down the road.

"Where's the medic?" Luke asked.

Isabelle moved nearer. "Here. Do you need something for the pain?"

"No." He really did want something for it, but he didn't know if draining a vampire would clear it from his system, and he didn't want to be drug-addled when they found the children. "When I give you the word, I need you to remove the clamps."

"I can't do that; you'll lose a lot of blood and then die." Isabelle's matter-of-fact tone nearly made Luke chuckle.

"No." He took in a few shallow breaths. Talking was a struggle right now. "Take them off. I can drain vamps…as we roll."

"Ah." Understanding dawned on Isabelle's face. "Then they'll be stuck in your arm."

As a werewolf, Isabelle would understand. That was one of the bigger dangers for their kind. Their fast healing often meant weirdly healed broken bones that needed to be rebroken or debris and bullets stuck in their body that had to be cut out from healed flesh.

"Ramon, my rudis."

"I'm going to need to lift up his shoulders to get to it," Ramon said. "Keep his arm protected."

A moment later, Luke's back lifted off the stretcher aided by strong arms. After they set him down, Ramon placed the rudis by his right hand, then helped him clasp it.

"We're going now," Sam called from the front of the van. "Hold him steady as we drive off the curb."

The van bounced off the curb and onto Willamette Boulevard, and he grunted in pain. He couldn't tell how fast they were going, but it didn't feel like the speed limit. They probably had to take a slow start to let the parents find the scent trail. While others handled that, he took in several steady breaths, trying to find some focus in his pain-addled brain. Once he thought he'd found enough, he pushed out his awareness, searching nearby for a nest he could drain.

He didn't know the maximum distance at which he could drain a vamp, but it didn't matter right now. He couldn't concentrate well enough to shove his awareness out that far, anyway. They'd have to be in a house on Willamette or maybe up to a couple back.

"What are those flashes of light down below?" Luke didn't recognize the voice who said it.

"Looks like gunfire," Sam said. "Shit. I think that's Roxi's team. I hope they have it handled. We're stretched a bit thin right now. Ramon, send a text to Pieter and ask for a status update when he can provide one."

"Got it." Ramon fished his phone out of his pocket.

"We're turning," Sam said.

Isabelle and Ramon braced Luke, so he'd stay steady on the stretcher. They rolled for a minute when Luke lifted his head off the stretcher, the first twinge of vampire pushing into his awareness. With each meter they drove, it grew stronger.

"Sam, stop," Luke gasped out.

"Sam, Luke wants you to stop," Ramon said loud enough for Sam to hear.

Luke lifted his arm, but it wobbled terribly. The normally light wooden sword felt like it was made of lead and generated higher gravity. He kept the arm up until he found the direction he wanted.

"Ramon, steady my arm. When I give the mark, remove the clamps."

Ramon's strong hands grabbed his hand and forearm, steadying him and supporting the sword.

Drawing in his concentration, Luke focused on the feel of vampire. "Mark."

He cringed as Isabelle removed the clamps but compartmentalized it as he drew in his power. Gasping, he struggled to grip onto the vampire's essence, but he couldn't tell if it was because of distance or his own weakness. Finally, it popped, and a gold line formed, extending through the wall of the van. The line disappeared as a globule of glowing light burst through the steel of the van's wall, illuminating the dark cargo space before it disappeared into Luke's rudis.

He inhaled loudly as warmth suffused his body, and the pain lessened.

"It's stopped bleeding," Isabelle said in wonder. "It's still pretty mangled, but the arteries have healed."

With more strength, Luke reached out, still sensing another vampire nearby. This time, it came much easier. Now, only a dull throb remained where before hot agony had dominated.

"Holy shit, it's… It looks mostly healed. How are you feeling?" Isabelle gently moved his arm to examine it.

"Better." He took a moment to reach out again, but didn't find a vampire nearby, though he could sense them in the vague distance now that his mind was working better. "Help me up. Sam, let's find those kids."

"Are you going to be able to fight?" she asked.

"As long as I don't have to fight left-handed, it'll work well enough." Next time, he'd pack his manix. The arm armor would have helped a lot, though normally he'd only wear it on his right arm. Maybe he'd have to procure some for his left arm, too.

The van rolled forward, making another turn. He wished he was riding up front so he could see what was going on, but he'd have to make do with at least being in the van to continue the hunt.

"Ramon, have you heard anything back from Pieter yet?" Luke worried about Roxi and her team. If they ran into heavy resistance, it could go badly for them. They weren't geared for a heavy fight, but for stealth and infiltration.

"Nothing yet."

"Damn."

"Luke, the teams at the house are reporting all clear there. Every-thing's cleaned up. Do you want to send them down to Swan Island? It's only a few minutes away." Sam made another turn.

He thought about it for a minute. "No. I don't want them blun-dering in and making thing worse. But... Split them. Have half catch up with us. Send the other half down to Swan Island, but have them holed up away from the warehouse until we get information from Pieter. They'll be close enough to jump in quickly that way."

"Sounds like a plan." Sam held up a thumbs-up so he could see it through the safety cage. "Ramon, you heard the man. Send out the orders and let Pieter know we have bodies standing by if they need them. Shit!" She turned hard.

Grabbing for the rail, Luke nearly slipped off his seat.

"Luke, do you sense anything? The parents are getting more agitated."

"Let me check." He put out his senses. "Maybe, vaguely off to the right and forward." He paused for a moment, holding onto the feel-ing. "We're getting closer." He handed his sword to Ramon.

"Can you drain them from here?" Ramon asked.

He shook his head. "I could, and I could use another one to heal, but I don't want to alert whoever has the kids that we're onto them. There could be werewolves there. They might resort to hurting the kids and fleeing."

"Right. I didn't think of that."

"That's a good point. We know a couple of vampires took off with the kids, but we don't know who they met and how many of them there are." Sam pulled over and parked. "Let's wait until our backup arrives. They should be here in a couple minutes."

"OK. Here's the plan when we find them. I'll drain the vamps as long as there aren't too many of them, I don't want to put myself back on that stretcher, then we'll pounce while they're freaked out about their friends dissolving in front of them. Capture as many as you can so we can interrogate them."

"If they don't want to give up?" Ramon asked.

"Rip them to shreds."

A feral grin spread across Ramon's face as a growl rumbled in his chest.

LUKE STARED through his binoculars at the house they'd tracked the kids to. It looked like any other Portland bungalow. Pushing out his senses, he felt several vampires nearby, some in another house a block or so to the north. But in front of him, he felt two distinct clusters, as if they were in neighboring houses.

They weren't sure which house it was since they'd had to stop before they could see where the trails led. Not wanting to give themselves away and endanger the children, they pulled back to reformulate their plan. Splitting their small team into two was going to be a stretch, but they couldn't risk picking the wrong house and the kids being whisked away a second time.

Sam slipped her katana and wakizashi under her belt. "Everyone's in place."

Luke cast a glance off to the east, the first faint glow of dawn's sun peeking over the horizon. "Any word from Pieter?"

"Nothing yet," Ramon replied.

"Damn."

Sam set her hand on his shoulder. "They'll be OK. You know Roxi. She's one tough lady, and she's got a good crew."

Luke's gut twisted in knots. "I know, but I can still worry. Too many bad things have been happening lately, and I couldn't handle it if something happened to her."

"I know. I do. But we need to focus in right now. The kids are alive, but really scared. They need us." Sam pulled her katana from its scabbard.

He unsheathed his gladius. "You're right. Let's get this done so we can sweep down to Swan Island."

"I'm going to send the teams."

He nodded, jogging out from behind the tree they'd been hiding behind. It was a good distance across the park to their target. A pair of wolves in the bipedal forms sprinted forward, carrying one of their battering rams. A matching pair ran towards the other house. He picked up his pace to keep up, his left arm still weak and in pain. It made it hard to run with proper form, but he managed because he had to.

Almost simultaneously, both front doors caved in to their battering rams, and the wolves burst in. A few second later he joined them.

A pitched battle already raged in the living room. Werewolves squared off against each other, clawing and snapping at each other viciously. Dodging out of the way, he ran upstairs and kicked in a door, finding an empty bathroom.

Something smashed into his back, driving him into the bathroom. The shower curtain tangled around his head and arms as he tugged it down along with the tension rod that had been holding it up. Claws scraped against his back.

Bent over the edge of the bathtub, he tried to free his hands so he could push off something. Freeing his right arm enough, he reared back with his elbow, delivering a glancing blow. Whatever was attacking him pulled back enough that he was able to pull his hand and sword free.

Swinging back, he made contact, though he didn't know if it cut. He doubted it had since it was such a weak blow, but the scent of burned flesh told him the blade had made contact with skin. He swatted at them again, drawing a hiss as they scrambled back. Pulling back, Luke spun around, grimacing in pain as he used his left arm to pull the shower curtain off his head just in time to see a set of gleaming fangs coming at his face.

Luke thrust up, letting the vampire's weight do the work as it impaled itself on his gladius. It exploded into a shower of goo, drenching him. Coughing and spluttering, he dragged his hoodie sleeve across his eyes, trying to clear them before something else could attack him.

Somewhere nearby, a high pitch scream focused him. It sounded like the voice of a child. He grabbed a nearby towel and quickly wiped his face, then threw it aside as he dashed out of the bathroom. Ahead of him, a werewolf in bipedal form stood blocking the hallway, growling and slavering. Behind it, a child cringed away from the creature, tears streaming down his face.

Raw anger flooded through Luke. Pointing with his sword, he snarled back. "Let the kid go and stand down. This will be your only warning."

The wolf leapt at him, not even taking a moment to think over the offer. Adrenaline pumping and rage flowing, Luke pivoted backward into the bathroom and slashed across his body hard as the wolf landed where Luke had just been. It yelped in pain from the silver tainted cut as whiffs of burnt flesh and hair filled the air.

Reversing directions, Luke brought the blade around, slashing a gaping wound into the werewolf's back. Before it could recover or force its way up, Luke kicked out, catching it in the face with a steel-toed boot. The werewolf flopped over onto its back, screaming in pain, the sound eerily human though still mixed with the growl of the wolf.

Twirling the blade in his hand into a reverse grip, he plunged down hard, sinking the blade up to the hilt in the werewolf's chest. A weak whimper escaped its lips as its body went limp and began its final shift to human. Grabbing a towel from the rack in the bathroom, he tossed it over the dead woman's face.

The child still cried in the corner of the hallway. Luke stepped over the woman, then squatted down in the middle of the hallway, using his body to block the dead woman from the kid's view.

"Hey, we have your parents outside." The kid didn't budge. "I'm Luke." He tried to remember what the conversation had been around the kids and their child safety code word. He'd been struggling to focus through the severity of his wound, and they hadn't been talking to him since it was unlikely he'd be too engaged in the next phase of the operation. "Ah, pumpernickel underpants."

The kid looked at Luke, squinting through the tears.

"Pumpernickel underpants is your family safety phrase. I'm Luke, and I'm here to get you back to your parents. Will you come with me?"

The kid shook his head vigorously, but his eyes shifted to the open door at the end of the hall for a brief moment before returning to the floor.

Understanding dawned. "OK. You wait here. I'll go fetch your parents."

He wished he had his shotgun, but his arm was still too fucked up to effectively operate the pump action.

"Luke, you up there?" Ramon shouted from downstairs.

It was times like this that Luke wished he could use the packlink. It would make this situation so much easier. Standing up, he took a step back against the same wall the kid looked toward.

"Yeah. I'm coming down."

He faked taking steps, trying to make them progressively quieter sounding, and waited in the shadow of the bathroom's doorframe. Keeping his breathing shallow and light, he kept an eye on the kid out of the corner of his eye. Something gray and large breached the line of the open door, taking a step closer to the kid. A low rumbling growl emerged from its throat.

Coiling, Luke sprang, diving on top of the werewolf in its full wolf form. He wrapped his right arm around the wolf's neck, careful not to stab himself with his gladius. The wolf bucked up as Luke looped his much weaker left arm under its front legs. As Luke's feet left the ground, he quickly wrapped them round the wolf's body, trying to loop them back to catch his foot behind the knee or back of the wolf's legs.

Growling and snapping, the werewolf tried to dislodge him. Luke arched his back, hauling back on its neck and stretching out its back to deprive it of some power. The wolf, trying to shake Luke, leapt up as hard as it could and rolled in midair, coming down hard on Luke.

The wolf's body crushed the air from his body and dislodged his weak arm and one of his legs. Scrambling desperately, he tried to reestablish some semblance of control while failing to get his lungs to inflate. Somewhere, dimly, he heard high-pitched screaming.

Gripping hard with his right arm, he forced his right hand into an angle where he could get his gladius's edge through the thick fur around the werewolf's neck. As his vision fuzzed from pain and lack of oxygen, the wolf kept its weight pressed against him, attempting to crush him to death. He summoned his anger and strength and ripped the sword across the wolf's neck.

The werewolf yelped before it was smothered by bloody gurgling as blood gushed out and air mingled with it as it entered and exited the sliced trachea. The only color he saw in his graying vision was the vivid spurts of arterial blood splattering the walls and ceiling as it gradually slowed and ran down the wolf's neck and chest to flow onto his body.

Without the werewolf wriggling around to smother the air from his lungs, Luke tried to shift the wolf off him, but with one bad arm, he couldn't manage it. Dropping his sword, he shoved with his right hand and thrust up with his body. The wolf slid to the side and landed on his bad arm as it made the final shift to human.

He screamed at the momentary shock of pain surging through the already wounded arm. For a second or a minute or who knew how long, the world turned to darkness.

CHAPTER
TWENTY-THREE

"Luke, buddy, you there?" Ramon said, lightly tapping Luke's cheek.

He drew in a deep breath, which was a change. Reveling in the feeling of unimpeded breathing, he took a few more deep breaths even though it hurt his ribs. No doubt the weight and force of the wolf and the landing had damaged his ribs.

"I think so." The kid. He tried to push up, but Ramon stopped him. "The child, where…"

"He's safe with his parents, along with his sister." Sam squatted down and moved wet hair off his forehead. He hoped it was just sweat and not blood. "You look like shit. Like you came from a way off Broadway production of Carrie."

"Good. Then I look how I feel. How long was I out?" He stared at the ceiling he'd turned into a Jackson Pollock using the wolf's blood.

"Less than a minute," Ramon said. "I was on the way up to help you out. I had to call for help to get the wolf off you. I didn't want to do any more damage to your arm by dragging it off.

Luke tried to move his left arm but found it immobilized.

"We strapped it down until you can get some more vampires or the docs can look at it. Look, I hate to rush you, but the sun is coming up and we need to get out of here before Portland's most corrupt show up with lights ablaze. We need to get down to Swan Island and find out what's going on with Roxi and her squad."

"Shit, yeah. Help me up." He stuck out his right hand and Ramon used it to pull him up. Leaning against Ramon, he let his head calm down as it swam from the sudden move to vertical.

"Help him down the stairs, Ramon. I have to get the teams ready to roll out." Sam patted him on the arm before running downstairs, calling out orders.

"You ready?" Ramon twitched his body to indicate movement.

"Whether or not I am, we have to go. Your big, strong arms can keep me moving. Shit. Swords?"

"We moved them down to the Penetrator."

Fortunately, the stairs were wide enough for both of them. Luke still had trouble managing his body after everything. He hoped there wouldn't be a call for him to fight more werewolves today. The first had nearly ripped his arm off. The second had nearly crushed him.

Someone met them at the front door with a blanket they draped over Luke's head and wrapped around his shoulders. It was probably best. He probably looked like a one-man slaughterhouse. Wolves ran back into the house carrying large gas cans.

"You want the stretcher? Or are you good enough to sit up?" Ramon stopped at the rear of the van.

"Sitting is fine. I'll be OK."

Again, Ramon's strength came in handy, providing some lift to aid Luke mounting the bumper to get into the back of the van. Crouching low, they moved Luke to the seat closest to the cage. It would let him talk with the driver and give him an extra wall to prop himself up against.

Soon, the Penetrator filled up with people until no more could fit in comfortably and the doors were shut. Sam fired up the van and didn't spare the gas as they sped away, flames visible through the windows in the back doors.

He grunted when the van flopped down onto the street and turned hard. A few blocks later, they zoomed down Willamette Boulevard on their way to Greeley Avenue and Swan Island.

"Hang on, everyone!" Sam called, hitting the brakes hard.

Luke did his best to comply with only one working arm. As they screeched to a halt with a slight lift to the back axle, he groaned as the vehicle settled. A shadow of an animal wobbled in front of the van, then flopped down.

Luke stared out the front window, slack jawed. "Did you hit a dog, Sam?"

"No. Whoever is in the back, grab the stretcher and get out quick." Sam turned to look into the back of the Penetrator. "Go!"

The doors flew open, and a pair of people jumped out, carrying the stretcher with them. A minute later, they carefully loaded the stretcher into the center between the seats running down both sides of the van. A wolf with bloody fur covered in plant debris breathed heavily, a tongue hanging out as they panted.

As soon as the doors were shut, Sam smashed the pedal down and sped off. "That's Erik."

"He was on Roxi's team, wasn't he?" Luke tried to keep the worry from his voice.

"Yeah. Once he catches his breath, we'll get some information from him. He scaled the bluff to get up here."

That couldn't be good. That was a serious climb up brush, over fences, and steep sides. Luke tried not to stare at Erik as he panted on his side, but he needed to know.

"That looks like a lot of flashing lights down on Swan Island. Like a lot," Isabelle said from the passenger seat.

Luke tried to twist around but couldn't get a decent enough angle to see through the cage and over the dash and down to Swan Island.

"What's happening on the packlink?"

"Not much that's comprehensible," Ramon said. "Some people are going intentionally silent, others are just chaos and fear. It's sometimes not the most reliable form of communication."

"Have you checked in with the team we sent to help?" He tapped his knee with has forefinger.

"They're trying to keep their heads down and see what happens with the cops."

"Why wasn't I told?"

"You were kind of busy or passed out, and this just went down." Ramon shrugged. "Everything just fell apart as we finished up at the houses."

Luke wanted to be angry, but knew it wasn't Ramon's fault. This happened in operations. And he could save the anger for later. Right now, he needed to be calm and cool because he needed to figure out a plan. "Has anyone checked in with Delilah and Simone?"

"They reported in about thirty minutes ago. They're already in Washington heading west," Sam said.

"So that leaves the two teams we took for the kid's rescue. And none of Roxi's team. Delilah's team is too far out of position if they turned around now." He stopped and guessed their routes at this time of morning. "Hmm, we could move them into position in maybe fifteen minutes at the best if they haven't gone too far."

Ramon, who'd been tapping away on his phone, looked up, a regretful look on his face. "There's a bridge lift at the Oregon-Washington Bridge. They'd have to back track all the way to the Glenn Jackson Bridge."

"Fuck." Luke gripped his fist until his knuckles hurt, then let it go, stretching out his fingers. "Any idea how many cops are down there?"

"No numbers. They're reporting lots of cruisers and a couple of SWAT vans." Ramon cringed back.

Seeing his friend's reaction, Luke closed his eyes and took a couple deep breaths. He needed to be calm and collected.

"Luke, we can't have a shootout on Swan Island with the police. We'd be trapped as they brought in more cops and probably werewolf allies." Sam slowed to turn onto Greeley Avenue. "Muscle isn't the answer."

"You're right. In that case, we need to find out where the cops are going to take whoever was captured. Has anyone been able to link up with Pieter?"

"He's not part of the packlink, Luke."

"Why?" He'd assumed his Belgian friend has officially been brought into the pack and all its connections. The news that he wasn't confused and worried him.

"Last time I asked him, he said he wasn't ready for that level of connection. I think he's still hurting badly from what happened in Belgium and Paris."

Luke sighed. He should have checked in more deeply with his friend, but he always seemed to be too busy or too focused on something related to the vampires. But he couldn't really blame them. He should have done better as a friend. Shaking his head, he pursed his lips and stared at his clenched fist.

And now Pablo was in the hospital still unconscious. Pieter had finally made a deep connection with Pablo and Tony, only to have that happen. No wonder he was a bit gun shy about taking the final steps of joining the pack. But it had to be lonely for him, profoundly so if what he'd learned from his other werewolf friends about how important pack was to wolves as a source of comfort and community.

To intentionally hold himself apart... Luke could understand that. He'd done it for most of his life. First, because being an elite officer running his own legion set him apart. Then out of loneliness after Marpesia's death as he wandered the world, mourning her. Finally, because of time and age and not knowing anything else after centuries of being mostly alone.

When the time was right, he'd talk to Pieter about not letting it go on too long and encourage him to plan his path forward. He didn't want his friend to forget the close bonds of family and community. He didn't want Pieter to end up like him.

"Luke," Ramon said gently to prod him. "Reports are the cops are packing up and moving out. What do you want to do?"

He shook his head to clear it. "Send out a few of the cars on Swan Island like they're naturally done with their work night. Pull over when the cops move by like good law-abiding citizens. Then follow. If the cops split up, they can sort out who goes which way."

"Got it." Ramon's fingers flew over his phone.

"Sam, are we close enough to get into the mix?"

"Yeah. I think so," she replied.

"Isabelle," Luke said. "Do you know the drivers of the other cars with us and their passengers?"

"Yeah."

"Good. Text someone and relay the plan. We'll try to do our best to sort out where they go. If we can narrow our options, it'll help make our next move."

"Luke, do we want Delilah to head back this way?" Ramon asked.

"No. Tell them they're done for the night. Get back to the farm and get some rest. We may need them later, and rested is better than not." Luke wished he was in the front with Sam so he could better see what was going on around them, but a blood-soaked weirdo in armor was a bit too suspicious.

They stopped on the overpass for Going Street as cop cars flowed toward I-5 while others merged onto Greeley, also heading toward I-5.

"I'm going to follow these since we're here," Sam said. "Isabelle, relay that we're going to stay with whoever merges onto I-5. If some of the cops split up onto Interstate, one of them can follow. And whoever is last in line, have them pull a U-turn and pickup anyone who goes north on Greeley. If no one does, they can catch up with us."

"Yes, ma'am."

"Ugh. You're in trouble for that."

Isabelle chuckled mischievously.

Once the stream of cop cars heading south on Greeley ended, Sam merged back into the southbound lane and followed at a discreet distance. Sure enough, some of the cops took the Interstate option. Sam kept behind the ones merging up onto I-5 South.

"I've got two more cars with us, Sam. What about the Broadway exit and I-84?" Isabelle asked.

"We'll take the Broadway exit if they use it. There's a big jail in Southwest, and this is a decent way to get to it. Send the other two south if the cops split up again."

"Yes, ma'am." Isabelle snickered.

Luke stared out the front window, watching the cops in front of them. He hoped they all stuck together. They only had so many cars available to handle more splits. But sure enough, about a third of the cops pulled off onto Broadway.

"Shit," Sam said, hitting the steering wheel.

Half of the cars that had pulled off onto the Broadway exit took the right turn toward the Broadway Bridge and downtown Portland. The other half went straight where they could either merge back onto I-5 South or head east on Broadway into Northeast Portland. They were already going to lose one set of cops.

"Has someone alerted Holly?" Sam asked. "We're going to need a defense attorney to get in and poke the cops about talking to their clients. Assuming we can figure out who was snatched." She mumbled the last.

A small wave of relief washed over Luke. He knew Holly was a defense attorney, but it was information he rarely thought about and never needed…until now. If their people were being processed into the system, Holly would be able to figure out where. Then, they might be able to come up with a plan to spring their people. Assuming the vamp's agents within the police force didn't get up to some shenanigans.

Luke had to hope that the vamps would retire for the day and the cops would be on their own, which would mean their people would be booked and sit in a jail cell. He never thought he'd have to put his hopes in police following procedures. If they didn't, their people could be in deep trouble. Roxi could be one of them.

He squashed down the panic that threatened to rise up from deep in his heart. If she were disappeared by the vampires, he'd bend all his will and resources to discovering where she was. He'd do anything to free her and get her back. Once he noticed his breathing growing shallower and faster, he took a deep breath and closed his eyes, sitting back against the wall of the van.

Letting the conversations about the reports from the other teams wash over him, he focused on getting his mind clear and ready. If they found an opportunity, he had to be ready to exploit it. Roxi was depending on him.

"Luke… Luke?"

Blinking his eyes open, he realized the van wasn't moving and when he looked through the cage and out the windshield, he only saw a nondescript gray cement wall. "What?"

Sam had twisted around in her seat to look into the back of the vehicle. "We're parked in a nearby garage. There's no one around."

He made to stand up.

"Where do you think you're going?" Sam looked him over. "You look like you were just in a slaughterhouse. You can't stand outside a police precinct like that. Isabelle can handle it. She's the only one of us who doesn't need a hot shower and a bucket of borax and steel wool to get the blood and gore off."

"Right." He shook his head and slumped against the wall of the van.

Isabelle popped out and quickly shut the door. Now that they were just sitting with no destination in mind, the back of the van felt cramped and none too fragrant. Sam was right, as per usual. They all needed serious time in a shower.

"Don't worry, Luke. We'll find Roxi and spring her. Holly will be here in time to get on top of it." Sam's eyes filled with empathy.

"I wish I could go with her. I feel so powerless sitting here." He sat up and arched his back as best as he could in his armor. Erik now laid on his back in his human form, a blanket covering him. He looked awake and alert.

"You ready to talk, Erik?"

"Yeah. Thanks for the breather." He sat up. "Where do you want me to start?"

"At the beginning." Luke's voice sounded clipped and curt even to himself.

"Right. We'd scouted the silver stash, checking it out from every angle while keeping away from their patrols. Roxi and Pieter determined it was too well guarded for our group to handle it on our own, especially without a plan. So we packed up and headed down to Swan Island to check out the warehouse down there. Roxi and Pieter wanted to take the cache of weapons we had there."

He picked up a bottle of water and took a swig. "When we got down to Swan Island, we had to stash our cars a ways away from the warehouse. There's not a lot of room to work down there, so they wanted to go in on foot. We put on our long coats and packed our duffels with our weapons and headed out."

"What was the approach like?" Luke asked.

"It seemed fine. We followed procedures and approached cautiously in small teams, trying to look like any other night shift people that might be around. We also didn't want to look too suspicious to any people who were there legitimately. When we arrived at the warehouse, we only found two pairs of vampires patrolling the warehouse. Roxi said she didn't sense more than that." Erik shrugged.

"We figured they hadn't discovered the false wall we'd hidden the weapons behind and were just guarding it because it was our property. We quickly took them out. Everything seemed to be going as planned. A quick search through the guards' pockets yielded keys to the locks, and then we were inside. The floor was empty and the false wall seemed undisturbed."

He took another drink, then tipped the bottle up again, downing the rest noisily. "That's when everything went to shit. Heavily armed men all in black swarmed out from the upper storage areas."

"More vampires?" Luke asked, leaning with his good elbow on his knee.

"No. Had to be humans. Roxi said there were no more fangers, and we would have picked up the presence of other werewolves, especially that many. They had to be human mercenaries."

"It's not the first time the vamps have used human mercs," Sam said.

Luke nodded. "Yeah. It's an effective counter to our abilities to sense our adversaries." He looked back at Erik. "Go on."

"It worked. There were a ton of them, and they all had lots of really big guns. Certainly enough to take care of us. Some of us wolves might have survived but would have been helpless when they came to give us the coup de grâce." He swallowed and looked down at his hands.

"That's when he came in." He looked up at Luke, anger burning in his eyes. "The one who we have the bounty on. Pieter's brother."

"Fucking Jan." Each word tasted bitter and poisonous on his tongue.

"Him. The piece of shit strolled in through the door we'd just come through, whistling a jaunty tune, smug expression on his face. I'd like to take it and shove it down his throat." Erik took a moment to regain his composure. "That's when he made the offer."

"What offer?" Luke asked.

"He said if Roxi turned herself in to him, the rest of us would be released. It didn't take Roxi long to think about it. She sheathed her sword and stuck her hands in the air and started walking toward Jan. Faster than you could blink, they tased the shit out of her and trussed her up like a turkey."

Erik looked a bit wild around the eyes. "That's when he saw Pieter. Seemed like he didn't expect to see him, but he adjusted quick enough. Said he was changing the deal. Roxi and Pieter for our lives. They already had Roxi moved outside the warehouse. I have no idea what Pieter was thinking. But I guess he had no intentions of going quietly. He screamed into our heads to 'Scatter, flee, run.'"

"What?" Sam held up a hand to the metal cage. "He's not linked to the pack."

"That's what I thought, too. But it didn't feel like a standard packlink communication. It felt...distorted. Like he'd hacked in. Either way, the authority was there, and we obeyed. That's when he dropped the spoons on a couple grenades. One he hurled at Jan and the other he tossed up into the air. Except it wasn't a frag grenade. It was a flashbang."

"How'd you get out without being stunned?" Luke asked.

"He'd given us a warning. I covered my ears and clamped my eyes shut as I scrambled for the back way out of the warehouse. That's when the mercs opened up, shooting blindly. I took a couple rounds, but nowhere serious." He sighed. "Guess I'll have to get them removed."

"Do you know if anyone else got out?" Sam asked, grasping onto the cage with both hands.

"I don't know. I got out the back door, then went full wolf and sprinted out of there as fast as I could. I knew y'all were nearby in Overlook."

Luke finished for him. "So you scaled up the hill and found us on Willamette."

CHAPTER
TWENTY-FOUR

Luke jumped in his seat, his heart thumping. When he looked around the van, everyone else appeared startled as well.

"Sorry about that," Isabelle said, settling into the passenger seat after opening the door. "I waved at Sam to let her know I was back."

Sam chuckled weakly, clutching her hand over her heart. "I guess we were a bit engrossed in Erik's story. What's the report?"

"Holly is here. She's in talking to the police now."

Luke felt a bit of the knot in his stomach unwind, though the fate of all his friends on Roxi's team, for the moment, replaced his worry about Roxi. She was alive and away from the action, though probably in a lot of pain if she'd regained consciousness yet.

"She said she's got several other lawyer friends coming down to join her. She figured more attention couldn't hurt," Isabelle said.

"And it'll keep them from snatching her and disappearing her along with Roxi and anyone else they might have captured." If Holly were taken… Luke didn't want to think about that.

Sam nodded. "She'll come through for us, then get out of there."

To Luke, it sounded like Sam was saying it pep talk herself as much as him and the others.

"What are we going to do about the others?" Ramon asked.

Sam cleared her throat. "Has anyone heard anything on the packlink?" She got back nothing but shaking heads. "Let me reach out to Holly."

She closed her eyes and concentrated. Nodding, she opened her eyes. "Let's head back to North Portland. I want to check in on a safe house or two, plus we need to gather up the cars we left parked. We'll be able to see if proximity will let us pick up the rest of Roxi's team."

"But—"

"What are we going to do here, Luke?" Sam snapped. "We can't rush the police station with less than a dozen people. We're low on ammo and rest." She took in a deep breath. "I'm sorry for snapping at you. I'm tired and just as frustrated as you are. Holly's right. We can't do anything here to help. It's all between her and her lawyer friends at the moment."

"But shouldn't we station people to watch in case they move Roxi?" Luke felt his panic rising again.

"It would be a true shot in the dark. We don't have enough people to watch every station and every vehicle." Seeing that Luke was about to protest, she held up a hand. "We're not giving up on Roxi. We're just setting up for the next stage. We need to clean up and get a bit of rest. None of us will be any use if we're covered in blood and too tired to see straight. I know you don't like it. Neither do I. But it's the best course right now."

Luke took several harsh breaths, then nodded, his eyes burning with unshed tears.

Sam turned on the van. "Thank you, Luke. I just hope the safe houses haven't been discovered. I need a hot shower."

LUKE STARED at his pink hands, stained with blood in contrast to his gleaming armor, freshly cleaned of blood and gore. A hand gently squeezed his shoulder.

"Luke, it's your turn." Sam toweled her black hair. She wore a fluffy white bathrobe.

Standing up, he numbly walked into the bathroom and stripped down, leaving a pile of gore-stained clothes on the pile Sam had already started. Cranking the water as high as he could stand it, he stood under the hard stream, resting his head on his forearm as he leaned against the tile of the shower.

The two safe houses the pack had set up hadn't been compromised. Splitting the teams between them, they showered in shifts while others prepared food from the stores of dried and canned goods. When it was their turn for a shower, a clean person would take over for them.

So far, they'd only heard from one of Roxi's team. Isabelle had zipped out to pick them up in the van since it provided a space that was hard to see into. They were in the other shower. Once they finished, Sam said she'd debrief them. Now, they played a waiting game for the backup teams they'd activated to come help with search and rescue. Though Luke had no idea how they'd be able to do much searching around Swan Island with a strong police presence still causing issues.

Maybe things would look a bit brighter after he scrubbed his skin off and put some processed food in his stomach. Right now, all he could focus on was that the woman he loved more than his own life was in the hands of Jan—a man he'd helped take everything from.

Luke hated that he was in a position where he hoped Jan was firmly leashed by his masters and would turn her over to them instead of simply venting his ire on her body. Pushing off the wall, he soaped himself up with his hands first to get the first layer or so of blood and dirt off his skin. Then he grabbed a clean washrag from the stack outside the curtain and started the serious scrubbing.

By the time he stepped out of the shower, the mirror was covered in a thick layer of steam, and his skin throbbed from the aggressive washing he'd given himself. Once he dried off, he availed himself of the giant bottle of lotion.

He did have to admit he did feel incrementally better. Perhaps the food would get him a bit further out of the despair pit he was in, at least enough to begin some serious scheming. He found a large white robe to put on. They had stacks of the things, which was good since all their clothes were currently in the washing machine. Good thing operations clothes were almost always black. Even if the blood had stained the fabric, it would be next to impossible to see. But knowing Sam and the North Portland Pack, there might even be a variety of clean clothes somewhere around here.

Following the scent of cooking food, he stepped into the dining room and found a bowl of beans, bacon, and mashed potatoes waiting for him. It was hot and tasted like a feast. The coffee didn't miss either.

Once he scraped his bowl clean, he pushed it away and sat back. "Where's Sam?"

"She's debriefing Rosa," Ramon said. "Back room, next to the second bathroom."

Nodding, he pushed away from the table and strolled back, knocking before entering.

"Thanks, Rosa. Go get some food and close the door on the way out." Sam waited until she left, then patted the seat Rosa had just vacated.

Luke sank into it. "What did she have to report?"

"Same thing as Erik, though she spent most of her morning hiding in the bushes."

"No werewolves?"

"No. Good thing, or they'd have had her. I'm surprised the police didn't have the K9 units activated."

He sighed. "Yeah. Maybe the vamps don't have control of them, or they didn't have time. Or didn't want to risk them."

"Yeah. Nothing draws the public's attention like harm to the dogs." Sam wiped a hand across her eyes and yawned.

"Did you get something to eat?"

"Not yet. I will. I'll send out the orders to patrol around Swan Island, if we can, and along the river."

"Then you should get a nap."

She snorted. "You first." She sighed, deflating a little. "She said she felt someone die next to her."

"What?"

Sam nodded. "She wasn't sure if it was only one person or maybe more. Just a general sense of death next to her. It's like a painful snapping of the packlink—like a sudden missing piece."

"I'm sorry, Sam."

Sam nodded, dashing a tear from her eye with the heel of her palm. "There's just so much death and cruelty. Why are they like this?"

He shrugged. "The vampires—warped creatures created by an even more warped god. The werewolves—yearning for power and willing to do horrible things to get it. The humans—money, greed, lust. It's all the worst inclinations of our species, and yeah, the vampires and werewolves all started as humans, though werewolves can create more werewolves without turning a human. But all of us have the seed of corruption in our human DNA."

"All of us?"

He'd never seen so much sadness in Sam's eyes. He reached out and caressed her cheek, smiling gently. "But not all of us give into it. Some of us, like you, are the finest of individuals. People who not only wish good upon the world, but actively do something about it. You made me a home when I had none. You gave of your resources and heart when the people we rescued had nothing and nowhere to go. You stood by my side through thick and thin."

The smile slipped from his face and his shoulders slumped. "You're the very finest and proof that the choice is there for us all."

"The choice?" She grabbed his hand and squeezed it.

"The choice to aim your face toward the light and keep your path steady and true, no matter what tries to push you off course."

Sam looked away. "I think you have a higher opinion of me than you should."

"It's rare that I get to say this to you, Sayumi Wakamatsu, but in this case, you're wrong. My opinion of you is straight and true, like an arrow fired from Roxi's bow—or your own." He sighed. "Sam. I'm so scared right now. If anything happens to her… I don't know if I'll be able to keep my face in the light."

"Don't even think that, Luke. First, we'll get Roxi back. She is family. She is your family and my family. I won't even address the other piece because it's not going to become an issue."

"But we don't know that, Sam."

"Hush, you. Nothing will happen to Roxi, and you are incapable of turning to a dark path. All the years you've walked in darkness, you've kept your soul pointed in the direction of right and justice. You are the incorruptible avatar of all that's antithetical to the forces of darkness." She grabbed his other hand, squeezing them both. "I'm honored to fight by your side and to be your friend, Lucius Silvanius Ferrata. Together, we'll get to the other side. I know it."

Pleading filled his eyes as he leaned closer. "You know it? How?"

"Because I have faith. Faith in what we're doing. Faith in my pack and my friends. Faith in Roxi. And faith in you."

"Faith?"

"I have to have it. I need it to keep me moving forward. I'm proud to be part of something bigger than myself. Something for the good of humanity. It keeps the light burning." She took a hand and tapped her chest hard enough he heard it. "Here." She took the same hand and tapped him hard in the same spot. "And I know it burns here, probably hotter and steadier than in us all. You've just built so many hard walls around it to protect yourself from the pain."

Luke swallowed hard, his eyes burning. If the first tear spilled, the rest would too.

"You're going to have to do something harder than killing all the vampires. You're going to have to break down the walls. Use them in a catapult. Throw them. Grind them to dust. But let loose the fire burning within. I know it's there. It's why we're guided to you."

"Moths fly to flames."

Sam chuckled sadly. "True. But we're not moths, and the destruction you fear isn't for us."

The tear fell, then another. "How do you know?"

"Because I have faith."

The last of Luke's reserves crumbled. Sliding off his chair, he sobbed. All the exhaustion and pain and loss came spilling out. Sam slid off the chair and pulled his head onto her shoulder, cradling him as he emptied himself of all the things that formed the mortar and held the bricks together. A crack formed. A bit of light shone out. A bit of Sam's faith soaked in. And the fire burned brighter.

CHAPTER
TWENTY-FIVE

Luke stared out the window of his bedroom, the yard beside the farm a hub of activity as families moved around the cabins and the medical staff dealt with the latest round of wounds after the rest of Roxi's team had been recovered.

All told, besides Roxi, they'd lost five more pack members. The news had reported four people killed by the brave action of Portland's police. They still hadn't found Pieter yet. In his heart of hearts, Luke held hope that he was still alive.

He mourned his lost packmates and friends while he waited for news on any developments in the whereabouts of Roxi. Holly and her platoon of lawyers had been working the system hard from every angle, trying to find where the cops had taken her, all to no avail.

He checked his watch again—still a while before moonrise. Behind him, the door opened and closed, and a moment later, arms slid around his waist. Clasping Maggie's hand, he pushed back into her, letting their connection soothe the pain of his missing piece.

"How are you doing, Luke?"

He gave a twitch of a shrug. "I'm alive, which will have to do for now."

Maggie squeezed him. "Come, lie down with me. The world out there can wait until it's time to go meet with Selene."

Nodding, he let himself be led back to the bed. It felt good to have Maggie in his arms, even if the circumstances weren't ideal. "I feel like I should be taking care of you after what happened at my house."

"And you did. Now it's my turn to take care of you. Not that we need to keep score. The point is, we're here for each other when we're needed." She reached up and stroked his cheek. "I've set my alarm for moonrise. You should take a nap. You're pushing yourself past your tolerance."

In truth, he'd have to put considerable effort into staying awake now that he was horizontal, and he had no interest in spending his limited reserves.

THE SHOWER HAD GONE a long way to waking him up and reviving him. The cool evening air of the Coast Range went a bit further. Maggie, her hand in his, walked alongside him. She'd volunteered to keep him company, and for that, he appreciated her.

Once they reached the clearing Luke liked to use to call the goddess, he dropped Maggie's hand, leaving her at the edge of the clearing. Turning his face toward the sky, he called out to Selene, asking her to join him if she could. He felt her assent.

A moment later, the goddess materialized in front of him, tall and luminous. "I am here, my brave soldier."

"Thank you, My Mistress," Luke bowed.

She reached out and lifted his jaw, running a thumb over his cheekbone. "I can feel your pain. What has brought you so low, Lucius?"

"It's Roxi. She has gone missing."

"What?" Selene's jaw dropped slightly and her eyes widened.

The weak flame of hope dwindled. If the goddess was shocked, then she hadn't heard from or seen Roxi. "She was captured by the local police, who've been subverted by Saubarag's minions. We haven't been able to get any trace of her through any of our means, both supernatural and mundane."

"Let me see if I can find her. I shall return." Selene blinked out.

Maggie joined him in the clearing, pulling his face down for a kiss. "She'll be able to find her."

"I hope so." Pulling her in tightly for a hug, he kissed the top of her head.

It wasn't long before the goddess reappeared. "I'm sorry, Lucius. I cannot locate her. About the only sense I get is that she is alive, but something interferes with my ability to go deeper."

"Do you think they've taken her to Saubarag?"

"I'm not sure. That could be causing the issue. Though as powerful as he is at this point, I would almost assume I'd get no trace of her if she was near him. His power would smother her and keep her well shielded from my sight." She squeezed Luke's shoulder. "I'm sorry I can't provide more information."

"At least she's alive, that's something," Maggie said. "Thank you."

"Of course, Magdalena. Now if you'll both excuse me, I must go. I'll see if I can ferret out any other information. If I find something, I'll let you know immediately."

"Thank you, My Mistress."

Once the goddess disappeared, they walked back to the house, hand in hand. Maggie's presence kept him from spiraling into the world of what-ifs. Roxi was alive. For now, that was a start. He'd get her back, no matter what.

"Are you still planning on going out tonight?" Maggie stopped, pulling Luke around to face her.

He nodded. "Yes. I need to check on the silver. If we can get it out, we can put it to good use and make sure it isn't used against us."

"Do be careful."

"I will, Maggie. I'm not looking to go out and make a point. I need to do something, but not something stupid."

"Good." She smiled. "I've grown quite fond of you."

Chuckling, he bent down and kissed her. "I'd say I'm more than passingly fond of you myself."

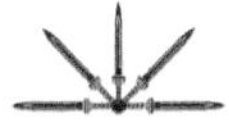

"THIS FEELS TOO EASY," Delilah whispered, handing Luke the night scope binoculars.

He watched the path of the pair of guards as they walked their patrol around the warehouse where the pack had stored a significant chunk of their silver. They'd split up a good amount to their ammo production facilities and into a few other storage options, but they hadn't had an opportunity to get the rest of it safely stored. Now it was in the hands of their enemies.

"Right," Luke said. "I'm only sensing a few vampires. Simone, are you picking up any enemy werewolves?"

"It's hard to tell. I think maybe, but not a lot." Simone's French accent was thicker than normal, as often happened when she was nervous or scared.

He was scared, too. "It feels like a trap."

"Would they repeat the same trap they used to capture… Like at the other warehouse?" Delilah asked.

"It worked." Luke watched the next pair of security guards. "They're trying to make the target too soft and tempting."

"We could always go with the other option—Owen's option."

"We could…"

As a failsafe, Owen had packed the warehouse with explosives, hiding it in all kinds of nooks and crannies. Luke had the remote in his pocket, though Owen had asked to be the one to push the button. But he was busy on the coast with his sister Lauren, setting up spaces for all the refugees from Portland.

"It's better than letting them get it," Simone said. "And we can probably scoop up quite a bit of it. Bombs won't vaporize the silver."

Explode. Dash. Grab. Flee. It had its possibilities. If they could lay their hands on a dump truck and loader, it would be a legitimate option. If…

There were too many ifs right now, too many options, too many choices, too many chances of catastrophic failure.

Luke grabbed his radio off his belt. "Let's send up the owl."

"Roger that," Jamaal replied.

In a few minutes, Jamaal's latest toy—a large drone fitted with infrared thermal imaging—would fly high above the warehouse.

Hopefully, whatever it was constructed with wouldn't block the imaging and would allow them a good idea of how many human bodies were inside.

"Not getting much. Going in closer," Jamaal said through Luke's earbud. "Alright. Bingo! There's a whole bunch of bad guys inside. I'm going to take another pass to see what else I can pick up."

A few minutes later, Jamaal announced that the owl was safely roosting.

Luke handed his binoculars over to Sam. "I'm going to run back to the siege van and see what Jamaal has for us."

"The what, Luke?" Sam asked, grinning at him.

"You know where I'm going."

"Nope. No clue. Where ya going?"

He pushed up, flipped her the bird, and crawled back until he could stand up without being seen from the warehouse. A couple blocks away, he found the black Sprinter van Sam insisted on calling "The Penetrator." Jamaal had an eye out for him and opened the back door to let him in. For this mission, they'd included batteries and a computer setup for Jamaal. The "owl" was already secured and out of the way.

Without preamble, Jamaal brought up images he'd gathered on one side of the long monitor. On the other side, he had a blueprint of the warehouse with figures marking where the ambushers waited.

"That's a lot of people to be standing around in a warehouse," Luke said.

"Yeah. Glad we're not funding that kind of security."

Luke slowly turned away from the monitor, catching Jamaal's gaze. "It's a warehouse full of silver. We *are* funding them."

"Oh, right. Sorry."

"No worries—"

A phone rang. All phones were required to be set to silent for missions. All phones except the one Jamaal kept away from the front lines. The tip line.

It rang again. Jamaal reached for it, surveying the screen. "I don't recognize the number."

Luke extended his hand and took the phone when Jamaal gave it to him. "Hello?"

"I hear you're looking for me."

Luke instantly recognized the voice. Though it lacked the zeal of fanaticism it had when he first met him, however the smug oiliness still remained. "Eusebius."

"Ah, Lucius. I'm glad we don't have to work through underlings."

"What do you want?" Luke tried to keep the open hostility out of his voice but failed.

"It's not what I want so much as what I can offer. One moment." There was a moment of silence. "Speak for the phone, my pretty."

"Fuck off and die, you blood sucking piece of shit."

Luke's heart dropped into his gut. Eusebius had Roxi.

"Charming," Eusebius said. "As you can see, I have your little friend. I'm willing to make a trade along with providing the information you seek."

"My associate as well as the location of your master? What do you want?" Luke asked.

"A simple thing that'll cost you next to nothing to give to me."

Luke rubbed his temples with his free hand. "Just spit it out."

"You always were a direct man, Lucius. But what can you expect from a peasant soldier? I want my life. Or, to be more specific, my undeath."

Luke's hand dropped from his forehead as he stared at the phone in his other hand, stunned and confused. "I don't understand…"

"Let's just say I've always excelled at reading the direction in which the wind blows. And I'm not too fond of what I see. And to be candid, it blows from two directions and none of them are particularly good for me. Unless…I choose a different…windbreaker."

Jamaal snorted, covering his mouth to stifle the sound. It was a humorous image—a fourth century Christian zealot wearing a members only jacket.

"That's it? You just want me to not kill you?"

"I'm prepared to sweeten the deal. Hmm. Let us continue this conversation soon. I'll send a new number via text. I'm not interested in having my conversations traced." Eusebius hung up.

"Well, shit…" Jamaal said.

"Agreed. And what does he mean by 'sweeten the deal'? If he gives me Roxi and Saubarag, that's all I need."

Jamaal shrugged. "Who knows, but he's throwing things in like there's a better offer out there. Hold out for a first-round draft pick and a cash offer, too."

"And a player to be named later?" Luke sank into the other chair in the back of the van. "Call in Sam and Delilah. We'll want to conference in Holly as well."

"What about the warehouse?"

"It's a means to end, and we were just offered a direct route to the destination. The warehouse can wait. I'll send out the order to abort and return to base."

TODAY'S MEETING was closed door and only involved the highest leadership—Luke, Sam, Holly, Maggie, Delilah, Simone, Jung-sook, and Owen, who'd finally been able to break away from the coast after helping his sister Lauren settle Portland's refugees. Mary, though not part of the leadership team, sat next to Owen. The two seemed to be inseparable these days.

"How do we know this isn't another elaborate setup? The last time we had inside information, it drew us out of town and they burned down our homes." Holly, her shoulders tense and rigid, had a deep furrow running down the center of her forehead.

"It's a valid concern," Luke said, resting his elbows on the table in front of him. "But that was an anonymous tip."

"How do we know Eusebius wasn't the anonymous tipster?"

Luke shrugged. "He very well could be. It's something to consider."

Sam cleared her throat, resting a hand on Holly's arm to calm her. "Ask him."

"What?" Luke asked.

"Ask him. Even if he gives an obvious lie, it's still useable information." She sighed. "But I'm inclined to say we take the chance"—she squeezed Holly's arm to forestall her—"with heavy precautions."

"I know this isn't pleasant to hear, but with the exception of the farm, the pack has been pretty much burned out of North Portland. What more can they trick us out of?"

Holly deflated. "You're right. Everything we built…"

"About the only thing they didn't attack," Sam said, "was the building Luke gave the pack to run to help the houseless community. I'm glad we never got around to filing the paperwork. That could have been an even bigger crisis."

Everyone around the table nodded at their good fortune regarding that building.

It was moments like this that Luke missed Pablo the most. His ability to inject levity into serious proceedings to lighten the mood was special. Too many of these meetings as of late really could have used his humor. Luke could have used it, too.

"Circling back, I like Sam's suggestion. Let's see what he says. Do I have a consensus that we proceed with the next call?" Luke looked from person to person, collecting nods. "Good. I'll text him the next burner."

A minute later, the burner phone rang. Luke stood up and answered it, setting it in the center of the table with the speakerphone on. "You're on speakerphone with my leadership team."

"Interesting. All these centuries later, and you still have an army. Though they're not the famed Black Legion."

"To sum up, you're offering back our associate, a 'special gift,' and the location of Saubarag in exchange for your life?"

"Well… And the lives of those who follow me."

Luke held up a hand to stifle the ripple of grumbling emerging around the table. "How many are we talking?"

"Not so many as I'm offering you." He sighed. "You're so distrustful."

Luke gripped the table hard. If he shifted, he could snap a chunk off. "I feel I have reason after all the encounters you and I and your acolyte have had. But I'll put that aside for now. I'll allow you an opportunity to earn a bit of trust from me and my associates."

"Interesting. Proceed."

Luke rolled his eyes at the pretentious prick. "Tell me about the night of the fire attack on North Portland."

"What do you wish to know?"

"Were you the informant that sent us west so it could happen?"

Eusebius sighed. "Yes. I was the informant." It was the first time since they'd started negotiations that the vampire didn't sound arrogant. He actually sounded weary. "But I didn't do it to betray you. I was betrayed. I trusted the wrong vampire."

He initiated a video feed, which Luke accepted. The ancient vampire wore his customary cassock. "Let me introduce you to the special gift and the vampire who betrayed me"—he waved the phone around to capture the tiny, rundown house he stood in—"and who is the reason I'm running from safe house to safe house and calling you on burner phones."

Eusebius walked to a closet and opened it. A figure was wrapped in chains and affixed to a heavy steel chair. A black bag covered his head. Keeping the camera fixed on the figures, Eusebius reached out and ripped the bag off its head.

Luke stared at the blindfolded face of Flavius Constantius. Luke's knees wobbled, and he sank onto the chair behind him.

"Does this answer some questions for you?" Eusebius asked.

Luke swallowed and tried to speak but couldn't. Licking his lips, he took a quick drink of water. "Yeah. That answers some questions. Give me one minute to speak with my people."

"Text back with your next burner." Eusebius didn't wait for an answer, hanging up.

"What's going on Luke? Who was that?" Holly asked.

"That is Flavius Constantius, known in the history books as Emperor Constantine II. He betrayed me and tortured me in the winter of 333. Eusebius is his vampire sire." Luke shook his head and sat up, draining the rest of his glass of water.

Maggie rested a hand on his thigh. "You think Eusebius is serious, don't you?"

Luke looked deep into her blue eyes. "I do."

Sam walked to the cabinet with the liquor bottles and pulled out a few bottles until she found the one she wanted. Delilah stood up and grabbed down glasses, handing them out. Sam walked around the table, filling everyone's glass.

"Thought we should have a little something special before we finish this discussion." Sam picked up her glass and sniffed it, sighing happily before taking a drink.

Luke followed suit, letting the burn of the fine whiskey settle his nerves. For the first time in his life, he might actually trust a vampire to fulfill his word.

Sam held up her glass. "I'll keep the vote simple. Do we make the deal? Yes or no. I'm a yes." She pointed to each of the people at the table, starting at her left. Each person said yes.

When she made her way to Holly, Holly stood up. "When the opportunity comes to win this, you have to take it. There are obviously some fine print we have to work out, but I'm a yes."

Nodding, Luke stood up and grabbed the phone, texting the next burner phone's number. It rang a few moments later.

Luke answered the phone. "Eusebius of Nicomedia, you have a deal."

CHAPTER
TWENTY-SIX

Luke swept his binoculars over the St. Johns Bridge from end to end and over to the east side. Through the trees, red and blue lights flashed on the streets leading to the various parts of the St. Johns neighborhood. The symmetry of his first big battle with the aid of the whole North Portland Pack felt odd and perhaps comforting, though this time they'd approach from the west while the vampires would approach from the east.

"That's a lot of bodies over there. A lot of bodies that could be used to betray us," Sam said, standing next to Luke.

Luke couldn't deny he'd had the same thought. "I know. And Roxi is the perfect bait to get me to show up."

"Then what are we doing here?"

"It's the best chance we have. Also, survival makes for a powerful incentive. And Eusebius is nothing if not a schemer and a survivor." He stopped and made eye contact with Sam. "This is our chance to end this."

Sam held his gaze for a moment, then nodded. "Then let's do it."

He squeezed her arm. "Everyone in position?"

"Yes. They've all checked in." Sam pulled her long black hair back into a ponytail.

Stashing his binoculars, he looked down at his watch. "It's time to move to the next spot."

Together, they worked their way away from the river back to Highway 30. Rhonda waited in Linnton in one of the pack's road runners—souped up heaps loaded with a variety of weapons and mods worthy of a Mad Max movie. Luke held the door for Sam, then walked around to the other side, jumping in.

Without a word, Rhonda put the car in drive and drove up Highway 30 to the road that led up to the St. Johns Bridge until they were parked near their own line of red and blue lights, though their vehicles merely impersonated official vehicles. Luke grabbed his steel helmet from the seat next to him and opened the door, climbing out.

"I'll pull 'er around so we're ready to haul ass if we need to," Rhonda called through the open passenger side window.

In response, Luke slapped the car's hard top roof twice. After he strapped his helmet on, he repositioned his gladius on his left hip and pulled the rudis from its scabbard. Sam assembled her naginata, pulling the blade's cover off and throwing it into the car when she was ready.

Reaching through the open window, Luke grabbed a heavy, steel tactical helmet and tossed it to Sam. "Humor me. It's got Selene's blessing on it. Got your heart armor on?"

Sam rapped her knuckles over the bulge covering her breasts and sternum. "Damn straight." She pulled the helmet on, adjusting the strap. She shook her head to settle it into place and to make sure it was snug enough, then gave Luke a wicked grin and a single firm nod. "I believe we have a date."

This date was nearly seventeen centuries in the making. Twirling his rudis once, he nodded and turned to walk through the line of cars and their packmates who held the west side of the St. Johns Bridge. They nodded or saluted Luke and Sam as they passed by. Once they made it to about the one-third mark, they stopped, waiting. A quick time check said they still had a couple minutes to wait.

"I hope they're timely," Sam said, leaning on the shaft of her naginata, doing her best to look casual.

He nodded. "Me too. I want to free Roxi. I'm not interested in extending this engagement any longer than we need to."

"Right, we don't need any flying piggies in their budget busting planes or helicopters checking out all the lights on the bridge."

Luke snorted. "I'm sure they spread the word to ensure our meeting remains a special invite only affair."

Checking his watch again, he scowled, squinting down the bridge. They were late. He was just about ready to complain about it when a light flashed at them from the eastern side of the bridge.

"Only a couple minutes late. Not bad."

Luke shrugged, pulling a flashlight out of his pocket to return the signal, though he was sure the vampires could see them well enough with the lights on the bridge and their supernaturally enhanced night vision. Once he received the ready signal, he waved Sam forward.

Normally calm the moments before an engagement, Luke's stomach writhed like a ball of worms. Too much could go wrong with the exchange. He tried to burn some of his nervous energy by swishing his rudis through a few maneuvers but settled down after a couple of swings. Sam sauntered along next to him, her naginata casually resting on her shoulder.

She always was calm under pressure, though he imagined underneath she was similarly nervous. Despite working out as many of the variables as possible, there were still plenty of opportunities for things to go wrong—betrayal being at the top of the list.

Trusting vampires to keep their word was a recipe for disaster, but Luke hoped the chance at self-preservation would keep them honest enough, at least until he got what he wanted—Roxi and the location of Saubarag. If this worked out, it would be the first time in his life he'd made a deal with the creatures that was actually worth the risk.

"That's far enough!" Luke called, pointing his rudis toward the poorly detailed shadows.

"Lucius."

Luke recognized the smarmy voice of Eusebius. "Keep the name my mother gave me out of your mouth, fanger. You may call me Centurio Ferrata or sir."

Eusebius nodded, acknowledging the point. "My apologies, Centurio Ferrata. We've brought the agreed upon prizes to seal the deal."

In the distance, four figures approached. A hooded and bound figure stood between one pair of them who looked like they were dressed as cops in riot gear. Another pair carried a long bundle that occasionally wiggled. Another figure emerged from the shadows, stepping in front of them and heading toward Eusebius. The nearer it drew, the stronger Luke's sense of vampire grew.

"You've got an extra attendant." Luke scowled. Trust a vampire to push the detail.

"As you can see, my other associates have their hands full. You don't expect someone of my stature to arrive without proper escort." He gestured behind him toward the four figures carrying a six-foot long bundle that seemed to be wiggling more vigorously and the hooded figure stumbling as she was shoved forward.

"Sam," Luke mumbled.

A moment later, a shot cracked the silence and the extra vampire dropped to the ground.

"What the hell!" Eusebius yelled, almost squeaking.

"You had a simple deal. Four escorts. Now the numbers are as agreed upon."

"I said they'd be safe." Eusebius looked back and forth between the fallen vampire and Luke.

"I guess you lied to them, too. The bullet is just steel. Your minion will recover. They won't recover from the next shot."

Another shot thudded into the fallen vampire's thigh. The fanger writhed, and smoke rose from the second wound.

"Next one goes in the heart." Luke twirled the rudis, light twinkling off the silver. "Do we understand each other?"

"Yes!"

"Yes…"

The vampire slumped slightly. "Yes, sir."

Luke had never seen the smug bastard anything less than cool, collected, and firmly in charge. A small, wicked grin spread across

Luke's face. It felt good to score the petty victory after all the man and vampire had put him through.

"I see you've brought one of the terms of the contract with you. Do you have the other?" Luke called.

"Yes." Eusebius tried to put some more steel in his spine. "How can we trust you?" He nodded toward the doubly shot vampire on the ground.

"I kept my word. I simply returned the engagement to our agreed upon numbers. You have your four escorts. I only brought one. And in all the years I've walked this earth, my word is beyond inscrutable. You will accept my word or you will die. Simple as that. Understood?"

"Understood, Centurio Ferrata."

Luke nodded. "First, release the woman. Return her weapons and let her join me by my side."

Eusebius looked over his shoulder. "Release the woman and return her weapons."

One of the men in riot gear hooked Roxi's swords to her belt and pulled the hood from her head. "March slowly."

Roxi, hands still bound behind her back, moved slowly toward Luke, walking a wide berth around Eusebius. When she made it to Luke, she turned around in front of him and opened her palm. Light glinted off a set of keys.

"Sam," Luke said quietly, stepping out of the way so she could unlock Roxi. He was too wary to want to take his attention off the vampires. "It's good to see you, dōšagīh," he whispered.

Rubbing her wrists, she stepped behind Luke, tracing her hand over his butt as she passed, to stand on his other side. She drew her rudis and sword.

"Good. We've made it through the first part. Now, I want your other two goons to come forward and drop their package."

"And you won't kill me?" Eusebius asked, a bit of a whine winding through his voice.

"If you've provided what I want, you will survive this encounter."

"And the next one?"

"There better not be another. You can spend the rest of your bloodsucking life running from my presence, but if you happen to pop up wherever I'm at, you can count your time as finished. Now send your goons forward, or I'll let my snipers practice on them."

Eusebius nodded hastily, murmuring something behind him toward the two holding the long bundle. They scrambled forward, jogging awkwardly with the writhing bundle between them. Once they reached the center of the bridge, they dropped it unceremoniously and walked briskly back to the other escorts.

Luke stared at the bundle. It moved some, wiggling like a worm out of soil. A faint rattle of heavy chains accompanied the movements. Stepping toward the bundle, Luke waved Sam forward. She waited a couple steps then followed Luke, her naginata held at the ready. Other than Roxi or Delilah, there was no one he trusted more as a fighter than Sam. With her long weapon, she'd be able to clear a lot of space around them and reach out with silver and goddess tainted death with ease.

Roxi, though she didn't know the plan, moved up with Sam, stopping when she did.

"You may come forward," Luke called.

Once they reached the bundle, Luke squatted over it.

"That's far enough," Sam said, her voice laced with menace. She shoved her spear out to emphasize the point.

Luke grabbed a wad of heavy canvas, shoved his rudis into it, and ripped down the middle toward the more rounded end. He tore the rest open, revealing a blindfolded face. It was a face he'd recognize anywhere. It was a face belonging to a man who'd betrayed him and tortured him, while trying to discover the secret of Luke's immortality.

Luke yanked the blind away. "Hello, Flavius, you little shit."

Despite being bundled up in chains and cheap canvas, the former emperor of Rome stared daggers at Luke. Reaching down, Luke grabbed the duct tape covering the vampire's mouth.

"I'll drain your blood and everyone you know!" Flavius shouted.

Luke brought his rudis into view, and the vampire clamped his mouth shut, his eyes going wide as he stared at the instrument of so many vampires' deaths. Feeling petty and hateful, Luke slowly lowered the flat of the blade toward the fanger's face. Flavius tried to turn his head away but couldn't move much as confined as he was.

Luke let the blade hover for a moment before pressing into the vamp's cheek. The stench of burnt flesh joined the agonized scream of the man who'd once ruled one of the mightiest empires on earth.

"I'd like to sit here and play with you, but I'm not that cruel of bastard, even if you deserve every bit of this and a whole lot more for what you've done to me and to the people of this world." Luke lifted the blade and stood up, taking a step back.

With his blade, he waved Eusebius forward. The vampire took a hesitant step forward, then another until he was nearly standing next to the man he'd turned into a vampire.

Luke wanted to laugh at the look of betrayal spreading across Flavius's face.

"Betrayal hurts, doesn't it, Flavius? You betrayed me and tried to take everything I valued away from me—multiple times. Now you can know I've paid you back with all the accumulated interest owed…almost." Luke looked to Eusebius. "Now, give me the other part of our deal. Give me the location of Saubarag."

Eusebius winced at the mention of the name.

Flavius, his eyes growing even wider, opened his mouth, his fangs growing long. "Don't betray the master!"

Luke reached down and swatted him in the face with the flat of the rudis, the blade catching and opening a deep gash in his cheek. Flavius yelped but clamped his teeth shut, his jaw clenching tightly against the pain he no doubt felt. The wound smoked and oozed a dark sludge.

"The location," Luke barked.

Eusebius looked down at the man he'd served in life and betrayed in undeath, then looked back up at Luke. He licked his lips lightly as he delayed.

"The location. Now!"

The sniper rifle barked out a shot, and Flavius screamed as it slammed into his gut.

For a creature who was nearly whiter than paper, Eusebius paled visibly. "The master is…" He gulped, wetting his lips again. "His altar is in a house north of White Salmon, Washington."

"And why do I care where his altar is?" Luke asked.

"It's his base, and he can be called back to it."

"How?"

"Slit the throat of a vampire and pray for his presence. He will return."

"You sacrifice one of your minions every time you need to speak with your master?" Luke sounded slightly incredulous.

Eusebius shrugged. "There are plenty, and it's easy enough to make more. The master likes to remind his children of their place."

Luke focused on Eusebius. He wasn't sure how, but he could find no lies in the vampire's words. The creature was so desperate to survive Luke's war that he'd betray his own god. Luke snorted, shaking his head.

"How often is the altar moved?" Luke asked.

"Infrequently. It requires too much sacrifice to set up after the move. Additionally, it can only be moved if the master wills it." Eusebius edged away from Luke slowly, a quarter step at a time, casting furtive glances over his shoulder to ensure his path still remained unblocked and held by his people.

Luke quirked an eyebrow. "Going somewhere?"

"I believe that is everything we agreed upon…"

Raising his rudis, he pointed it at the nervous vampire, then aggressively pointed to the pavement next to Flavius. "I didn't dismiss you. I have one last thing to address."

Nodding nervously, he reluctantly took a step forward, returning to the place he'd been only a moment before.

Luke turned around, took a step, before spinning back around. Pointing his rudis at Flavius, he made eye contact with Eusebius. "Don't watch me. Watch your little protégé. I want you to closely mark the rewards of betraying me and keep them firmly in the front of your mind in case you get an urge to cross me ever again." Luke waited, but Eusebius stared back at Luke like a mouse caught in the snake's gaze.

"Look!" Luke ordered.

The old vamp forced his eyes down to the son of the man he'd served, to the man he'd sired into vampiredom. Luke adjusted the aim of his rudis to Flavius but kept his gaze firmly on Eusebius. As Luke concentrated, it sharpened the scowl on his face. Once he felt the connection snap into place between his rudis and the vampire lying bundled up on the ground, the telltale golden thread lit up the face of Eusebius as it slipped from anticipatory to horrified.

Wanting to extend it as long as possible, Luke attempted to throttle down on the draw, straining against his body's urge to pull the vampire's energy in all at once. Instead of the standard large globule of golden energy, smaller bits worked their way up the stream, disappearing into the rudis. Flavius screamed. Luke's scowl shifted to a vindictive grin as the former Roman emperor flecked to dust in small pieces, the night breeze carrying them away from Luke and dusting Eusebius's black cassock.

As pieces of Flavius's face sloughed off and blew away, the scream withered into a dusty gurgle until there wasn't even enough left for that. When the last marble of energy disappeared, the golden connection blinked out, leaving a skiff of dust swirling around the bridge, some of it landing on Eusebius.

"Know my power, vampire, know it and fear it. For if I ever find you again"—he nodded toward the ground—"that will be your fate."

Behind Eusebius, one of the people in riot gear worked around behind the other escorts. Luke caught Sam's attention. She nodded before speaking into her radio. A second later, a shot rang out, thudding into the pavement near the quartet.

"I don't know what you're doing, but stop moving, or the next shot will be silver and aimed to kill," Luke yelled.

The cop in the riot gear stopped behind one of the escorts who'd carried up Flavius. He looked down, a ball cap obscuring his face.

"I'd like to alter the deal slightly," the cop in riot gear called back.

Luke raised his rudis and pointed toward the man. "Who are you to alter this deal?"

Reaching up, he unbuckled the helmet with the facemask and peeled it off, letting it drop and roll behind him. In the blink of an eye, he slung his arm around the cop in the ball cap's neck, grabbing him in a choke hold.

"Pieter…" Luke whispered.

The other escorts edged toward Pieter. Two more shots rang out. The other figure in the riot gear hit the ground, writhing in pain. The next shot hit pavement, encouraging everyone near it to stop.

Reaching up, Pieter pulled off the ball cap and dragged the head up by the hair. "Hello, little brother. You thought you could escape me by allying yourself with this piece of shit?"

Jan growled, but it was halted as Pieter tightened his grip on his brother's throat.

Luke, thinking quick, pointed his rudis at Eusebius. "As my associate said, we're altering the details slightly. We'll be taking that werewolf with us."

"There's no need for that, Luke. We won't be taking him with us." Pieter let go of Jan's hair and something glinted in his hand. Quick as lightning, Pieter dragged the blade across Jan's neck—the wound hissing and smoking—then pushed him forward enough to create some space. He rammed the blade into his brother's back and twisted. Jan fell to the ground, landing on his face. A pool of blood spread around his head.

Reaching down, Pieter pulled the knife from his brother's back and wiped the blade on Jan's shirt. "Burn in hell." Pieter spat on Jan's corpse and walked toward Luke. "And now I shall think on you no more."

At the far end of the bridge, Luke saw movement. No doubt curious about the sudden outbreak of violence, Eusebius's people might decide to investigate. Eusebius stared at Jan's corpse.

Luke snapped his fingers, catching Eusebius's attention. "We're done here. Now, run."

Eusebius shook his head lightly, seemingly dazed. It took a moment before recognition dawned in his eyes as they grew wider, his jaw trembling as he took a stuttering step backwards.

"I said run!" Luke bellowed, pointing his sword toward the vampire.

The old vampire spun around and tripped over his cassock but scrambled up and sprinted away from them. Despite having the appearance of an old man, Eusebius was still a powerful vampire and could muster all the speed of one of his kind. Luke watched him flee, a vicious grin splitting his lips. When the vamp who'd betrayed his god disappeared into the haze of swirling lights and darkness, Luke shook his head, then spat into the last bit of dust left on the bridge.

Roxi slid up next to him, pulling him tightly. "It's good to see you." She kissed him. "Thanks for springing me."

Luke chuckled. "I'm glad you're free."

Pieter strode toward them, looking odd in a police uniform.

Luke smiled at his friend, relief at seeing him alive washing over him. "I'm glad to see you. I've been worried sick for days, thinking the worst had happened. How did you..." He gestured toward the other end of the bridge the vampires had occupied moments ago.

"I got away in the confusion and took out a cop or someone dressed as a cop and took their uniform. I blended in and followed them back to their base. There are so many unattached werewolves there, no one thought anything about me." Pieter shrugged but held up his hand to stop anyone from saying anything. "Please, don't ask me anything else or offer a hug. I can't right now."

Luke thought he understood. Pieter hadn't wanted to be the one who brought justice to his brother. And Luke didn't want Jan's blood on Pieter's hands. But whatever must have transpired since the last time he saw Pieter must have changed his mind. Right now, offered camaraderie and affection would have probably caused the man to lose what little control over his emotions he had right now.

"You three ready to head back?" Sam asked.

"Um, we should probably dispose of the garbage before traffic resumes," Roxi said, pointing her sword toward Jan's corpse.

Luke nodded, sweeping the bridge for the downed vampire. The remaining escorts must have picked it up and carried it after their master.

"Roxi, take Pieter back to the cars. Sam and I got this." Luke sheathed his rudis and started toward the corpse.

Sam handed her naginata over to Pieter, then joined Luke. Together, they grabbed Jan's body by the ankles and wrists and carried him to the edge of the bridge. They tossed him over the side and let the water claim him. At least in death, he'd feed the wildlife of the Willamette River. Dusting his hands off, he waved Sam after him, and they jogged back to the group.

"All done?" Roxi asked.

He nodded, grabbing her hand, and turned toward the sidewalk on the south side of the bridge. "Sam, send the order to open the bridge for now."

The swirling red and blue lights on the west side of the bridge began to break up, some taking off in different direction while others turned off, leaving only their head and brake lights to reveal their destinations.

"What about our snipers?" Sam asked after sending the order to their blockade team on the west side of the bridge.

"Let's keep them in position for now. I don't want them to be vulnerable on the descent. We'll give the fangers a few more minutes to make sure they've cleared off." Luke leaned against the railing along the sidewalk, staring off to the east.

"Those were some excellent shots." Sam chuckled. "I almost jumped out of my skin. That was closer than I like to be to their handiwork."

"Jung-sook and Connor are exceptionally competent."

He watched as the last few vehicles he thought were the vampires disappeared. Once he no longer felt even the slightest twinge of the presence of vampires, he gave the order for their snipers to pack up. It wasn't until the first obviously civilian vehicles crossed the bridge that Jung-sook and Connor appeared, carefully working their way down from the western tower of the bridge along the main cable.

Sam shook next to him. "Blech. That gives me the willies watching them walk down that cable."

"I sure don't envy them the round trip," he mumbled. He knew he should be more nervous about watching his dear friends and packmates in such a precarious position, but mostly he just felt numb. Maybe a bit angry, or more than a bit. Angry and numb. He'd hoped he'd feel relieved or vindicated after ending the seventeen-hundred-year life of one of the most powerful vampires he'd ever met. Flavius was certainly the second oldest—the third oldest, actually, after Eusebius and Cassius—he'd known in life and then as a vampire.

"What's the matter, Luke?" Roxi asked. "I thought you'd be a bit more excited about getting rid of Constantius."

"Me too."

He shook his head. Even though he was a couple centuries older than either Eusebius or Flavius, his old buddy Cassius had never risen higher than what amounted to a middle manager position in the vampire hierarchy. It had been a while since he'd thought about the man who'd been his closest friend in their early days in Emperor Trajan's legions. Though it made sense. He'd used the same rudis to drain the stolen life force from his former friend just a little further down on the same bridge.

"The symmetry is uncanny," Luke mumbled.

"What?" Sam asked.

"Oh, nothing much. Just thinking about Cassius and how I killed him"—he pointed down toward the middle of the bridge and a little further east—"just over there. What was it? Five and half years ago?"

"That sounds about right. The winter of 2018." She sighed. "It's been a busy five years. I hope we can take a break when we track down your dark god."

"Yeah. Me too." If he survived it.

The dark entity—Saubarag—had nearly stripped Luke of his immortal life almost a half dozen times, if he ignored the countless attempts his underlings had made over the nineteen plus centuries he'd been hunting vampires.

He shook his head. "One thousand nine hundred and six years, give or take a few months."

Sam narrowed her eyes and tilted her head slightly to the side.

"The number of years I've been a vampire hunter, Sam. Nineteen centuries." He gestured toward Roxi. "The same for her since we both signed up for it the same winter."

"I can't imagine that length of time doing any one thing, included living. You amaze me sometimes." Sam reached over and squeezed his shoulder.

He shrugged. "I'm not sure I had much of a choice in the matter."

"You could have given up. That was always an option."

"I guess. I almost went out the other way more than a few times. With luck like that, I should have bought a lottery ticket or two."

Sam chuckled. "I'm not sure being competent at fighting and surviving translates into winning the lottery."

"Besides"—he gestured toward Sam then toward Roxi—"I think I did pretty good with the lottery that really counts. I am loved and appreciated. I've got Gwen and you and Roxi and Maggie and Pab —" A surge of sadness and anger burned in his stomach. "And all my other friends. All in all, I'd say that's good enough."

Roxi bumped into him affectionately. "Ah, you say the sweetest things."

Sam slipped inside his arms and hugged him. "You're right, Luke. You can't ask for too much more, and there's little more you could need."

"Hey!" Jung-sook called. "A bridge is no place for gratuitous PDA."

Snorting, Sam shook her head and stepped back. "Gratuitous?"

Jung-sook and Connor chose to shimmy down one of the cables to land on the railing before jumping down to the sidewalk next to Luke, Roxi, Sam, and Pieter.

"Ready to get out of here?" Luke asked.

They nodded, heading toward their getaway vehicles. Pieter tucked in behind everyone, keeping his distance.

"We've got plans to make."

TWENTY-SEVEN

The farm's kitchen table wouldn't work any longer for their planning needs, so they set up a large tent in the back of the clearing near the farmhouse and the little cabins where the pack's dispossessed families stayed and the wounded recovered. Room at the farm was at a premium with tents serving to house those who could handle living a bit rougher. The pack's kids mostly took the tents, enjoying the adventure of it, allowing more adults to take the limited beds. When they were done with the planning session, the tent would be turned into a field hospital.

Luke knew the decisions he made here would determine how busy this tent would be in the coming days. It wasn't the first time he'd had to make such decisions, far from it, but no matter how many times he'd taken the lives of his troops into his hands, it never got easier.

The last person had filtered in a few minutes ago. He was just waiting for the all clear that there weren't any eavesdroppers loitering about.

Sam poked her head out of the tent and spoke quickly with someone. "We're good to go, Luke."

He stood up and walked around the table he'd been sitting behind. "Thank you all for joining me here. Today is going to be about making tough decisions. Some of you I've known for years. Some of you I've only met a handful of times. But today, we must come together and create a plan that will ensure not only our survival, but the future of our communities. Look at those around you. These are the people who are going to look out for you and by extension, your people."

Luke waited until everyone looked around them. Some smiled at familiar faces. Others nodded or exchanged small waves.

"This is going to be the biggest operation we've ever attempted, requiring more coordination and using more personnel than at any other time since I started working with the North Portland Pack."

Sam coughed. "Since you joined the pack." She coughed again. The room chuckled.

"I stand corrected, Sam. Since I joined the pack. And Sam brings up a valid point. Going forward, we can't afford to be separate entities. Yes. You'll still maintain your own packs and use your own packlinks, but we must act as one organism with one goal—survival.

"Those of you from different packs, you'll be responsible for leading your people and working with my people from the North Portland Pack. By keeping your packs together and assigned to the same missions, it will help with unit cohesion and make sure the orders are carried out quickly."

He reached behind him and grabbed a glass, taking a drink. "I know most of you haven't worked intimately with many of the people here who will be leading the missions, but I trust them explicitly. They've stood by my side time and time again and know what to do. Place your trust in them and in the plan. Owen, for those of you who don't know, is the second of the Coast Pack. He's volunteered to take on the warehouse job. Owen?"

Owen stood up and made his way to the front of the room. "Thanks, Luke. I've already assembled my people and the equipment we'll need. After much discussion, here's the plan."

Owen outlined his heist mission and the specific points each team would be responsible for and how it fit in with the bigger mission. In essence, it was a much more detailed version of Luke and Jamaal's smash and grab scenario. As his friend spoke, Luke wondered how many of these people he'd just met he would never see again. He wondered how many of their family members would curse him. Once Owen finished, Luke stepped forward.

"This is the last opportunity to make any suggestions or bring up any potential issues." Luke waited for anyone to bring something up. Since only some of the new people in the room had worked on the plan, it was a good opportunity for outside views to spot any holes in their plan, though no one spoke up. "OK. Thanks, Owen. Next, Pieter."

Luke waited until Pieter joined him at the front of the room. "Pieter represents the Belgian contingent of the North Portland Pack. His commando training will definitely come in handy as he leads the assault on the vampires' leadership compound."

The address of a valuable target to hit as a distraction had been one of the "fine print" details they'd extracted from Eusebius. Most of their resources would be going toward this assault, both to distract from Luke's mission, but also to pull bodies away from the silver warehouse. It was by far the most complex since Pieter had to handle both the assault and any relief the vampires would be sending from outside. It certainly presented the most opportunity for casualties because of the potential for things to go wrong and because the bulk of their numbers would be dedicated to the mission.

Tutyr had volunteered to join this part of the expedition, adding his limited god powers to the mix. Having his strength there would add weight to the mission, though Luke hoped the god wouldn't have to use his limited abilities in the healing department.

When Pieter was finished, only a couple people asked questions, though simple answers took care of their concerns.

"OK. You've heard your missions. You know the details. Each one of you is key to our success. Without you, we wouldn't be able to make our run at the king. To continue the chess metaphor, your dedication to executing your tasks will make it possible for me and my infiltration team to achieve a checkmate and end this war for good.

"And this is something I've said to my people many times, but I'll say it to all the new people here who haven't heard it. You don't win a war by dying for your country. You win a war by making the other poor, dumb bastards die for their country."

That line got a few nervous laughs.

"But I am serious about that. Don't make stupid sacrifices. Rely on your teams and the people standing next to you. Work together to get the job done and get each other home safe. Don't make me speak at your funerals. Let me toast you at the celebration party."

Sam stepped forward. "Synchronize your watches!" She leaned over to Luke. "I've always wanted to say that." Turning back to the crowd, she continued. "Report to your team leaders and good luck."

The people assembled around the room stood up, looking surer and more confident than when they'd walked into the tent. Pieter and Owen moved through the room, collecting their lieutenants and assembling their personnel to head to their staging zones. It took a few minutes to get everyone pointed in the right direction, but eventually the tent emptied out, leaving Luke and Sam sitting at the table at the head of the tent.

In ones and twos, his infiltration team filtered into the room. Delilah and Simone sat next to each other, their shoulders touching. He'd wanted Delilah to lead the assault on the vampire compound, but she'd refused. Deep down, he was glad she had. They'd started this phase of his vampire war together; it felt fitting that they finish it together. Plus, she was one hell of a fighter and would increase their chance of success. Add in Simone, and they were a terror as a duo.

Sam could have easily led either mission, but she'd volunteered to go with him before he could even ask her. She'd become his sister and one of his closest friends. He'd die for her, and he knew she'd do the same for him.

Jung-sook had been by his side almost from the beginning and had turned into a world-class sniper. She'd also become a dear friend. He never quite felt comfortable on a mission if she wasn't somewhere out there hidden. Armed with the new silver alloy bullets their ammo team had created, she'd rain death from afar. Though her presence would be missed on the other missions, she'd trained Connor and her other proteges well.

Roxi finally pushed into the tent, a broad smile spreading across her face when she saw Luke. Before he could stand to greet her, she sank into his lap, wrapped her arms around his shoulders, and gave him a kiss. "Hello, handsome." With a wink, she stood up and grabbed the chair next to him.

For a split second, he looked up, hoping to see Pablo making his way to the head table. Without his best friend by his side, Luke felt like a piece of himself was missing. Pablo's friendship had saved his life. He'd insisted on sticking his nose in Luke's life and adopted him whether he wanted it or not. If Pablo hadn't, Luke had no doubt he would have died in the gutter that first winter.

Luke would see this through so that no one else had to lose a friend thanks to the vampires. He'd do it so that when Pablo woke up, it would be a world in which they could be friends without having to cruise around town looking for vampires to stake. Luke would do it because he hoped when he came back, he'd find his friend awake and fully on the mend. He'd do it because he had hope. And it was because of Pablo that he had hope.

Ramon poked his head into the tent, then walked in, taking a seat near Luke. Ramon had been his shadow, looking out for him, since he'd carried Luke away from their confrontation with the dark entity outside the arena in the mountains of western Wyoming. It wouldn't feel right to not have his shadow. Ramon had felt the same, quietly showing up and refusing to be sent off to another mission.

Reaching out, Luke grasped Roxi's hand. "Who else are we waiting for?"

"Our explosives man. Roldie should be along soon." She turned back to her conversation with Sam.

Roldie still hadn't returned home to Maine, not that Luke was disappointed about that. He'd installed himself with their ammo folks, working on integrating some of their stolen silver into explosive ordnance. Though, if rumors were true, Roldie was rarely seen out of the presence of Isabelle. Once Roldie went over some of the tools Luke had requested, he'd join Owen on the silver assault where his explosives expertise could best be used.

He watched Roxi as she chatted amiably with everyone. Of all the things that had happened to him in the last few years, her presence in his life might be the most surprising. He'd honestly thought he'd never find someone to share his life with. For the average human, that was fifty or sixty years. For him, that had the potential to be centuries. The fact that she was the only other surviving hunter Mithras had created felt ironic and fitting all at once. He loved her absolutely.

Motion out of the corner of his eye caught his attention; Gwen was trying to sneak into the tent. The young trans woman had been one of the other great surprises of his recent years. They'd found each other, two wounded creatures, and had bonded into their own little found family. He loved his adopted daughter and would do anything for her. Except let her join in the front line fighting like she wanted.

She was absolutely exasperating in her single-minded determination to use the skills he'd taught her when he was looking for a way to bond with her when she'd first moved into his life.

Taking a deep breath, she stood to her full height, raised her naginata, and strode purposefully across the tent. When she made it to the table, she knelt down, resting her naginata across her shoulder.

Luke stood, but before he could start what he'd know would be a heated argument with his ward, Holly burst into the tent.

Breathing heavily, she jogged up to the front of the tent. "There you are. I've been looking everywhere for you, Gwen. Didn't Luke tell you?"

Gwen twisted her head to look at Holly. "Tell me what?"

"I've requested you as my aide-de-camp. I need someone to be my liaison with our defensive positions. I need someone I can trust who knows how to fight, so I asked for you."

If he didn't think Sam would slug him in the arm, he would kiss Holly right now. His daughter had been lurking about trying to be included in the missions but had been kept at arm's length. And there was no way he'd let her go. She wasn't ready for infiltrating the lair of a dark god, and if he had anything to do with it, she'd never have to. He wished he could have tied her up and locked her in a closet to keep her safe.

The chatter around the table stopped, everyone holding their breath. Roxi squeezed his hand almost to the point of pain. Her relationship with Gwen had been particularly turbulent since she'd returned after trying to find a solution to her corrupted rudis.

"Aide-de-camp?" Gwen asked, looked between Luke and Holly.

"It's a big job, if you think you're up for it." Holly smiled reassuringly. "You'll be part of our last line of defense and protecting the wounded and those who can't fight."

"Last line?" Gwen stood up, turning to face Holly. "Really?"

"Are you my person?" Authority slipped into Holly's voice.

Gwen nodded, standing up straight. "Yes, ma'am."

"Alright, I want you to visit each of the defense points into Birkenfeld and get their readiness reports. If you notice anything that can be improved, add it to the report and bring it to me. I'll expect your report by 17:00 sharp. Got it?"

"Yes, ma'am. 17:00 sharp. I won't let you down." Gwen turned and marched out of the tent, her head held high.

Holly followed her, but stopped halfway, turning to wink at Luke. He kissed the tips of his fingers and extended them to her. A palpable sense of relief washed over him. That was one loose end tied up.

He only had one more before they packed up and headed out. The brief respite of relief flitted away as sadness replaced it. Squeezing Roxi's hand, he stood up. "I'll be back."

"Pablo?" she asked quietly.

He nodded. The love and sympathy in her eyes nearly undid him. Bending over, he kissed her then marched out of the tent and across the clearing to the farmhouse.

Pablo and the other wounded people had been moved out of Portland. He now occupied the room he usually took when he was at the farm.

Knocking quietly, Luke cracked the door. "Is it OK to come in?"

Maggie, looking over Pablo's vitals, waved him in. "I'll give you some privacy after I finish."

"Take your time." Luke was glad Tony wasn't there. He was busy on errands for Holly. Luke wasn't sure he could deal with Tony's angry glare, though it had softened somewhat, at least in intensity. It wasn't Tony's anger that got to him, but his own guilt at seeing Pablo lying unconscious in the bed.

Maggie stood up and smiled softly at Luke, leaning in to kiss his cheek. "Come see me when you're done visiting with Pablo."

He nodded as he sank into the just abandoned chair. Slipping his hand under Pablo's, he grasped it gently. "We're going after Saubarag. Finally. I know it doesn't mean much if anything, but I'll make sure he pays for what he did to you." He sighed. "I wish you were going with us. As bad as this is going to be, you'd make it better just by being there. Who is else going to joke with Sam and make us all laugh when we're in the middle of the dark shit?"

He wasn't sure what else to say to his friend, so he sat quietly holding his hand. They weren't violent screed kind of friends. Luke was the straight man to Pablo's jokester. Pablo was the best kind of friend. The kind that made the world a brighter place. The kind that set him up with Maggie because he knew it would be a good match and Luke deserved the joy of her company. Pablo was the best kind of person who'd lived a hard, and at times, sad life and come out of it joyous and vibrant.

Luke sat there in silence, just being present with his friend, hoping deep down his presence would be felt by Pablo.

Someone knocked and opened the door. "Luke," Roxi said quietly. "It's time to go."

Nodding, he gave Pablo's hand a squeeze and bent down and gave Pablo a kiss on the forehead. "Wish me luck."

Once he pulled the door shut, Roxi enfolded him in a hug. "Are you ready?"

"As I'll ever be." He squeezed back, kissing her.

"Good. Maggie's waiting in her room. Go see her then come down to dinner." Roxi patted his cheek companionably.

He nodded, running a hand down her cheek, then turned to head down the hall to the room Maggie and Zel shared. He knocked on the door. "It's me. Luke."

"Come in."

He slipped into the room, shutting the door quietly behind him.

Maggie, setting a book aside, rose from her chair and stood in front him, clasping her hands in front of herself, then she slid forward and pulled him into an intense hug. He wrapped his arms around her, pulling her tightly into his body.

They stood like that for a while. He didn't want to let her go, but he had things that only he could do. His team awaited.

Without having to push back, Maggie seemed to pick up on the moment and stepped back, raising a hand to caress his cheek. "I love you, Luke. Do be careful and come back to me."

"I love you, too. I'll do all I can." He left it at that, then leaned forward and kissed her, letting all he felt for her flood out through his lips. When he thought he'd disappear entirely into the kiss, he pulled back. They leaned into each other, resting forehead to forehead, their breath mingling.

Finally, he sighed and turned around, exiting the room and leaving Maggie to prepare for the wounded that would soon be streaming in. He walked down into the house's common area, dodging around a hub of activity as people came and went on their various tasks and missions, and slipped into the kitchen for a hearty meal with his strike team. Over the centuries, he'd participated in many of these dinners before heading out on a deadly mission. Although people laughed and joked, there was always brittleness to it because in the back of everyone's mind was the thought that it might be the last such meal.

But it also served to add to the bond among those at the table, though after all they'd done together, their bonds were deep and tight.

"Hey, Luke?" Gwen stood outside the threshold to the kitchen, her hand clasped in front of her.

Luke stood up and walked to his adopted daughter, folding her in a tight hug. "I'm glad to see you."

"I just wanted to say good luck before you leave, and I hope everything goes good." Gwen sounded nervous and scared. Having been jailed by vampires and seeing bits of Luke's world, she knew what kind of danger he faced.

"Me too. Thank you."

Backing up, she held up a folder. "I have to run. Holly needs this report."

"Sure. I'll see you later."

"Later." Gwen turned and jogged off towards Holly's office.

The report probably wasn't that important, but it allowed the kid to excuse herself before she started crying or showed too much distress at the thought that this might be a mission Luke and most of her favorite people might not return home from.

Returning to the dinner table, he grabbed a bit more food while he had the opportunity. Though they weren't going that far, filling up on good quality food before departing had become ingrained in his being. He'd been on lean rations too many times, forced to live on the fat of better days. After everyone finished eating, coffees were spread around the table while they waited for their mark to leave.

As one, everyone's phones vibrated with their synchronized alarms announcing it was time to go. Last bathroom breaks were taken by nervous peers while everyone headed out to their rental vehicles. They had two nondescript passenger cars and a cargo van painted with the logo of a made-up plumbing company.

As his team settled into their assigned vehicles, the joking made way for silence and fidgeting. The mission had begun.

CHAPTER
TWENTY-EIGHT

Their little caravan wound its way through the forests of the Coast Range emerging in Astoria so they could cross the Columbia River at the Astoria-Megler Bridge. For Luke, the bridge held unpleasant memories.

"You going to be OK?" Sam asked as she pulled onto the loop winding up to the bridge.

"I still miss my Volvo," Luke said.

It had been a couple years since the Volvo had been blown up by vampires on the Washington side of the bridge, but the old car had given its life in order for Luke to fake his death so he could go off the grid in an effort to bring down the vampires and werewolves who'd betrayed him and his friends in Belgium.

Luke sighed. "If Pablo where here, he'd make a joke about pouring one out for our fallen homie."

Roxi and Sam chuckled, nodding sadly.

"He was always good for a well-timed and probably inappropriate joke." Sam held up a hand gripped as if it were holding an invisible bottle and made a pouring motion as they neared the Washington side of the bridge.

Now they just had to link up with Highway 4, which lead them to I-5 south where they'd skirt around Vancouver, Washington to get to Highway 14. It wasn't the fastest way to get to White Salmon, Washington, but it would keep them out of the Portland area, where the other two missions would be taking place. He hoped things were going well, and Maggie wouldn't be too busy.

The clear night made for a beautiful drive down the Columbia Gorge. When they left the lights of Vancouver and Portland behind, the stars shone in a thick quilt of twinkling lights. With good music on the car's sound system and two of his favorite people with him, it almost felt like the start of a wonderful road trip leading to adventure. But in their case, the adventure was a deadly mission to slay a god and anyone who stood in their way.

Once they neared White Salmon, they followed a series of more and more remote roads until they were deep in the hills overlooking the Columbia Gorge. Parking briefly, they waited for Ramon to pop out and cut the lock of the barrier gate blocking a private logging road. After they pulled through, they replaced the gate and placed a fake lock in place of the cut one so things would appear undisturbed. Turning their lights off, they continued up the road.

They drove slowly since they had no lights, and the trees blocked a lot of the moon and starlight as the clock approached twenty-three-hundred hours. At least the drivers had excellent night vision thanks to their lupine nature. Once they hit the desired GPS coordinates, they parked their vehicles and opened the box of the cargo van to gear up.

For their mission, Luke brought all his armor—his lorica segmentata, his manix, the greaves, and his helmet. Roxi had a similar array. After helping each other dress, they loaded up their weapons, each of them putting on a dizzying array of edged weapons, explosives, and firearms, and of course, bows for Roxi and Sam. They had enough ordnance among them to take on both a terminator and a predator.

Once they were fully loaded, the drivers who'd ridden in the van and the car Delilah drove climbed in the two vehicles and returned the way they came. They'd head into White Salmon and find a place to park out of the way and wait. The van would likely be abandoned.

After their small party was fully armed, Ramon wiped down the van for prints and locked it up.

Casting his face to the sky, Luke let Selene know they were ready for her aid. They'd prearranged their needs with her so she wouldn't have to descend to take care of it. While their werewolf friends didn't need help in the night vision department, especially as the moon neared full, Luke and Roxi did, even with their enhanced vision. Selene, goddess of the moon, blessed them, letting their eyes use more of her light.

Luke shook his head as the greenness of the forest faded to more silver and gray tones with only hints of green, but he could see the detail of needles and bark in the distance. The descent to the compound would still be rigid and arduous, but at least he'd be able to see it.

They gathered in a small circle, taking hold of each other's hands.

Luke cleared his throat to get himself started. "Alright. We do this together. We look out for each other. We've worked closely together. We take care of each other, and we'll come out of this alive and successful. I believe in each of you."

Sam raised everyone's hands in the air. "Yay, team God Smoters!" she called out in an intense whisper. They let go of each other's hands and spread out. He really should have revoked her naming rights.

Sam and Roxi melted into the shadows, heading down to their target. Together, they'd scout the way, and the rest would follow along after giving them a ten-minute head start. He wished he could be working with Roxi, but she was a far better scout than he was. When it was their turn, they slipped into the woods.

AS THEY NEARED the wall of the compound, they caught up to Roxi and Sam who hid behind a couple of large Douglas Fir trees. They were still well back from the fence and the lights illuminating the border of the compound.

Roxi, using hand signals, told them there were four werewolf teams of two patrolling the fence. Acknowledging the intelligence, he signaled for Jung-sook to head up the tree. She took a moment to put on a bit of tree climbing gear to help her make it up to the level where she should use the branches to aid her ascent.

Each time the tree shimmied or a branch cracked, Luke cringed, glancing up then toward the compound. But so far, the nearest patrol hadn't reached the section of the fence they hid near. Once the tree stopped shaking, a few faint clicks and clinks wafted on the breeze as she assembled the small canvas covered rigid framed platform she'd use as a sniper nest. Once she was situated, silence returned to the tree.

Setting down their guns and heavier equipment, Roxi and Sam crept forward, stopping at a thick rhododendron bush. Luke, Ramon, Delilah, and Simone tucked themselves behind their hiding spots as the first patrol neared their location.

Once it passed, Roxi and Sam emerged from their hiding place and slipped up behind the patrol. Moving as one, Roxi and Sam snatched the chins of their targets and slid their knives across their throats. But instead of letting them go to crash to the ground, they lowered them carefully. Ramon and Delilah ran out and between the four of them, they carried the bodies into the brush. A couple quick stakes ended the wolves quickly.

With the first patrol neutralized, they waited and watched. If the wolves managed to get off a message on their packlink, even assuming the wolves here had a pack to link to, then the other wolves would descend on them to investigate. But if they'd been quick enough, the wolves wouldn't know until they arrived at the spot and found blood. They might be able to cover the sight of it up, but not the scent.

When the other patrols kept their steady pace, Luke exhaled softly in relief. The first encounter had gone off well. Roxi and Sam rejoined them and they moved upwind from their first kill, leaving Jung-sook hanging out in her sniper tree. From up in her nest, she could command the entire back of the compound, including the other patrols, but they wanted to save her for when she was needed. If they opened fire now, it would alert everyone to their presence.

Using the same procedure they'd just used, Roxi and Sam took down the next patrol and they reset further upwind.

As they waited for the third patrol, a bat flew overhead and directly into the fence. The poor creature sizzled and fell to the ground.

"Fuck," he whispered. They'd planned for an electrified fence, but he'd hoped they'd get lucky. But not tonight.

Either way, there was little they could do about it until they neutralized the last couple of patrols. By the time they took down the last one, they were nearly at the corner of the compound. Tucking back into the woods, they silently worked their way back to the tree where Jung-sook waited.

Once they checked in with Jung-sook, they waited for the radio click that said it was all clear. They didn't know how long the check in intervals would be for the patrol teams, so they had to work on a short timeline and hope for the best.

Ramon dropped his backpack and pulled out the class 4 linesman gloves. They were as heavy duty as one could buy and would protect the wearer from up to 36,000 volts AC or 54,000 volts DC. He took a deep breath before pulling them on. Luke reached into the backpack and pulled out the bolt cutters, handing them to Ramon.

With shotguns ready, Luke and Delilah snuck up toward the fence, spotting up behind nearby bushes. After they waved their readiness, Ramon dashed in and tremulously laid the back of his glove covered hand on the fence. Nothing happened. Taking his hand off the fence, he stepped back and slowly pushed the bolt cutters toward the fence. Again, nothing. Reassured that the gloves would protect him, he started at the ground and snipped the links of the fence to create a hole wide and tall enough for them all to slip through with their gear.

As Luke swept his gaze along the fence, looking for trouble, he breathed shallowly. It seemed to be taking forever for Ramon to cut the fence. Luke had tried on the gloves. They were thick. All things considered, his friend was making good progress. When the last link was cut, Ramon carefully reached through and folded up the cut piece of fence, dragging it through the hole, he ran back and hid the piece of fence in the brush and stripped off the gloves, stashing them and the bolt cutters back in his backpack in case they needed them again.

Again, they took a moment for Jung-sook to make sure their handiwork hadn't been noticed. All clear.

One by one, Luke waved in the rest of the team, then followed when they'd set up a defensive perimeter at the opening. While they'd been dealing with the patrol, Jung-sook had used the time and her powerful sniper optics to survey the back of the compound. Their next stop, as directed by Jung-sook, was the generator.

Working in twos, Luke and his people swept across the open space of the compound, doing their best to aim for shadows. So far, they'd managed to slip in with only minimal intervention. It always made Luke nervous when things went too smoothly. He felt it was the universe saving up to counterbalance the ease with even bigger difficulties. He tried not to be a superstitious man about such things, but he'd lived a long time and seen a lot of bad shit go down.

But despite his misgivings, they arrived at the generator without incident. The team surrounded it and Luke, forming a protective ring as he opened up the covers and sabotaged the expensive piece of equipment. A moment later, the generator sputtered to a halt, and the compound was plunged into darkness. And that's when all hell broke loose.

CHAPTER
TWENTY-NINE

"Luke, incoming," Roxi called.

Off in the distance, Jung-sook's Steyr SSG 69 barked to life, spitting lead in a steady rain of death.

Picking up his shotgun, he moved slowly around the generator, poking his head around the corner blocking him from the open space of the backyard of the compound. Shadows swept toward them, moving like trained soldiers. He wondered why he didn't sense their approach, but neither had anyone else.

He ducked behind the generator and moved to the other side. As he turned, he pulled back, a yelp nearly escaping his lips as a figure in tactical gear drew a bead on him. Jung-sook saved him, blowing a hole in the side of the soldier's head.

Luke reached out and grabbed an arm, dragging it behind the generator as Roxi, Delilah, Sam, and Simone opened fire. They'd been smart to save their shots until their targets were in range of their shotguns. They only had a limited supply and no chance of easy resupply.

Looking over the dead man, Luke guessed it was probably a human mercenary. He stripped off the automatic rifle, its magazines, and a couple of fragmentary grenades, which he quickly stowed on his person.

With his friends covering the approach to both sides, he needed a better vantage point. The ladder running up the side of the generator would do nicely. He climbed up and flopped down on his belly before he could give his position away.

Off to his left, a group of mercs worked in teams, advancing toward Luke's position. They still hadn't reached shotgun range. Starting at the outside, Luke laid down strategic bursts of fire, aiming more for location than to hit anyone, and herded the platoon of mercs together. Once he was satisfied, he pushed up, grabbed a grenade, and pulled the pin. Giving it a couple seconds, he hurled it toward the cluster of men, then flopped back onto his stomach.

As they tried to break from cover, he opened fire again, this time aiming for flesh. The chaos he created worked. The grenade exploded and had plenty of meat to grind. With that side momentarily handled, his people could take care of the mercs who'd moved closer, he swung around to the other direction.

A quick burst of gunfire slowed their progress as they dove for cover. Jumping up, he grabbed another grenade and flung it as hard as he could. It bounced on the tin roof of an overhang once, twice, and then settled and rolled off the edge to explode in the air right above where the mercs had dove for cover.

Luke grabbed his radio. "Spartacus calling Ma Bell. What's our situation?"

Ma Bell had been one of his favorite of Sam's assigned nicknames since the old phone company's slogan had been "Reach out and touch someone," which Jung-sook did so well, but instead of a call from a loved one, she delivered hot lead.

"Looking good. Just a last few." Jung-sook signed off by taking out another merc.

Crawling to the edge of the generator, Luke popped up on his knees and took some pot shots at the nearest mercs. Between him and his teammates, they eliminated the last few. Moving forward, he sat on the edge and jumped down, landing nimbly. There were times when advanced reflexes and strength came in handy.

"Scrounge what you can, then we're moving out." Luke went looking for anyone carrying the same gun he'd picked up, taking as many magazines as he could carry. He also picked up any grenades he could. They always came in handy.

After a minute, they were ready to go. Jung-sook hadn't spotted a door on this side of the compound they could aim for, so he waved his people after, as he jogged in the direction most of the mercenaries had come from.

"I'll watch your back," Jung-sook said over the radio.

"Roger," Luke replied.

When they neared the corner of the building, Luke held up his fist, stopping their advance. "Ma Bell, corner check, please?"

"You're beyond what I can see at this angle."

Handing his gun to whoever was behind him, he pulled out his small periscope from his utility pouch and extended it around the corner. After a couple seconds, he drew it back and stowed it. He waved everyone over and grabbed a stick, then drew the layout in the dirt. Mercenaries waited in ambush. Using hand signals, he assigned everyone's tasks.

Luke, Delilah, and Ramon pulled out grenades and pulled the pins. Letting go of the spoons and counting two, they darted out and chucked the grenades at their targets, then dove behind the wall for cover as shots rang out from multiple points.

Three explosions followed by screams signaled Sam, Roxi, and Simone to move around the corner and open fire with their newly pilfered automatic weapons. With well-aimed bursts, they stifled screams and created more to replace them.

Luke pushed himself off the ground and joined them, running behind them and away from the building. He hoped to draw some fire and reveal anyone who might still be trying to hide. Delilah and Ramon were right behind him. Once they reached a stack of firewood, they held up, providing cover fire for Roxi, Sam, and Simone as they made it to the first embankment where the mercs had set up. It would work well to protect his people from the ambushers.

With only a handful of mercs left, they easily outflanked them from their position behind the woodpile. Roxi and her team advanced to the next spot and finished a couple stragglers to silence them while Luke and his squad kept their wide approach and moved to the next bit of cover.

From here, he could see the next corner, and beyond it, a door. The compound was sizable and had several buildings attached with roofed walkways. This back building they'd been working their way around appeared to be some sort of utility building.

Pointing at it, he sent Roxi and her squad in to clear it out if there was anyone in there. While they waited, he moved his people around so they'd be closer. Though they'd met a decent amount of resistance, they still hadn't come across any vamps or wolves, and he expected to be overwhelmed with the ominous presence of Saubarag.

So far, he didn't hear any gunfire from inside Roxi and her team. A minute later, Roxi reappeared and joined him.

"Looks like it was being used as a barracks for the mercs. If the beds match the bodies, we may have taken out most of them. Doesn't look like there were any secret doors or alternate routes to an altar," she said.

"Good." His brow furrowing, he looked around the compound. "Do you feel anything? Vamps? Saubarag?"

Roxi looks puzzled. "No... No, I don't. Do you think we were hoodwinked?"

He shrugged. "I hope not. Let's hit the next building. If there's nothing there, we'll hit the house."

The house would be the most likely place for the altar to be. He just hoped he didn't have to sweep all the floors and rooms of the large mansion. Though logically he wanted the altar to be in the basement since Saubarag was a dark sort who belonged in a musty basement with a mold and mildew problem, he could be in the attic or in the largest bedroom. Hell, the altar could be set up on the back of a toilet, though that seemed more absurd than an actual possibility.

After he sent Roxi in to clear out the second building, his anxiety grew steadily, not because he worried for her—he did—but because everything about this felt too easy...too wrong. While Ramon and Simone watched his back, he took a minute to consolidate a couple partial magazines he'd switched out to ensure he had a full mag before their engagements. Dropping the empties so he didn't have to carry them, he watched the door until Roxi and her squad popped out. She gave him a thumbs up.

"Ma Bell, update," Luke whispered into the radio.

"All clear."

A new wave of tension caressed his already wound tight nerves. Once Roxi, Delilah, and Sam rejoined his group, they swept forward in their squads, not letting their guard down as they approached the house for all the good it did them. They could have walked up and knocked like a delivery person.

As they gathered around the backdoor, Luke on one side and Roxi on the other with the rest of their people spread out further down the wall, he raised an eyebrow and mouthed, "Sense anything?" at her.

She shook her head. He didn't like it, and he could tell she didn't either.

Since they had all these extra grenades, they spread out around the building and picked different windows. When they were in position, Jung-sook counted out their mark.

Glass shattered as the butts of guns were used to break them out. With holes opened, everyone pulled a pin on a grenade and tossed them in. If anyone waited inside, they were about to have a rude evening.

Luke tossed his grenade in and dove to the ground, covering his head. Nearby, a thump of a body hitting the ground told him someone else was likewise hugging the ground. A few seconds later, several grenades went off in rapid succession, sending glass and other debris flying out shattered windows.

Since there was a convenient opening, Luke bounced up, used his manix covered right arm to knock any remaining shards of glass from the frame, and pulled himself in. Rolling to his butt, he brought his machine gun around and swept it around the room but found nothing moving in the smoky interior. Careful not to cut himself, he placed a hand on the ground and pushed himself to kneeling then to standing.

The grenades had done a hell of a job redecorating the interior, shredding upholstery, breaking wood, and peppering the walls with shrapnel. At least the broken windows were venting the explosives smoke.

Creeping to the door, he twisted the knob slowly, peeking out of the crack before opening it all the way. Roxi and Sam stood in a hallway, each of them having entered from their windows. Sam walked over and shut his door, then spray painted a red "X" on the door to indicate it had been cleared. The three of them checked the other rooms attached to the hall but found them empty as well.

The sound of a creaking floorboard drew Luke's attention as he swung around, his gun raised and ready. Ramon held his gun in the air and raised his other hand. Luke lowered his gun. They just had to collect Delilah and Simone.

With all the rooms checked and marked off, they proceeded deeper into the ground floor of the house and found the last two members of their party in a central sitting room.

"Find anything?" Luke whispered.

Delilah shook her head.

Luke shook his head and exhaled an exasperated breath. He was about to open the discussion about the next part of the plan when his knees collapsed and he smacked the floor.

Vampires. Above. Below. Moving in from the sides.

Vaguely, he heard someone calling his name, but he couldn't hear them over the violent thudding of his heart. The reptilian part of his brain tried to take over, telling him to get up and run, flee, escape. Death and doom approached.

"No…" Luke was the master of his body, not his amygdala. He would not let his enemy drive him off.

Forcing himself to sitting, he tried to draw in his focus and push out the darkness threatening to drown him. "I. Am. Lucius. Silvanius. Ferrata. I. Am. Luke. Irontree. I am."

He rolled onto his hands and knees and pushed himself upright, his head clearing with each moment he fought off the crushing feeling that had literally floored him.

"Help him," Roxi said.

Sam and Delilah took a step toward him, but he held up his hands. "No."

With first one leg, then the next, he forced his body into the standing position. Drawing in a harsh, deep breath, he exhaled loudly, then repeated it two more times. By the third time, his heart slowed, and he could see and hear straight.

All around him, vampires writhed like a maggot pit, though he didn't know what kept them from swarming him. The sense of doom that had overcome him momentarily shifted slightly, almost like it was chuckling.

"I'm OK… I think." He looked for his gun and grabbed it off the chair where it'd fallen. "Vampires."

"Where?" Delilah asked.

"Everywhere," Roxi said, looking around frantically. "Did anyone see the stairs up or down? We need to make a decision and get to it or we'll be sandwiched."

Luke closed his eyes and concentrated, trying to follow the tendrils of darkness laughing at him. Despite the pervasive sense of fanger, he thought he felt a core of dark power below them. He let go and opened his eyes.

"The basement. That's where we need to go."

"Follow me." Delilah jogged off, waving them after her.

When they dashed toward a set of steps heading up, Luke stopped. Now that they moved, the vampires moved with them. He heard footfalls above them. Grabbing a grenade, he armed it and threw it upstairs, bouncing it off a wall so it rolled out of sight down a hall. It exploded, spraying debris and screams in its wake.

"Quick, give me your last few frag grenades." Luke held out his hands. He stuffed them in his pockets as they handed them over. The last one, he pulled the pin and threw it after the first one. The sound of pain washing down the stairs after the explosion further contributed to clearing his mind. "Take the last two and clear the path down. I'm going to use the rest and try to even the odds. Roxi, set a few traps but don't arm them until I'm with you."

This wasn't something they'd discussed, but they nodded and ran toward the basement stairs. Marking the location, he returned to his new pastime and lobbed another grenade upstairs. This time, he drew few screams. But shattering windows and yells to jump told him the fangers had given up on the stairs down. They'd soon be swarming into the house from all directions like he and friends had.

Backing down the hallway toward the basement stairs, he saw the first signs of his enemies as they poked their head into the hall. Not waiting for them to react, he threw a grenade, banking it off the door and into the room with them. The door flew open with the explosion, the inside newly painted in gore.

As he neared the door to the stairwell leading into the basement, he heard gunshots. Hopefully Roxi and company could hold their position until he joined them. He only had two grenades left. The hallway took a ninety-degree turn toward the other side of the house. Out of the corner of his eye, he caught a bunch of vampires trying to sneak down and ambush him from behind. Not giving away that he'd seen them, he pulled the pin surreptitiously, carefully removed the spoon, then hurled the grenade into the middle of the cluster.

Before it could explode, he spun around and ran down the stairs two at a time. Once he reached the bottom, he pulled the pin on his last of the stolen grenades and waited until he heard footsteps tromping towards the door. Letting the spoon fly, he waited a full three second then lobbed the grenade through the door. It bounced once before exploding, ripping limbs and screams from those who'd been in its way.

He'd tucked himself around the corner, then hustled to find the source of the gunfire. As soon as he saw Roxi, she ran back down the hall. Skidding to a halt, he followed her, providing protection as she armed the simple traps she'd only had a couple minutes to set up. If the vampires were too eager to get revenge on them, they'd walk right into it. Luke had to hope leveler heads didn't prevail.

As they backed away, Luke took a moment to concentrate on the vampires. They'd thinned out the numbers some, but not enough. More swarmed in from the distance. He hoped Jung-sook just kept quiet and stayed hidden. She couldn't make much of a difference against this horde. Her shots would only serve to reveal her.

"Luke," Roxi said quietly. "Where's the light coming from?"

He looked around. She was right. There seemed to be a glow emanating from above them. "Perhaps some backup lighting?"

The contrast of the glow, the tall ceiling—odd for a basement—and soft evenness of the light made it hard to pinpoint if there were fixtures or what. Either way, it was better than having to use the headlamps, though Luke preferred the beacon he had attached to his chest.

Ahead of them, a door shattered as someone bashed it in. Sam, Simone, Delilah, and Ramon had been advancing down the hallway. They must have found a room that needed to be cleared if they didn't want to get flanked.

When he caught up to them, the room had been marked, and they'd reached a junction leading off in opposite directions.

"What do we do now?" Sam asked.

"I'm loath to split up, not when there's only six of us and who knows what down here." Going to the inner place where he could concentrate, he focused on homing in on his target. "Left."

To emphasize his decision, he led the way, proceeding slowly. The feeling of dark wrongness grew stronger as they delved deeper until the hall ended at another stairwell down, though this one didn't match the materials or architecture of the house in any way. One didn't usually see wide, granite steps leading deep into the earth in Western Washington.

"I don't like this," Roxi whispered.

"Me neither. But we don't have much of a choice."

"Guys…" Sam called over her shoulder. "We got company. Lots of it."

Luke reached out and set his foot on the first stone step and dread and darkness pulsed up through it. Looking at Roxi, he shook his head. "This isn't for them."

He began stripping off his stolen gun and ammo, setting it in a pile. He only kept his swords, the Winchester M12, his shotgun ammo, and two of the special silver scrap frag grenades Roldie had made. Roxi, understanding Luke's decision without having it explained, stripped down to the same mix.

"Where are you going?" Sam asked.

"Take everything here and push down the hallway. What's down those stairs is not for you. Trust me on this. If you go down there, you won't come up again. Hold them off as long as you can."

An explosion sent light, flames, and a shockwave down the hall. They'd found Roxi's first booby trap. That would slow them down.

"Hurry, before you're pinned back here."

"Right. You heard the man," Sam said, bending over to hand out the various weapons. When she'd distributed everything, she darted in and kissed Luke on the cheek then Roxi. "See you on the other side."

Delilah made eye contact and gave him a single nod. Simone smiled sadly and gave a little wave, then followed Delilah. Ramon grinned jauntily and gave a matching salute before jogging after everyone.

Luke turned to Roxi. "Right. Ready?"

"Not yet." She pulled him in to a passionate kiss that lasted too long and not nearly long enough. When they finished, they rested helmet-covered foreheads against each other, sharing their breaths for a moment. "Lead the way, dōšagīh"

Taking each other's hands, they stepped down onto the steps and the basement hallway disappeared.

From the recently constructed basement, Luke and Roxi descended into dimly lit stone until they stepped off the last step and settled on a cave floor. A familiar cave. Looking around, Luke narrowed his eyes. It was hard to tell if his memories were playing tricks on him—dimly lit caves shared a lot of features that could confuse a person. But this one still felt strangely familiar.

"Is this…" Roxi whispered. "Is this Mithras's cave?"

Luke nodded uncertainly. "It could be. But…how?"

She reached out and tentatively touched the wall. Her hand pressed up against the wall and didn't sink in. "It feels real enough."

Wondering if he could find the entrance to the tunnel leading to Mithras's temple, he took a step forward, letting go of Roxi's hand. He turned around to see if Roxi was following him, but she'd disappeared. Yanking his gladius from its scabbard, he spun around quickly, his heart beating double time. He wanted to yell out her name but didn't know who else might be listening.

Before he lost control, he sank to one knee and laid his empty hand flat on the ground. In front of him, Roxi's boot prints remained in the dirt, but she'd disappeared—no drag marks or a third pair of footprints to indicate what might have happened. Following her boot prints backward, he expected to the see the stairs, but instead there were only boulders from what looked like a cave in.

A hand placed against the boulders found no give and no indication of the stairs and door they'd just walked through. He narrowed his eyes, looking closer, then on a hunch, laid the flat of his gladius against the boulder directly in front of his face.

He didn't see anything, but the feeling running around and through him gave a momentary shudder. In response, he shivered.

Turning around, he stared into the dark abyss, holding back the panic that wanted to take hold. He'd wandered this path over nineteen-hundred years ago and it had led him back to it, but how? The mountain had been in the Caucus Mountains in Armenia. The house they'd infiltrated sat in the foothills of the Cascade Mountains in Washington.

Seeing no other choice, he took one step forward, then another. Feeling insecure in the dark surroundings, he reached over his shoulder and grabbed his rudis. He'd never been fond of caves and such, even on a philosophical level as a Celt who believed in Dubnos —the dark underworld and the place of birth, death, emergence, and rebirth.

Stopping for a moment, he forced his eyes closed, despite the fear of what might choose to pounce if he weren't watching, and extended his senses. He couldn't feel any vampires. But it didn't feel like Mithras's cave had, if he could bring back the memory of centuries ago. It felt... Oppressive. And under that, a malicious current seethed.

A delighted and unhinged laugh rang through the cave, and his eyes shot open. The glow that emanated from above pulsed and almost twinkled in time with the laugh. Before he could take another step, the cave collapsed, crushing him to the ground.

Weight pressed on him from all sides. He whimpered, his breathing shallow and raspy. Tears burned in his eyes and ran down his cheeks. The laughter grew louder, more satisfied.

He couldn't move as pressure squeezed every bit of his body. Except for his hands...

Twitching his wrists, the pressure shifted slightly. A growl of anger and fear rose up in his throat. With all his strength, he rotated his wrist and flicked his rudis out. Instead of impacting harmlessly on stone, the collapsed cave writhed and grunted in… pain?

Before the cave could return its full pressure to his body, he flicked both wrists, slashing out with his swords. The weight on him eased slightly, freeing more space. With the ability to move his arms, he struck harder, grunting at the impact when his swords met resistance that still wasn't hard, unforgiving rock.

More space opened up around him, allowing him to force his way to his knees. As his anger pushed back the fear, he struck out harder and harder, growling and snarling as the cave tried to reassert its power. The laughing ceased.

Luke wasn't sure if it was the silver in his blades or the magic contained within them that had driven back his tormenter. The more space Luke regained, the harder he fought, driving the cave up and away so he could stand. Once he had the room, he started a defensive pattern more common in Chinese sword arts than in western methods that allowed him to carve the air around him in all directions—top, sides, back, and front. The focus on form and precision helped push the panic back into the recesses of his mind.

As his muscles flowed freely and he reveled in the feeling of being free of the oppressive weight, he failed to notice a tendril of darkness sliding up his legs and onto torso until it attached itself to several points where he'd been pierced in his fight against Saubarag. As soon as they linked up, he was pulled down harshly, slamming to the ground.

You are mine!

Luke scrabbled to grab his weapons, merely inches out of reach. His fingers scraped in the dirt of the cave floor. Despite the dark tendrils pulling at his torso, their grasp wasn't as strong or oppressive as the collapse of the cave had been.

Grunting under the strain, he pushed up on his knees and elbows, then surged forward, snatching his rudis and gladius. The weight in his hands and the magic of the blades allowed him a breath. He used it to roll over and flail around his body with the blades. One by one, the tendrils frayed and snapped until he was free again, though still on his back.

Stabbing upwards, he slashed out to each side, then stabbed up again and sliced up and down. Around him, the darkness groaned and receded. He took advantage of the respite and surged to his feet.

He couldn't keep up the tug-of-war and win. Bold action was required. Reaching into his pocket, he pulled out one of the silver loaded grenades Roldie had made. The dim light glinted off a silver line around the middle of the explosive ball. Ripping the pin free, he bowled it underhand as hard as he could, using the space he'd opened up to send the grenade as far away from himself as possible.

Diving back onto the ground, he covered his ears and curled into a ball. The helmet would protect the rest of his head. A couple sends later, the grenade loaded with sliver shrapnel exploded and the darkness shrieked in agony, withdrawing further.

For the first time since he'd stepped off the last step, he felt like he had a bit of control. Rising to his feet, he grabbed his sword and tried to regain his composure.

When the dim light returned, he once again stood in a cave, though not the cave he'd first seen when entering. He took a moment to focus in and reach out with his senses. The power that had been playing with him had backed away, but now that it wasn't so all-encompassing, he thought he could detect a directionality to it. Taking a deep breath, he moved toward what felt like the point of origin.

He'd only taken a few steps when the sense of vampires hit him like a runaway truck. He'd wondered where the vampires he'd felt below him earlier when the shield had been ripped off went.

Slipping into a versatile stance, he readied himself and slowed his pace. The first vampire flew out of a dark nook, fangs dripping and eyes filled with bloodlust. Stepping aside, Luke speared it on the tip of his gladius, then flowed with the motion as the vampire dissolved around his blade.

Soon, he had no time to tell from where the vampires came. His blades struck like lightning—indiscriminately and brutally. Most of those who attacked were young, weak, and inexperienced. But a few older ones were mixed in. It didn't matter to Luke. All died on his blades, but the flow didn't slow.

Ducking under a clawed swipe, he dropped his gladius and pulled out his last silver grenade and yanked the pin. By now, he could pick out where the majority of the fangers were coming from and launched the grenade in that direction before snatching up his gladius and deflecting the next blow aimed at his head.

He struggled back to his feet and cut his way ward a nook and tucked in just in time as the grenade exploded. Tearing limbs, undeath, and screams from the vampires. Yet they still came.

Breathing heavily, he reengaged. He had no idea how much more he had left in him at that point. His arms burned from the exertion. Soon, he'd have to choose between death and potential self-destruction. But if he delayed in making the decision, he'd likely not have enough left to finish why he'd come here.

He cut his way back into the center of the cave and set up a defensive pattern to create a bit of space, then focused his concentration and thrust it out through his rudis. The incantation surged through his mind and out through the wooden blade. The room burst into light as golden threads connected with the horde of vampires. Before they could recover, he yanked back on the rudis and ripped every last bit of life force from them.

The golden globules slammed into his rudis, knocking him to his knees. He couldn't lower his arm, the rudis and energy feeding through it into him locked him into place until the last one disappeared into the wooden sword. He fell onto his hands and vomited until he was left with nothing but dry heaves.

Random trembles shook through his body as he held himself aloft on his hands and knees. He needed to move away from his mess. The stench of bile was becoming overwhelming. Instead of risking standing and falling into his mess, he opted to push to the side and roll onto his back. At least he could face away from it.

He wanted to lie there and gasp in breaths, but the dark entity beckoned to him. He had work to do still. Rolling onto his belly, he pushed himself up and stumbled to his feet.

His entire body vibrated as if it were going to fly apart at the seams. Sucking in a harsh, deep breath, he closed his eyes and focused. He could fly apart later. Right now, he had to find Saubarag, and maybe then, the energy threatening to shatter him would be useful.

Staggering forward, he followed the tendrils, looking for their origin. With each step and each breath, he found a way to contain the energy ricocheting around inside him. Not even really seeing where he went, he homed in and followed the trace like a blood-hound. Occasionally, he bounced off a wall as he picked up speed into a shambling run.

"Luke? Luke!"

Shaking his head, he focused on the sound. Roxi? It was her. A relieved cry fell from his lips as he pulled her in tightly. "What... what happened?"

"I don't know. One minute you were there, then the next you weren't. Then I..." She let out a ragged exhale. "I had to watch you die over and over again. All the while, the smug bastard promised me he could save you if...if I gave myself to him and brought you with me."

Pushing back a little, he saw a glint of light catch on a tear streaking down her cheek. He reached up with trembling fingers and wiped it away. "I'd never let him take you, and I'd never go to him."

"I know." She kissed him desperately on the cheek and forehead and finally his lips. "It just felt so real."

He had no true idea what Saubarag had been trying to accomplish by torturing him, other than weakening him enough to seek mercy. But the petty god had bitten off more than he could chew. Shaking his head to clear it, he clenched his hands into fists to stop the trembling.

"I'm here now, Roxi. Together, he can't hurt us. Together, we're stronger." He hoped she didn't notice the shaking in his voice.

"I know." She took a moment to breathe deeply and collect herself. "I know."

The presence of the dark god pulled at him. They had an appointment.

"Are you ready?" he asked.

"Can you find him?"

He nodded. "Follow me."

Taking her hand, he hoped contact with her skin would help calm the energy bursting through him, or at least still the trembling in his bones. Together, they moved through the last bit of the twisting cave until they found what looked like a regular house door.

When they stepped within reach of it, he heard the faint sound of gunfire in the background. Turning his head, he looked back in the distance at the stone steps leading up to the hallway where he'd left his friends what felt like hours ago. Gunfire meant they were still alive, still fighting.

But for every moment Luke didn't go through the door, the chance of his friends being overwhelmed grew. It was now or never.

CHAPTER
THIRTY-ONE

L uke reached out, pausing a moment. The familiar darkness of Saubarag pulsed off the door handle, a tendril of it slithering through the air, searching for Luke. For something in him. Behind him, Roxi stared up the stairwell. Gunfire and small explosions drifted toward them.

Gripping the door handle, he pulled hard, stepping back but keeping his sword ready.

A dark voice chuckled from the unlit recesses of a vast cavern. "Welcome. I'm glad to see you've returned to me."

Behind Luke, Roxi flicked on a flashlight, shining it between them. He took a step, entering the room.

Though the flashlight was a good one with an intense beam, the darkness swallowed it, letting little of it escape to show where they were going. After draining so many vampires out of necessity, Luke practically hummed with energy.

Concentrating, he forced a trickle out of himself into the blade. The silver-steel alloy pieces glowed gently, stopping at the tip. When he was sure he could control it in a refined manner, he drew a bit more power from himself and pushed it into the blade until it glowed far brighter than the flashlight.

Roxi clicked it off and put it away. "That's handy."

The darkness receded some, seeming to writhe and growl as it did so.

"My, you have become powerful, glutting on the essence of my children. You're even more magnificent than I could imagine." A shadowy outline emerged from the darkness, striding forward confidently.

Once the figure breached the shell of the orb of light Luke's rudis had created, it resolved into a dark-haired man with slicked-back shoulder length hair. He wore black leather with bits of dark steel riveted on it. His thick beard was tightly cropped, though it wasn't thick enough to hide a weak chin.

"Nice Sheriff of Nottingham cosplay," Roxi said. "But where's the spoon?"

A momentary flash of annoyance interrupted the calm façade he kept draped over his face. He gestured around him. "Welcome to my home."

"Your hospitality is a bit lacking," Luke said, since there was no one around to criticize his banter.

"If you'd just waited for an invitation, you could have been the guest of honor." Saubarag looked him up and down. "And what a fine guest you would have made, too. You are indeed the finest of my creations."

Luke snorted. "I'm not your creation."

Saubarag laughed, the sound oily and hollow. "How can you claim that? Because of the creation of my children, you were brought before that fool Mithras and made a hunter. Because you feed off my children, you are immortal. You've honed your skills on their bodies over the centuries. Stolen their lives and picked over their clothes for your wealth. Who else can claim to have contributed so much to who you've become? Now you've come to pay homage to me and join my forces and fight at my beck and call."

"It's a pretty story you spin, but it's a lie. My parents forged my character. The legions forged my arm. Mithras gave me a mission. Selene blessed and guided me. My friends have aided me over the centuries. All you've contributed was pain and misery." Luke spat on the ground between Saubarag and himself.

"But pain and misery are the truest emotions. Constant and universal. They've driven you along your journey. They've caressed you while you've slept at night. Comforted you when you were alone. Guided you into the arms of others." He chucked his chin toward Roxi. "Now, join me, or die."

"The answer is the same, you disgusting little sneak thief. No. A thousand nos. So fuck off with your offer."

"Oh? Fuck off, you say?" Saubarag raised his hand, holding it open. Then, he crushed his fingers into a fist.

Luke's body seized up. His muscles wouldn't respond to his brain. Pain seared every nerve ending. A scream tried to erupt through teeth clenched so tight, Luke worried they'd shatter. Saubarag yanked his hand down, and Luke fell to his knees.

"Do you like that? Your weak little god friends missed something when they pulled out the spikes I left in you." He barked a sharp laugh. "It's been flowing through your veins. It's the reason you've grown so much since our last encounter. The reason you're able to dominate my children. It was my insidious little gift to you. Festering and metastasizing inside you. It won't be long until your soul will be as beautiful and dark as mine. Then, you'll belong to me wholly."

Tears burned from Luke's eyes. Roxi knelt next to him, stroking his hair and whispering calming words.

Saubarag lessened his grip slightly. The relief of slightly less pain was splendid. Luke gasped in several gulps of air before the twisted god gripped his fist again, forcing the air from his lungs in a ragged scream.

"Let him go!" Roxi screamed.

"Why? He is mine to do with as I will. But perhaps he'd be more willing to join me if you had already done so, my dear."

"I'd rather die." She spat on the ground and reached for her sword.

"No..." Luke groaned. Those words should never be spoken to a villain.

"That can be arranged." Saubarag yanked Luke out of the way, keeping him tightly contained, and shot out black tendrils at Roxi.

She leapt to her feet and drew her blade in one smooth motion, slashing at the nearest tendril, lopping the end of it off. The dismembered portion dissolved into smoke and dissipated. Her blade moved in fast, precise movements, carving off bits of the tendrils. But for every one she cut, two more replaced it as if she were fighting a hydra.

One wrapped itself around her ankle, and her blade arced down to slice it. But two had clamped onto her other wrist and a third had her other ankle. They pulled and ripped her off the ground. Screaming in fear and fury, she slashed at the dark ropes grasping her limbs, but soon another batch of tendrils grabbed her sword arm and shook her until she dropped it.

She punctuated her frustration and anger with screams as she tried to reach one of her other weapons. When she couldn't reach one, she tried to bend her body to bite at the tendrils. When she got too close, one lanced out and wrapped itself around her head, muzzling her.

Despite all her limbs being captured and her mouth blocked, she fought on, thrashing and tugging with all her might. Her chest expanded and contracted like billows working too hard, her desperate breath hissing and whistling in and out of her obstructed mouth and nose.

Saubarag laughed. "My, she's a feisty one, isn't she? I can see why you like her. It'll be a shame to destroy such a fine creature, but if she's no use to me, there's no reason for her existence to continue."

The dark god flung Roxi against the nearest wall. Her head slammed into it and she instantly stilled, slumping and dangling from Saubarag's creepy tentacles.

Finding a way to compartmentalize the pain being inflicted on him, he stared at Roxi, watching her chest and stomach to find out if she was still breathing. A drop of blood rolled out of her hairline and down her forehead to drip on the ground. It was joined by another and another…

Fury built inside of him, roiling in him like an explosion of flames, and he shoved the pain aside. Saubarag hadn't created him. The god hadn't made him more powerful. Luke was powerful. Luke was power.

The god, a smirk on his face, stared at the blood dripping, licking his lips. Fixated on his handiwork, Luke used the distraction, not sure when or if he'd get another shot at regaining control.

Gathering in all the energy he'd drained from the vampires, he built a brick against Saubarag's control and pain, then another. Each brick grew and strengthened the wall. The more Luke stared at Roxi's blood, the faster the work went until he'd surrounded himself in an impregnable fortress. Each breath combined with his will to add another brick.

Not used to working internally in such a manner, he needed a rest to catch his breath, though time was not a luxury he had. He hoped Saubarag was too involved with watching Roxi's corpse, so he wouldn't notice Luke marshaling his strength, the stolen essence from the vampires, and his fury. Whether he was truly ready or not, he had to go. Ragged energy buzzed inside him, the wall also keeping it in for the moment. Drawing in a deep breath, he forced himself upright onto his knees. Then lifted one knee to brace for the next movement.

Saubarag's attention snapped to Luke. It was now or never. Taking his gathered power, he pushed outwards with his mind in all directions, white hot light exploding throughout his body, burning and searing every nerve with a pure hot flame. A scream erupted from his mouth, shredding his throat as he momentarily lost himself in the cleansing flames, until it wheezed to a trickle of laughter.

Relief flooded through Luke as Saubarag's control over his body melted before the intensity coursing through his veins. Finally able to draw in a deep breath, he stoked the flames licking at the wall he'd constructed and poured in his rage at all the vile god had done to him.

Bits and pieces of the wall chipped away, turning brittle against the flames of his fury until it lost integrity and blasted outward in a surge of power. The black tentacles disintegrated before the fires of Luke's anger, and the wall of power smacked into the god, flinging him against the back wall.

Leaping up, Luke dashed over to Roxi, ignoring the slight wobble in his legs. In the short time he had, he looked her over for vital signs but saw nothing in the dark room. Fear started to wind its way around his heart, but he could do nothing about it with Saubarag ready to strike at any second. Closing his eyes for a split second, he shoved the fear aside. Fear was a keyhole Saubarag could pick, and Luke couldn't let him in again.

Wanting to keep the god off kilter, Luke dove back to where his gladius lay on the ground. Tucking and rolling, he snatched it up on the way by and came to his knees with the swords extended toward the god. The god's attention was firmly fixed on Luke. Jumping to his feet, he advanced.

"You've made the last mistake you'll ever make," Luke growled out.

"See how powerful you have become thanks to me." Saubarag straightened his tunic and strolled casually to the side, keeping the distance open between himself and Luke. "You are my creature. In time, you'll see it." He cackled, the noise high-pitched and unhinged. "You'll have no choice. It would be better if you came to me now and willingly. It would be less painful for you, and you'd retain more of yourself."

"I am not your creature! I am Lucius Silvanius Ferrata, Princeps Primus Centurio—first among centurions. Leader of the Black Legion." He took the stolen vampiric energy coursing through his veins and pushed it into the two blades he held. They ignited with buzzing flickering energy. "Beloved of Selene, a soldier of Sol Invictus and Mithras. And one of two spears of light defending against the darkness. I am the last Gaul. The last Roman."

With each word, the power vibrating over his sword crackled and surged. "I am my own man. I am Luke Irontree, the most feared vampire hunter ever. I am the wood-fanged demon—and more feared by your minions than you are. I am my own man, and your death I shall bring!"

Luke charged.

But before he could make contact, Saubarag blinked away, reappearing thirty yards away in full armor. In one hand, he bore a long sword in the other, a heavy mace. While the sword could cause some problems, the mace would crush his armor and shatter bones. But he didn't care. Saubarag had hurt Roxi and maybe... He couldn't finish the thought. The god would pay.

Luke ducked under the lumbering swing of the mace and parried the slash of the long sword. Throwing a shoulder into Saubarag's side, Luke came up close and dragged the blade of the rudis across the underside of the god's arm. Saubarag yowled in pain but threw his elbow backwards at Luke. Instead of ducking it, he shouldered it up so it was robbed it of most of its force as it slid over his helmet.

Pushing away with the shoulder he'd just used to deflect the blow, he smashed the gladius into the side of Saubarag's armor, leaving a deep dent and discoloration where the energy warped the metal. Instead of facing Luke, the god blinked out and reappeared, though blood still dripped from his arm and the dent still cratered in the side of his armor.

Tossing his blades into the air, he snatched them in the opposite hands so the rudis was in his right hand. Though it was a shorter blade, it more readily wanted to accept the power Luke forced into it. And while the gladius would also take the power, he doubted he had an infinite supply of it. The gladius would have to serve as his shield and weapon of opportunity.

Stalking forward, Luke pushed more power into the rudis, drops of lightning dripping from the edge to splatter on the ground into sparking pools and sending the scent of ozone into the air. The god's eyes shifted to the blade and the remnants of power spilling from it. Flicking the blade at the god, Saubarag jumped back as globs of silvery power flew toward him.

Luke sprinted forward, leading with the rudis held high and the gladius low and partially hidden behind his leg. Continuing to backpedal, Saubarag caught his heel, stumbled, and opened his arms to catch his balance. With a high thrust of the rudis at the god's visor-covered face—the god flinched back violently as he flailed for balance—Luke followed through with the gladius, aiming the tip at the gap between the chest armor and the plates covering the hips and waist.

The blade bit true, and Saubarag screamed in agony. Black smoke roiled from the wound, and Luke gagged on the stench of burnt, rotting flesh. But sound slammed into Luke, knocking him backward and dislodging the blade before he could go exploring in the god's internal organs. What blood had been on the blade hissed and sizzled as the coursing energy burned it away.

Luke laughed. "I assumed if you were going to dress as a warrior, you'd know what you're going. But like everything you do, it's all shadows and lies."

Saubarag growled, the sound reverberating through the chamber. A wave of fear washed over Luke, but he shook his head to clear it and pushed it away. More trickery. To spite the god, Luke flushed more power into the rudis and flicked its tip into the air, sending balls of silver lightning at the god.

Dancing to avoid them, the god bellowed when one found flesh. A putrid scent drifted from the burning flesh, causing Luke to gag again. Despite his body giving a half-hearted involuntary shiver of a retch, he pressed his advantage and thrust the gladius into the Saubarag's face to distract him. Prepared for it this time, he knocked the blade away with his heavy mace and countered with a thrust of the longsword.

Luke stepped into the thrust, twisting his body at the last second. Saubarag's blade skittered over Luke's armor, screeching with the contact. Though the god was ready for the first thrust, a repeat from an earlier attempt that had worked, he wasn't prepared for the lower thrust into the side of his guts.

Fired by Luke's fury and hatred for the dark god and the power burning along it, the rudis pierced the plate armor and found flesh to devour. A ghastly smoke billowed from the hole in the armor, gagging Luke. This time, he was prepared for the scream of pain and twisted the blade to add to it.

Saubarag momentarily faded to nearly invisible but snapped back to full substance. Bashing his head forward into Luke's helmeted forehead, the god brought up his knee into Luke's thigh, knocking him backward. The god screamed again as the blade withdrew from his body.

Luke had wounded the god badly, goading him into desperate measures. But he hadn't been able to blink away and reform. The rudis and its power had pinned the god in place. Not wanting to lose the advantage, Luke charged in, his legs a little wobbly from both blows. Tapping into his full speed, Luke thrust and slashed his sword, knocking aside the god's clumsy counters. The only thing that saved the god was his thick armor combined with his divine strength and speed, but Luke made contact with steel and flesh more times than not, and soon the god was breathing hard, dripping smoking blood, or whatever vile sludge flowed through his veins, from too many cuts to easily count. If Luke couldn't get the killing blow, he'd do it with a thousand cuts. Dead was dead.

Saubarag had other ideas. Bellowing, he swung his mace hard at neck height. Luke dropped to his knees as the most expedient way to avoid it without having to give up ground. Though the blows weren't powered with all his strength, Luke brought both blades into the sides of the god's knees.

With the momentum of his swing and the slashes to his knees, Saubarag collapsed, falling over Luke's shoulder. He shoved off a leg and pushed away from the falling god to avoid getting tangled or absorbing any wild blows. With a grunt of pain, Saubarag kicked out, but the attack had no power and his leg collapsed to the ground before it reached Luke.

Standing up, Luke lowered his gladius but kept his rudis pointed toward the god.

Saubarag dropped his mace and lifted his longsword with both hands, pointing it at Luke. "Please. Spare me. I'll give you anything…"

Luke's eyes flicked toward Roxi's body heaped in an ungainly pile against the wall. "You already took away the one thing I want."

Kicking out, he knocked aside Saubarag's longsword, flipped the rudis to a reverse grip, and surged forward, plunging the burning rudis into the god's chest, through his armor, and into his heart. The god convulsed and screamed.

Luke's eardrums popped, and he added his yell of pain to that of the god he'd just stabbed. He held on, tossing aside the gladius to bring both hands into contact with the handle of the rudis so the dark entity's convulsions wouldn't dislodge him. Sludge flowed around the blade, spilling over the armor and filling the air with its stench. The acrid smoke rising from the wound burned his lungs and eyes. He felt like his head would explode from the agony filled screams and waves of power pouring off the dying god, but he couldn't cover his ears or curl up in a ball for fear of the god reviving himself.

Instead, Luke grabbed the power he'd taken and dumped it into rudis. Saubarag's body thrashed harder and vented a noxious black smoke from his mouth and nose along with the wound. Careful to keep the blade in place, Luke crawled onto the god and straddled his waist, using his feet to keep Saubarag's legs from bucking as hard. Luke's arms burned from the exertion of keeping the rudis planted in the god's chest, and his hips groaned from clamping tightly against the death throes of the god.

He wasn't sure how long he sat there after the god stopped twitching, but he finally realized he could unclench his body. Rolling off the god, he slid into a pool of acrid smelling sludge as it evaporated. He'd have to burn these clothes. Scrambling to get away from it, he came to his knees. Seeing Roxi against the wall, he dashed to her, using all four limbs when necessary, in his animalistic effort to get to her faster.

Tears burning at the corners of his eyes, he straightened her out, rolling her over. He grabbed her wrist and checked her pulse but found nothing. He wasn't always the best at that method, and he was growing frantic. He placed his hand over her heart, then his ear, but pressing it to her scale mail-covered chest hurt his damaged ears. Still, he could find no signs of her life.

Scooping her into his arm, he stroked her hair, panic beginning to take hold. "Help..." he mumbled. "Please... Selene... My Mistress."

Selene. She could help. She had to.

"Please, My Mistress. I need you. It's Roxi..." He cast the words into the ether. Pulling on his power, he repeated the message with amplification.

A faint shimmering blur appeared in the middle of the room. The silver blur pulsed, getting stronger, then weaker. Finally, it burst into a radiant explosion of silvery light. When Luke's eyes cleared, Selene stood in the center of the room.

"Lucius, what is it? Oh... Oh, no..." Selene swept across the room. Touching Roxi, she examined her body. "Lucius. I... I don't think I can do anything. But we have to release her. Whatever Saubarag did, her soul is trapped inside of her body."

The air froze in Luke's lungs. He couldn't. He wouldn't believe it. He needed Roxi. He'd gone to hell and back and threatened a god to save her. He couldn't lose her now. Not when they were so close to the life they wanted.

Luke eye's homed in on the body of Saubarag, his rudis sticking out of its chest. He stared at it, a possibility sparking to life in the dark recesses of his heart. Gently pushing Roxi's body toward Selene, he handed her over to the goddess, then scrambled to the god's body.

Wrapping his hands around the rudis, he lowered his forehead to the pommel.

"Lucius, no! You can't handle that much power."

He didn't care. He'd rather die trying to save Roxi than not try and live. As he finished the incantation, a massive light burst from Saubarag's chest, forcing Luke to clamp his eyes shut. The power vibrated up the blade shaking like an earthquake. As soon as the power touched Luke's head, a connection was made between their bodies, the rudis functioning as jumper cable. He gripped with all his might on the rudis as it shook violently, the power slamming into him.

The power roared through his head like a jet engine. His body vibrated so hard he thought it might dissolve into its component atoms and fly apart. Standing, he stopped to stabilize himself. With his first step, he nearly collapsed. He could barely see. Sweat flooded from his pores, dribbling down his skin. He felt like his blood boiled and his organs cooked. Another step.

He had to lock his knees to keep from falling, lifting one weak leg to transfer his weight to the other and back again. Losing the power to control his knees, he collapsed but crawled forward on three limbs, cradling the rudis to his chest.

"What have you done?" Selene whispered.

"Her… rudis…" he rasped out.

The goddess looked confused, but she pulled Roxi's rudis from its scabbard.

Once he judged he was close enough, he let his body do what it wanted, and he collapsed to the ground, landing on his chest. He reached out, his hand shaking violently, and took the rudis from Selene by the blade. It bit deep into his flesh. He gripped harder, fearing he'd lose his hold because of the violent tremble and the slickness of his blood.

"Hold her hands…on the handle."

"Lucius, please… You can't do this," Selene pleaded.

"Please, I need her." His voice rasped out over battered vocal cords as trembles pulsed over his body at random intervals. It was all he could do to get the words out. "Please try."

Though Selene was nothing but a silvery blur in his failing vision, he held her gaze, trying to pour his desperation into it.

Selene nodded, picking up Roxi's hands and clasping them around the handle of her rudis. Letting go of his own rudis and lifting his other hand, Luke tried to grip the other side of the blade but missed, overshooting it. Careful to not move too quickly, he ran his hand down his other arm until it met the wood of the rudis, then he slid it down and gripped the blade tightly. He didn't have to move his hand to cut. The uncontrolled shaking did it for him.

"I'm going to have to cut one of her hands."

He nodded, moving a hand to make room. With a quick efficient move, Selene slide Roxi's palm up the blade, then returned it to the pommel.

"Can you move so we can place the pommel on her head?" Selene asked, her voice gentle but filled with pain. "Quickly."

Selene tugged the blade up toward Roxi's head. Forcing himself onto three limbs, he kept his grip on the rudis and moved forward. His body almost beyond control, he let gravity do the work and fell over Roxi, settling into her side. He gripped the blade desperately, afraid to lose contact with the only hope he had.

Tilting Roxi's head up with one hand, Selene pressed Roxi's forehead into the pommel of the rudis while still keeping one hand wrapped around the hands on the handle.

"Focus," Selene said.

As his thoughts buzzed around like a drunken bee, he tried to bring his will to bear on the rudis blade in his hands and the power quickly eating away at his body and mind.

A surge like electricity tingled his palms as Selene brought her power to bear. Roxi's body jolted as if hit by a defibrillator. Blinking hard to focus his eyes, he stared at her chest, waiting for it to inflate with air and rise.

"Again," he mumbled.

Focus. He'd overcome the vile god of the vampires, he could do it again. He felt the surge of Selene's power and, like before, nothing happened.

"Lucius—"

"No! Again!" he slurred.

Roxi's face flashed through his mind. Her kind smile. The laughter in her eyes. The joy of their love. Her warm, callused hand squeezing his. The feel of her body in his arms. The vibrancy of her laughter.

Holding onto all they'd shared and the future he hoped to build with her, he reached out for the power, trying to rot his soul and grabbed it by the metaphorical throat.

"Now!" he gritted out between clenched teeth.

This time, the tingle in his hands was a roaring inferno, extending down his arms and into his chest. His heart thumped fast and hard as if it were about to explode in his chest.

A dark pain exploded in his gut as the last remnants of Saubarag rebelled against Luke's control. Every muscle in his body contracted into a massive full body cramp, and his lungs ceased to pull in air, instead squeezing out what was there in a rising scream until he felt like his vocal cords would rip.

Next to him, Roxi's body shook violently. Her body arched, only her shoulders and heels touching the ground. She drew in a shuddering breath, then coughed, a whimper escaping her lips.

"Lucius, stop. Lucius. You have to release," the goddess pleaded. "Luke, please. Unclench."

"Luke…" Roxi whispered.

Grunting, he forced his hands to open. Selene yanked the rudis away, disconnecting him from Roxi and the goddess. His body sagged into a muscleless puddle as he gasped desperately for oxygen, his lungs heaving and his heart pounding to circulate blood to his depleted body. And he did feel depleted.

He'd given everything to this fight. All the power he'd drained from the vampires had been pushed into his swords and Saubarag, then all the power he'd taken from the god had been used to save Roxi. What he had left was all Luke. For the first time in a long time, his body had nothing vampiric powering it. He felt empty, but in a way that felt clean and wholesome. He'd recover and be himself.

Gently setting Roxi's head down, Selene looked around for a moment before stopping and closing her eyes. Her face fixed into a mask of concentration and some clean bandages filled her hand. Taking a pot of salve, she spread it across Luke's sliced up hands, then wrapped his hands with the bandages.

"It's not as fast as draining a vampire, but we seem to be suddenly short on vampires. It'll work to close the cuts, though." She moved some sweaty hair from his forehead. "You did it, my brave soldier. You saved her."

He nodded, still unable to get enough air to satisfy his body. He mouthed, "thank you," to the goddess.

Roxi, breathing heavily herself, rolled over onto her hands and knees and crawled to Luke. A sheen of sweat covered her face. She collapsed into the space between his body and his arm, resting her head on his shoulder as she wrapped her body around his.

"We did it, dōšagīh." She chuckled weakly. "You killed a god."

Allowing them to have a moment of privacy, Selene stood and walked over to the prone body of the god who'd dominated their lives for so long and squatted down beside his head. Saubarag no longer looked slick and handsome, reverting to his original form—weak chin, greasy hair, and a thin, scraggly beard—the lying sneak thief.

Raising her face upwards, Selene drew in a deep breath, a calm placidity washing over her face. A moment later, the dark cavern filled with a bright golden light, forcing them to clench their eyelids shut against it. When the dots dancing in his vision cleared, Sol Invictus had joined them, standing over the body of the dead god.

"He created so much trouble and despair just to aggrandize himself," Sol said, shaking his head. "At least it's done."

"You felt it, too?" Selene asked.

Sol nodded. "There are still a few vampires in the world. I don't know how they managed to break free of Saubarag's grasp, but that's a curiosity for another day. Is there anything left of this piece of filth?"

"No. Not after being twice distributed and filtered through two rudises. His essence is gone and all that remains is this husk." She grabbed Luke's rudis and handed it to Sol.

Concentrating, he turned the blade over in his hands as he stared at it. He nodded, then set it down next to Luke's hand. "It's still laced with the compulsion. I fear for our hunters without a ready supply of vampires."

Selene pursed her lips, nodding. "We'll have to deal with this."

Sol nodded. "Shall we call him?"

"Yes, let's get this over with." Selene rose and extended her hand to her brother. He took it and they both closed their eyes.

A moment later, Mithras appeared in the room, choosing to appear taller than the other two deities.

"Mithras. It is done," Sol said.

The god removed his Phrygian helmet and ran a hand through his dark, curly hair as he squatted down next to the body of Saubarag. Closing his eyes, he laid his hand on the dead god's forehead and focused, wrinkles radiating out from the corners of his eyes.

"This is naught but an empty shell." He opened his eyes and stood.

"Lucius drained the god's body and used the energy to revive Roxiustana," Selene said. "Saubarag's life force has been distributed and there is no more. He is forever gone from this world."

Nodding, Mithras stepped over to Roxi and Luke, squatting down next to their heads. He looked over to Sol. "Dispose of that pile of offal."

Sol reached down, placing his hands on each side of Saubarag's head. A whiff of smoke drifted toward Luke as flames spread over the dead god's body.

Reaching down, Mithras placed his hands on Luke's and Roxi's foreheads. Luke's eyes shot wide as pain seared through his body. Next to him, Roxi twitched, then convulsed.

Selene's eyes flashed wide, and her jaw dropped. "No!"

The world around Luke grew hazy and gray. The last thought Luke had before the world around him disappeared was that their master had betrayed them.

CHAPTER
THIRTY-TWO

Floating to surface on the rage and indignation that after all they'd done in the name of Mithras's mission, the god had betrayed them at the moment of their victory, stealing them away from the basement in Washington and the protection of Selene and Sol Invictus.

A gentle squeezing in his left hand told him that he wasn't alone, and relief flooded through him, pushing aside the anger. Tipping one eye open a crack, he waited for the blaring white uniformity to resolve into a vision of the battlefield they'd just fought on. It didn't.

Opening the other eye and lifting his head, it took him a while to realize he was in a white void. He couldn't make out walls or a ceiling or even a floor. The only thing not conforming to the white emptiness was Roxi lying next to him, unmoving.

Luke sighed in relief when he saw her stir, her long black eyelashes fluttering before her eyes opened.

"Lu…Luke? Where are we?" Roxi asked.

"I don't know. How do you feel?"

"Weird, shouldn't I be hurting? I remember falling pretty hard."

He hadn't thought of that, the oddity of the situation overwhelming any other thoughts. "Yeah, we hit hard. I'm going to try to sit up." He rolled enough to push himself into a sitting position while still holding Roxi's hand, afraid if he let go, they might be separated.

Roxi turned her head to look at Luke, a thick eyebrow arched. "Well?"

"I didn't feel much when I sat up, but if I think about it there's something around the edge, like the beginnings of pain or stiffness." Luke focused in on it, feeling more of it.

"If you don't feel anything until you think about it, don't think about it." She tugged lightly on his hand. "Help me sit up."

He braced and pulled, aiding her quest for seated verticality. She wore the same dirty clothes covered in mud and blood she'd had on moments ago in the basement. Looking down, he wore jeans and had his hoodie over his armor. As Roxi shifted around some, he could hear the rustle of her scale mail under her padded outer coat.

"What is this place?" Roxi asked, her head moving around slowly as she tried to take it all in.

"I wish I knew..." He tried squinting, but they were the only thing in the clean white void.

"Are we... Did we die? Are we in the afterlife?" It sounded like she was feeling around the edges of the concept.

"I don't think so, but then again, I've never been dead before." He didn't want to be dead, not when there was a life to build in a new world with his friends. His stomach clenched slightly and his breathing shallowed. "Do you feel the presence of Selene or Sol?"

She shook her head. "I don't feel anything but your hand in mine."

"Should we look around? Investigate?" He kept his face pointed toward Roxi's but looked around with his eyes as if he could catch sight of something in the corner of his eye if he were sneaky enough.

He started to roll onto his knees, but Roxi tightened her grip on his hand.

"Don't let go of me." The note of panic in her voice was matched by his own.

He nodded and carefully pushed himself up, still hunched over enough to keep his hand in hers. Reaching out, he took her other hand and helped her to her feet. Stepping into him, she pressed her body against his.

"It's disorienting," she said, looking at the ground. "I can feel something under my feet, but I can't see anything. We could be floating in the middle of…wherever, or there could be something there."

She bent her knees and bounced as if testing the solidity of the floor. Next, she lifted her left foot, closed her eyes, and reached out with the raised left foot, squatting some on her right leg while holding onto Luke tightly. He looked down, seeing her wiggle her foot around without meeting any resistance. She squatted lower, and a pit opened in his gut as he watched. With a small scream, she lunged toward him, grabbing onto him tightly, her breathing panicked and ragged. Luke tried to keep his breathing in check as adrenaline surged through his veins.

"There is a floor…there is a floor…there is a floor…" she repeated over and over to herself in a low voice, holding her left foot in the air

Ready to lunge after her if needed, he held his breath. Tentatively, she pushed her left foot down, finding purchase.

"What did you do?" Luke asked once his breathing calmed some.

"I was afraid there wasn't a floor under that foot and when I lowered it, there wasn't. I guess I leaned down a little too hard and lost my balance."

"Is there floor under your foot now?" He looked down at her foot —it appeared to be standing on something solid.

She nodded weakly.

"OK, so we need to always make sure there's a floor to stand on in our thoughts."

She nodded more vigorously.

Concentrating, Luke brought an image of solid stone to his mind —thick and stable—then pushed it under them and out. When he looked down, they were standing on a rock floor about ten feet in diameter.

"You can open your eyes, Roxi. We're standing on stone now." He squeezed her reassuringly.

Looking down, she gasped. "Did you do that?"

"Yup. I thought of stone and then put it there."

"This is bloody weird. I don't like it."

Luke snorted. "That's a fucking understatement."

"Now what?" Roxi asked, looking out into the distance.

Luke closed his eyes again and imagined what he wanted, constructing in his mind's eye down to the last detail. Opening them again, he looked to the right and saw the moving sidewalk trailing off into the distance, its conveyor belt moving steadily away from their current position, an infinite line in an endless white void.

Roxi laughed. "I guess it saves us from having to walk."

"Just one more detail." She closed her eyes, squeezing them tightly.

Rails popped up on both sides of the sidewalk with a runner along the top of both sides moving at the same pace as the sidewalk's floor. He laughed, kissing her forehead, feeling more secure about being surrounded by an infinite maw of nothingness.

"I mean, it's you and me, but safety third, right?" Roxi smirked.

Though he avoided thinking about possible injuries or pain, seeing the state of his clothes forced on him the feeling of damp clothes and the smell of blood and mud. Seeing if he could affect a wardrobe change, he closed his eyes. When he opened them, he looked like the Princeps Primus Centurio once again.

From the ground up, he had on a set of calligae, his ornate greaves, a black tunic that dropped to a few inches above his knees, the tasseled under armor padding, his singulum, and his lorica segmentata. His favorite phelera, attached to a leather harness, covered his chest. Over it all, he wore the black cloak with the black bear fur shoulders Marcus Aurelius had given him. Each side of the cloak was linked with a gold chain with Aurelius's seal on each side. His gladius and rudis hung from a baldric over his left hip.

"You look magnificent, Roman. Now it's my turn."

He watched as her clothing sloughed off and was replaced. She wore baggy dark red trousers—tucked into a rich dark brown leather soft-soled boots—covered in delicate, colorful embroidery that featured flowers and plants with mythical creatures intermixed.

Her scale mail gleamed, the bronze at the sleeves, hem, and neckline glowing. The sleeves of a long tunic poked out of the ends of her scale sleeves. The embroidered motif continued. Around her neck and draping over her shoulders, she wore a blue shawl the color of lapis lazuli. Likewise, it was embroidered in a delicate botanical theme. Around her waist, she had a sash that matched the color of her trousers, her sword's grip poking above the sash at her left side.

Still holding her hand, Luke bowed before. "You look spectacular, my lady."

Roxi chuckled. "'My lady'? My, aren't we being formal?"

"Just showing my regard for the woman I love." Underneath, the constant, never-ending blank void tugged at his awareness, but for a moment, he could center himself and appreciate the image Roxiustana chose to present to him.

"You're very sweet." Her eyes flicked toward the moving sidewalk, then looked around nervously. "Aren't we being a bit blasé? Shouldn't we be more terrified about where we're at and what's going on?"

"I thought all us hero types were supposed to be unafraid and too cool?" Maybe if he said it, he'd believe it too.

"But you and I aren't those kinds of people." She rested her head against his chest. After a moment, she blew out air, then snurfled before raising her head. "I inhaled bear fur. This cloak is really quite dashing, but it's tickling my nose." She sighed and looked deep into Luke's eyes, fear pouring from them and connecting with the same emotion in his. "Because I'm scared, Luke, really scared."

"You're right. We aren't those kinds of people. I'm just trying to hold it all together, Roxi." His hand trembled slightly as he raised it to caress her cheek. He gripped it into a fist to steady it before touching her soft cheek. "Inside, I'm terrified of where we're at. If we're dead, I don't really want to be here. After all this time alone, I have a family and community to live for. If we're not dead, where are we and what awaits? Maybe I'm trying to bravado myself into courage."

"You've never been short on courage, but I do appreciate the effort. It's always nice to get a compliment." She sighed, her eyes tracing the line of the moving walkway and never wavering to the side as it trailed off into the distance. "Shall we?"

They stepped back from each other, but Roxi gripped his hand tighter.

"Just don't let go of my hand, Luke."

"I need your hand in mine as much as you need mine."

Together they stepped onto the walkway, letting it carry them into the distance and into the unknown, unchanging white void.

CHAPTER
THIRTY-THREE

L uke was unsure about how long they rode their silent, moving walkway, but Roxi's hand never left his. He couldn't tell which was causing him anxiety—the possibility of finding something or the fact that he still hadn't seen anything they hadn't created themselves.

"Are we going the wrong direction?" Roxi said, breaking the silence.

"I don't know. We're in a three-dimensional space. We could be going in any direction—wrong, right, or parallel."

The conveyor belt slowed and stopped. Turning, they faced each other.

"Have you tried reaching out to Selene?" Roxi asked.

He shook his head. "I have not." He sighed. "I guess I've gotten used to relying on her as a last resort, and despite the weirdness and my fear, it doesn't seem desperate."

Roxi laughed. "How messed up are our lives that an infinite void isn't desperate enough to cause us to call for help? Selene loves you and has to be worried about what happened."

"You know, she loves you, too. She'd respond to your call."

Roxi blushed. "It is a weird thing to be beloved of a goddess. And though I do believe you, you are her chosen favorite. You carry out her will on the earth. It is through you that she accepted me."

"Don't think so low of yourself. You do her works as well, Roxi. She accepted you because you are worthy of her love all on your own. You didn't need me. It is through your strength that she has regained a large portion of her own strength." He grazed his fingers along her jaw to raise her head up.

"I do need you, but I understand what you're saying. Together?" She held out her other hand.

Taking her hand, Luke kissed her forehead, then straightened, closed his eyes, and called to Selene. *"My Mistress, can you hear me?"*

He waited, sending out his presence along the connection he could always feel—like a string—when he called to the moon goddess. Concentrating, he felt the gentle touch along the connection, though it felt strained, as if either the string was overly taught or not taught enough.

"My brave soldier? I can feel you, Lucius, but there's a barrier or something pushing us apart."

The sound of her voice in his head felt distant and somewhat distorted.

"Roxi, did you reach her?"

She nodded. "But it's weak.

He leaned forward, resting his forehead against hers. "Focus with me on Selene. Focus through me. I need to boost our connection."

"I can feel you, Lucius. And Roxiustana, too." Selene's voice sounded clearer with Roxi's aid. *"I think I can find you now."*

Relief flooded through him, loosening the knot in his stomach slightly. Then, he felt a heavy presence push against his brain. *"Will you come to us? We are lost in an endless, empty void."*

"I will, but give me some time. There is something of keen importance I must attend to you before venturing into your void," Selene replied.

"Thank you, My Mistress." Luke could feel Roxi sending her thanks along the connection the three of them shared. "Could you hear her?"

"Yes," Roxi said. "And feel her alongside you." She looked

around. "Can we wait somewhere besides this conveyor belt? I feel like sushi waiting to be selected."

Luke chuckled. "Sure. Build us a place, and I'll connect our walkway to it."

Roxi concentrated, looking off in the distance behind Luke. When he turned, he saw an island come into existence, thin and insubstantial, until it pulsed one last time before solidifying completely. It wasn't a huge island, but in its center stood a large tree. With a brief thought, Luke split off a sideline to their island. It was becoming easier for him to control things inside the void the more he worked at it.

"What kind of tree is that?" Luke asked.

"Persian Ironwood. I was always fond of them. They always meant I was getting close to home, to Parthia." She squeezed his hands and led him to their island.

The tree had a large canopy created by multiple stems covered in smooth, pinkish-brown bark that peeled in places, leaving patches of various colors ranging from greens to cinnamon. The foliage was a bright, rich green made of oval leaves.

"Do you think we have time to sit in the shade?" Roxi asked.

"I don't know, but we're spry enough as long as we don't get distracted or fall asleep." Luke helped Roxi to the ground, then joined her.

Together, they stared off in the distance, trying to cover as wide of field of vision as they could. He couldn't tell if it would be easier to spot something new in the endless white void or if the monotonous sameness would dull his mind and cause him to miss anything. When the leaves rustled above him, he looked up sharply, his breathing and pulse quickening.

"Sorry about that. Just thought about how nice it would be to have a breeze move through the leaves." Roxi looked apologetic before looking up. The sound of the leaves rubbing against each other and the branches groaning delicately washed over her, a serene mask settling over her face.

Luke closed his eyes for a moment and let the peaceful moment soak into his being. "It's lovely, Roxi. Though if thoughts become real that quickly, we'll have to be disciplined about what we think."

She nodded. "But the breeze *is* nice."

Their oasis didn't erase all the tension in the back of his neck, but he felt more in tune with himself and with the woman sitting next to him as he scanned the horizon for any sign of the goddess or anything at all. What could be taking her so long? She'd always appeared quickly.

"I've been thinking," Roxi said. "What would Selene have to do before finding us?"

"I was thinking the same thing. I don't—"

"Luke..." Roxi trailed off, pointing into the far distance.

Following the direction of her finger, he squinted, trying to make out what she might have seen. Finally, he settled on something that looked like a small flaw in the distant, unmarred void. At first, it looked like a speck or perhaps an insect, except it didn't flit about in random patterns on its unknown mission. It gradually increased into a larger, darker spot, steadily moving toward them. Luke stood and helped Roxi up.

"I wish I had a bow," Roxi said, unable to take her eyes away from the approaching smudge.

"Then wish for one."

She snorted. "Of course."

"No worries. Nothing about this makes sense, yet here we are." He wished for a pilum and a moment later, one appeared in his hands.

Roxi pulled a strung recurve bow from a bow case strapped to her left hip along with a handful of arrows, holding them all in her left hand.

"I'm going to let go of your hand," Luke said, not wanting to just tug it out without warning.

"Yeah, it'll be hard to shoot with only one hand, though I could try drawing with my teeth." She clacked her teeth for him to see.

"Four out of five dentists do not approve of that method of drawing a bow."

Roxi laughed, the free sound bringing a small smile to his lips. "I do love you, Luke, and no matter what is coming, I'm glad you're by my side. There's no one else I'd rather have by me."

He pulled her into a fierce, passionate kiss, then stepped back. Staring into her eyes, he tried to match the love he saw there, then dipped his head to kiss her again. They had a moment, and who knew what approached on the horizon, so he'd use the time to express his love for her. When they finally pulled back, it was with regret and longing in their eyes. They smiled at each other, then nodded, their faces returning to business mode.

They turned and found the spot moving toward them. With a quick thought, his helmet appeared on his head, the long black hair of the transverse crest caught in the wind and floated behind him. In his left hand, he created a broad scutum painted black save for a silvery white crescent moon in the middle. A few eight-pointed stars were scattered about the black field. Likewise, Roxi had manifested a helmet on her head, though hers was pointed with a red tail streaming out of the top spike. Around it, she'd wound a blue scarf of the same shade as her shawl that draped down over her neck and formed a veil, though he could see a mail veil peeking out of the top and bottom of the scarf covering her face. They were ready to face whoever approached.

Stepping forward, Luke hefted the shield and prepared to defend Roxi so she could fire her bow unmolested until it was time to hurl his pilum at his enemy and draw sword for close combat. He took a quick glance back to make sure no one else was coming up from behind. Nothing.

Nervous sweat dripped down his back as they waited. He tried to relax his muscles, but he couldn't manage it. This unmarked world was too eerie and deserted. Gripping his pilum, he picked it up, testing its haft and weight. Its balance was perfect.

"When will it be in range?" Luke asked.

"I have no idea. It's nearly impossible to mark distance with no landmarks to compare them to."

"Try a shot and see what happens?" he suggested, nervous that he couldn't control his surroundings to his satisfaction.

"I guess so..." She stepped back and angled her bow to forty-five degrees, releasing the arrow. It shot into the sky, a bright bolt of light sizzling around the edges. They reminded him a bit of how his swords had behaved in the fight against Saubarag. It continued up into the void until it disappeared. "Huh. Wasn't expecting that."

She flattened her arc and aimed. With a twang, the arrow shot forward, screaming toward the blip in the distance. It was hard to tell against the constant white of their surroundings, but it appeared to miss to the left of the growing speck.

"You missed."

"No. It went where I intended it to. We don't know if they're friend or foe. I'd rather not turn the former into the latter by skewering them with an arrow, especially nasty ones like these."

He nodded. "Fair enough." Sighing, he spun the pilum before returning its butt to the ground. "So we wait."

"Looks like it."

Since there seemed to be no immediate rush, he sat down facing whoever was slowly approaching their position. At that pace, they'd have enough warning to get up. Roxi joined him, sitting to his right.

He had no idea how long they'd been waiting—there was no sun or moon to mark the passage of time—but it was definitely making a straight line for them.

"Is that… Are those oxen?" Roxi asked, standing up and shading her eyes with her hand.

He got to his feet and squinted into the distance. "I can't quite tell. Your eyesight must be a bit better than mine."

"Yeah. It's oxen."

Luke relaxed. "It's Selene. She often uses an oxen-pulled chariot."

"I don't know if it's time to relax yet. It could be anyone using her image. We imagined our gear into being. Someone else could be using a form pleasing to our eyes so they can get in close."

She was right. He'd apologize to Selene later if their greeting was a bit on the frostier side than the goddess deserved.

He sighed, pursing his lips. "So back to nervous waiting. I hate waiting."

Roxi chuckled. "Isn't that most of what being a soldier is about? Waiting for something or the other?"

"Yeah. But when I was a common legionnaire, complaining to my comrades about waiting was my right, but no one cared. As a commander, you rarely get to complain about anything as mundane as waiting since you have to maintain a certain façade of dignity. Now. I can do what I want. And I feel like complaining about waiting."

"Nervous?" she asked.

"Yeah. Aren't you?"

She nodded. A smirk on her face, she leaned over and kissed his cheek. "Complain away, my handsome man."

"If nothing else, it's something to do."

He wasn't sure if they'd managed to keep their minds occupied, or if the approaching figure was now moving faster, or somehow, the distance had shrunk the nearer they came to meeting. But either way, he could clearly see Selene holding the reins of the chariot as the oxen plodded along. One of the beasts gleamed white while the other looked a gray smudge next to its companion. The chariot glowed with a silver aura that highlighted the crescent moon at the center of the vehicle.

While the chariot and oxen were the same he'd seen before, Selene had eschewed her normal raiment and was geared for war. She wore a Corinthian-style helmet with its wide cheek guards and nose guard. On top, a silver crest ran from front to back. Her silver cuirass featured her crescent moon and stars. Strapped to the left side of her chariot, a large, round shield protected her side. He could see the handle of a sword peeking above the rim of the chariot but couldn't tell what kind of blade she favored. A bundle of spears and javelins rested on the other side of the chariot, ready to be brought to hand.

Raising his scutum, Luke stepped in front of Roxi, standing tall to block as much of her as possible. He'd have to rely on his greaves to protect his lower legs and his helmet to protect his face and head since he couldn't crouch behind the thick wood of his shield.

"Identify yourself and state your business," Luke called out loudly.

"I am Selene, goddess of the moon, and I come to your aid, Lucius and Roxiustana." She raised her hand and sent out a gentle silvery beam that floated toward them.

The closer it got, the more sure he was that it was indeed his mistress and patron. Once the silver beam stopped in front of his face, he could feel the goddess's love and protection. He'd felt it countless times over his almost two millennia and knew it as well as he knew himself. Relief flooded through his veins and his shoulders dropped a bit, though the knot in his stomach still remained. He wouldn't have to fight her, but that didn't mean there would be no fight in his near future.

Lowering his shield, he dropped to one knee and bowed his head. "My Mistress, please forgive my wariness."

Roxi lowered her bow and joined Luke.

"Rise, my children. You are wise to be cautious. No offense has been taken." Pulling back on the reins, she dismounted and removed her helmet. Brutus in his Gampr dog form hopped out from behind the goddess, his tongue lolling out.

Luke shook his head, reminding himself it was Tutyr. He'd just gotten used to that dog form being Brutus. As if the thought of his true name called him, the dog shimmered and grew taller until Tutyr stood before them in bronze scale mail over brown trousers made from a rough weave. He had a double-headed battle axe strapped to his back. He reached into a pouch on his belt and pulled out a handful of his favorite kibble and popped some in his mouth, crunching them noisily with a grin on his face.

Roxi stashed her arrows but left her bow strung. "Where are we?"

"This is an in-between place. A place of power." Selene nodded toward Luke and Roxi. "I see you've already learned to harness some of that power. But be careful. It can also be a place of illusions and lies. You were right to question our appearance, critical thinking and a healthy dose of caution will stand you in good stead."

Luke nodded. "Now what? Why are we here? I'm assuming you

didn't bring us here to this 'in between place.' The last thing I remember is Mithras touching my head. Did he bring us here? Do we just wait until our host shows up?"

"No, I didn't bring you here, but I can feel a power off that way. And to answer your second question, I don't know why you were brought here or what Mithras's intentions are toward you, if he indeed is the one who brought you here. Though, if it's hostile, he may have made a mistake allowing you here. Your minds are strong and disciplined."

She chucked her chin off to the side. "Roxi, you shall ride next to me. Your bow will be best used there. Lucius, Tutyr. You ride behind us so you can dismount quickly."

"Aye, My Mistress," Luke said, grabbing his shield.

Tutyr nodded. Placing her helmet back on, Selene climbed into the chariot and Roxi followed. Once they were settled, Luke and Tutyr stepped onto the back of the chariot, gripping the side railing to hold themselves steady as the goddess flicked the reins to start her great oxen moving.

Luke had never ridden to war in a chariot. It was antiquated technology long before he joined the legions. They were pretty much only used for ceremonies and racing. He'd also never done so with two gods. This was a new experience, and a weird one at that. Choosing to hold on to the wonder of the riding to war with gods in a chariot, he could return to worry and tension if needed in a moment's notice. He was an expert at that.

With his left hand holding steady on the rail, he longed for the feel of his gladius in his right, but it was currently occupied by the pilum. Closing his eyes, he transformed the space where his hand rested on the shaft so it matched the feel of gladius. It wasn't quite the same but would do until it was time to draw blade and join battle.

He didn't know what awaited them, but he'd be ready to defend his goddess and his love. Together, they could meet any challenge. Together, they could overcome who or whatever had drawn them into this white void.

CHAPTER
THIRTY-FOUR

"There!" Roxi pointed ahead and just off center.

Leaning into the middle to look between Roxi and Selene, he had to squint to even see the tiny dark speck in the distance. Though, unlike Selene and her chariot, whatever approached was coming toward them at a far faster speed.

"Tutyr, let's get off here and walk alongside the chariot," Luke said.

"Right. No sense being out of position," he replied, hopping into the air and landing on the ground behind the chariot. He grabbed his axe off his back.

Luke chose to step off cautiously instead of trying to match the god's panache. Adjusting his grip on his scutum and pilum, he jogged out to the left side of the goddess's chariot.

By now, the distant speck had grown enough that Luke could make out its odd gait as it ran toward them. It didn't look like the smooth stride of a horse on the run. His eyes flicking to the oxen pulling the chariot, realization dawned on him. He'd seen a few charging bulls over the years. This definitely matched his memories, though the shape looked slightly off—taller and narrower on top. A rider. Someone was charging toward them on a massive bull.

Licking his lips, he returned to a jog and moved up until he'd drawn equal to the head of the oxen pulling the chariot. "What's our play?"

"Roxi, a warning shot, if you please," Selene said casually, though her voice sounded slightly distorted as she spoke through her helmet.

In one smooth motion, Roxi pulled an arrow and released it toward the oncoming bull and rider. The arrow sizzled through the air, narrowly missing the rider's head by a couple feet. If it had been any other archer, he'd have chalked up the brilliant shot as luck, but Roxi had nearly two thousand years of experience with a bow and was using the magical one for all it was worth.

"That doesn't seem to have dissuaded him," the goddess said. "A little closer."

"If I try to get much closer, he'll be able to pick his teeth with it." Roxi grabbed another arrow.

"If the rider won't desist, perhaps his beast. Put it in his shoulder. I'll create the angle." Selene flicked the reins sharply, and the oxen surged forward.

They didn't gain momentum like a normal animal of their size, slowly and at a rumbling gait, but instantly. Before the rider could adjust his aim, Selene had taken them toward the left, leaving Luke and Tutyr behind.

Luke returned to a jog, keeping his path straight at the rider and its bull. Tutyr flared out to the right, adding a slight angle to his forward movement.

The bull bellowed, tossing its head as Roxi's arrow plunged into its front right shoulder. Reaching down, the rider yanked it free, the bull screaming again, and tossed it aside. The charge only faltered slightly before returning to its previous gait.

Selene and Roxi had outflanked the bull and rider as they dashed past each other. The goddess was in the process of bringing the chariot around and had put them in an awkward position for Roxi to effectively fire.

Tossing the pilum up, he reversed his grip and snatched it from the air then jogged faster, bringing his arm back and taking aim. When he judged his speed and the angle right, he hurled it into the air. It flew straight and true.

Slowing after his throw, Luke willed another pilum into his hand as the one he'd thrown reached the apex of its arc and descended toward its target. If the bull's rider had brought them here thinking them unable to tap into the power of the place, he'd made a serious mistake. Luke hoped it was arrogance and not that something nastier waited.

Focused entirely on his pilum, Luke stopped, his jaw dropped as the heavy pyramidal point plunged into the forehead of the massive bull. Its steady charge faltered at first with a slightly off step, then a stumble, then it fell forward onto its chin, the momentum hurling the rider off its back. The gigantic bull slid to a stop, dead.

Tutyr barked out a laugh. "Good throw!"

Shaking his head at his companion, Luke had to remind himself that the bull wasn't the only source of danger. Raising his shield and preparing the pilum, he stalked forward toward the heap that was the rider.

At first, Luke thought the rider must have been killed by the throw, breaking his neck in the fall. But movement told him otherwise.

A tall figure wearing a bright blue cloak pushed itself up, dusting itself off. When it stood straight, Luke recognized him immediately. It was Mithras—the god who'd turned Luke into a vampire hunter. The god who'd enslaved Luke and Roxi to the power of the rudis which forced them to hunt vampires whether they wished to or not. The god Luke had served loyally only to be abandoned when he needed the god to save Roxi.

"Why have you brought us here, my Lord? We have slain your enemy and destroyed the vampires' power." Even though Luke didn't feel respect for the god anymore, he could still show respect to avoid making matters worse. He moved the pilum to his left hand, setting it in a clip on the back of the scutum in hopes the gesture would be seen as a move toward nonaggression. Though he had no idea what the situation was now that Mithras was there.

"Now it's 'my Lord'? You weren't so respectful last time we spoke, mortal," Mithras said, voice low and deadly.

"Respect is a two-way street. It was given for a long time, but you neglected to return it. Especially when you were needed. If I hadn't challenged you then, we wouldn't have completed your mission. I could not have done it without Roxiustana Surena. Together, with the aid of divine Selene and Tutyr, we have ended the tyranny of Saubarag. His creatures are no more. We have fulfilled our oaths to you."

Mithras barked out a laugh devoid of humor. "Not all of them. There are still some in the world, those who broke free from Saubarag's clutches. You still have a task to complete."

Perhaps Eusebius had managed to break free from his master and take some vampires with him. "If some few do still remain, there are plenty of newly trained vampire hunters who can manage them. Without the driving power and corruption of Saubarag, they are much diminished."

"Will you shirk your duty, Roman? You made an oath to me. I expect it to be fulfilled to the letter."

Luke, narrowing his eyes, let his right hand drift to the pommel of the gladius strapped at his left hip, his index finger bouncing in a steady rhythm on the pommel button. "We've given you nearly two-thousand-years of service. We've achieved what no one else could, what you couldn't. Release us. Remove the compulsion."

"No."

Luke pulled his gladius. "Remove the compulsion. It isn't a request."

Mithras's nose flared and his eyes burned. "Who are you to give me orders, mortal? I could crush you like a bug."

Luke laughed hollowly. "Can you though? I've overthrown one god today, casting his lifeless corpse down at my feet. I can make it two."

"Would you cast me down and raise yourself up as a god to replace me?"

"What do I need to be a god for?" A wicked grin spread across his lips. "I'm already a devil...a demon actually, a wood-fanged demon, so named by my enemies. I have brought ruin to the vampires. I don't need to replace some petty god of old."

Mithras shifted his focus to the goddess of the moon. "What's your position in this, Selene?"

Behind him, Selene's chariot rolled to a halt, her oxen stamping and snorting. "Release them, Mithras. They have been true to their word and have earned their freedom…many times over. It is right and just to reward them for all they've done. No longer being subject to the compulsion is the least you can do."

Tutyr stepped up next to Luke. "They have served loyally. Be a gracious god."

"I don't recall asking the opinion of the lord of fleas," Mithras spat out.

"Where do you stand on this, woman?" Mithras pointed toward Roxi. "You were once my most devout follower until you fell in with this blasphemer."

Roxi, an arrow nocked and ready on her bow, stepped up on Luke's other side. "And how did you reward that loyalty, my Lord?" She filled the honorific with invective, rendering it into an insult. "You would have let me die after all the honor I've paid you over the centuries. Free us. Or fight us. We have no more time for petty gods of cruelty."

Mithras sneered at the moon goddess. "Are you proud, Selene? You've stolen them from me."

"I have stolen nothing. You did not care for them or attend to their needs. I cannot steal what you've cast aside."

"Where you provided a cold shoulder and contempt, My Mistress supported me and aided me countless times. I owe her not only my loyalty, but my love. She stood by my side and helped me save Roxi from your cruelty." Luke shook his head and spat on the ground in front of where he stood. "I'm tired of talking. Do the right thing or —"

"Or what? Mithras spat out.

"Or die."

A Persian long sword appeared in Mithras's hand while a long dagger appeared in the other. Luke reached to his shoulder to unsheathe his rudis.

"No," Roxi said. "The rudises belong to him." She grabbed her sword and unsheathed it, handing it to Luke.

Luke took it. It was a bit longer than his gladius, but he'd leave it in his left hand. He could fight equally well with either side, and perhaps the different presentation might throw the god, who seemed inflexible and static after so many centuries of decline. Stepping forward, he brought both blades to the ready position. Tutyr raised his axe and made to follow.

"No," Luke barked. "This is between me and the godling."

"Fight well, my friend." Tutyr stepped back, taking up a post next to Roxi.

Mithras took half a step forward, raising his long sword to halt Luke. "You are really going to challenge me?"

Luke was tired of the god's voice. "If you didn't want to fight, you should have listened to us or not bothered showing up."

Before the god could prepare, Luke dashed forward, sprinting straight at the god. Instead of charging at Luke, Mithras steadied his stance and moved his weapons to a ready position. Nearing the god, Luke waited until the last moment when he thought the god had committed to his defensive stance and leaped to the left and spun in toward the god's sword arm. A quick slash and Luke landed and danced away, avoiding the divinely quick counter.

Mithras raised his dagger hand and ran it over his shoulder, drawing back blood on his fingers. Luke had drawn first blood. Not giving him time, Luke darted in, feigned a slash with his gladius, but dropped to his knees and dragged Roxi's sword across the god's thigh. Shifting his weight to the other knee, he rotated around and brought both swords inward like a pair of great shears, aiming for the god's hamstrings.

Diving forward, Mithras tried to roll, but came up awkwardly thanks to the two wounds he'd already taken, though he evaded being hamstrung.

Luke pushed backward and hopped to his feet, shifting the position of his swords to keep the god guessing. "You're going to have to do better than that."

Mithras opened his mouth to say something, but never got the chance as Luke thrust his gladius at the god's stomach, which was parried aside by the god's dagger. However, Mithras didn't see the other sword slash in. But he felt it as it bit into his other thigh, opening another line of blood. Yelling in pain and lashing out, Mithras caught Luke in the head with his fist and the hilt of his sword.

Luke staggered back, keeping his swords up. Shaking his head, he cleared his vision and hearing but didn't advance. He wanted to make sure the helmet had absorbed enough of the blow so he didn't do something foolhardy.

Mithras's eyes worked side to side, his face drawn into a mask of uncertainty. Luke let one side of his lips quirk up. The god had no idea how to handle Luke. He'd trained in dozens of different sword styles over the centuries, honing the skills regularly. Mithras might be a warrior god, but Luke was the most trained sword fighter the world had ever known.

Twirling the sword in his left hand, Luke telegraphed a clumsy swing with the one in his right hand. Mithras caught it easily with his sword and dagger, trapping Luke's gladius between them. The god didn't see the left sword thrusting upward.

Luke stopped the blade, letting it draw a bit of blood from Mithras's neck just below his chin. "Drop your weapons, or I turn your skull into a kebab."

The god froze, his eyes wide.

Luke pressed a touch harder with Roxi's sword, a tiny rivulet of blood running down the blade. "This is your last chance. I don't actually want to kill you. I just want to be free of you."

A bright light flared into existence behind Luke. He had to squint, though he wanted to clamp his eyes shut, to keep an eye on Mithras.

"Drop your weapons, my old friend," a new voice said. "You have been defeated."

Luke pulled his gladius free from the grip of Mithras's sword and dagger but kept it ready to strike.

"Even you have betrayed me, Sol?" Mithras bit out carefully so as not to spill more of his own blood down the sword held to his throat.

"In what world would I ever side with you against my sister of the moon? You are disgracing our dignity and the mission. Drop your weapons, or I give the word for our instrument to strike," Sol Invictus said, his voice filled with annoyance colored by weariness.

To encourage the god, Luke pressed the gladius into Mithras's stomach, though not hard enough to draw blood.

"Mithras. Now!" Sol barked.

The god sagged and let his weapons fall to the ground. Not trusting him to not have a dagger hidden up a sleeve, Luke kept his weapons in place.

"Lucius, you may withdraw your weapons," Sol said in a much more companionable manner.

Luke held Mithras's gaze and gave one final push of his blades to remind the god who had the power in the situation, then moved back one step, keeping his blades raised and poised.

"Luke," Roxi said.

Reorienting himself to Roxi's voice, he sidestepped and took another step backward, then another. Once he felt safely out of range of the god, he lowered his weapons and backed the rest of the way until he stopped by Roxi's side.

Selene, her blade naked and her shield strapped to her arm, stepped out of her chariot and walked toward Mithras.

Sol Invictus, likewise armed, angled toward Mithras from the other side. "You have suffered a defeat here today, my old friend. But don't let it taint our victory. The god of the vampires is dead. Most of his spawn are gone. Humanity is safer from the scourge of vampirism than they ever have been since their twisted creation."

Selene stopped next to her brother. "You brought us together in this purpose, and now your vision is fulfilled. Share with us in this joy. Reward the vessels of our mission with the freedom they so richly deserve. Remove the compulsion. Let them enjoy the fruits of their immortality and keep their abilities. As long as there are vampires upon this earth, we may need their arms and wisdom."

"That is the least we can do for them. You were wise in setting this course all those years ago. Be wise and gracious in victory." Sol shoved his sword into its scabbard as a gesture of goodwill.

"Without the compulsion, how can we trust they'll return if we need them?" A note of whininess slipped into Mithras's voice.

Selene scowled, her beatific face darkening as if a storm cloud eclipsed the moon. "They have fought on for many generations of humans. They have proven their mettle and willingness to execute their duties. And Lucius is right. There are vampire hunters of all stripes around the world thanks to his work. Knowledge of the dark creatures may not be fully in the open, but there are more than enough to answer the call. Lucius and Roxiustana deserve a rest and a choice in the matter."

Raising her sword to point at Mithras, she glared at him. "I will plead upon your higher reason no more." Her sword blazed to life, a fiery silver glow shimmering down its length.

Mithras stared at her, then lowered his head. "Fine. Bring me their rudises."

Tutyr dropped his axe into a loop on his belt and held out his hands, winking at Roxi and Luke so that Mithras wouldn't see the gesture. Sliding his gladius into its scabbard, Luke grabbed his rudis and flipped it around, offering the handle to Tutyr. Roxi, her bow still nocked with an arrow, did the same.

Luke appreciated Tutyr's willingness to step in on their behalf so they didn't have to approach the god they'd just fought and defeated. Once Mithras took the wooden blades from Tutyr, Selene lowered her blade but didn't sheath it. The silver filigree and the silver and steel alloy of their wooden blades glowed brightly for a moment then returned to normal.

As the glow receded, Luke felt a slight tug in his guts as a lightness descended over him. He stood straighter, as if a huge weight had been lifted from his shoulders. Roxi, a silly grin slowly spreading across her face, looked at him. She'd felt it, too. His mind a jumble, he focused in on the present. He and Roxi could explore what this change would mean for them later…in great depth. Right now, he had to make sure there wasn't any last-minute treachery.

"There. They still work to draw power and heal, but now there is no compulsion. They are free to live until the sun burns out for all I care." Mithras thrust them out.

Tutyr took them and returned to Luke and Roxi quickly, as if fearing that Mithras would change his mind. By the time they'd sheathed the wooden blades and looked up, Mithras was gone.

Selene and Sol turned and walked toward Luke and Roxi. Luke dropped to a knee and set the tip of the sword on the ground, holding the handle in both hands. Roxi joined him, resting her bow across a knee.

"My Mistress." Luke bowed his head to the goddess, then to her brother. "My Lord, Sol Invictus."

Reaching down, Selene set a hand on Luke's right cheek and her other on Roxi's left cheek. "You have far exceeded my expectations. And in more than just your ability to fight and kill vampires. You are examples of the very best of humanity, and I salute you both." She bowed and kissed them on their foreheads one at a time.

Sol Invictus bowed to them, resting a hand over his heart. "Let me add my congratulations to my sister's. You both possess my fire in your hearts. You are indeed truly exceptional in all the best ways. I'm pleased to have met you both."

Tutyr, standing behind the other two gods, smiled warmly, nodding in agreement.

The god of the indomitable sun straightened and flared brightly, forcing them to close their eyes. When Luke opened them, the god was gone, though he'd left spots dancing in his eyes.

"Thank you, I owe you so much, My Mistress," Luke said, reaching out to grasp Roxi's hand. "You've given me my life back and someone to share it with."

"Thank you," Roxi stated simply.

"You two owe me nothing. Love each other well. I shall be there if you need me. When I depart, you shall be returned to where you were pulled out of the world. Are you ready?" Selene held out her hand to Tutyr, who took it.

"Aye," Luke said.

"Yes," Roxi confirmed.

The moon goddess's glow gradually increased but never reached the aggressive blast of the sun god's, though Luke had to close his eyes against it.

CHAPTER
THIRTY-FIVE

When Luke opened his eyes, he stared into a brilliant blue morning sky, the rubble of Saubarag's mansion strewn about him. Birds serenaded the glorious late summer day. Best of all, Roxi's hand was still in his.

They'd done it. They were free.

A chuckle bubbled up from his lips. It quickly turned into a full-on joyful laugh.

"They're over here!" someone shouted.

Roxi rolled over and hugged Luke fiercely. Unable to resist, her soft laugh soon grew louder as she rested her head on Luke's armor-covered chest. Around them, feet scrabbled over rocks and debris. More shouts filled the air, but Luke didn't care.

He'd killed a god, and with his death, destroyed the vampires who he'd claimed. Then he'd defeated another god. But most importantly, they'd freed themselves from the tyranny of their rudises. They could choose or not whether they wanted to fight vampires.

And right then, Luke didn't want to fight vampires for a good long time.

"Luke! Roxi!" Sam called, scrambling down into the crater, Delilah and Simone hot on her tail. Covered in blood and with a bit of a limp, Ramon sauntered up behind Sam with a sardonic smile on his face and a jaunty wave to say hello. A moment later, Jung-sook joined them, a broad smile on her face.

"What happened?" Sam's eyes bugged out a bit. "The vampires just…exploded. Well, they didn't explode. I mean, some of them did. But others turned into goo and some poofed out. Then the mansion… I thought we were all goners."

Luke couldn't remember if he'd ever heard her quite this frantic and discombobulated. Squeezing Roxi hard, he tried to take a deep breath but kept chuckling. So instead, he hugged Roxi again.

Delilah stopped, crossing her arms. Simone chuckled joyously by her side. "What's so funny, old man?"

"We're alive, and we're free!"

EPILOGUE
THE FOLLOWING SPRING

THE HALLERBOS, BELGIUM

Luke and Roxi strolled through the bluebells, holding hands and listening to the spring breeze rustle through the trees. Birds chirped their songs of nests and eggs while small creatures moved along unseen paths under the leaves.

"I used to hide here when I was a boy, avoiding my chores," Luke said quietly, breaking the silence.

Roxi chuckled warmly. "I can't imagine you as a boy. Carefree and avoiding your duties."

"I'd lie on my back and watch the clouds through the limbs of the trees. Sometimes I'd take a nap." He smiled fondly at the memory. "My mother would come find me and bring me something to eat since I'd invariably have forgotten to bring my lunch."

"It sounds idyllic." She sounded wistful. "Childhood for me was competing against my siblings to impress our father. Martial studies and education. I rarely got the chance to be a carefree child. Then I became a young adult with responsibilities to king and empire."

Luke winked at her. "Chasing down handsome Romans in the mountains of Armenia?"

"Yes. Hunting a wily centurion and two children. I still can't believe you got the better of me." She laughed and pulled the band keeping her hair contained and freed it so the breeze could play through her wild curls.

"I was just running to save my life and my new mission. You'll have to blame Ariazate for stealing me away. She's the one who raised a small army and set an ambush for you."

"Well, since I can't talk to Ariazate, maybe I'll have to have a word with Anne-Marie." She laughed and pulled Luke in for a warm kiss that seemed to stretch into deeper passion.

When they resumed their casual stroll, Luke directed their path toward a fallen tree and sat down, patting the spot next to him. "Maybe it's time I sit down with Anne-Marie and tell her about Ariazate. She's pregnant with a daughter. Perhaps it's time for the name to live on."

"You loved her very much, didn't you?" Roxi asked, an eyebrow slightly raised.

"I did. She and her brother Tigran were the siblings I never had growing up, though she and I were always closer than I was with Tigran. He longed for home and a throne he'd never be able to sit on. Zate accepted her fate and threw herself into her new life, finding joy and purpose." He paused, lifting his face to the breeze and closing his eyes. "They were my first chosen family."

"Now you have a much larger chosen family."

"It's the only option open to us, who have lived for too long to have any blood family left."

"I've always thought about submitting DNA to one of those ancestor places to see if I have any relatives from my many siblings."

Luke barked out a laugh. "How badly would that fuck with the results to have two-thousand-year-old DNA suddenly injected? You have a relative…from however many generations ago!" He shook his head, chuckling.

"I'm almost tempted to do it for that alone." She sighed. "You know what, Lucius of the bluebells? I think I'd like a proper lesson in how to slack off and avoid my chores."

"What do you mean?"

She gestured around her. "There's this lovely meadow of blue-bells in full bloom. Let's go find a patch."

He nodded and stood up, offering his hand to her. She took it, and he walked them deeper into the woods until he found a sun dappled meadow. Squatting down, he fell backwards onto his butt then stretched out with his full body, accompanying it with a noisy yawn. He did his best to ignore the vague sounds of civilization and Brussels in the near distance, though those noises only intruded if the wind was just right.

Smiling, Roxi shook her head and crossed her arms. "Is the whole rigmarole required?"

"You wanted lessons. Now get down here and start relaxing." He patted the spot next to him as he focused through the trees toward a blue sky with clouds skittering across it slowly.

Roxi flopped onto the ground next to him, performing an exaggerated stretch and yawn. A moment later, she found his hand and intertwined her fingers with his. "Are we supposed to find images in the clouds?"

"If you wish."

He breathed deeply, holding the fresh spring air in his lungs for a few moments. For the first time in ages, maybe centuries, he felt truly at peace as he watched the delicate spring leaves dance on the breeze. Somewhere nearby, a bee buzzed from flower to flower, collecting nectar.

"I think I saw them disappear somewhere over here," said a distant voice drifting on the breeze.

"It appears we're about to be found by our family," Roxi whispered.

"Moments like this are best shared," he replied.

"There they are!" Gwen called, jogging over with Olivia Adelisa in tow. Together, they flopped down in their own patch of sunlight.

Shifting his eyes over, he saw Maggie smiling down at him, Zel beside her, holding hands. He patted the empty space next to him. A moment later, he grabbed Maggie's hand, squeezing it.

"It really is lovely here," Maggie said.

"Mhm," Zel agreed.

A shadow eclipsed his view as Delilah and Simone stood over him briefly before joining everyone else on their backs. The two spoke to each other in French as Delilah worked to pick up the language of her new home under Simone's gentle tutelage.

He wished Holly and Sam could be here with them, but they were too busy reestablishing the pack in North Portland. Though they promised to visit and stay with Luke and those who'd moved with him into the cottage as soon as the opportunity arose. Jamaal, as the new second, would handle things in their absence. Maybe someday Holly would pass leadership of the pack to the next generation, and she and Sam could join them in their little commune. Then his family would be complete. Also, he secretly suspected Holly would be a lot of fun without the weight of leadership pressing down on her shoulders.

"Watch out for that limb, dear," Tony said, guiding Pablo toward the group of skivers.

Luke lifted his head in time to catch Pablo roll his eyes. Pieter, holding Pablo's other hand, smiled indulgently and shook his head. Together, the trio found a spot nearby and stretched out to join their friends. Amiata walked beside Pieter, her hands held behind her back.

Luke hoped Pieter, Pablo, and Tony would make the move to Belgium permanent. Tony had largely forgiven him. The few other wolves who had moved with Luke to Belgium had talked of forming a mini-pack with Pieter leading it. Luke had ensured the Belgium Pack would let them exist autonomously. Also, Amiata wished to move back with her daughter and wanted her stepson there so Olivia Adelisa had all her family together.

Pablo seemed mostly recovered, though he still hadn't really spoken to anyone, and he'd seemed to have lost the usual humorous quirk to his lips and spark in his eyes. Luke was just happy to see him up and moving about. It had been one of the best things about returning to Portland after killing Saubarag.

Once everyone settled in, the birds returned to their earlier songs. Someone snorted and gasped as if they'd momentarily drifted off and startled awake. Luke chuckled quietly to himself before returning his gaze to the clouds drifting by.

"And you did this a lot when you were a boy?" Pieter asked.

"As often as I could get away with it," Luke replied dreamily.

"I somehow can't picture you as young and carefree."

"We all start somewhere. I wasn't born in armor." Luke stretched, groaning happily. "This is where I started—in a village not far from here. I came back here after my first war in the legions. I visited it anytime I brought my legion through the region…until I was exiled from the empire. By the time I returned, I'd lost that something that drew me back here. Now, it feels like the right place to start the rest of my life."

Roxi rolled over so she hovered above him. Stroking his cheek, she bent down and kissed him. "It's a perfect place."

After the brief kiss, she returned to her back, resting her head on her hands as she stared at the sky and the clouds.

For the first time since those heady days as a boy, Luke felt free. He and Roxi were no longer beholden to the power of the rudis and could choose when and how to use it. Or they could enjoy their immortality without even thinking about the wooden sticks. No longer would they have to suffer the pain and indignity of withdrawal from lack of using it.

There were still vampires in the world. Saubarag's death hadn't taken those who'd split away at the end. Luke had no idea how they'd managed to achieve that or how many had done it, but for the moment, he didn't care. They were little more than a minor pest that could be handled as needed. He didn't even have to be the one to do it—not with the army of vampire hunters he'd raised around the world.

Now, he could find a new purpose for his life. He could be there all the time to help Gwen as she grew into adulthood, helping her learn the French and Flemish of her new home. He could be with Roxi and Maggie without the constant threat of vampire hunting disrupting their lives. He could continue working with his therapist on his centuries of trauma in earnest now that he wouldn't be called off to fight.

A small smile spread across his face and grew into a broad grin at the thought. He could just be.

"That cloud…" The voice that spoke sounded rusty and weak from disuse. "That cloud looks like that time when Luke got shot in the butt."

"Pablo?" Tony said, hope and fear in his voice.

Tears of joy prickled at the corner of Luke's eyes. Pablo had spoken.

"I didn't get shot in the butt, Pablo," Luke replied.

"Right in the ass," Pablo said, his voice a bit stronger.

"It just grazed my hip. Barely worth mentioning."

Delilah laughed. "Your very high hip, just below your waist."

"Luke got shot in the butt?" Olivia asked, a giggle coloring her Flemish accent.

Luke sighed. "'Twas merely a flesh wound."

His friends laughed, the sound joyful in his ears. Pablo could make that joke as much as he wanted. He still had a long road to recovery, they all did, but today had been a big step forward.

Today had been a good day.

The End

THE RED CITY REAPER RIDES FOR THE FIRST TIME IN...

A SHOT FOR DEATH

CHAPTER ONE

Dax

Dax leaned up against the scarred wooden bar top, looking over the sparse mid-morning crowd. Each time the front door opened, the knots between his shoulder blades tightened. Something had felt off since he'd parked his motorcycle, something that felt all too familiar.

Death was present everywhere all the time, especially in a place like Red City. But today, something about the constant undercurrent niggled at the back of his mind. Every time someone came or went, a whiff of the thread entered, teasing him, taunting him.

He checked his watch. Tomi was late, which was unlike him. Dax swallowed nervously and pulled in a deep breath through is nose, breathing slowly so as not to make noise. Even concentrating on every detail he couldn't it sort out, he couldn't identify where the thread came from, went, or to whom it belonged. He figured that if it belonged to someone he knew well, it would be easier to find the owner. At least that's what he hoped. He stopped a frustrated grunt from escaping his lips. Still nothing.

With a quick scan down the bar to distract himself, he pushed off and strolled to the balding white patron at the end of the bar. "Can I get you another round, Bill?"

"Yeah. I got one more in me," Bill replied, slugging down the last swallow before sliding the glass the short distance toward Dax.

Setting the glass by the sink, he grabbed a clean pint glass and filled it with Pabst before setting it in front of Bill. Four dollars were already waiting on the bar. Dax grabbed them, dropped one in the tip bucket and deposited the other three into the till.

A gust of cold, moist air and another hit of impending darkness blasted through the freshly opened door. He whipped his head around to the door. Still no Tomi. Dax's worry compounded. His manager was never late. Well…rarely.

"I didn't expect to see you in today, Red," Dax said. "What can I get you?"

Red ran a hand through his shaggy, wet ginger hair, flinging away some of the accumulated rain "Hadn't planned on it, but got home after work and heat's out in the fucking building. The super has no idea when it'll be back on." Red hung his coat up on the hook under the bar.

"That's unfortunate. The usual?"

"Yeah, the usual." Red turned toward Bill. "Hey, Bill."

"Yo, Red."

Dax grabbed a bucket glass and poured in a heavy shot of Jim Beam then filled a half pint for the beer back. After he set it down, he refilled his coffee from the carafe on the counter, cradling the cup in both hands to warm them as he leaned up against the back bar. After he felt it had cooled enough, he took a sip and made a face.

"Gack," he tossed the coffee into the sink then followed it with the rest from the coffee maker's carafe. He couldn't tell if it was just bad coffee or the increasingly bad mood he found him in as he tried to home in on the sense of death. He couldn't even tell if it had happened or was only the potential of future events.

Bill laughed. "You've got to get better coffee."

Dax scowled. "It's fine when it's fresh."

"Do your taste buds work, bro?" Red asked. "Even fresh, it tastes like shit."

Shaking his head, Dax shrugged. "If you want good hot beverages, I'll make you tea. Coffee is just wakeup juice."

"You can keep your hot leaf juice," Red replied, with a coarse laugh.

Bill chuckled along, nodding at his friend down at the other end of the bar. "It's cold as fuck out there. Get some better coffee. I might want a Spanish coffee sometime."

Dax narrowed his eyes and looked between the two men. Coffee cocktails would be an up charge compared to their usual PBRs. He'd have to talk it over with Tomi, if he ever showed up. Looking up at the clock, the ball of tension in his gut tightened further.

Movement out of the corner of his eye drew his attention. A tall, fat black man stepped out of the hall leading from the back of the bar. He'd shucked his coat in the office already, but the black beanie he wore glistened with rain. Dax sighed in relief, his shoulders dropping, but only fractionally.

"Sorry, Boss. Had to help my mama with something this morning and she insisted on making me breakfast." He shrugged. "You know you can't say no to her when she insists on offering food."

Dax nodded. "No worries. How is your mama?"

"The same. But when does she ever change?" Tomi washed his hands in the sink before drying them off. "Looks like I missed the morning rush."

"You didn't. This is it. If you can handle this unruly crowd, I'm going to head to the bank." He'd hoped Tomi's arrival would alleviate his sense of dread, but not only did it linger, it had intensified.

"Have fun. It's nasty out there."

Dax grunted and stepped back into the hall and down to the office, pulling his keys from his pocket. After he threw on his black leather coat and a scarf, he opened the safe and pulled out the deposits from yesterday. His brow furrowed. The envelope was much thinner than he'd have preferred. Stuffing it into the custom zipper pocket inside his coat, he padlocked it closed. He grabbed his helmet and pulled it over his shoulder length black hair.

Shoving the back door open, he pushed it shut and paused under the awning. The rain had picked up since he'd opened this morning. It poured off the awning in rivers. Sticking his pale white hand out, he let the rain wash over it. An involuntarily shiver ran through him.

He sighed. "I need to get a car."

Inhaling deeply, he narrowed his eyes. The thread lingered. He shook his head, frustrated with his inability to track it. About to close the visor of his helmet, he stopped when he thought her heard something. Looking down and to the left, he almost missed the movement in the shadows.

"Mew." A tiny kitten stepped out of a half-soaked box—the awning provided protection to part of it—but the rain was quickly winning the battle as it wicked into the rest of the cardboard.

In the dark gloom of the rainy day, the black kitten looked like a smudge. Pursing his lips, Dax squatted down. The kitten looked curious but stayed back. Holding out his hand, he left it hanging until the kitten approached and sniffed his fingers. He gave it a scratch under the chin. The kitten gave a half-hearted purr then shuffled back toward his box, giving a looking over his shoulder before disappearing into its shadows.

Shrugging, he flipped down his visor and walked to the end of the long awning and mounted the big, custom chopper motorcycle. Kicking it to life, it rumbled loudly, adding its sound to the rain and the few cars moving down the street. He joined traffic and headed toward Redemption City First National Bank. Fortunately, they had a parking garage nearby so he didn't have to park in the rain.

After he made his deposits, he slipped into a nearby coffee shop and picked up a proper cup and sat down to warm up. Bill and Red were right. The coffee he served was shit. He'd have to get something better. When he finished, he tugged his helmet on and darted outside to run toward the parking garage. He really needed to get a car if he was going to make it another winter in Red City.

He hoped Tomi had the inventory finished before he returned to the bar so he could call in his order to his beer distributor and the liquor store. If it was still dead, he wanted to get his tasks finished so he could head home and leave the bar to Tomi for the day.

After parking under the awning, he glanced toward the box. The kitten raised its head then returned it to its paws as it curled into a ball. Sighing, Dax headed into the bar and shucked his coat, shaking the excess water off it before hanging it in the office along with his helmet.

When he popped his head into bar, the same handful of people were exactly where he'd left them. Without a word, Tomi handed him the clipboard. Nodding, he returned to the office and closed the door, turning on the small space heater. He tossed the clipboard onto the desk and sat down. As he ran his eyes over the pages, he realized he hadn't assimilated any of the information.

He looked toward the back door and sighed. Standing, he slipped out of the back door and propped it open with a brick. He squatted down next to the box and folded the flap back, revealing the kitten within. It lifted its head and gave a weak "mew." He gently laid his hand on the kitten's back, closed his eyes, and reached out.

Tracing the thin tendrils backwards, he felt only severed connections and death, even the largest of the threads led back to nothingness. Pulling back his awareness, he pushed forward this time but only found a short, fraying thread that ended abruptly... If he did nothing.

He shook his head, making a decision, and scooped up the kitten. It felt like nothing but skin and bones. Wrapping his awareness around the kitten, he found a few fleas eking out a meager existence on the poor kitten. As he homed in on them, he clipped the threads tying them to life. Once the last tiny life winked out, he pulled the brick out of the door and stepped in, letting it close behind him as he returned to the office. Holding the kitten, he stared around the office, wondering what to do. His eyes settled on the stack of sixteen ounce cans he kept for back stock.

With one hand, he took out the four six-packs of tallboys from a flat and tossed the shallow cardboard tray onto the floor. Then he grabbed a package of bar towels and peeled off the wrapper and wadded up the towels into the bottom of the flat. Once he had what looked like a good nest built, he grabbed another bar towel, carefully dried the kitten off, and set it in the box, covering it with a towel. Finally, his eyes settled on the space heater, so he turned it to face the box.

While the kitten snuggled into its box, he pulled up a browser on the computer and looked for the nearest pet store. When he found one between the bar and his apartment, he sent the address to his phone, then called in his orders to his vendors. He'd never had a pet before. He wasn't sure if he'd keep the sad ball of fluff, but he couldn't let it die on his stoop. It felt too soon to send the little orphan on to join his mother and siblings who'd already crossed the veil.

When he finished the few last pieces of paperwork for the day, he pulled on his leather coat then scooped up the kitten in a towel, stuffing him into the same pocked he'd stashed his bank deposit in, though he didn't zip it all the way. The kitten didn't seem interested in fight him. It wiggled around for a few seconds then settled into a ball. A faint purr vibrated just under Dax's chest as he walked out front.

"Tomi, I'm heading home. Call me if the things get busy." The speech had disturbed the kitten who wiggled around again before resettling.

"You…uh…got an alien about to burst through your chest there, boss?" Tomi smirked, gesturing toward Dax with his head.

Dax pursed his lips and shrugged. "Don't worry about it. Office is locked." Then he pointed at Bill and Red. "And I'll get some better coffee."

" 'Bout time," Red mumbled before throwing back the rest of his Jim Beam.

Dax turned and raised his middle finger before disappearing down the hall. He grabbed his helmet and scarf, throwing them on quickly before stepping back into the frigid pissing rain. When he sat on his bike, he patted his pockets looking for his keys, but came up empty. As he dismounted, a shot cracked out from across the street, spraying cinder block shards from the wall.

A second shot sounded and pain exploded in his chest near his right shoulder. The shot knocked him off balance as he tottered backwards, slipping on the wet concrete of the alley. A third shot whizzed over his head, grazing his helmet before it smacked into the ground. Stars exploded across his visor like an iMax astronomy show except in far greater detail and clarity.

Through the fog of his ringing ears, he heard tires spin out, rubber screeching against wet pavement. Behind him, the back door squealed open. He would need to remember to get some silicon lubricant for it. The mundane thought made him laugh.

"Ow! Knock it off, you little shit," he mumbled as the kitten growled and dug in his claws.

"You OK, boss?" Tomi said quietly.

Groaning, he lifted his visor and pushed himself to sitting then patted his chest over the kitten. "Calm."

The hand seemed to steady the puny kitten as he settled back into a still lump on his chess. He jolted up as Tomi scooped him up under the shoulders, sending blinding pain radiating from the gunshot wound.

"Fuck!"

"Shit, did they hit you?" Tomi asked, nearly dropping him in the hurry to stop causing his boss pain.

Dax staggered to the other side of the other side of the alley, propping his good, left arm against the wall to stabilize himself. He wasn't in danger of falling over, but the rain cascaded over him, seeking out any dryness he had left.

Red poked his head out the door. "Should we call the cops or an ambulance?"

Pushing off the wall, Dax waved him off with his left hand. "No. I just landed funny on my shoulder. Let's leave the fucking authorities out of this. They cause more problems than they solve."

Red snorted. "Need a belt of whiskey, then? I'll go grab one for ya."

Tomi pointed aggressively at the bald white man. "Hey. You stay way from my side of the bar, you hear me?"

Raising his hands in the air and backing away, Red winked. "I'll be good. I'm just going to go back and nurse my Pabst."

Once the door shut, Dax sagged back into the wall, letting it prop him up. "You better go make sure they don't decide to serve themselves while we're out here."

"You sure, boss? You don't look too steady."

Not wanting to worry Tomi too much, Dax pushed off the wall and stumbled before righting himself. The kitten, apparently not liking being tossed around in his secret hideaway squirmed before letting off a weak growl.

"What the hell's moving around inside your coat, Dax?" Tomi crossed his arms and stared at the lump moving around inside the leather coat.

Leaving his right arm dangling, he carefully unzipped his coat, then dropped the pocket's zipper a couple inches. The kitten shoved his head out the gap and hissed.

"Hush, you." Dax tapped it gently on its nose.

With a final grumpy growl, the kitten pulled its head back in and settled down again.

"What are you doing with a kitten?"

Dax shrugged, hissing and wincing at the pain in his right shoulder. He reached across his body and touched his shoulder, drawing back a bloody hand running thin from the rain.

"Shit, you did get shot," Tomi said.

"It didn't hit anything too vital. I'll be fine. You know that."

Tomi furrowed his brows, his lips drawing into a thin line across his face. "Whatever you say—"

They both perked up at the distant sound of sirens.

Dax shook his head. "Looks like someone around here still has hope Johnny Lawless will still do something." He sighed. "I'd better get out of here before they arrive. You know the drill if they come in."

"Yeah. You know the regulars do, too." Tomi scowled briefly before fishing his keys out of his pocket.

"Tomi," Dax called to halt his manager. "Can you grab my keys off the desk and hand them out to me."

The Black man nodded, ducked inside then reappeared a couple moments later and handed the keys to his boss. "You better hurry up."

He nodded and took his first steps carefully as water sluiced down the alley toward the gutters running nearly bank full alongside the sidewalk. As he straddled the motorcycle and kicked it to life, he cursed as the vibrations rattled his bones and jarred the wound. For the third time that day, he wished he drove a car. A nice easy automatic that he wouldn't have to shift.

Flipping down his visor, he reached out with his right arm and wrapped his fingers around the grip on the handlebar. The movement brought tears to his eyes as he gritted his teeth through the pain. The ride home was going to be hell.

Join Dax in A Shot For Death, the first book in the Red City
Reaper series.

ACKNOWLEDGMENTS

First, I'd like to acknowledge my lovely and talented partner Amy Cissell. She encouraged me to start working on my novels and supported me through the whole process, providing a sounding board and editing throughout the process. She really is awesome. You should check out her books.

Second, a big thanks to all my readers who have made it this far. We've gone on a journey together, and I hope you thought it was as fun as I did.

There are a lot of other people that contributed to this series, but I'd like to mention a few specific people. Dan—Thanks for your support and excitement about this series. You're the best friend and fan a person could have. Sue—you saw the first inklings of Luke in The Centurion Immortal and have provided top notch edits throughout the entire series. My ARC Team—Thanks for all the reviews! I hope you enjoyed the journey.

To my author friends in FAKA, your support and counsel have been invaluable. To my first writing group, you're a big part of who Luke has become.

To all the bars and coffee shops in North Portland, you have no idea how many words were laid down inside your walls. The Chill n Fill - Luke first drew breath on the page under your roof. I can't not include the others—Tiny Bubble Room, Leisure, Great North, Slim's, 45th Parallel—you've all been a home away from home when I needed to shake up the tedium of writing in the home office.

ABOUT THE AUTHOR

C. Thomas Lafollette is a student of history and a world traveler. He's dined with a Prime Minister, read poetry with Yevgeny Yevtushenko, and drank beer with monks. He's the author of the action-adventure urban fantasy series Luke Irontree & The Last Vampire War and the forthcoming Red City Reaper series. Besides reading and writing, he loves a good action movie, be it a Hollywood blockbuster or a classic Samurai flick, as well as the occasional rom-com. He lives in Portland with his partner – the devastatingly talented author Amy Cissell – his stepdaughter, and their two jerk-face cats.

facebook.com/CThomasLafollette

bookbub.com/authors/c-thomas-lafollette

amazon.com/C-Thomas-Lafollette/e/B09JMTR7W7

goodreads.com/cthomaslafollette

tiktok.com/@cthomaslafollette

instagram.com/CThomasLafollette

ALSO BY C. THOMAS LAFOLLETTE

Luke Irontree & The Last Vampire War

Book 0 - The Centurion Immortal

Book 1 - Dark Fangs Rising - March 22, 2022

Book 2 - Dark Fangs Raging - April 19, 2022

Book 3 - Dark Fangs Descending - May 17, 2022

Book 4 - Blood Empire Reborn - August 23, 2022

Book 5 - Blood Empire Avenged - September 20, 2022

Book 6 - Blood Empire Infiltrated - October 18, 2022

Book 7 - Blood Empire Burning - November 15, 2022

Book 8 - Ancient Sword Falling - March 21, 2023

Book 9 - Ancient Sword Unyielding - August 22, 2023

Book 10 - Ancient Sword Shattering - January 4, 2023

The Luke Irontree Historical Adventures

Rise of the Centurio Immortalis - April 5, 2022

Fall of the Centurio Immortalis - May 31, 2022

The Moonlight Centurion*

The Highway Centurion*

Red City Reaper - A Dark Urban Fantasy Adventure

Book 1 - A Shot For Death* - March 5, 2024

Book 2 - Death Orders a Double* - Winter 2024

Book 3 - Death on the Rocks* - Sprint 2024

*Forthcoming

Titles and release dates may be subject to change.